# THE TRAFFICKERS

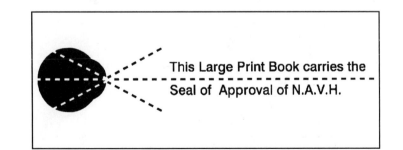

This Large Print Book carries the
Seal of Approval of N.A.V.H.

# THE TRAFFICKERS

## W.E.B. GRIFFIN
### AND WILLIAM E. BUTTERWORTH IV

**THORNDIKE PRESS**
*A part of Gale, Cengage Learning*

GALE
CENGAGE Learning™

Detroit • New York • San Francisco • New Haven, Conn • Waterville, Maine • London

Thorndike Press® Large Print Core.

The text of this Large Print edition is unabridged.

Other aspects of the book may vary from the original edition.

Set in 16 pt. Plantin.

Printed on permanent paper.

**LIBRARY OF CONGRESS CATALOGING-IN-PUBLICATION DATA**

Griffin, W. E. B.
    The traffickers / by W.E.B. Griffin and William E.
Butterworth IV.
        p. cm. — (Badge of honor) (Thorndike Press large print
core)
        ISBN-13: 978-1-4104-1564-6 (hardcover : alk. paper)
        ISBN-10: 1-4104-1564-3 (hardcover : alk. paper) 1. Payne,
Matt (Fictitious character) — Fiction. 2. Police — Pennsylvania
— Philadelphia — Fiction. 3. Gangs — Fiction. 4. Philadelphia
(Pa.) — Fiction. 5. Large type books. I. Butterworth, William E.
(William Edmund) II. Title.
PS3557.R489137T73 2009
813'.54—dc22
                                                         2009019761

Published in 2009 in arrangement with G.P. Putnam's Sons, a member of Penguin Group (USA) Inc.

Printed in the United States of America
1 2 3 4 5 6 7 13 12 11 10 09

★

## IN FOND MEMORY OF

SERGEANT ZEBULON V. CASEY

*Internal Affairs Division
Police Department, the City of
Philadelphia, Retired*

★

*There came a time when there were assignments that had to be done right, and they would seek Zeb out. These assignments included police shootings, civil-rights violations, and he tracked down fugitives all over the country. He was not your average cop. He was very, very professional.*

— HOWARD LEBOFSKY
Deputy Solicitor of Philadelphia

# I

## [ONE]
## 7522 Battersby Street, Philadelphia
## Wednesday, September 9, 1:55 A.M.

Tony Harris returned to his bed, silently cursing himself for not having hit the john before he'd crawled under the sheets two hours earlier. Harris — a thirty-eight-year-old homicide detective in the Philadelphia Police Department who was slight of build and starting to bald — then clicked off the lamp on his bedside table. As he put his head on his pillow and sighed, wondering when — or even if — he'd start to drift off back to sleep, a monstrous *BOOM* shook the house. It reverberated through the darkened room, knocking loose a picture frame from the wall, its glass breaking when it hit the floor.

"Holy shit!" he said aloud, sitting bolt upright and clicking on the lamp.

He looked toward the front window.

*What in hell was that?*

*Did a damn gas leak just blow up the middle school?*

Austin Meehan Middle School was a half-block down the tree-lined residential street.

Harris quickly got out of bed, crossed the room, and pulled back the curtain to look out the window. On either side of Battersby, the Northeast Philadelphia neighborhood had a series of nearly identical, neatly kept comfortable two-story brick duplexes with large lawns. The homes — some of which now with their lights flicking on — had stone façades on the front and garages in the rear, on a common alleyway. Because Harris's garage served more as a storage unit than a car park, he left his city-issued Ford Crown Victoria sitting at the curb in front of his house.

It took Harris no time to locate the direction of the source: In the sky some blocks to the east, he saw a bright glow that he recognized as that from an intense fire.

*Maybe a gas station on Frankford went up?* he wondered as he automatically started picking up his clothes from the chair where he'd tossed them at midnight. He quickly pulled on his wrinkled pants and short-sleeved knit shirt, then slipped on socks and shoes. He watched as the glow from the fire seemed to pulse even brighter, as if the fire were being fed more fuel.

"Jesus!" he said aloud.

Harris double-checked that he had his wallet and badge and pistol, then ran down the stairs as fast as he dared and out the door.

He drove the Crown Vic up Battersby, turning right onto Ryan Avenue, then followed it the seven blocks to Frankford Avenue, where Harris could clearly see that the intense glow was to the south. He was about to make the turn when he heard the wail of sirens — and then the huge horns blaring — of two fire department emergency medical vehicles. The red-and-white ambulances flew up on the intersection, braked heavily as they lay steadily on their horns, then accelerated through it.

Harris checked for any other vehicles headed for the intersection. He saw that it was clear and turned to follow the ambulances.

As he went south on Frankford, the sky became a brighter orange-red mingled with black and gray smoke. And then, down on the left side of the street, he saw the first of the flames. They were coming from the back of the Philly Inn, an aging two-story motel that had been built long before Anthony J.

Harris had been born at Saint Joseph's Hospital.

He pulled into a parking lot to the north of the motel, to where he had a better view of all the activity. He also enjoyed more than a little of an olfactory assault from the awful smell filling the air and now entering the car via the dash vents.

*That's the smell of burning wood, for sure, and plastics.*

*But I'd bet that's also a bit of human flesh . . . you can damn near taste it.*

Philadelphia Fire Department Engine 36, from the station just up Frankford, already was on the scene. It had hoses snaking everywhere and the firefighters were laying down an impressive amount of water. Other firemen were going door to door, methodically clearing the motel's rooms and herding what people they found inside to a parking lot to the south. Doors that no one answered were busted open with twenty-eight-pound metal battering rams and the hammer-headed pry bars called Halligans.

The pair of ambulances that had flown past Harris at the intersection were parked close by, their paramedics pulling out equipment — first-aid kits, backboards — with a well-practiced efficiency. A minute or so later, Engine 38 came roaring in from

its station a mile away on Old State Road —
followed by an articulated ladder fire truck,
which Harris thought a bit of overkill for a
lowly two-story structure.

*But, hell. Can't blame them.*

*Everyone loves a little adrenaline rush, espe-
cially these guys getting to play with all their
toys.*

*And this damn fire seems to offer plenty of
excitement.*

*It's got my pulse beating. No way I could go
back to sleep now.*

Harris noted that the Philadelphia Po-
lice Department was well represented, too.
Cruisers practically surrounded the place.
There was even a flatbed wrecker from the
Tow Squad, which was being waved toward
the back of the motel.

Harris looked to where the wrecker was
being routed and saw a half-dozen firefighters working feverishly at an SUV. It was on
the backside of the motel, at a room with its
door blown outward, where the flames appeared to be the hottest.

*And where the blast took place.*

The firemen were in the middle of a row
of vehicles parked outside the motel rooms,
and were inserting a heavy fire-resistant
blanket in through the framework that once
held the SUV's front windshield.

The wrecker raced up to the back bumper of the SUV, and a heavy-linked stainless-steel chain was quickly slung from the SUV's bumper to a tow hook bolted on the front frame of the wrecker.

The driver ground the gearshift into reverse and carefully took up the slack in the chain. At a firefighter's rapid hand signals and shouts of *"Go! Fuckin' go, go, go!"* the diesel engine then roared and the wrecker started tugging the SUV away from the fire.

The wrecker didn't slow until it had slid the SUV practically in front of Harris's Crown Vic, leaving a trail of black tire marks across the parking lot.

*That's one of those really fancy Mercedes-Benz SUVs.*

*What the hell is it doing here?*

*And how the hell is it connected to that explosion?*

*There's absolutely no question it has to be. . . .*

One of the emergency medical vehicles then pulled alongside the passenger side of the SUV. Floodlights mounted on the side of the unit were switched on, brightly illuminating the SUV. Two firefighters almost instantly appeared, carrying a heavy metal device with hydraulically powered pincers that Harris recognized as the Jaws of Life. The rescue tool proceeded to cut the right side of the Mercedes to pieces as other rescuers worked feverishly from inside the left-side doors to stabilize whoever was unlucky enough to be in the vehicle.

There suddenly was more shouting at the motel, and when Harris turned his attention to it he saw the impossible — a man on fire came staggering out of the motel room that had the blown-outward door.

One fireman rushed to the man. As he tackled him to smother the fire, a fire hose was trained on the both of them, instantly flooding the flames. Then the fireman stood and seemingly effortlessly slung the man over his shoulder. He ran with him — slipping twice — to the second ambulance, where the paramedics waited, ready to go to work.

Forty-five minutes later, twenty minutes after the motel fire had been brought under control if not put out, Harris watched the emergency medical personnel remove from the SUV someone they'd strapped to a rescue backboard. The victim looked to Harris to be a young woman. She had IV hoses dangling from her arm and wore an oxygen mask.

Five minutes later, the doors of the ambulance slammed shut, and its siren wailed as the unit began to roll. As if on cue, the other ambulance did the same only a minute later.

Harris scanned the motel and saw that the firemen were putting what Harris thought of as their toys back in their trucks. And he saw that the yellow and black POLICE LINE — DO NOT CROSS tape was being strung up, signifying the scene was being turned over to the police.

*Well, now that all the excitement's over,* Harris thought, reaching for the door handle, *professional curiosity overwhelms me.*

## [TWO]
## The Philly Inn
## 7004 Frankford Avenue,
## Philadelphia
## Wednesday, September 9,
## 1:15 A.M.

Forty minutes earlier, Becca Benjamin, despite having to wait in her silver Mercedes-Benz G550 at the back of a lousy Northeast Philly motel, had just reminded herself that she could not believe how much her luck had changed.

Becca — a trendy twenty-five-year-old brunette with olive skin who was five-foot-seven and just under 140 pounds, having recently started winning her battles to keep the bathroom scale from tipping 150 — not only had reconnected with her prep school boyfriend two months earlier but they had found that they still enjoyed what first had brought them together: partying, mostly booze-fueled but with the occasional recreational drug.

They had first dated nine years ago when in the Upper School at Episcopal Academy. She had been a voluptuous sixteen-year-old in IV Form (tenth grade) and J. Warren Olde, known as "Skipper," then eighteen and in VI Form (senior year), had begun flirting with her in the back row of an International Politics class. He was taking it for the second time, having yet to meet even the lowest threshold of the academic standards for passing the required course.

Skipper had a slender athletic build — he was a star player on the academy's championship lacrosse team, a midfielder who seemed to float effortlessly from one end of the 110-yard field to the other — and stood five-ten. His sandy hair was cut to his collar, with long bangs that he regularly swept out of his eyes. He was genuinely gregarious, quick with a laugh. And Becca, herself outgoing, had been immediately taken by his attentions.

Their relationship had lasted, though, only until the end of the school year. It had been a wild ride — literally — as an inebriated Skipper, driving Becca home after a graduation party, had misjudged a Dam View Road curve — actually wound up going down an estate's driveway at a high rate of speed — and put his little Audi in Springton Reservoir. Becca wound up with a broken collarbone and a trip to the Riddle Memorial Hospital emergency room in Media.

The Benjamins and Oldes — both families of significant means and, accordingly, connections with which they arranged to get the incident forgotten in the legal system, if not in their own tony community — were not amused. His parents declared Becca a wild child, albeit one in a woman's body, while her parents deemed the older boy a bad influence, unfit for their impressionable sweet sixteen-year-old — and thus absolutely off-limits.

Neither Becca nor Skipper was thrilled about the forced separation. But then, while Skipper's angry old man was still dealing

16

with the lawyers and having the sports car fished from the reservoir, Skipper's mother had sent him off early to the small private university he'd been set to attend in Texas — her alma mater in her hometown of Dallas. And so neither teenager had been prepared to fight the inevitable. They'd agreed to stay in touch, but even that turned out to be short-lived. They simply lost contact.

Then, two months ago, at a Fourth of July party on the Jersey shore thrown by a mutual friend from their prep school days, they'd run into each other. Becca had first noticed Skipper — who'd been standing beside the beer keg cooler on the beach — mostly because he wore, in addition to flowery Hawaiian-style surfer shorts and aviator-style sunglasses, a frayed straw cowboy hat and a white T-shirt emblazoned with a running red horse and block lettering that read S.M.U. MUSTANGS LACROSSE.

They had found that their outsized personalities were still in sync — with their appetites somewhat matured — and they damned near immediately picked up where they'd left off years before.

The party was back on.

Now Becca sat in the front passenger seat of the boxy Mercedes SUV; she'd had Skipper drive because she'd been shaking too

17

much from the drugs. She hated that down-side, which included her being stressed, as she was now. But she told herself there was no question that the upside's euphoria was worth it, not to mention the added benefit of a killed appetite that helped her finally lose — and keep off — those damned ten-plus pounds.

Despite the night, she stared through dark bug-eyed sunglasses at the motel door to Room 52. Then she punched the map light switch in order to read her wristwatch. The white-platinum diamond-bezel Audemars Piguet had cost her parents more than most of the battered work trucks and cars parked near the Mercedes were worth, never mind the six-figure sticker of the SUV itself. Her arm twitched a little, but she could tell by the position of the watch's hands — there were no numbers, just four dots of diamonds, twin-kling in the map light, to represent the 3, 6, 9, and 12 on the face — that it now was just after one-fifteen.

Her hands and feet were cold — another side effect from the drug — so she sat with her feet tucked under her thighs, her arms crossed, with her hands resting and warm-ing in her armpits. She wore cream-colored linen shorts and a tan silk blouse that was cut low in the front, revealing her ample

18

bosom, which now was rising and falling more rapidly than normal.

*He's been in there fifteen minutes.*

*He said it'd take only one: "In and out, baby."*

*What's taking so long?*

*Is he okay?*

*Should I go in?*

*Hell no, I shouldn't go in — who knows who's in there? — and I sure as hell don't* want *to go in that fleabag room.*

*But what if he's not okay?*

*What if —*

Her cellular phone, resting on her lap, simultaneously vibrated briefly and made a *ping* sound, announcing the receipt of a text message.

"Damn!" she said, startled. It caused her to uncross her arms and kick out her feet.

She quickly glanced at the phone's screen, thinking the text might be from Skipper. She saw — barely, as her sleep-deprived eyes had trouble focusing on the backlit small print — that it was from her girlfriend Casey, who was asking WHERE R U??

Becca threw the phone onto the leather-covered console between the front seats and sighed loudly.

She looked back at the motel door, wondering if she should shoot Skipper a text message. Maybe something along the lines of WTF???

*Yeah, Skipper — What The Fuck?*

The only movement she saw was from the motel room curtain, which was pulled closed over the open window and gently swaying, as if being blown by a breeze.

She crossed her arms and tucked her feet back under her and closed her eyes. After a while, she glanced at her watch again.

*One-thirty!*

*That's it. I'm going in there.*

She had just clicked off the map light and reached for and found the button that would release her seat belt when the door of Room 52 swung open. Out came Skipper Olde, holding a white handkerchief over his nose and mouth.

Olde wore a baggy navy blue T-shirt, khaki shorts, and sandals, and his aviator sunglasses hung from the front of the collar of his T-shirt. At twenty-seven, he still had his athletic slender build and his sandy hair collar-length, but no bangs, as he was thinning noticeably on top.

He pulled the motel door shut, then stuffed the handkerchief in his pants pocket. He glanced at the Mercedes, and Becca saw him flash his usual happy-go-lucky grin at her.

He quickly walked to the driver's door of the SUV and got in.

She then hit the button that simultaneously locked all the doors.

"What happened?" Becca said softly. "I was worried. I was just about to come after you."

"Sorry, baby. They were having a little trouble in there." He reached into his T-shirt pocket and pulled out a white plastic bag, heat-sealed at each end, that was about the size of a single-serving sugar packet. "I should've brought this out to you first, then helped them."

She pulled the bug-eyed sunglasses from her face and slipped them up on the top of her head.

Skipper Olde placed the white bag beside her cellular phone on the leather-covered console. She looked at it, then at Skipper, then nervously glanced out the darkened side windows, then the rear ones, to see if anyone was watching them.

"Go on," he said, smiling. "It's yours."

She smiled back weakly, then leaned over in her seat and kissed him quickly on the cheek.

"Thank you," she said, picking up the packet, then biting off a corner and removing the cut stub of a plastic drinking straw from it. She looked at Skipper. "What about you?"

He looked a little embarrassed, then nodded toward the motel room.

"I had a bump when I first went in. And there's more cooking. That's what they were having trouble with."

He nodded at the pouch she held and said encouragingly, "Go on, baby. It'll take your edge off."

She smiled slyly and said, "You don't have to tell me twice."

Becca Benjamin — who at age fourteen had been the Commonwealth of Pennsylvania's top Girl Scout cookie salesgirl, which she later listed under ACCOMPLISHMENTS on her University of Pennsylvania application to the Wharton School's master of business administration program — straightened herself upright in her seat. With the effortlessness of one who'd had some practice, she cupped the white packet with her hand so that it could not be seen, then took the straw stub and slipped an end in the hole she'd bitten, then placed the other end halfway up her right nostril. She pinched her left nostril closed and snorted.

"*Shit,* that burns!" she said after a moment, vigorously rubbing the outside of her right nostril after removing the straw.

But Skipper saw that she was smiling.

He also saw that all of the off-white powder had not been fully ingested. Some, mixed with mucus, was trickling toward her upper lip. With a fingertip, he wiped it from there, then licked it off his finger and grinned at her. She shook her head in mock disgust.

His cellular phone rang, and when he looked at its screen, he said, "Damn!" then answered it by saying, "Sorry. Running late. Give me ten minutes. It's still in the office safe." He listened for a moment, added, "No, no, I want you to have it before Becca and I leave town," then hung up without another word. He put the phone on the center console.

"I need to go inside and put together some more," Olde said as he opened the driver's door. He looked back in at her, said, "I'll be right back, baby. Promise."

She held up her left index finger and said, "Wait a sec."

She then snorted through the straw again, working it around the packet as she did so. Then she held out both to him. "Don't need this empty bag in my car."

Wordlessly, he took it and the straw, then got out and closed the door.

Becca hit the master locking button for the doors as she watched him go into the room.

The motel lights hurt her dilated eyes, and she pulled the sunglasses from her hair and slid them back over her eyes.

Skipper's cellular phone started ringing again. She grabbed it, then held down the button on top labeled "0/1," turning it off. Then she reached for the switch on the door that manipulated her seat's position, reclined the seat back almost flat, and lay back while enjoying the sudden pleasant flood of warmth that the methamphetamine triggered by tricking her brain into creating the chemical dopamine in overdrive.

## [THREE]
## The Philly Inn
## 7004 Frankford Avenue, Philadelphia
## Wednesday, September 9, 1:40 A.M.

Skipper Olde unlocked and entered the motel room, which had the cat piss stench of ammonia and stank of other caustic odors. He put the handkerchief back to his face and quickly stepped around a heavy cardboard box that had been moved by the door. Then,

24

tripping over the coil of clear surgical tubing next to it, he let loose with a long, creative string of expletives.

That caused the two Hispanic males in their twenties at the stove of the kitchenette in the back of the room to laugh from behind the blue bandannas tied over their noses and mouths.

And that in turn caused Skipper to bark, "Fuck you two *and* the cocksucking donkey you rode in on!"

Then he laughed, too.

The pair grunted and shook their heads, then turned their attention back to the stove.

Olde — stepping past the box fan with its switch set to HIGH to help the window unit circulate the air, and causing the tan curtain to sway — looked around in an attempt to find an obvious path to follow to the kitchenette. It wasn't that the motel room was small. The problem was that the room was packed, to the ceiling in places, with boxes and barrels and assorted materials. It was what could be described as a haphazard-warehouse-slash-makeshift-assembly-line.

The Philly Inn's management advertised the facility as modern. But in fact it had been built more than fifty years earlier and was an older two-floor design — "low-rise,"

25

its advertisements called it, playing on the nicer image that tended to come to mind with the term "high-rise." It was of masonry construction, each of the 120 rooms basically an off-white rectangular box with a burgundy-painted steel door opening to the outside, a plate-glass window (with tan curtain) overlooking the parking lot, and, under the window, an air-conditioning unit.

In its heyday, the Philly Inn had served as short-term, affordable lodging for traveling salesmen who used it as their base on U.S. Highway 13 — which was what Frankford was also designated — and for families who took their vacations in Philadelphia, enjoying the historic sites and museums in the city, and the entertainment of the various themed amusement parks nearby.

Each large room — all identical and advertised as "a De-Luxe Double Guest Room" — had a thirty-two-inch TV on the four-drawer dresser, a round Formica-topped table with four wooden chairs, two full-size beds separated by a bedside table with lamp and telephone (though the phones mostly went untouched, as an additional cash deposit up front was required to make local and long-distance calls). The mosaic-tiled bathroom held a water closet and a tub-shower combination. And taking up all of the far back wall was an ample kitchenette with a three-burner electric stove and oven, a single sink, a full-size refrigerator, and a small countertop microwave oven secured to the wall with a steel strap so that it might not accidentally wind up leaving with a guest at checkout.

Depending on one's perspective, the Philly Inn wasn't exactly seedy. Skipper Olde himself had spent the night there more than a few times, though it had been mostly out of necessity, as he'd been far from sober enough to drive. But it damn sure was sliding toward sleazy. It had long ago lost the steady business of the salesmen and families on holiday to the shiny new chain hotels nearer Philadelphia's Northeast Airport, mere miles to the north, and on Interstate 95.

Now the Philly Inn had an entirely different demographic of guests, ones who tended to stay more long-term. The motel had become temporary housing for those who needed some really cheap — but livable — place to stay during the period, say, after having sold their row house and not yet able to move into the next one, or while waiting for family members or friends who were receiving medical treatment at the many nearby hospitals, such as Nazareth, Friends,

Temple University, even the Shriners for Children.

The Philly Inn's posted rack rate was still the same seventy-five dollars a night that it had been for at least the last decade. It was, however, not unheard of for management to agree to a negotiated rate of as little as twenty-five bucks a night, even less for those staying thirty days or longer and paying — usually with cash — each week in advance.

There still were quite a few couples or families staying as guests for days or even as long as a week. But there were many more long-termers. These latter ones were mostly transient laborers, men working in construction — you could tell them by all their pickups in the parking lot late at night — and other seasonal work, such as mowing the countless lawns of suburban offices and homes, and harvesting the fruits and vegetables of the farms nearby and the ones across the river in New Jersey.

The motel management was as conscientious as it could be about keeping some separation between the workers and the families, assigning rooms to each in their own part of the motel and leaving vacant rooms between as a buffer.

But as far as the owner of the property was concerned, none of that really mattered.

The reality was that the Philly Inn's days were numbered. Its demise was inevitable, and about the only real reason the damn place had not been boarded up — or torn down completely — was that it could be made to show a profit. Enough to cover the bills, from its utilities to the assorted taxes levied upon it, which was not the same thing as saying that the motel did in fact earn a profit.

Its owner — Skipper Properties LLC, of which one J. Warren Olde, Jr., served as managing principal — had bought the place in a deal that included two other aged motels and a string of laundromats.

Skipper Properties LLC already had plans drawn up to build fashionable condominiums on the ten acres of land presently occupied by the Philly Inn. Being a self-proclaimed civic-minded company, Skipper Properties LLC was trying to jump-start a gentrification of the area. It was arguably mere coincidence that the company had also quietly bought up nearby parcels, including practically stealing a strip shopping center, to flip later at a huge profit.

Skipper Properties LLC announced that this so-called jump start would take place just as soon as His Honor the Mayor of Philadelphia convinced the goddamned lame-

29

brain city council to come to its senses and grant said civic-minded Skipper Properties LLC the "fair and just" tax abatement and other incentives that had been requested so as to make such a project viable — which was to say profitable — and build a more beautiful city.

There were secondary reasons that Skipper Olde was in no hurry to tear down the place — ones he certainly was not in the habit of sharing freely. Chief among these was that the inn was a mostly cash business now, and books were easily cooked when a lot of cash was involved. Also, most of the laborers living at the inn and at the two other aged motels the LLC had bought earned that cash by laboring for companies that were more or less indirectly controlled by Skipper Olde. Though, again, with Skipper not sharing such information freely, particularly with his silent partner-investor, and keeping those connections at arm's length, few knew many, if any, of those details.

So, as far as Skipper Olde was concerned, the how and why of that, if shared with others, would only create problems for him. The bottom line was that the various companies had plenty of work for the laborers, and the laborers were ready and willing to do it — and for low wages. But they could not do so if they had no place they could afford to live on a semipermanent basis.

Thus, the Philly Inn — the vote of the damned Philadelphia city council notwithstanding — was worth more standing as-is than demolished.

For the time being.

Skipper Olde began blazing a path through Room 52 by pushing aside a stack of cardboard boxes — one box was labeled 4 ROLLS POLY TUBING, ALL-VIRGIN FILM, USDA- AND FDA-APPROVED, 2-MIL 1-IN X 1,500- FT, the other BUN-O-MATIC COFFEE FILTERS — ONE (1) GROSS.

As he squeezed past a short wall of more than a dozen boxes stacked three and four high, some imprinted with LEVITTOWN POOL & SPA SUPPLY. HANDLE WITH EXTREME CARE! HYDROCHLORIC ACID. 2 1-GAL BOTTLES, the wall wobbled.

He called out to the pair standing at the kitchenette stove: "Hey, you amigos need to move these. If this fucking muriatic acid spills, it'll eat you to the bone!"

He pointed to two plastic orange jugs, at the foot of the beds, that were stenciled in black ink HYPOPHOSPHOROUS ACID. HAZARDOUS! USE ONLY IN WELL-VENTILATED AREA!

31

"Same with that shit!" he added.

Then he worked his way around the stacks of clear plastic storage bins containing various boxes of single-edge utility razor blades, some plastic gallon jugs of iodine, and heavy polymer boxes of lye.

*At least that caustic soda is safe in those thick plastic boxes.*

One clear plastic storage bin held gallon cans of Coleman fuel, refined for use in camping stoves and lanterns. Yet another was filled with ten or so smaller tubs of white pellets, hundreds of pills per tub, on top of which was a commercial-grade stainless-steel blender coated in the white dust of the pellets. And, beside a home-office paper shredder, which was overflowing with confetti, was a pile of opened plastic blister packs common for holding individual doses of medication.

When Olde reached the kitchenette, he wasn't surprised to see that one burner of the electric stove was still in pieces — the crusty coil cracked in at least three places — as the damage had been done by his hand when he'd tried getting it to work during his earlier visit to the room.

The other two burners each now held a large nonstick skillet and clearly were working just fine. Not only was the milky fluid in each at a fast boil — giving off a remarkable mist that floated up and hung heavily over the stove — but the thermometers clipped to the lip of each pan indicated a temperature of 450 degrees Fahrenheit.

The two Hispanic males, both wearing blue rubber gloves, now paid Olde no attention. They carefully poured a honey-yellow fluid from a square Pyrex glass baking dish into a paper coffee filter that had been placed over the mouth of a Mason jar.

There was a line of the heavy glass jars, ones with lids screwed on. These contained various colored fluids at different stages of a separation process, with solids settling to the bottom and the fluids rising to the top. After filtering the honey-colored fluid and spinning on a lid, the Hispanic males then methodically went about measuring and adding fluids to the various other jars, then resealing and shaking them, then letting them settle and cool, then using the surgical tubing to siphon off the top fluids.

Skipper Olde walked over to the folding table that had been positioned beside the stove. It had been set up as an assembly station. On it was a plastic bowl containing some partially crumbled whitish cakes and a plastic measuring spoon imprinted with "1 tbspn" on the handle. Next to that was a one-foot-square glass mirror that had some residue of the whitish powder on it, an electronic scale with a digital readout in ounces and grams, a package of the single-edged razor blades, and a quart-size plastic jar of methylsulfonyfoyl-methane — labeled "MSM dietary supplement." And there was an unwrapped spool of the flat plastic tubing, right next to which was the wandlike iron that first snipped the tubing into single-serving-size packets, then was used to heat-seal them closed.

Skipper Olde smiled. When he'd been in the room earlier, there had been nothing in the plastic bowl on the folding table. Now he was in business.

He pulled one of the wooden chairs to the table, then with the measuring spoon scooped up some of the crumbled cake from the bowl and put it on the mirror. Using a razor blade held by a ten-inch-long polymer handle, he quickly chopped at the powder, turning what little clumps and chunks there were into a fine powder.

He then bypassed the usual next step — mixing in the MSM to cut the pure meth, then measuring out "eight balls," exact portions of one-eighth ounce, each bringing these days $200 "retail" on the street. Instead, he used the razor blade to shovel the neat pile of powder — easily a half-ounce —

34

into a white packet he'd snipped from the roll of plastic tubing. He then sealed that packet shut and repeated the process, filling three more and putting them in his pocket.

*That's about two ounces,* he thought, then grinned. *Uncut, an easy fifty Franklins. But I hope the bastard's got something smaller than all hundreds, even though they're easier to carry than bricks of twenties.*

Skipper Olde then got up and walked over to the two Hispanic males.

Olde glanced at the broken coil on the stove.

"One last try," he announced, which earned him dubious looks from the Hispanic males.

He turned the dial that controlled the burner's temperature, setting it to low so that in the event he was successful he wouldn't burn the shit out of his fingers. Then he grasped the cracked coil and jiggered it, pulling its plug end from the receptacle on the stovetop, then reinserting it, then jiggering it again with more gusto.

Nothing happened.

"Fuck it," he finally said, frustrated. He smacked the coil, breaking it in pieces. "One of you go get one from another room's stove."

Then he nodded at the bathroom.

"I'm hitting the *baño* and then it's *adios, pendejos!*"

As Skipper Olde entered the bathroom, a crackling sound came from the plug receptacle of the broken coil on the stove, followed by an enormous electrical spark.

The spark immediately met the rising mist of phosphine gas that was being released by the overheated hypophosphorous acid in the milky fluid of the pans. And that instantly triggered an intense explosion — making Skipper Olde's declaration of "Goodbye, assholes" profoundly prophetic.

At almost the same time, Becca Benjamin, feeling flush from her quickened heart rate, was enjoying the warmth coursing through all parts of her body. With the meth heightening her urges, she'd been entertaining the thought of a nice romp with Skipper in her Center City luxury loft overlooking the Delaware River — *Or maybe right here right now in the backseat* — and gently stroked herself through the front of her cream-colored linen shorts.

*Let's go, Skip.*

She glanced at her watch.

*Almost two?*

*Dammit.*

She pushed the lever on the door that

caused her seat back to begin returning upright. Then, as the motel window came into view, there was suddenly a horrific blinding flash, followed immediately by the plate glass exploding outward and a concussion that rocked the box-shaped Mercedes.

In what seemed like a dream, Becca felt the vehicle shake violently, then watched the windshield go from clear to crazed as shards of plate glass struck it, and then felt the crushing sensation of the windshield, blown free of its frame, as it pushed her against the seat back with such force that the seat back flopped back with her to the reclined position.

And then her world went black.

The explosion had triggered the vehicle's alarm system and, as the chemical-fueled flames from the motel room roared and there came the *thuuum! thuuum! thuuum!* sounds of the secondary smaller explosions that were the cans of Coleman fuel cooking off one after another, the horn of the Mercedes bleated its steady warning.

# [FOUR]
## Delaware Cancer Society Building, Fourth Floor Rittenhouse Square, Philadelphia Wednesday, September 9, 4:46 A.M.

"Oh shit," Matt Payne muttered as he put down the stainless-steel thermos. Payne, a twenty-seven-year-old with dark intelligent eyes and conservatively cut dark thick hair, was sitting — shirtless, wearing only boxer shorts on his lithely muscled six-foot, 170-pound frame — at the notebook computer on the desk of his Center City apartment. He stared at his cellular telephone, which had caused him to utter the obscenity. It was vibrating and, on its color LCD screen, flashing: SOUP KING — 1 CALL TODAY @ 0446.

*Not good,* he thought.

With his body clock still not reset to local time after his return from France, Payne had been up since four and, counting the last drops from the thermos, drunk five cups of coffee.

Near the computer were a pair of heavy china mugs. The one that actually held coffee was navy blue with a crest outlined in gold that had gold lettering reading PHILADELPHIA POLICE and HONOR INTEGRITY SERVICE and, above the crest, in gold block letters, DETECTIVE MATTHEW M. PAYNE. The other cup — with a chip on its lip, and holding pens and pencils — was black and emblazoned with the representation of a patch. The center of the patch had the likeness of the downtown Philadelphia skyline, complete to a statue of William Penn atop City Hall, behind which stood a black-caped Grim Reaper with a golden scythe. Circling this scene was, in gold, the legend PHILADELPHIA POLICE HOMICIDE DIVISION.

Sergeant Payne, Matthew M., Badge Number 471, Philadelphia Police Department, was in fact on leave from the department in general and its homicide unit in particular.

That Matt's relationship with the Philly PD — with police work — had created a quandary for him was one hell of an understatement.

On one hand, being a cop was in his blood; his family had a long history with the cops.

A long and tragic history. When Matt was still in the womb, his natural father had been killed in the line of duty. Badge 471 — assigned to him only recently — had belonged to Sergeant John Francis Xavier Moffitt when he'd been shot dead while answering a silent burglar alarm. And, five years ago, Matt's uncle, his father's brother — Captain Richard C. "Dutch" Moffitt, commanding officer of the Philadelphia Police Department's elite Highway Patrol — had been off-duty at the Waikiki Diner on Roosevelt Boulevard when a drug addict tried robbing it. Dutch was killed when he thought he could talk the hopped-up punk into handing over the .22-caliber pistol.

Yet, on the other hand, Matt had been indisputably raised in a life of privilege. Fact was, he did not have to work at a job — and certainly not risking his life as a cop — thanks to an investment program established for him at age three. It had made him a very wealthy young man, and for that he could thank the man who'd adopted him.

Following the death of Matt's natural father, his mother had had to find employment, and after taking classes she'd become, with some effort, an assistant at Lowerie, Tant, Foster, Pedigill & Payne, one of Philly's top legal firms. Soon after, the young and attractive Patricia Moffitt came to meet Brewster Cortland Payne II, son of the firm's founding partner. "Brew" had recently become a widower, one with two infants, his wife having died in an automobile accident on the way home from their Pocono Mountains summer place. One thing led to another with Patricia, and Brewster Payne had then felt it necessary to leave the firm to start his own, particularly after his father expressed his displeasure of "that gold-digging Irish trollop" by boycotting their wedding.

The union of Patricia and Brewster produced another child, a girl they named Amelia. It was not long thereafter that Brew approached his wife with a request to adopt young Matt, whom he loved as his very own flesh and blood.

Matthew Mark Payne had grown up on a four-acre estate on the upper-crust Main Line, attended prep school, and from there went on to the Ivy League, graduating summa cum laude from the University of Pennsylvania. And, accordingly, it was more or less expected, certainly reasonably so, that Matt would go on to law school, and from there very likely join the prestigious Philadelphia law firm of Mawson, Payne, Stockton, McAdoo & Lester.

Matt, however, had felt the pull of service to his country, and went out for the United States Marine Corps. Yet when he'd failed the Corps's precommissioning physical examination — thanks to a quirky complication of his vision one no one knew he suffered from, nor had cared about since — everyone then was convinced that the writing was on the wall: He'd now simply go back to school.

Everyone but Matt, who confounded them all by taking, just after his Uncle Dutch had been killed, the civil service exam for entry into the police department.

Matt's passing the exam shocked no one — he was as far as anyone knew the first, very possibly the only, summa cum laude university graduate to apply to the department — but many were surprised at his passing muster during his thirty-week stint in the demanding Police Academy.

And that had really worried more than a few, because there was talk that the only reasons he'd joined the cops was to prove his manhood — failing to make it into the Marines had damaged more than a little pride — and to avenge the deaths of his natural father and uncle. And, further, behind the worry was the genuine fear that not only would walking a police beat leave Matt, the product of such a privileged background, less than satisfied, it damn well could leave him hurt, or dead.

One such person who'd shared this fear was then–Chief Inspector Dennis V. Coughlin. The last thing Coughlin wanted to have to do was tell Matt's mother that there'd been another shooting — Denny had been the one who knocked on her door and delivered the news that John Francis Xavier Moffitt, her husband and his best friend, had been killed in the line of duty.

Coughlin had toyed with the idea of hiding Matt in the School Crossing Guard Unit and getting him bored to tears helping snot-nosed second graders make it to the next curb — making Matt bored *and* pissed off enough to quit the department — then decided it was safer to have him assigned to a desk as administrative assistant to Inspector Peter Wohl. Wohl, it was hoped, would keep an eye on him and make sure he suffered in the line of duty nothing worse than a paper cut.

And that had worked. But only for a short time. A very short time.

Neither Matt's godfather (Coughlin) nor his rabbi (Wohl) on the police force, despite all their efforts to the contrary, anticipated that Officer Matt Payne would find himself in shoot-outs with bad guys — and they sure as hell had no idea that he'd ultimately come to be known as the Wyatt Earp of the Main Line.

First, with not even six months on the job, he'd been off-duty when he spotted the van used by the doer whom the newspapers had dubbed the Northwest Serial Rapist. Matt had attempted to question the van's driver, at which point the driver had tried to run him down. Matt responded by shooting the sonofabitch in the head. Then, in the back of the van, he'd found the rapist's next victim — a neatly trussed-up, and naked, young woman.

The reaction of Matt's godfather and rabbi — and damned near everyone else on the force — was to quietly declare Matt impossibly lucky that (a) he'd stumbled across the rapist and (b) that he hadn't died from the blunt-force trauma of the van's bumper.

And so they redoubled their efforts to keep Matty safe until he came to his senses, recognized that he damned well could have been killed, and rejoined civilian life.

But not a year later, in the middle of a massive operation designed to arrest a gang of armed robbers on warrants charging them with murder during a Goldblatt's Department Store heist, Matt again made headlines. He'd been assigned to sit on a *Phila-*

*delphia Bulletin* reporter in an alley that was deemed to be a safe distance from where the arrests were going down — for the reporter's safety but, conveniently, for the safety of the reporter's "escort," too.

The foolproof plans unraveled when one of the critters, who hadn't been made privy to the foolproof plans, stumbled into the "safe" alley and started shooting it up. One of the ricocheting bullets grazed Payne's forehead, and he returned fire.

In the next edition of *The Philadelphia Bulletin,* the front-page photograph ("Exclusive Photo By Michael J. O'Hara") showed a bloody-faced Officer Matthew M. Payne, pistol in hand, standing over the fatally wounded felon. Above the photograph — written by Mickey O'Hara, who well knew Payne's background, as he'd written the *Bulletin* piece on Dutch Moffitt's death — was the screaming headline "Officer M. M. Payne, 23, The Wyatt Earp of the Main Line."

And again came the quiet accusations, particularly considering that the vast majority of cops over the course of a twenty-year career on the beat never found cause to pull out — let alone fire — their service weapon at a murderer or rapist or robber.

Yet here was a cop — *a goddamned Richie*

*Rich rookie at that!* — with two righteous shootings proverbially notched on his pistol grip.

It didn't help that not long afterward, Matt Payne had taken — and passed, the summa cum laude college boy's score having placed him first — the exam for the rank of detective.

The quiet accusations gave way to those on the force who made it loud and clear that they regarded Matt Payne as a rich kid who was playing at being a cop, and whose promotions and assignments were thanks to his political connections, not based on his abilities.

And then there were those who weren't quite so accommodating and mindful of their manners — and more than happy to share their opinions directly to Matt's face.

There hadn't been a helluva lot that Payne could do about them, of course, except just stick it out and do his job to the best of his ability. And Matt had found that he not only liked being a cop but thought that he was good at it, further proof of that having come twice in the last six months.

The earlier episode had involved one Susan Reynolds, a beautiful blue-eyed blonde with whom Payne saw himself winding up living happily-ever-after in a vine-covered cottage by the side of the road. However, Susan, blindly loyal and trying to protect an old girlfriend, stupidly got caught up in a group that included Bryan Chenowith, a terrorist hunted nationwide by the Federal Bureau of Investigation. Payne set it up for Philly's FBI special agent in charge to take down Chenowith behind the Crossroads Diner in Doylestown. They bagged the bad guy — but not before Payne saw his dreams with Susan literally die when the lunatic Chenowith cut her down with a stolen fully automatic .30-caliber carbine.

The second episode had happened in the last thirty-odd days, and the Wyatt Earp of the Main Line again had made headlines.

Payne and his date had been in his Porsche 911 Carrera. They were headed for his apartment, about to leave the parking lot of La Famiglia Ristorante, when they came across a middle-class black couple who only moments earlier had left the restaurant and been robbed by two armed men. The doers had pistol-whipped the husband, knocking out teeth, and had gotten only as far as the end of the lot.

Sergeant Payne, Matthew M., Badge Number 471, Philadelphia Police Department, automatically gave chase — and almost immediately his car took the brunt of two blasts from a sawed-off shotgun. Payne then pulled his Colt .45 Officer's Model pistol and put down the shotgunner with a round to the head and severely wounded the accomplice, who had fired at Payne with a .380-caliber Browning semiautomatic pistol.

Payne's date — the extremely bright and attractive Terry Davis, a heavy hitter in the entertainment industry in Los Angeles — had not been badly hurt, but their budding relationship died in that parking lot.

While Matt Payne's shootings were all righteous ones — ones in which he not only was found to be justified by the system but also ones in which he'd been hailed a hero by the public — they haunted him.

And this last shooting had put him over the edge.

It set up a series of events that found him hospitalized and briefly under psychiatric care. After careful examination — and a more or less completely clean bill of health — he was ordered to take a thirty-day leave of compensatory time. The purpose of this leave was (a) to fulfill the prescription for recovery that the psychiatrist said was necessary for such an overworked and overstressed police sergeant, and (b) to be a period of reflection, in which said police sergeant could consider if he might be better suited to another career path at the somewhat tender age of twenty-seven, such as that of a lawyer.

Sitting at his computer in his Rittenhouse Square apartment, Matt Payne had begun his morning — after making coffee and filling the thermos — reading e-mails and the online edition of *The Philadelphia Bulletin*. Then he'd moved on to reviewing the files saved from websites he'd studied the previous night. These had extolled the virtues of various law schools he'd looked at across the country, from Harvard Law — a short scull ride from the Atlantic Ocean via the Charles River and Boston Harbor — to Pepperdine Law, overlooking the surfers in the Pacific Ocean at Malibu. He also had a yellow legal pad on which he'd listed the pros and cons for each of the schools he was considering — or not considering, as there were more schools marked through than not.

And, just as last night, they had begun to bore the shit out of him.

About the time he had poured coffee cup number three, Payne started clicking on another website that he found far more exciting: 911s.com. It had, among other things, a search engine that required the user's home zip code. Payne had first punched in and searched his home zip code, 19103, and almost instantaneously was offered a listing of twenty one-year-old and two-year-old Porsche 911s offered for sale by dealers and brokers and individuals within twenty-five miles of his apartment.

He scrolled through the list, clicked on a few Carrera models, idly wondering as he read the pages how much of their histories were truly factual — "Only 10,250 pampered miles! Always garaged! Never driven in rain!" — and how many of the cars actually, say, had been raced from Media down I-95 to Miami Beach, or run in last month's Poconos Mountain Off-Road Rally then hosed off for resale before the tires — as the stand-up comedian Ron White was famous for saying — *fell the fuck off!*

Matt had grinned at the thought of the comedian's shtick — not a day went by, especially when on the job, that he couldn't apply at least one of White's hilarious observations to a particular situation, most often "You can't fix stupid" — and then he had thought: *Or an even worse abuse — the cars used as daily commuters, rain or shine.*

*Porsche actually built their cars to fly down the highway at the hammers of hell.*

*Stop-and-go traffic is the equivalent of a slow death.*

*Especially in salt-laced snow sludge.*

Figuring he would search major cities that had no snow, and thus no road salt to rust out body panels, he'd punched in 90210, 85001, and 75065, and read the results from those. They belonged, respectively, to Beverly Hills, Phoenix, and Dallas. And each offered three times as many 911s as did 19103.

*Ones with no road salt.*

*Maybe I could get one shipped back here.*

*Or maybe go get one, and drive it back here at the hammers of hell. Now that would be fun . . . .*

He then punched in 33301, which was one of Fort Lauderdale's zip codes. In the search field that asked for a radius in miles from that geographic point, he'd typed in "50."

*Fifty miles easily covers Miami to the south and Palm Beach to the north.*

Then he'd chuckled as he clicked the SEARCH button.

*And plenty of Everglades swamp to the west and Atlantic Ocean to the east.*

*If there's a Porsche in either, it's going to be worse off than my shot-up Carrera.*

*Maybe I should donate mine as an artificial reef. It'd sink like a rock with all those shotgun pellet holes. . . .*

It took a long moment for the page to completely load on his computer screen.

*Jesus! Look at all those Porsches for sale!*
*Ninety Carreras alone!*
*Who the hell is buying them?*
He took a sip of his coffee.
*Stupid question. Who the hell else?*
*All the goddamned drug-runners.*

It had been then that his cellular had started to vibrate, flash Soup King — and cause him to worry.

Matt Payne looked at the cellular phone and said aloud, "What's he want at this hour?"

Payne told himself that it wasn't the time of day that bothered him; rather, it was what it suggested. For as long as he could remember, certainly since his early teen years, his parents had told him that calls in the late of night or early morning almost never announced good news. And his experience as a Philly cop sure as hell had only proved their point, time and again.

*Maybe he accidentally hit my auto-dial number?*

*And if that's the case, and if I'd been sound asleep, I'd be pissed he's waking me up.*

Payne had been pals with the "Soup King" — Payne's nickname for Chadwick Thomas Nesbitt IV — since they were in diapers, when Chad was merely the Soup Prince-in-Waiting. Later, they attended prep school together before both graduating from the University of Pennsylvania.

Had Payne's cellular phone volume not been muted, the phone, having linked "Soup King" with the audio file Matt had saved to its memory chip, would have blared from the speaker their alma mater's marching band playing:

*Tell the story of Glory*
*Of Pennsylvania*
*Drink a highball And be jolly*
*Here's a toast to dear old Penn!*

The Soup King crack came from the fact that Chad's family was Nesfoods International — his father, Mr. Nesbitt III, was now chairman of the executive committee — having succeeded his father, who'd succeeded his — and Chad was recently named a vice president, having worked his way up in the corporate ranks, just as his father and Grandfather Nesbitt had.

And Matt's father and Chad's father were best friends.

Chad never had lacked in the self-esteem department, and Matt often found it his duty to help keep him grounded.

Payne grabbed the phone from its cradle, which automatically answered the call. He put it to his head and by way of greeting said: "My telephone tells me that the Soup

King is calling at four forty-six in the morning. Why, pray tell, would anyone — friend or foe or vegetable royalty — wish to awaken a fine person such as myself from a peaceful slumber at this ungodly hour?"

"Matt? Are you awake, Matt?"

Payne pulled the phone from his head and looked at it askance; it was as if Nesbitt hadn't heard a word he'd said. He put the phone back to his head and replied: "Such a query calls into question the intelligence of one who asks it. Because, it would follow that if one were to telephone a person, and said person were to answer, then, yes, it could be presumed that that person was awake. Or perhaps rudely awakened."

Nesbitt didn't reply.

"Actually, you're lucky," Payne went on. "I wasn't rudely awakened. I was, instead, accomplishing multiple tasks, from plotting my future to looking for a new car. All with the wonders of this miraculous thing called the Internet that's ready at any hour of the day or night. I don't know about you, but I think this Internet thing might be around for a while. Wonderfully handy. And you can go anywhere on it, even in just your underwear."

Nesbitt either ignored the ridiculous sarcasm or again didn't hear what he'd said.

"Look, Matt. I need your help. This is bad."

Payne thought that Nesbitt's voice had an odd tone to it, and that caused a knot in his stomach.

*"What's* bad, Chad?"

Nesbitt did not address the question directly. "I'd heard — Mother said at dinner last week — are you still a cop or not?"

"Well, the days of the Wyatt Earp of the Main Line very well may be numbered. I'm thinking of taking a road trip. Any interest in —"

"So," Chad interrupted, "does that mean no?"

"No. It means technically, yes, I'm still a cop. The real question, though, is: 'Will I continue to be a cop?' I've been put on ice to take time and consider just that —"

"Dammit, yes or no?" he interrupted.

"Yes. What the hell's got you upset? And at this hour?"

"Can you meet me?"

"Now?"

"Now. Remember the Philly Inn? On Frankford?"

*Remember it?*

*No way in hell could anyone forget a party like we had that night — what? — ten, eleven years ago.*

55

*Damn. Has it been that long?*

"Sure, Chad, I remember. Who could forget Whatshisface diving off the roof into the pool?"

"What? Oh, right." His voice tapered off. "Skipper did that . . ."

"Yeah, that's who it was. So, what happened? Did Daffy finally have enough and throw you out?"

Daphne Elizabeth Browne Nesbitt was wife to Chadwick Thomas Nesbitt IV, and Matt was godfather to their baby girl, Penelope Alice Nesbitt, named after the late Penelope Alice Detweiler, with whom, before she shot up her last vein of heroin, causing her to breathe her last breath, Matt had fancied himself in love.

Payne heard only silence, then said, "What's the room number?"

"No. I'm at the All-Nite Diner, by the shopping strip just south of it. Thanks, pal."

"Be there in —" Matt began but stopped when he realized the connection had been broken.

# [FIVE]
# 2512 Hancock Street, Philadelphia
# Wednesday, September 9, 5:01 A.M.

Hancock, off Lehigh Avenue, was only a couple miles southwest of the Philly Inn. It was in the section known as North Philly, which of course was due north of Center City — downtown proper — hence North Philly's name. If the area around the Philly Inn could be described as seedy and sliding to worse, then it would be no less than a kind and charitable act to call North Philly, particularly the more and more Latino neighborhood containing Hancock Street, a miserable godforsaken slum with zero to zilch chance of redemption.

And in a dilapidated row house on Hancock, Ana Maria Del Carmen Lopez — a petite pretty seventeen-year-old Honduran with light-brown skin, long straight black hair, dark eyes, and soft facial features, including a smattering of freckles across her

57

upper cheeks and pixie nose that made her appear even younger — was startled awake from an uneasy sleep by sounds outside her open second-story bedroom window.

Ana was lying with two younger girls from Mexico on a dirty mattress on the wooden floor of the bedroom. She first heard the familiar rattling of a lawn care utility trailer, then the squeaking springs of the dirty tan Ford panel van pulling it over the curb, across the sidewalk, and through the open gate of the vacant lot next door — where two abandoned row houses once stood before burning and being torn down — and then the white rusty Plymouth minivan with its darkened windows that followed the van and trailer into the lot.

Ana's pulse quickened as she then heard Latin music coming from another vehicle that was accelerating up Hancock Street. While she was not surprised, she was scared. This had happened nearly every night for the two months she'd been here: One of two vans would bring the girls and others back to the house — she wasn't sure why they had the trailer of lawn mowers out so late — and El Gato would be right on their heels to collect the cash. If everyone was lucky, he then would just take the money and drive off into the dark humid night.

At five feet eleven inches tall and 180 pounds, twenty-one-year-old Juan Paulo Delgado moved with the grace and power of a big cat — thus his nickname, "El Gato." He had the toned, muscular body of one who worked out regularly with gym weights, which he'd learned to perfect during a short stint in the prison system. He was as fastidious as a cat in his appearance, keeping his black hair cut short and neat, his face clean-shaven, his body — with one exception — absolutely unmarked.

The exception was a small black tattoo — a gothic block letter D with three short lines on either side representing whiskers — at the base of his palm. The location made it more or less unnoticeable to the casual observer unless El Gato chose to show it. It was the same tattoo he convinced each of the girls to get when he first met them — "To show my love of family," El Gato told them. But each girl's whiskered D was tattooed on the neck behind the left ear, at the hairline.

The girls — at first, while they still were under his influence, desperate to believe his bullshit ruse of "love of family" — had enjoyed flashing the tattoo by pulling back their hair and smiling appreciatively, if not seductively, at El Gato.

And Juan Paulo Delgado had another cat-like trait: He carried himself in such a way that one moment he could be all charm, his deep, dark eyes almost smiling — then the next moment his short Latin temper turned him intimidating, his eyes cold and hard. When his anger erupted, it made him seem much older than his twenty-one years.

Ana felt the two other girls, Jorgina and Alicia, both fourteen years old and with attractive features somewhat similar to hers, snuggle in closer for protection. Yet they all knew that there would be no protection from whatever was to come.

*Of course they know,* she thought. *And they, too, are scared.*

*My bruises are almost gone.*

*Theirs are still dark, still fresh and with much pain . . .*

There was the grating of the wooden slats of the gate as it was being slid closed on the vacant lot. And when that was done — and only after the gate was closed and its chain locked — there came the slamming of the van's front doors and the sliding open of the rusty side doors of the minivan for the half-dozen girls to exit.

Footsteps could be heard as the girls were herded through the backyard to the back door of the row house, then into their bedrooms. There they, like Ana and Jorgina and

60

Alicia, were kept more or less warehoused, guarded under lock and key until sent out to work — which could be any hour of the day or night.

Ana did not think that the round-the-clock watch was really necessary. If the fear of being beaten again was not enough to keep the girls from trying to get away, then the threats made against their families certainly was. Proof of that was that almost no one tried to get away.

*No one but Rosario, may the Holy Father protect her wherever she ran off to.*

And then there were the other invisible barriers, among them not having any papers proving who they were — those girls who actually had, for example, a birth certificate had them taken by El Gato "to keep them safe." Also, the girls could speak only Spanish — and with no real formal education could barely read it — and so they had no understanding of exactly where they were and especially where they could go. Certainly not to the police, whose screaming *woop-woop* sirens they heard piercing the night. Back home, they'd learned *policía* could not be completely trusted.

And so the fear of the unknown was as strong a deterrent as any of the iron shackles or guarded doors.

Ana listened closely for what would happen next.

Usually, El Gato simply stopped in the street, and Amando or Omar or Eduardo or Jesús handed over to him the cash — usually in a backpack — and exchanged a few words — or none — and then his Chevrolet Tahoe accelerated up Hancock and made the turn onto Lehigh Avenue as he headed toward his nice converted warehouse apartment in Manayunk, a gentrifying middle-class section on the banks of the Schuylkill River in Northwestern Philly.

Occasionally, however, he came into one of the houses and dealt with whatever problem there had been that night — most often a girl who had not performed for a client as expected or another who needed "encouragement" to work.

*El Gato,* Ana thought, *always says he does not like raising a hand to us girls.*

*But I think the reason is not because he doesn't like to hurt people — I think he does, and pray that God may punish him — it is because the marks he puts on us make the men not want to pay.*

*So we stay locked up till the marks go away . . .*

Ana heard the sounds of tires climbing the curb — El Gato liked to park his SUV off the narrow street, its right-side wheels crushing the weeds growing in the sidewalk cracks — then the engine being turned off. Next came a door being opened and shut, followed by a short *honk* that reported a button on the remote had been pushed to lock the SUV's doors and activate its alarm.

Ana suddenly realized that the sounds had caused her palms to sweat and that she had begun to slightly shake. She felt one of the girls, who apparently recognized the shaking for what it was, rubbing her back in a calming fashion.

*Dear God, please do not let him come up here.*

*I told him again and again I do not know where Rosario went.*

*Another beating will not change that.*

She next heard the unlocking of the front door, then the heavy footfalls quickly pounding up the flight of wooden steps. Finally, the bedroom door swung open.

Faint light from the streetlights up Hancock bled in through the open window, which had been wedged open to provide the room with some — *any* — air circulation on the hot humid night. El Gato was dimly lit in the doorway.

*Maybe with my bruises almost gone he is taking me to work?*

*Please, no . . .*

As El Gato approached the bed, she saw something fall from his hand, then heard it make a soft bump as it hit the wooden floor. Ana suddenly curled up defensively in the fetal position. Then, when he grabbed her by the collar of her T-shirt, the two younger girls back-crawled off the mattress to a dark corner of the room.

"No . . ." Ana softly said, and whimpered in anticipation of what was about to come.

Breathing heavily, Juan Paulo Delgado hovered ominously over her.

Ana smelled the alcohol on his breath, some beer probably and what had to be tequila. She could visualize his cold hard eyes in the dark even though she could not clearly see them. Then she heard him grunt — and saw his right arm in silhouette suddenly swing back, then forward, his palm finding her face. As she recoiled, her T-shirt ripped in his left hand.

*"No mas! No mas, por favor!"* she cried out, wishing that this all was just another nightmare. But she then felt the sting of his backhanded slap, and she understood with painful clarity that this was building to be the real thing. Again.

"You fucking bitches! Every one of you!" Delgado yelled in English, then swung again,

64

this time striking her with a balled fist. He switched to Spanish: "I helped you, made you family, and how do you repay me?"

Ana looked away from El Gato, trying to hold her small hands to her face as protection.

"You want to see your cousin?" he went on in Spanish, and hit her again. "I take you to Rosario! I'm through with the both of you!"

Ana began to sob. She did not understand; for months now she had been doing the disgusting work for El Gato, selling her body to repay her passage debt — and now her room and board — to him. As had Rosario. And it was not Ana's fault that Rosario had had enough and finally run off. Though Ana knew that it was futile to try to make that point now.

El Gato again cursed her, and her cousin, then hit her again.

The salty taste of sweat on Ana's lips now mingled with a metallic one — and she recognized the warm sticky fluid as her blood.

As El Gato yelled — there was a furiousness in his voice that she had never before heard, even during the other beatings — she silently prayed, *Holy Mother of God, please make him stop.*

But he began striking her repeatedly, the

sickening thuds of his fist on her face triggering whimpers of sympathy — or fear, or both — from Alicia and Jorgina, who were clinging to each other in the corner of the bedroom.

Then she stopped sobbing, made an awful groan, and went limp.

And Ana Maria Del Carmen Lopez's prayer was answered; he stopped beating her.

Alicia and Jorgina, fearful El Gato would turn and unleash his fury on them, tried to silence their whimpering. They watched in the dimness as he walked back to the doorway, picked up what he'd dropped on the floor, then returned to Ana.

The sound of a strip of heavy tape being ripped from its roll came next. Delgado applied that over Ana's mouth and nose. He then took the roll of heavy tape and wrapped her wrists behind her back, then bound together her ankles.

He threw the roll of tape back on the floor, then grunted as he dragged Ana's limp body out the door and let it fall with a dull *thud.*

A moment later, he came back into the room.

Alicia and Jorgina recoiled.

El Gato walked over to them in the corner. He got down on one knee and in Spanish softly said, "It will be okay now," then reached out with his left hand and stroked Alicia's hair, his fingers brushing her tattoo in the process.

Then he pulled from the front pocket of his blue jeans two paper packets and tossed them to the floor by the girls. Without looking, the girls knew what they were.

Each small packet — the size of a business card — was white and had a rubber stamp imprint in light blue ink of a cartoonish block of Swiss cheese, on either side of which were three lines that shot outward — not unlike the lines of their D tattoos — and above the cheese the legend QUESO AZUL.

"If you're good, and I know you will be, I will bring you more," he said, then stroked Jorgina's hair and stood and left the room.

Alicia and Jorgina heard the *thump, thump, thump* of El Gato dragging Ana down the stairs. Then the back door opening, then the sliding of the minivan door, then the grating of the wooden slat gate of the lot. There was a banging of metal tools in the lawn care trailer, then the slamming shut of a minivan door.

The Plymouth spun its wheels in the dirt and gravel of the lot, the tires chirping as it quickly drove off the sidewalk and up the street.

In the now eerie silence of the dirty bedroom, fourteen-year-old Alicia and Jorgina clung to each other and started crying uncontrollably.

After a few minutes, Jorgina reached for one of the paper packets. She opened the flap at the end, took the tiny straw from inside, put that to her nose, and snorted the brown powder contents of the packet.

# II

## [ONE]
## Rittenhouse Square, Philadelphia
## Wednesday, September 9, 5:10 A.M.

After Matt Payne had gently lowered the screen of his notebook computer, closing it to put it in sleep mode, he'd gotten up from the desk and crossed the room to go into his bedroom. It had been a short trip.

"Small" didn't begin to describe the apartment, which actually was the garret of a brownstone mansion, 150 years old and recently renovated. The first three floors had been converted to office space, the current occupant being the Delaware Cancer Society. The garret had been turned into an apartment — no more than a bedroom barely able to contain its king-size bed (and nothing more, the few lamps and shelves wall-mounted), a bath not large enough for a bathtub, a kitchen separated from the dining area by a sliding partition stuck half-open, and a living room from which a small area of historic Rittenhouse Square could be seen if one stood high on tiptoe and squinted through one of its two eighteen-inch-wide dormer windows.

Payne pulled on a pair of lightweight khakis, a black T-shirt, and then a short-sleeved striped cotton shirt that he left unbuttoned down the front and the shirttail untucked. He slipped his wallet and badge into the back pockets of his pants, and his cellular phone and two magazines of .45 ACP ammo in the front ones. His bare feet went into a well-worn pair of boater's deck shoes. Then he pulled back the tail of his striped cotton shirt. He snugged his loaded Colt Officer's Model semiautomatic pistol — six rounds in the mag, one in the chamber — inside the waistband of his khakis so that it rested comfortably on his right hip. He felt the cold of the stainless-steel pistol through his clothing.

*That won't last long.*

*There'll be a sweaty spot there the second I step out of the air-conditioning.*

He then took the stairs down to the third-floor landing, where he pushed the button to summon the elevator.

Getting off the elevator in the basement garage, he walked toward his rental car. It was a nondescript Ford midsize sedan that he had come to loathe for its utter blandness, the car's only redeeming quality being that it was so nondescript, and so white, that no one tended to notice it, making it an unlikely candidate for key-scratched doors and other such abuse afforded nicer cars in the city. He wasn't sure if the New York State license plates were a plus or a minus. But he had decided that the best thing about the rental car was that his insurance company was paying for it while they decided what to do with — which meant how much they were going to cough up to fix or replace — his shot-up Porsche.

Payne looked somewhat wistfully at the empty parking spot that normally held his 911. He really missed the car — it was a helluva lot of fun driving it hard on Bucks County's two-lane country roads. Yet even if he had it now, he sure as hell would not use it, as where he was going was not the place for a nearly new sports car of any kind. While Rittenhouse Square had some of the oldest and most expensive real estate in Philadelphia, if not all of Pennsylvania, Frankford Avenue — though only miles away — cut through some rough neighborhoods that were a world removed.

Matt pulled out of the garage, cursing the sloppy feel of the Ford's front-wheel drive as he drove to Eighteenth Street, deciding at the last moment to take Eighteenth and not Broad Street north, the latter of which would have submitted him to the circle jerk of traffic that was around City Hall. He'd long ago decided it was best to avoid that, even at this very early hour.

His mind wandered as he drove north on Eighteenth through the heart of Center City. Force of habit almost had him turn right on Race Street, his usual route when driving from Rittenhouse Square to the Roundhouse — the decades-old Philadelphia Police Headquarters, at Eighth and Race, which was built in a circle design and was said not to have a single straight wall, including in the elevators.

Payne stopped himself from turning just as he'd flipped the flimsy turn-signal stalk — *If it wasn't for me noticing that, I'd have automat-*

*ically made the turn, and I really don't feel like seeing the Roundhouse right now in my frame of mind* — then jerked the wheel back left to stay in his northbound lane. This act earned him the wave of the driver in the Chevy sedan behind him — the "wave" consisting of but a single digit and complemented with a burst of horn.

*Chalk another one up to Ford.*

*And maybe score one for the New York tags.*

*That guy probably thinks I'm just a poor schmuck lost in his rental car.*

*If I'd been in the Porsche, he'd have ridden my bumper and his horn forever.*

Two blocks later, he turned east on Vine Street and followed it to Broad, then hung a left on Broad. A few blocks later, crossing Spring Garden, he glanced to the right at Lodge No. 5 of the Fraternal Order of Police — the cops' labor union — and wasn't surprised to see the building dark and the parking lot empty.

Farther north on Broad, however, he was surprised to see that another building was being more or less renovated — residents trying against the odds to seed some good in another neighborhood that long had been and, if history was any indicator, probably would remain blighted.

The decay of the city depressed him, and that caused him to think about the reason why he lived in Philly anyway.

Matt Payne, who had grown up in the wealthy comfort of Wallingford, outside Philadelphia proper, lived in Philly because he had to: It forever had been a rule that in order to apply to be a member of the Philadelphia Police Department you had to show proof that you had been a legal resident of the City of Philadelphia for at least one year prior.

But recently that fifty-year-old rule had been changed somewhat. And there were at least a couple very good reasons for that, not the least of the which was that the Thin Blue Line was getting thinner and thinner in Philly. The city needed not only to recruit more cops — and, it went without saying, more good cops, "good" clearly meaning candidates who were best qualified — but needed to actually hire those recruited and then retain them after their probationary period. Preferably for twenty or more years, until retirement.

When cops did quit the force, the City of Philadelphia Office of Human Resources approached them with a one-page form, "No. HR-106-B, Questionnaire, Upon Separation of Civil Service Employee," the ultimate purpose of which was to learn of any possible problems that existed and, it was hoped, could be corrected. While it certainly was too late to stop the man or woman from quitting, the information from the completed form might help fix what had caused their decision to leave the force in the first place.

Or, at least, so went the logic of the HR midlevel bureaucrat who had come up with the idea of the form, which had come to be known as the Don't Let the Doorknob Hit You in the Ass Exit Interview. It was arguable if the form had effected any genuinely helpful changes in policy, or if it just created some paper-pushing, number-crunching bureaucrat — or bureaucrats, plural — with job security.

Matt had heard time and again that it cost the city significant money to train the new cops. Particularly during the recruits' time in the academy, where it still managed to surprise even the most hardened of the veteran instructors how many recruits only six months prior had not, for example, ever had a driver's license, or had not handled a firearm — or both. Thus, the particular recruits had to be taught the basics of driving an automobile and firing a pistol before moving on to more refined skills required of a Philadelphia Police Officer in the execution of his or her duties when using a vehicle or a loaded weapon.

*Maybe even,* Matt thought with a grin, *when using a car and gun at the same time.*

Matt also had heard that more than a few of those who either had quit or had turned down offers to join the force, when polled for their reason or reasons why, had said that chief among them was having to live — and try to raise a family — in, as one wrote, "the very crime-infested cesspool of a city" they would have been sworn to protect.

That sort of description was hard to hear, particularly for one who loved Philadelphia as much as Matt did. But hearing the truth often was hard, and Matt knew that the crime-infested cesspool was not limited to the ghettos. There was plenty of crime to go around. People were being robbed and raped and stabbed from South Philly to Far Northeast, even in Center City.

*Bad guys are equal-opportunity offenders.*

And so the city officials in their sage way found it within themselves to change that requirement for joining the police department — yet, in their usual half-assed manner, went only so far as to waive the one-year prior-residence requirement, allowing the applicant a six-month period after being hired to become a resident.

*So every cop still has to reside in the city.*

*And I've never understood that.*

*A lot of cities allow you to live elsewhere than in the actual city you serve, say within a half hour of your assignment.*

*That forty-grand salary a Philly police officer recruit gets could stretch further in the suburbs.*

*Then again, a lot of cities like Philly wanted their cops close and handy to their crime-infested cesspool. . . .*

Matt's mind, as he continued northbound on Broad, wandered back to his conversation with Chad Nesbitt.

*Hell, there're a lot of things I don't understand.*

*Starting with what's going on now with Chad?*

*And it was Skipper — J. Warren Olde — who jumped into that pool at the Philly Inn. One helluva cannonball.*

*Now, there's a real dipshit. Always had some con going, thinking he was more clever than he really was, and sometimes getting bit in the ass because of it.*

*Not a bad guy, and could be funny, especially drunk, which lucky for him was often.*

*And he'd really been boozing it up at the motel when he jumped off the roof.*

*Or, maybe, when he fell.*

*But his biggest problem was that he couldn't stick with anything. First they blamed it on his trust fund taking away any motivation. Then they found out he had some slight mental imbalance that pills would fix — if he just took the damned meds and stopped self-medicating with booze and whatever else.*

*And Chad, for whatever reason, maybe because they were the hotshots on the academy squash team, was always bailing him out.*

*Always.*

*Like after that time Skipper drove into the reservoir with that really nice Audi — and that gorgeous Becca Benjamin.*

*Dad said he'd heard Skipper's lawyer say that it'd cost a small fortune to make that go away.*

*An absolutely gorgeous girl.*

*Still hurts to remember the day I heard they were dating. . . .*

Matthew Mark Payne had known Rebecca Stockton Benjamin longer than J. Warren Olde had, though certainly not as intimately. The Paynes and Benjamins had worshipped at the same small Episcopal Church in Wallingford. Its sanctuary physically was more chapel-like than church-size, and its parishioners numbered no more than five hundred. Thus, while growing up, Matt and

Becca had seen each other practically every Sunday. They often were in the same youth group meetings, retreats, camps, and the like. Matt had always liked the spunky, outgoing girl — few didn't — and even thought that there had been some sort of mutual interest.

*A crush?*

Then, when Skipper took up with the blossoming sixteen-year-old, Matt had been really pissed. Especially when he saw the direction Skipper was taking her . . . and she was blindly following.

At Cecil Moore Avenue, Matt hung a right, skirting Temple University, then about a mile later he picked up Frankford and followed it north another mile or so — until he saw the flashing emergency lights.

*Jesus! Look at all the fire trucks.*

*Even a HazMat unit.*

To the side of that heavy-duty red Ford truck, a fireman was using a fire hose to wash down two men wearing bright orange HazMat "moonwalker" bodysuits, rubber boots, and full-face hoods. Another was respooling smaller HazMat hoses onto the roof of the truck's equipment box.

*What HazMats are at a motel?*

*And judging by all the cruisers, there can't be a cop left at the Roundhouse.*

His pulse quickened at the sight.

*Is my heart beating faster because I want to rush in?*

*Or because it wants me to run away as fast as my feckless rental Ford can go?*

A pair of police cruisers, their roof light bars flashing, was parked at an angle across the northbound lanes of Frankford just south of the Philly Inn. A cop stood in the street beside them directing traffic to detour onto a side street.

Payne looked ahead and saw the neon sign for the All-Nite Diner, then the diner itself and the crowd gathered in front of it. He hit his turn signal to go into the diner parking lot, and when the cop saw it blinking, he motioned approval for the nondescript Ford sedan to take its turn.

# [TWO]
## 1344 W. Susquehanna Avenue, Philadelphia
## Wednesday, September 9, 5:35 A.M.

Paco "El Nariz" Esteban, a heavyset, five-foot-two twenty-seven-year-old with coffee-colored skin and a flat face whose most prominent feature was a fat nose twice as wide as it was long, stood in the middle of the brightly lit, newly renovated laundromat. He had his stubby fingers splayed on his ample hips as he surveyed his midnight-to-eight work crew feeding motel bedsheets and towels to the machines.

Built into one long white wall were twenty stainless-steel commercial-quality washing machines. Another interior wall held a line of twenty-five commercial-quality clothes dryers. Waist-high four-foot-square thick-wire baskets on heavy-duty casters either were waiting in front of a washer or dryer, or were full and being wheeled by Latina women in jeans and T-shirts from the wall of dryers to a long tan linoleum counter at the back of the room. There, an assembly line of more Latinas folded and stacked freshly laundered sheets and towels before sliding them down the tan counter to be sorted and packed for transport back to the various motels. The large windows and front door to the street were papered over, and milky paint-splattered plastic sheeting sealed off a side room that was still under construction.

Paco "The Nose" Esteban soaked up the atmosphere of the laundry at this early hour — the soft conversations in Spanish of the workers, the Latin music station playing on a clock radio in the back corner, the hum of washers and dryers. It created an almost peaceful sound, the kind of rhythm that came when good people were accomplishing honest work.

El Nariz took a quiet pride in his crews — he also had ones working as housekeepers at the motels — and what he thought of as his role as their mentor and protector — indeed, their *paterfamilias,* as he could trace his relationship by blood to a majority of his workers.

Like El Nariz himself, those in his hand-picked crews were simple hardworking people. Almost all had fled the raw-dirt tin-shack squalor of the slums of Mexico City.

El Nariz — whose own formal education would be described as the School of Hard Knocks in a place like South Philly, where he now lived — had no idea about official census numbers. Moreover, he did not give a rat's ass about them. He simply understood that what he had now was a helluva lot better than what he'd lived in in Mexico.

Had he even the slightest interest, however, Paco Esteban easily could have learned that Philadelphia, founded October 27, 1682, was the largest city in Pennsylvania. That in its 135 square miles the population numbered — officially, not including those such as El Nariz and his illegal immigrant crews, who wished to remain under the radar and therefore went uncounted — nearly 1.5 million, or roughly more than 11,000 people in every square mile, with about one in four in poverty. That Philadelphia was the fifth-largest city in the United States. And that its urban area, with some 5.3 million people, was the U.S.'s fourth largest.

Also with a cursory search, Paco Esteban could have as easily learned that Mexico City had nearly six times as many people (8.8 million) as Philly within an area only a little more than four times as large (573 square miles), or 15,400 people per square mile. And that Mexico City's metro area swelled with nearly 20 million people — 40 percent of whom lived in poverty with no better than a snowball's chance in hell (or Mexico) of ever enjoying a finer quality of life.

But Paco Esteban didn't need numbers to tell him what he already damn well knew: that life here, while not perfect, was far better than in Mexico. As it was of course for everyone in his crews. They had come to America via various routes — not a damn one of them legal — most planned and financed by El Nariz himself, as had been done for him seven years earlier.

■ ■ ■ ■

Esteban had been twenty-two years old when he'd hopped across the U.S. border — literally, as his smuggler had led his group of four Mexican nationals to the flimsy rusty fencing that separated the two countries and showed them how to boost one another over it into Nogales, Arizona. The smuggler had announced that his amigo — like him, another "coyote," so named because of their wily, evasive traits — waited on the other side to take them to a nearby drop house.

At the small four-bedroom ramshackle house, where coyotes armed with shotguns and pistols guarded doors leading to the outside, they had joined dozens of other illegal immigrants. These were almost all men, but some women and children, too. The majority were dark-skinned ones Esteban recognized as being from Mexico and elsewhere in Latin America, but there also were ones with much lighter skin who appeared to be European, Middle Eastern, and, clearly, because of their eyes, Asian, all keeping clustered to their own kind and very quiet.

While everyone so far had successfully evaded arrest by the various U.S. agencies policing the border — that alone, El Nariz quickly came to understand, was a significant accomplishment — they still were in danger. He saw that except for mostly moving during the night, not much effort was given to discreetly carrying out the smuggling; this was simply a numbers game to the coyotes, and the coyotes even warned them point-blank that not everyone was going to make it, so they damn well better give it their best shot.

Surveying the groups in the house, El Nariz had comforted himself with the thought: *You don't have to be the fastest — just not the slowest.*

Cellular telephones — ones the smuggled immigrants had brought or ones provided by the drop house for an added fee — were being used by the immigrants to call their benefactors in the United States to wire payments of $1,500 to $2,100 via Western Union to the smugglers so that the immigrants could move on to the next leg of their journey.

Western Union promised, for a fee of about a hundred bucks, that anyone could "Send money in minutes by telephone, online, or from one of our 320,000 Western Union Agent locations worldwide! We accept cash, credit, and debit cards!"

Depending on their funds and desire to do so, the journey's next leg could mean being taken in a car or a bus — or packed miserably in the back of an eighteen-wheeler trailer — on to California, New Mexico, Texas, or even far across the country.

Paco El Nariz Esteban had made his way, under a tire-topped tarp in the back of a Ford pickup with SMITTY'S ROADSIDE SERVICE, SERVING SOUTHERN ARIZONA SINCE 1979 painted on its doors, up Interstate Highway 19 the forty-odd miles to Tucson, Arizona. There he'd joined his uncle, himself a Mexican national illegally in the United States, and who'd floated El Nariz his smuggler's fee of $1,700.

El Nariz began working at construction jobs. It was brutal, menial work in the Arizona sun, but in six months he'd scrimped together four grand, more than enough to repay his uncle. El Nariz then made contact again with his smugglers, and used the rest of his savings to bring up his wife from the Mexico City slums and, with a small loan from the uncle to cover the difference, his wife's brother.

Not two weeks later, they were all celebrating the arrival of El Nariz's wife and brother-in-law. And not quite nine months later, the reunion that El Nariz and his wife had enjoyed that night found them, courtesy of the Primeros Pasos Clinic at Saint John's Hospital of Tucson, the parents of a newborn son.

And immediately upon his birth on American soil, Ricardo Alvarado Esteban, in accordance with the Fourteenth Amendment of the U.S. Constitution — to wit: *All persons born or naturalized in the United States, and subject to the jurisdiction thereof, are citizens of the United States and of the State wherein they reside* — had become a legal citizen of the United States of America.

When the proud papa, now twenty-three years old, was presented with the "First Steps" clinic's bill for services rendered to Señora Esteban — said bill having been translated to Spanish for him by the bilingual aide from the hospital's financial office — he could not begin to understand such an enormous dollar figure, never mind try to figure out how to repay it. If it had taken six months to save $4,000, he figured that was looking at five-plus years' savings just for this one bill.

El Nariz decided his next steps after Primeros Pasos were to pack up the family and move to another state.

He felt bad about not paying the bill. But his uncle — a carpenter's helper whose wisdom came from being three years older and in America for four more — helped him rationalize it by saying El Nariz should feel even worse about the laws of the United States that had caused him to have to risk his life and that of his family by sneaking into America as a criminal, then for little money sneaking around to do the difficult work that the gringos seemed more than happy to hire him to do.

The uncle rationalized that if they as immigrants were treated better — treated as El Nariz's son would be as an American citizen — then they, too, could be better paid and more able to repay such debts.

"It is really the fault of the *norteamericanos* and their unfair laws," El Nariz's uncle concluded simply. "*Comprendo?*"

The uncle then reminded El Nariz of other family he had in Pennsylvania — ones who'd helped with the uncle's coming to America — and they were in a place outside Philadelphia that was friendly to immigrants. It was called Norristown, and, as in Tucson, there was an established community of Mexican immigrants, but unlike in Tucson, they were more or less left alone by *la migra,* the various authorities enforcing the laws of *inmigración.*

And there was plenty of work up there, including construction. Perhaps best, there wasn't a desert sun to suffer under as he toiled.

In Pennsylvania, El Nariz started out doing day laborer jobs. Then, through a family referral, he'd found work renovating a hotel in Philadelphia's Center City. He secured the job of swinging an iron-headed sledgehammer to bust out each room's old bathroom tiling because he agreed to the pay. He later learned that it was next to nothing that the other laborers were being paid, but he did not complain — it was far more than the four dollars *a day* that the minimum wage in Mexico City had paid, which damn sure was nothing.

The demolition job in the city had caused him to find nearby housing for his family — whom he'd then sent for, wife and son arriving a month later by bus at the Philadelphia Greyhound Terminal in Center City — and that turned out to be a South Philly three-bedroom row house, one in disrepair on Sears Street, between the Mexican markets on Ninth and the Delaware River.

They shared the house with two other illegal immigrant families from Mexico, subletting the place — no signed lease, cash only — from a relative of one of the families. He was a punk, all of twenty-one years old. But he had been born in the United States and thus had the appropriate papers to satisfy the owner — a tough Vietnamese, an immigrant himself who had become a proud nationalized American and who'd moved out near his two shopping-strip restaurants in the upscale suburb of King of Prussia — in order to sign the original lease.

While the living conditions — particularly the crime — of Philly's run-down neighborhoods were hardly postcard perfect, the Estebans found them no worse than the rough Tucson barrio in which they had lived. And they were, of course, a vast improvement over the hopeless impoverishment of the third-world slum that they had fled. Just having reliable potable running water and sanitary sewer systems was a gift from God. And here there was the availability of free public schooling and, as they had found at Saint John's in Tucson, medical care at clinics and hospitals.

During the renovation job, the hotel had reopened in stages, and well before its laundry room was complete, thus requiring that the sheets and towels and tablecloths and anything else in need of laundering be taken off site. Paco Esteban was offered — and quickly took, having tired of the pain from swinging a bone-rattling sledge — the job of collecting the large laundry bins, then loading and off-loading them when the trucks came.

In the year that Esteban's family had been in Philadelphia, his wife's brother also had arrived at the Filbert Street bus terminal, and they had pooled their savings and paid for the passage of more of his wife's family members — a male cousin in his late twenties who escorted his two teenage nieces — up from Mexico City. For various reasons, the first of the other families in the row house had moved out, then the second, and Esteban's extended family filled their spaces.

The new arrivals found work, but, as El Nariz had experienced, it was spotty and sometimes dangerous, and, if it could get any worse, it wasn't unusual to work for days — and then never to get paid.

To what authority could they complain and not have to explain their situation?

El Nariz believed that he could do better, especially now that he saw how many damn towels got dirty in one hotel in a single day. He knew he couldn't personally handle such a large volume — not yet — but maybe he could do the towels and sheets that came from a smaller place.

He'd gotten the idea because one of the cousin's nieces now worked as a housekeeper at a motel in Northeast Philly. And after learning from her how many sheets and towels the motel needed laundered on an average day, he'd worked up some numbers and put together a proposal. He then approached the head of the motel's housekeepers, a plump, balding Puerto Rican woman in her forties who, most important, spoke both Spanish and English.

She agreed, after haggling for a handling fee in cash up front, to present El Nariz's proposal to the motel manager, a white male of sixty who was so morbidly obese that his engorged gut had popped off two buttons on his greasy polyester shirt, and his striped polyester necktie hung only as far as the bottom of his rib cage, unable to cover his sweaty T-shirt exposed by the missing buttons.

El Nariz had had no real idea of what such a job ultimately could bring. But apparently it was more money than his proposal requested. The manager had asked El Nariz a few perfunctory questions, which were translated by the Puerto Rican head of housekeeping. The manager then had grunted, and after some moments declared, "Aw, why the hell not? Less for me to deal with, especially keeping the damn employee books."

Esteban's initial excitement was tempered by the fact that the manager had been slow to pay for the laundry services. But Esteban did not complain — he quietly had begun using the motel's machines to clean the laundry of another motel that had accepted his proposal, this one more lucrative.

Apparently, though, the late-paying manager was nonetheless pleased with Esteban and his crew's work, as he eventually did pay and, further, offered Esteban the laundry detail of another motel, one across the river in Camden, New Jersey, that he managed.

Not long after that, El Nariz had offers of more work than he could handle. His limitation wasn't manpower. His stable of available workers continued to grow. And with more in the process of being brought up from Mexico City — including two who'd been caught by the U.S. Border Patrol near Laredo, Texas, and sent back south, only to get across the Rio Grande unnoticed on their next attempt — they soon filled additional South Philly houses, the rent paid of course in cash.

El Nariz's limitation was, instead, infrastructure. The motel's old machines, even if they weren't breaking down, simply could not keep up with demand.

So, as Esteban found himself having to feed coins to the heavy-duty machines of a real laundromat, he came up with another idea. He again worked up a proposal, and not only had the laundromat manager accepted it — leasing the facility during after hours on a cash-only off-the-books basis — the manager, who Esteban learned also was the owner, offered him the same deal with some other laundromats that he had in Philadelphia.

El Nariz suddenly found that he had more machines than he could use in one location, and when ready to expand, he had others that would be closer to the various motels he serviced.

# [THREE]
## All-Nite Diner
## 6980 Frankford Avenue,
## Philadelphia
## Wednesday, September 9,
## 5:40 a.m.

Matt Payne worked his way through the crowd milling in the parking lot and along the sidewalk outside the diner. He noticed that they appeared to be those displaced from the motel, mostly a mix of black and Hispanic males, as well as a few Anglo families. Some wore night clothing, some had on street clothing, and all looked haggard.

*These people really were rudely awakened.*

Inside, he found the place packed with more of the same, and it took him a minute to find Chad Nesbitt. That was mostly because Chad was slumped down in a booth by one of the front windows and more or less hiding under a red Philadelphia Phillies National League Champions ball cap, the tip of its brim pulled down almost to his nose.

Chad Nesbitt looked very much like Matt Payne, only a little shorter and a little heavier. He wore faded blue jeans, athletic running shoes, and a gray T-shirt with big black letters spelling BRUUUUUCE! The shirt had been bought six years earlier at a Springsteen show. Matt knew because he'd bought one, too, and that made him think of that well-built, very high-maintenance blond Aimee Cullen wearing his — and damn little else — as she left his apartment one Saturday morning, promising to give it back. But their relationship hadn't lasted long enough for that to happen.

When Matt reached the booth, Chad did not get up or look up. Instead, he stared out the window at the pulsing red and blue lights. Matt slid onto the red-vinyl bench seat opposite him. On the table in front of Chad, next to his cellular phone, was a cold plate of fried eggs and bacon and toast, all of it barely touched. He had his left hand wrapped around a cheap plastic coffee cup that was nearly empty.

Chad finally slowly turned to look at Matt, and Matt could see that he hadn't shaved and that his eyes were sleep-deprived.

"Thanks for coming, pal," Chad said in a flat, tired tone. "I wasn't sure who to call first."

Matt tried to lighten the mood. "Nice shirt. I miss mine, but I think losing it when Aimee left was worth the price just to see her go before she bankrupted me."

Chad glanced down and shrugged. "First damn thing I grabbed in the dark —" He stopped when he looked across the street toward the Philly Inn.

Matt Payne glanced around the crowded noisy diner, and when he saw a waitress, a plump black woman in her forties snapping orders to a young Latino busboy, he waved and got her attention, then pointed at Chad's plate and coffee, then pointed at himself. She curtly nodded her understanding of his order.

"Oh, Christ," Chad exclaimed.

Matt looked to see what caught his attention.

At the motel, one of the Philly cops was

walking to undo from a light pole one end of a length of yellow and black POLICE LINE — DO NOT CROSS crime-scene tape.

Behind the tape, next to a fire department hazardous materials unit, waited a flatbed unit from the Philadelphia Police Department Tow Squad, the doors of its white cab having the same scheme of the police cruisers, bold blue and gold stripes running diagonally up the door with a large blue-and-gold Philadelphia Police Department crest centered on the door. The wrecker's light bar on its roof was flashing red and blue, as were the wigwag strobes at the front and back of the vehicle. Chained down on the flatbed was a silver Mercedes-Benz SUV, the nose of which showing burned paint, the windshield missing, and the front and rear right-side passenger doors cut completely free, revealing the interior of the vehicle.

"Ouch," Matt said. "Besides being outrageously expensive, I've always thought that that Generalissimo Benz — it looks like something the dictator of some sub-Saharan country would drive — could not get any uglier. Yet it appears that it can."

"That's Becca's," Chad said.

"'Becca's'?" Matt parroted, his shocked tone evident. "Becca Benjamin?"

Chad nodded.

"What the hell's it doing here, Chad? Stolen? What?"

Nesbitt shook his head but didn't reply. He just watched as the tow truck pulled out of the motel parking lot and onto Frankford, then headed north.

He took a sip of his coffee, then put the cup on the table. "I don't know where to begin, Matt. There's a lot I just don't know myself. Didn't want to know."

Matt looked at him and said, "Well, the beginning's always a good start."

Chad looked out the window and appeared to be considering that.

The plump waitress appeared with a steaming pot of coffee and a cup for Matt, then wordlessly filled both of their cups as she glanced out the window at the motel before moving on to the next booth.

"Okay," Chad said, turning and looking at Matt. "You know Skipper."

"Not really very well, but, yeah, enough to know he could be funny —"

Chad nodded.

Matt went on: "— and a real dipshit."

Chad cringed.

"You know, Matt, I've known you all our lives and sometimes you can be a real asshole, too." He paused. "Sorry. I'm just upset about this whole thing."

"Well, you've been bailing out the bastard since we were at the academy. 'No good deed goes unpunished.' Ever hear that?"

Chad made a face of frustration.

"We were teammates, Matt. And I couldn't say no to him; he's just got that kind of personality. Endearing, you know? I should have, but didn't. You may remember that he had a real tough time with his father, who cut him absolutely no slack, often unfairly. Anyway, I didn't hear much from him after he put the Audi in the reservoir —"

"The Audi *and* Becca," Matt interrupted.

"— and he took off for school in Texas," Chad went on, nodding his agreement. "But a little more than a year ago, out of the blue, he called me at the office, said he'd be back in Philly that week, and wanted to get lunch. Said he had a business proposition."

"Tell me you didn't buy it."

"No, I didn't," Chad said, somewhat smugly. Then he added, "Not what he wanted to start, anyway."

"Which was?"

Chad Nesbitt looked cautiously around the diner and its patrons, then with a low voice said, "He wanted to supply me with migrant workers."

"For what? Last I looked, you and Daffy had domestic help. And whatever yard work that needs doing gets done by the building management."

The Nesbitts lived east of Matt's Rittenhouse Square place, in Society Hill, at Number 9 Stockton Place, a triplex constructed behind the façades of four of the twelve pre-Revolutionary brownstone buildings.

"No, Matt. Large numbers of laborers. For Nesfoods International. He thought we needed workers for harvesting the vegetables and fruits, and more workers for the processing lines at the plants. He said he could supply as many as we needed, at a price that was unbeatable."

"And?"

"And I wanted to tell him he was speaking out of ignorance again. He's the type who gets excited about something, decides it's the absolute best thing since sliced bread — but then doesn't think it through."

Matt was nodding. "Yeah, I remember."

"But I told him, instead, that I didn't do that, that Nesfoods didn't do that. The farms supply their own labor; we simply buy the product to process. And our processing plants, due to the various federal laws, are very careful in strictly hiring only those who were legal, with the proper papers. He said that that wasn't a problem, that he had it set up. He'd been doing it for years in Texas, running crews building custom houses for his father's company there, and now bringing them to do it here. I told him I wasn't interested — my job is sales, expanding the company internationally — but made a few calls and gave Skipper the names of some of the managers of the farms we buy from."

Nesfoods International had a few manufacturing facilities in the Philadelphia area, but many more Nesfoods establishments elsewhere in the United States — including one in San Antonio that made Tex-Mex salsa, a condiment far hotter in both taste and sales than ketchup — as well as outside the country.

The waitress approached with Matt's breakfast of bacon and eggs and a fresh pot of coffee.

"Here you are, sweetie," she said, sliding the food before him.

"Thank you," Matt said, and moved his cup closer for her to refill it.

She did, topped Chad's cup, placed the check upside down on the table midway between them, then said, "Let me know if you need anything else," and left.

Payne picked up two strips of bacon, made them disappear in a few bites, then said: "And that was the first proposal he made?"

"Yeah. The next one was better. It had

promise. It made sense. But I couldn't get involved with anything that might embarrass Nesfoods, even as only an investor. So my lawyers vetted it, said that if it were set up properly in a Limited Liability Corporation, it'd pass the arm's-length and smell tests and clear some other hurdles. And it required only a fairly small investment on my part. When it started to take off, I mean really generating serious income, I was both happy for him and not unhappy with myself. Not that I was going to get rich from it, but I felt good that Skipper was finally finding himself successful and that I was able to help him do it."

"What was it?"

"Something he'd started with one location just off his school campus in Texas. 'Sudsie's'?"

He looked at Matt, who was polishing off his eggs, to see if that registered.

After chewing and swallowing, Matt said incredulously, "That sports bar with the laundry machines? 'Get Sloshed With Us'?"

"Actually, for legal purposes it's technically a laundromat that has been sexed-up with a sports bar — TVs, beer on tap, snacks. But you're right. That's the place. And the concept — the LLC had only two here to start — rang all the bells with hitting the target choice demographic of young adults eighteen to thirty-five. It proved to be an unbelievable cash cow."

Matt raised his eyebrows and shook his head. He said, "Fancy buzzwords, Mr. Corporate Man. You always did talk in tongues, even in preschool."

Chad shrugged. "I'm in sales. It comes with the territory. Anyway, then Skipper found a package of real estate for sale that had a half-dozen laundromats." He glanced out the window. "It also had three motels."

Matt looked out the window, then at Chad. "You *own* the Philly Inn?"

He nodded. "The LLC does."

"What the hell are you doing with seedy motels?"

"Hey, don't be so fast to judge. Ever hear of PEGI?" Chad said, pronouncing the acronym phonetically.

"'Peggy'?" Matt repeated, then shook his head.

"Philadelphia Economic Gentrification Initiative. Big money, both local bonds and fed matching funds. The LLC's going to put up one hell of an upscale condominium when the Philly Inn's gone. When it's time, I'll get you in on the predevelopment pricing." He looked at all the emergency vehicles at the back of the inn. "Which now may be sooner than later."

"So, what's the problem, Chad?"

He shrugged. "It all just looks so bad. I just don't know. Skipper called around nine last night, said he was going out of town —"

"So then it was Skipper driving Becca's Mercedes?"

Chad shrugged again. "Maybe. But he said, 'Becca and I,' so she could've been with him. Anyway, he wanted to drop off a check, which was my quarterly payment on the LLC investment."

"Guess ole Skipper hasn't heard of the United States Postal Service. Or, for that matter, electronic bank transfers."

"That's not how Skipper is, Matt. He takes it personally; when he promises to give you something, he wants to hand it to you personally."

Matt took a sip of coffee, then said, "My recollection is *if* he hands it to you. I seem to recall he has trouble with following through on things. You just admitted he doesn't think things through."

Chad made a face, then said, "True. But his intentions —"

"Intentions my ass. Come on, Chad. You're covering for him. It's what the shrinks call 'enabling.'"

Chad sighed, sipped his coffee, then said,

"Maybe. Maybe not. Anyway, Daffy put Penny in her crib and then went to read in bed. I clicked on the late-night news, waiting — and promptly fell asleep. When I woke up, it was after one — there was some rerun of a late-night comedy on the TV — so I called his cell phone. He apologized —"

"He's good at that," Matt interrupted. "Lots of practice over many years."

"Are you finished?"

Matt slowly said, "Enabler," then made a grand gesture for him to continue.

"He apologized, said he was running late, but he'd be over 'in ten' with the check. He said it was still in the motel safe. I tried to tell him it was already late and could wait till this morning. But Skipper insisted he wanted it done before he — *they* — went out of town."

Chad looked toward the motel office and added, "Who knows when I'll get in there."

"So I gather he didn't show in ten minutes?"

"Or in four hours, when I woke up again, this time from a sore neck from the way I'd fallen asleep in my chair. Then I couldn't sleep. So, half pissed and half worried, I decided to go see if he was maybe passed out in one of the rooms here. Figured I'd bang on his motel room door and wake him up.

What's good for the goose . . ."

"But you never found him?"

Chad shook his head, then touched his phone. "And I tried calling at least a half-dozen times." He paused. "The cops wouldn't let me near the place, so I came in here, tried to think of who to call —"

"And I won."

"You're a cop, Matt. You understand this better than I do, than anyone I know does."

Matt Payne didn't say anything.

Chad went on: "Two ambulances, sirens blaring, came out from the back of the motel right before I called you. For Christ's sake, Matt, did you not see her vehicle?"

Matt suddenly had a mental image of what horror could have happened to the gorgeous Becca, and it was clear from the looks of the right side of the SUV that the rescue crew had had to use a powerful hydraulic Jaws of Life metal cutter to remove the B-pillar and the front and rear doors in order to rescue — *or, if dead, to recover* — whoever was inside the SUV.

Then Matt's mind suddenly flashed a Technicolor image of another beautiful young woman who'd suddenly been horribly mutilated — Susan Reynolds, her head grotesquely opened by a .30-caliber carbine round in that diner parking lot, blood and brains blown everywhere.

Matt immediately felt himself get clammy and tasted bile in his throat.

*Dammit, not that now!*

*Don't lose it.*

He took a deep breath, swallowed hard, and drained his coffee cup.

Then he looked out at the motel and all the police activity.

Behind the yellow Police Line tape, he saw a familiar cop, one in plain clothes and his usual well-worn blue blazer. Detective Anthony C. Harris was slight and wiry, not at all imposing, but was, Matt knew, one of the best homicide detectives, right up there with Jason Washington, who was the best of the East Coast's best, from Maine to Miami.

*Jesus, that's not a good sign.*

*If Tony is working the job, something big is up.*

He looked back at Chad and bluntly said, "Okay."

"Okay?"

"I'll do it. Do whatever. But not for Skipper. For you. For Becca."

"Matt, you can hate him —"

"Dammit, Chad, I don't hate him," Matt interrupted with more anger than he expected. He lowered his voice: "However, if he hurt Becca, that is subject to absolute immediate fucking change." He sighed. "I'll find out what I can."

"That's all I'm asking. Thank you, pal."

Chad reached out for the check and slid it back to himself.

"I'll get the tab. The LLC owns this diner, too."

Matt just shook his head at that as he pulled out his cellular phone, scrolled down its list of phone numbers, and then hit the CALL button.

He looked back out the window as he put the phone to his ear and listened to the sound of ringing. He saw Homicide Detective Anthony C. Harris begin shuffling the pen and notepaper pad he held so that he could reach with his left hand and retrieve his cellular phone from its belt clip.

"Hey, Tony," Matt said after a moment. "Matt Payne."

Then: "Yeah, sorry to bother you. I know you're more than 'a little busy' with a job. I'm at the diner next door."

He saw Harris, still holding the phone to his ear, turn and scan the diner.

Matt went on: "Inside the diner. I can see you. Look, I might be able to give you some information on the scene."

He listened, then said: "Sure. Of course.

But can you answer me one quick question?"

Then: "I know. Did you get a positive ID on who was in the Mercedes?"

Matt saw that Chad was watching him closely for any sign.

Matt met his eyes but remained stone-faced as he said, "Thanks. I'll be over. Tell 'em to pass me through, will you?"

Then: "Yeah, 'should' isn't the same as 'would,' and for all I know rumor in the Roundhouse and around the FOP lodge is that I wimped out and quit a long time ago. See you in a moment."

Then he hung up and waved for the waitress.

"Well?" Chad said.

Matt watched out the window as Tony Harris signaled for one of the officers standing at the crime-scene tape to come over to him. The cop did, at a half-trot.

The waitress appeared, and Matt told her, "I need a couple large black coffees to go, please."

After she walked away, Matt looked at Chad and said, "You were right: It was her Mercedes, or at least one leased to Benjamin Securities. And —" He forced back the lump that appeared in his throat, and his tone turned colder. "And it was her driver's license in the purse. So there's no reason not to believe it was her in the vehicle. They'll confirm it at the hospital. But he said it's hard to tell right now — she got hit pretty badly."

Matt saw that Chad was on the edge of tears.

# [FOUR]
## 1344 W. Susquehanna Avenue, Philadelphia
## Wednesday, September 9, 5:46 A.M.

Walking around the laundromat and surveying his workers, Paco Esteban considered himself a very lucky man indeed. Assembling his crews had not only gotten easier, the quality of his workers, being family, of course, had gotten better.

Yet he well knew that so many other immigrants were not so lucky. There were those who were devoutly grateful for a chance to better themselves, yet they just did not enjoy what El Nariz considered the opportunities that he and his extended family had.

And then there were the truly unlucky

ones who were preyed on by other immigrants, some legal and some not, unbelievably mean bastards with evil intentions who shamelessly — without any conscious whatever — took obscene advantage of their own.

*Treating them like animals, profiting from them, worse than the gringos, who could be bad enough.*

Esteban had seen examples with his own eyes — occasionally he suffered the nightmares, the vivid flashbacks of the bloated sunbaked bodies in the desert — and had heard of so many other examples. The worst were the coyotes who simply stole the smuggling fees they were paid — leaving the males to wander and die in the desert, and raping the females, sometimes selling them into prostitution — never intending to fulfill that for which they'd agreed.

He found those particular bastards despicable beyond description and made a quiet oath that if he could — within reason, of course, as he could not jeopardize his family and all that he'd worked for — that he would save the needy from the evil ones.

And El Nariz had done just that. As he glanced around the room, his eyes fell on his most recent rescue, a teenage girl who now was working at the folding station.

■ ■ ■ ■

It all had happened the previous Thursday afternoon, when El Nariz had been driving the minivan with a load of dirty laundry he'd just collected from the Liberty Motel in Northeast Philadelphia.

On Castor Avenue, the engine of the minivan had started to sputter. Despite the needle of the fuel gauge resting past the F, he knew that the tank was not full — it never was filled more than halfway, for fear the fuel would be stolen — but instead was bone damn dry.

He had seen Gas & Go signage on the corner up ahead, and was able to roll to its island of fuel pumps.

El Nariz had no credit cards, which required him to prepay with two ten-dollar bills. When he went inside the store, he was not surprised to find, in addition to the arrogant young Asian man behind the register and the pungent smell of kimchee and garlic that hung heavily in the air, that there was a pair of more or less attractive and young Latinas. They were filing their nails at a folding table, clearly bored. In a nearby corner, under a sign with an arrow to the XXX video room, stood a midtwenties Hispanic male with arms crossed and keeping a somewhat intense watch on the door.

El Nariz was not surprised, because he had seen the same situation at the Gas & Go next door to the Susquehanna Avenue laundromat: a shopkeeper, hookers, and their guard. Considering himself a principled man, he'd stopped going into that Gas & Go when he'd learned what they did — Paco Esteban took pride in helping people, not enslaving them — and had it not been for the minivan running out of gas right then and there, he would have chosen to buy his fuel at some place — *any* place — other than a damned Gas & Go.

Paco Esteban had made no eye contact with the guard. He did catch himself glancing at the girls, but only out of sadness for them. One, who had a cold hard expression, paid him no attention. But the other one caught his eye, and he saw in hers both fear and hope — the hope likely coming from not having long been forced to do what she was doing.

After paying the young Asian man at the register, El Nariz began walking toward the door. He made eye contact again with the girl. This time, her expression turned to one of sad desperation.

She quickly glanced over at her guard. He had noticed her look and made a face at her that showed he was at once annoyed and menacing.

Outside, as El Nariz pumped his gas, he thought about what had just happened. He had heard that girls in such a situation who did anything but what was expected of them faced harsh consequences. He'd wondered if what this girl had just done would result in that.

He'd shaken his head at the thought of all the misery in the world, and was glad that he didn't have to go back inside the store and again witness this small pocket of it.

After a few minutes, the pump shut off at eight dollars, not the twenty he'd prepaid.

This was not the first time that El Nariz had experienced this. The first time, not sure of what to do and having just arrived in the big city, he had simply driven off and tried to forget about the lost hard-earned money.

But then it happened to him again two weeks later, and at a different gas station. He kicked himself for not having earlier figured out the scam: The setting of the pump at a lower cutoff amount had been done intentionally, on the assumption that if the person pumping gas was an illegal alien, he'd almost certainly not be stupid enough to want to make a scene over a couple bucks.

Rather, he would, as El Nariz had done the first time, simply drive off.

If, however, the person did come back inside the store and called the attendant on the discrepancy, the attendant would blame the faulty machinery, or offer up some other bullshit excuse, and with a knowing smile hand over the money in dispute.

Back inside the Gas & Go, El Nariz saw that the girl had not been punished for her look — at least not yet.

After he explained to the young Asian male at the counter that he'd been shorted, the clerk said nothing. The young Asian simply peeled twelve bucks from a wad of cash he pulled from his own pocket. He handed the singles to El Nariz with a look of utter disgust that anyone would worry about such a paltry amount.

Paco Esteban said nothing, just pocketed the cash and started to leave, making an effort not to look again at the girl. Then the front door of the Gas & Go swung open and all eyes turned to it. A swarthy thirtyish Hispanic male in baggy blue jeans and white T-shirt swaggered in through the door.

The newcomer was drinking from a bottle of Budweiser. That earned him an admonishment from the Asian that there was no drinking beer in the store and to throw it away.

El Nariz saw the newcomer make eye contact with the Hispanic male who was keeping guard from the corner. He then drained the bottle and casually tossed the empty into a trash container. The guard looked at the girl with the cold expression, which seemed suddenly to turn even harder. Then she turned on a patently artificial smile, put down her nail file, and, without a word, got up and crossed the floor in the direction of the XXX video room, then made the turn to disappear behind the door labeled LADIES.

The newcomer passed El Nariz, then went past the guard and into the dimly lit room beyond the signage reading XXX VIDEOS MUST BE OVER 18 TO ENTER.

As El Nariz pushed the handle of the front door, he saw that the guard had stayed where he was until certain that El Nariz definitely was leaving. Then he followed the newcomer into the XXX room.

El Nariz shook his head sadly as he got behind the wheel and started the engine. He knew the odds were very high that money was being paid to the Hispanic male guard for fifteen minutes with the girl — probably twenty bucks, about the same amount he'd paid to put gas in his tank, with ten for overhead going to the Asian, even more if any coke or meth was sold — and that the girl and the newcomer were now in a dark, discreet space somewhere between the ladies' room and the XXX video room.

As Paco "El Nariz" Esteban put the van in gear and tried to shake the image from his mind, the passenger door swung open. Instinctively, trying to evade whoever he believed was probably trying to rob him, he'd floored the accelerator. The passenger door slammed shut with the force of the sudden forward movement — but whoever it was had managed to make it inside, onto the floor.

A horn blared angrily, and El Nariz swerved to miss hitting a car that was turning into the parking lot. Then he slammed on the brakes.

He turned to look toward the passenger floor, bracing himself for the view of a gleaming knife or the muzzle of a pistol being pointed at him.

Instead, he saw the young girl from inside the Gas & Go staring up at him, her eyes now at once terrified and pleading.

*"Vaya! Vaya!"* she cried, begging him to go, to drive.

El Nariz glanced around the parking lot. He could see no one coming after her — or him — but he floored the accelerator again anyway.

Paco Esteban smiled as he now watched that teenage girl, Rosario Flores, being quick but meticulous with her folding and stacking. Within the last week, she had worked hard to prove her thanks to El Nariz for his kind act of rescue, and for him and his wife taking her into their home. If she had not quite become as dedicated a worker as all his others, she was very close.

Slowly, first with El Nariz's wife, then with them both, Rosario had shared her story. It was sickening — her being fed drugs and forced to have sex with up to ten, twelve men in the course of fifteen-hour workdays. If only a small part of it was true — and El Nariz had no reason to believe she'd made up any of it — it was one of those horrors beyond description that he, as a God-fearing human being, despised to his very core.

And so Paco Esteban now smiled again, not only for Rosario in particular, but for all that he'd accomplished in general, both for himself and for his people.

They all had risked much, and they all had come far in their lives, and while — God forbid — some mistake they might make could send them back to that which they left far behind, they were being careful and invisible and integrating well in their adopted country. He'd even begun mailing small payments — no return address on the envelope, but his account number on the Western Union money order — to Saint John's Hospital in Tucson.

One of the workers came up to El Nariz and told him that she had heard a knock on the pair of steel doors at the back of the building.

Esteban looked at his cellular phone's clock, nodded appreciatively, and thanked her. The six-thirty delivery apparently was early, which meant his crew would have that much longer — nearly an hour — to process it before quitting at eight.

El Nariz went to the back door and looked out the peephole. All he saw was a darkened loading dock. So he went over to the electrical breaker box and opened its door. When he found the breaker, to throw that would power the mercury floodlamps that bathed the loading dock in a gray-white light, he saw that there was no red line on the breaker, indicating that the breaker had tripped. Still, he rationalized that with the recent renovation, anything was possible, so El Nariz threw the switch to the OFF position, then back to ON, then closed the door of the box.

At the steel doors, as he started to look out the peephole again, there came a steady and hard — bordering on impatient — banging. The mercury bulb was still out. El Nariz knew it took them a little time to come fully on, but thought that he could make out the silhouette of the laundry's minivan and the driver gesturing for him to open the door.

Paco Esteban sighed. He did not want to lose the advantage that the early delivery afforded him. There was a wooden brace, a heavy square timber that rested in U-brackets bolted to the wall on either side of the set of double doors, that secured them shut. With some effort, he removed the brace, then unlocked the lower deadbolt, then the upper one.

The door suddenly flew open, its leading edge striking Paco Esteban in the forehead and causing a great deal of blood to start flowing down his face. He staggered back as in strode a tall muscular Hispanic male in black boots, pants, shirt, and hooded sweatshirt, the hood pulled up on his head.

Hanging from a thin black sling on his right shoulder he had what El Nariz thought looked oddly like a long pistol or a short rifle. Whatever it was, it was futuristic-looking, unlike any weapon he'd ever seen.

In the man's left hand, El Nariz saw what looked like a wet brown ball hanging from a black rope — although, with Esteban's vision blurred, he could not tell if the blood he saw belonged to the object or to him.

"Rosario! Where is Rosario?" the man called out in almost happy singsong Spanish as he trained the muzzle of the weapon on El Nariz, then walked purposely past and on to the front of the building. Then his tone changed. "Rosario! Where the *fuck* are you?"

When the man reached the big room of washers and dryers, the workers moved to the side, out of the man's way, in effect creating a path for him. The man looked to the end of this path, to the folding station along the far wall, and grunted at what he saw.

He held up the grotesque ball by its black rope.

"Let this be a lesson to all of you," he bellowed as he swung it around.

Then he slung it, in a fashion oddly like that of a bowling ball, down the polished concrete floor toward Rosario, then turned to walk out the way he had come.

As he passed El Nariz, who was trying to get up from being down on his hurt left knee, his right hand holding his bloody forehead, the man again waved the muzzle of

120

his futuristic-looking gun at him — but this time let off a burst of fire. The fifteen rounds loudly made a neat arch of pockmarks in the newly painted white brick above El Nariz's head, pelting him with chips of masonry.

The man went out the door, and moments later the minivan roared off in a squeal of tires.

The bloody object had slid the length of the room and left a long, sloppy trail. As the crew of workers had recognized what exactly it was, they started wailing and shrieking — and running past El Nariz to the back door.

The object had stopped just short of Rosario's feet, and when she looked down and saw that the rope was a ponytail and the ball was the bludgeoned decapitated head of Ana Maria Del Carmen Lopez, its lifeless gaze staring up at her, Rosario Flores fainted to the floor.

# III

## [ONE]
## Room 52
## The Philly Inn
## Wednesday, September 9,
## 6:05 A.M.

"Detective, it's murder, is what it is," Javier Iglesia said. "No question in my mind."

Homicide Detective Anthony Harris, standing outside the motel room and looking in through the hole that once held a plate-glass window, was watching the technicians from the Medical Examiner's Office work the scene.

The masonry walls and ceiling of the interior — and practically everything therein — had been burned at such a high temperature that there were no distinct colors and almost no shades — just the grayish-white hue of ash everywhere. Harris saw that the mattresses had been scorched to such a degree that only their metal frames and coils remained, and these were melted almost to a point of being unrecognizable.

Two shiny black vinyl body-transport bags — open on the floor in the middle of the room, each containing a charred body — were a stark contrast to their surroundings, as were the technicians methodically documenting the scene.

One representative of the Medical Examiner's Office was a photographer, an attractive black female in her midtwenties wearing slacks and a dark blouse. She had slender features, and stood right at five feet, maybe a hundred pounds. She moved with her camera — a bulky professional-grade Nikon digital model, its strobe firing off flashes that washed the room in a pulsing light that bordered on the surreal — in such a graceful fluid manner that it looked to be a natural extension of her.

Harris had worked crime scenes with Javier Iglesia, the lead technician, and was aware of his well-earned reputation for being somewhat loquacious. He was a beefy but fit thirty-year-old of Puerto Rican ancestry. He wore black jeans, a white knit polo, and a frayed and stained white thigh-length lab coat with two big patch pockets on the front. Both he and the photographer had transparent blue plastic booties over their black athletic shoes and tan-colored synthetic polymer gloves on their hands.

"It's Shakespearean, is what it is," Iglesia then announced.

Harris shook his head, not understanding. "It's what, Javier?"

"'Cut his weasand with thy knife.' From *The Tempest*. William Shakespeare. Weasand's another word for the windpipe, which is the trachea." He paused. "Of course, it's for Dr. Mitchell to decide if death was ultimately caused by loss of breath. Or by loss of blood. Or by the blast."

Dr. Howard Mitchell was the medical examiner. Harris knew the balding, rumpled man, usually found in a well-worn suit, likely would be the one performing the autopsy. Or certainly overseeing it.

Iglesia squatted between the body bags. He pointed to the one on his right.

"But I can tell you that that one died from the blast," he said, then reached over to the body bag on the left. He pulled down on its opening so that Harris, standing outside the window, could have a better view of the remains. "And this one had what I call a circumcision."

The photographer chuckled.

Harris said, "What the hell are you talking about, a circumcision?"

Iglesia put two gloved fingers under the

dead man's chin and applied pressure. It caused the head to tip back and reveal the grotesque gap that was a slit across the neck.

"See?" Iglesia said with a grin. "A circumcision, 'cause he's a damned dickhead."

The photographer snorted her agreement.

The gash was so big that Harris could easily see that the carotid artery had been neatly severed, too.

*That certainly meets the Latin meaning of "homicide"* — homo *for "human being,"* caedere *for "cut to kill."*

*So then the fire was a cover for a murder?*

*But who did it?*

*So far as we know, only one person came out alive.*

*And he's not looking like he's going to make it to lunch.*

Iglesia pulled back his fingers and the head bobbed back forward.

He then reached into one of the patch pockets of his lab coat.

"I'm betting," he said, "that the cut pattern of the flesh will be consistent with the wavelike serrations on the blade of this. And of course that makes it murder."

He held up a heavy clear plastic bag that contained what was left of a folding pocket-knife. It was open, and its blade looked to be about three inches long, the sharpened edge serrated the whole length. The intensity of the heat had discolored the metal of the knife and turned the plastic handle into a melted blob of black goo, at least what remained of it.

*Good luck getting a print off that,* Harris thought.

"Me, personally?" the talkative Latino went on without prompting, "I'd like to see more of them die, is what I'd like. These drug dealers, they're all scum —"

"Amen to that," the photographer chimed in as she fired off another series of shots.

"And you know what they're doing now, man?" Iglesia went on. "These damn dealers?"

Harris realized that Iglesia had paused, and then it occurred to him that the reason for the pause was that Iglesia was trying to engage him. He wanted Harris to answer.

*Which I really don't want to do, because it'll only encourage Javier to go on.*

*And on and on. . . .*

After a moment, Harris reluctantly said, "What, Javier?"

With more than a little anger, Iglesia said: "They're now getting teens, young ones, hooked on horse, is what they're doing. Kids in my neighborhood doing Mexican

126

black tar heroin, man. And not knowing it, 'cause it's mixed with candy sugar." His face showed genuine disgust as he shook his head. "I hope these bastards kill each other, every last one of them. And I can't think of a better way for them to go down than getting blown up in their own damn meth lab."

Harris nodded and, not wanting to get into details, said, "I've heard something about that."

"Damn right," Iglesia said. He sealed the body bags, then looked at Harris. "And you know what else, man?"

*Jesus, he's not going to stop.*

Harris suddenly had an inspiration, and held up his left index finger in a *Hold that thought one second* gesture.

As if responding to the vibrating of his cellular telephone, he pulled it from its clip on his belt, put it to his head, and a little louder than normal said to absolutely no one, "Harris."

He pretended to listen for a second, then looked at Javier Iglesia, who was watching Harris while he impatiently held his thought a second. Harris mimed that he had to take the call, and Iglesia, looking disappointed, nodded and started to finish up with the job.

As Tony Harris walked away from the

motel room window, he realized that pulling out the phone wasn't exactly a charade. He needed to make a call.

Like all major city police departments, the Philadelphia Police Department was a complex organization. Just its uniformed police numbered nearly 7,000, making it the fourth-largest force in the United States.

The top cop was the commissioner. An appointed position, the commissioner served at the pleasure of the mayor. Under the commissioner were his deputies. Each was responsible for various bureaus — narcotics, special operations, internal affairs, among others — which in turn were commanded by a chief inspector.

There were six patrol divisions, each led by an inspector. And each of the twenty-three patrol districts, commanded by a captain, had four platoons made up of a lieutenant, a pair of sergeants, and some forty officers.

The upper ranks — lieutenant to commissioner — were referred to as "white shirts" because that was the color of their uniform. Likewise, the lower ranks — police recruit to sergeant — were the "blue shirts."

Their insignia more or less followed that of the military's. Among the white shirts, the commissioner wore four gold stars, his deputy had three stars, and so on, down to a lieutenant's single golden bar. And the shoulder of a blue shirt sergeant would bear a patch showing three blue chevrons outlined in silver, while a corporal's would have two chevrons.

Thus, keeping absolute order was absolutely critical for such a large and complicated department to operate efficiently and effectively. That of course meant the faithful and rigorous following of various protocols and systems and rules, many of which had been in place, or certainly improved upon, since the first foot patrol in the late 1600s.

One such system was the manner in which detectives in the Detective Bureau were assigned a job. The Detective Bureau, as its name suggested, included all the department's Detectives Units around the city — Central, South, East, et cetera. It also included Special Victims Unit (what in pre-politically correct times had been called Sex Crimes), Major Crimes Unit, and so on.

And it included the Homicide Unit.

The system, known as "The Wheel," was designed to distribute equitably the jobs that came in to a particular unit. Philadelphia had far more murders than most big American cities. Averaging a killing a day — the wee hours of weekends and full-moon Fridays being especially bloody — there was plenty of Homicide work to go around. Sure as hell, no one wanted to be unfairly assigned another job when they may already have more on their plate than the next guy.

The Wheel wasn't an actual wheel. It was, instead, a roster listing the detectives on duty at the moment. The detective at the top of the roster was assigned to "man the desk." When a telephone call came in with a job to investigate, the detective "deskman" got it. Then he consulted the roster to see whose turn it was "next up on the Wheel," and that detective became the next "deskman."

It was a logical system. One faithfully followed.

And Detective Tony Harris was about to throw a wrench in the Homicide Unit's Wheel.

Harris had gone around the corner of the Philly Inn to the line of rooms along the motel's south side. Next door, near the All-Nite Diner, he could see a large number of the people who'd been evacuated from the motel during the fire.

*And that's where Matt Payne said he is.*
*And he said he's got information on this?*
*What the hell is that all about?*

He pressed the key on his cellular phone

that caused the device to speed-dial the Homicide office on the second floor of the Roundhouse.

The deskman finally answered the phone on its fifth ring.

"Homicide," he said with no enthusiasm. "Detective Bari."

Tony Harris did not dislike Aldo Bari — a heavyset thirty-five-year-old of Italian descent who wore cheap suits with his necktie always loosened and the shirt collar unbuttoned — but he was far from his biggest fan.

Bari was a strict by-the-book type who could quote chapter and verse of police department procedure. It had carried him along just fine on the force. No one could ever accuse Aldo Bari of straying outside the lines of any policy.

Nor, Tony Harris knew, would anyone ever suggest that Bari actually stuck his squat fat neck out for anything. Bari found comfort within the established boundaries. He put in his hours, and not a nanosecond more than he absolutely had to.

"Good morning, Al. Tony Harris."

"Hey, Harris. What can I do you out of?"

"You're up on the Wheel?"

"Yeah. Lucky me. I'm off the clock in under two hours, though. Whatcha got?"

"There's a job coming in. I'm already on the scene —"

"That's not exactly kosher, is it?" Bari interrupted.

"— I'm on the scene *watching from a distance* the guys from the Medical Examiner's Office. This one's really got my attention."

"Really. What is it?"

"You know the Philly Inn on Frankford?"

"That old motel?"

"Right. A meth lab blew up in a room on the back side of the place about two o'clock this morning. The blast rocked my house, damn near blowing me out of bed."

"An *alleged* meth lab? No fooling?"

*"Alleged" my ass,* Harris thought. *Go ask the HazMat guys what toxic soup of caustic chemicals they had to clear out of there, Bari.*

But Harris ignored him and went on: "When I looked out the window, I saw the glow of flames. So, I drove over to see what'd happened."

"And?"

"And cutting a long story short, a white female got nailed outside the room that went 'boom.' She'd been waiting in one of those really fancy Mercedes SUVs. Apparently she's hurt pretty badly."

"Damn drugs."

"Yeah. Then, as the fire department was

battling the blaze, a white male, surprising hell out of everyone, came staggering out of the burning motel room. He and the girl were taken to the Temple ER."

"That's it?"

"No. When they got the motel room fire put out, inside they found two bodies, white Hispanic males, charred to a crisp."

"Nice."

"One of the critters had his throat slit."

"Ah. Very nice. But wait. The white guy was the doer? Then he torched the place?"

"I don't know, Al. If he did, it sure as hell backfired on him."

Bari chuckled. " 'Backfired.' "

Harris ignored him again. "Anyway, Al, there's a lot of very interesting questions, all unanswered. Which is why I want the job."

There was a perceptible pause as Bari considered what he'd just heard.

Tony Harris imagined Aldo Bari checking the black Casio watch on his fat wrist, looking at its oversize digital readout to see how close it now was to quitting time and wondering if he could dodge this bullet of a complicated case.

*Bari's probably breaking into a sweat trying to decide which desire to go with — play by the rules, or avoid a new job.*

After a moment, Bari said, "Gee, I don't

know, Harris."

Harris could hear real ambivalence in Bari's tone.

Bari went on hesitantly: "I'd have to get it cleared first. And the Black Buddha won't be here for another hour. Or more."

Lieutenant Jason Washington — the highly respected, articulate, superbly tailored, and very black detective who stood six-foot-three and 225 pounds — was known in Homicide, usually behind his back, as the Black Buddha.

Harris shook his head, more in disappointment than disgust. The clock already was ticking on the first forty-eight hours; outside that window, homicides got harder and harder to solve.

"I understand, Al. Look, the call itself probably won't come in for at least another hour, anyway. I just need someone to wind up the machine — get the paperwork started for a search warrant, run the pair who're in Temple Hospital for priors, get their backgrounds. You know, the usual. I just want to get moving on this while it's fresh."

Aldo Bari now did indeed check his watch. And he thought: *With any luck, that call won't come till after eight, and then it won't be my problem.*

*It'll belong to the next guy up on the Wheel.*

Bari cleared his throat and said, "Yeah, sure. Let me get back to you when either the Black Buddha gets here or the call comes in on the job. We're talking only an hour, right?"

Tony Harris shook his head again.

*Jesus! He's stalling, which means he's play-ing by the rules and avoiding the job.*

*What a chickenshit.*

After a moment, he said, "Okay, Al. Just let me know either way, right away, okay?"

"Absolutely," Bari said a little too eagerly.

Tony Harris shook his head a final time as he looked at the phone and angrily broke off the call with a stab of his thumb.

*I won't hear from him again for a month of Sundays. . . .*

*To hell with it. And him.*

Tony Harris decided to proceed as if he had the job, if only by starting with making notes on the small spiral-top pad he kept in his blazer's inside pocket.

He put his phone back in its belt clip, then pulled out the pad.

As he looked up and glanced across the parking lot, he saw a familiar face approach-ing the POLICE LINE yellow tape from the direction of the diner.

"And so the mystery thickens. . . ."

# [TWO]
## The Philly Inn
## Wednesday, September 9,
## 6:15 A.M.

Matthew Payne was carrying two foam cups of black coffee and sipping from one's top. When the uniform from the Fifteenth Police District standing behind the tape saw him coming toward the motel, the uniform started to hold up his hand to stop him. But then Payne pulled back his shirt to flash his badge on his belt. He pointed toward Tony Harris at the back corner of the motel, indicating that that was where he was headed. The blue shirt nodded his understanding. Then, no doubt remembering that Harris had told him to pass Payne, he went so far as to hold up the tape for him to duck under it.

"Hey, Tony," Payne said as he walked up to Harris.

Harris stood on the sidewalk in front of Room 44, scribbling furiously on his spiral-top pad.

Having written his share of them, Payne recognized what Harris was doing — making notes for a "White Paper." It was an unofficial memorandum for internal use in Homicide, and since it was unofficial, it would not be available to defense counsel as a "discoverable document." The White Paper was a report that was less formal and less precise than the "Activities Sheet." This latter document listed every move that the Homicide detectives made in the case; it was discoverable, which meant it would be made available to the defense counsel of anyone brought to trial in the case. The two documents together would present the details of the case as it developed.

Harris did not respond for a moment as he finished what he was writing.

"Sorry about that. Didn't want to lose my train of thought." Then he looked at Matt and smiled warmly. "It's good to see you, Matt."

"Thanks, Tony. You, too." Payne held out the cup with the lid. "Don't say I never gave you anything. Coffee, black."

Harris tucked the pad under his right armpit, took the coffee, and sipped from its plastic lid.

"I knew there was a reason why I missed having you around the office," he said with a smile. Then he squeezed Matt's shoulder. "It really is good to see you, and not just for the coffee. You look good. Relaxed. That time off has been good for you."

Payne shrugged, and forced a smile. "I guess."

"So, not that I'm not glad to see you, but what the hell are you doing here? And you said you had some information on this?"

As Harris sipped his coffee, he saw Matt's eyes were pained.

"Kind of a long story, Tony. A lot of it I don't know, and what I do know I don't fully understand."

Harris nodded appreciatively. "I probably could say the same about this job." He looked at Payne and thought he detected some interest. "You want to see it?"

Payne immediately nodded.

"Yeah," he said. "Yeah, I do, Tony."

Harris thought, *That's not just morbid interest on his part.*

*It's professional.*

*And maybe something more. . . .*

"The guys from the Medical Examiner's Office are working the scene. It'll be called in to Homicide anytime now."

"It's not your job?"

"No. At least not yet."

Payne considered that, then asked: "How'd

you wind up here?"

"I live over off Ryan. Across from the middle school?"

Payne nodded. "Oh, yeah."

"When the room went boom, it about blew me out of bed."

"No shit," Payne said, then after a long moment: "So, who's on the Wheel?"

"Bari."

Payne frowned and shook his head.

Harris thought, *And that damn sure was a professional assessment.*

*Great minds think alike, which explains why I've always liked Payne.*

"I hear you, Matt."

Harris motioned for Payne to follow him.

"C'mon. Let's go have a look. Maybe you'll see something I didn't."

When Payne had approached Harris standing in front of Room 44, he'd noticed that all the rooms from there to the front of the motel had appeared more or less normal. But now, as they walked down the sidewalk and turned the corner, he had a clear view of the back side of the motel.

*It looks like a war zone.*

Debris was strewn — blown out from the building in an irregular semicircular pattern — all through the parking lot. Everything was coated either in water or what remained of the foam that the firefighters had sprayed to suffocate the flames. One room eight doors down from the corner looked to have taken the brunt of the damage — its broken and burned door hung outward at a great angle, only the bottom hinge holding it to the door frame. And both the plate-glass window and its frame were missing from their place in the masonry wall.

They followed the sidewalk that ran the length of the back side of the motel. The doors to all of the rooms they passed were wide open, and Matt knew that the rooms had been cleared by the first responders. By the look of the interior of the rooms, though, no one had occupied them recently, and certainly not in the last night.

The acrid odor of burned plastic, fabric, wood, and more hung heavily in the air. And it got heavier as they moved toward the middle of the building.

There were two cars and three pickup trucks, all showing various amounts of body damage, all with their windshields either shattered or completely blown inward.

Almost exactly in the middle of the vehicles, where clearly another vehicle had been parked before forcibly being removed — *Becca's Mercedes,* Matt thought — there was a white Ford panel van backed up to the scene, doors open. A blue and gold stripe ran the length of the vehicle, with a representation of a police department shield on the door and, to the right of the driver's window, MEDICAL EXAMINER in blue block lettering.

Harris saw Payne looking at that and gave him an overview of what he'd seen that morning, including the rescuers pulling the girl from the Mercedes and the white male who had run out from the burning room.

"It looks like a bomb went off, Tony," Matt said as they walked up to the room with the missing window.

"May as well have been. Pretty much the same result," Harris said as they looked inside.

Javier Iglesia stood in the middle of the room. His hands gripped the tubular frame at the end of a heavy-duty gurney, on top of which was strapped one of the black body bags. The other bag was gone, already loaded into the back of the medical examiner's panel van. The photographer was in the van's front passenger seat, downloading the digital files of her photographs onto a notebook computer hard drive and packing up her camera gear. Both the bodies and the images were going to the morgue, where Dr. Mitchell, or one of the medical examiner's assistants, would perform the autopsies and review the crime-scene photos.

Harris and Payne's appearance in the window caught Iglesia's attention.

"Hey, Detective Payne! How the hell are you? Shot any bad guys lately?"

Payne grinned and shook his head. "Not in the last couple hours, Javier. But keep it up and I might have to use you for practice."

Iglesia laughed appreciatively as he started pushing the gurney toward the blown-out door.

"Glad to see you back," Iglesia said. "The cops need a classy guy like you, is what they need —"

"This isn't my job, Javier. But thanks."

"— and, as I was telling Detective Harris here, we damn sure need someone like you to put a bullet in these godless *pendejos.*"

Iglesia either let pass or did not hear what Payne had said. Instead, he loathingly slapped at the body bag with the back of his left hand, then pushed the gurney through the door.

"Hold up a minute, Javier," Harris said as he walked to meet him at the back of the Ford van. "Show Matt the bag, would you?"

"Are those the new-style ones?" Payne said.

Iglesia smirked and nodded. "You know

about them?" he said.

He then reached down and tugged at the foot of the bag until it turned enough to reveal the manufacturer's tag. It was imprinted in a white rectangle designed to resemble a cadaver's identification toe tag.

Payne leaned forward and read it:

---

**Remains Recovery Unit**
**SIZE ADULT X-LARGE — MAX TESTED**
**CAPACITY 700 LBS.**
**MFG BY 2 DIE 4 INC., PHILA., PA.**

---

Then he smirked, too. "Clever company, all right. I'd heard these were coming. A retired Philly detective came up with the idea, right?"

"Yeah," Iglesia said. "Don't know what he got paid for the patent, or maybe he's got a piece of the company. But at forty, fifty bucks a pop, someone's making a mint. Every agency with any budget is stockpiling the biohaz version, with the feds buying semitrailers full 'just in case.'"

He tugged at the bag and with some professional pride added: "These really are better than the old ones, in every way. The old ones, they had zippers, and those could get really messy."

Payne understood what he meant. The zippers allowed for the risk of contamination of the evidence, or for the viewer possibly to be exposed to any biological or chemical hazard that may be part of the remains, or both.

Not so with the new design. The bag — made of heavy-duty vinyl, oval-shaped and ringed with padded loops that doubled as lifting points and tie-down points — had two unheard-of features that made it unique and, more important, preserved the chain of custody.

The first was that the top of the bag had a black flap running its length that, when folded back, revealed a clear vinyl viewing panel. One could examine the bag's contents without having to open the bag, which was important, as there was no zipper on the bag.

And that pointed to the bag's second main feature: a chemically sealed main flap. Once the remains went into the bag and the clear panel was closed, a chemical reaction occurred as the seams touched, heat-sealing them securely closed. If someone opened the bag, it could not be resealed. A new bag, with a new, unique serial number, was required. And, as an added bonus, no zippers also meant no zipper teeth for bodily and other fluids to seep out through.

Harris pulled back the solid black panel, uncovering the clear vinyl viewing one.

"Actually, Javier," Harris said, "what I meant was for you to show Matt the critter, not give a sales job on the damn bag."

"Oh."

The clear vinyl panel, despite being somewhat smudged on the inside by viscous fluids, did its job of allowing a remarkably clear view of the remains.

So clear that, for a moment, Matt Payne feared that he — and everyone else — was about to see his breakfast again.

But he gulped his coffee, pushing down the feeling in his gut while trying to maintain a detached inspection of the remains.

He saw that the Hispanic male victim's face was disfigured beyond belief. And from head to toe the outer layer of skin was blackened and blistered. There were crude cracks and gouges in his darkened flesh, particularly about the face and arms and hands, which at points were scorched to the bone.

*Scorched and seared, like a steak on a hot grill.*

*It would take more than a little imagination to piece this guy all back together for an ID shot.*

*Right now he looks like something out of a*

*really bad sci-fi flick.*

"Javier," Harris went on, "is that the one with —"

"The circumcision?" Iglesia said, smiling. "Yeah."

In Harris's peripheral vision, he saw Payne looking between him and Iglesia, trying to decode what was being said.

"Give Detective Payne a peek, would you?"

Payne thought: *I don't want to see what's left of his damn —*

Javier Iglesia slipped his hand under the bag, at the point just under the back of the dead man's neck, and lifted.

*— Oh, Jesus!*

Payne felt the lightness rise in his stomach again. It went away when Iglesia pulled back his hand and the neck wound closed.

"Go on, Javier," Harris egged him on, "tell him."

Iglesia looked at Payne and, clearly pleased with himself, said, "The *dickhead* got himself circumcised."

Then he unceremoniously flipped the body bag's top flap back in place and rolled the gurney to the back bumper of the van. He aligned it there, and with a shove collapsed its undercarriage and slid it in beside the other gurney holding the other body bag.

Watching Iglesia close the van's back doors, Matt suddenly thought:

*. . . forgive us our trespasses, as we forgive those who trespass against us; and lead us not into temptation, but deliver us from evil. For thine is the kingdom, and the power, and the glory, For ever and ever. Amen.*

*Jesus. Where did that come from?*

*Where else? From years of reciting the Lord's Prayer — sitting in the same sanctuary as Becca.*

Then he thought: *How bad can Becca be?*

Matt looked at Harris and said, "Was Becca, the girl in the Mercedes —"

Tony Harris shook his head.

"Nothing like that, Matt. Curiously, what hurt her is also what saved her from something worse. When the windshield blew inward and struck her, it appears to have also acted like a shield that deflected the brunt of the blast."

They walked back to the window. As they surveyed the scene, Harris put down his coffee and pulled out his notepad, flipping to a fresh page.

"Matt, how about giving me that information you said you have? You asked about the Mercedes. Do you know the Benjamin girl well?"

"Yeah, fairly well. We grew up in Wallingford. Went to the same church. And she was two years behind me at Episcopal Academy."

Harris started writing on his pad, then said, "Any reason to believe she's involved with running drugs, specifically meth?"

"No reason at all. And I sure as hell hope she's not. Her boyfriend, however, is another case. . . ."

"What about the boyfriend?"

"I haven't seen Skipper Olde since we graduated from Episcopal Academy."

"'Skipper'?" he said, and spelled the last name aloud as he wrote.

"Right. J. Warren Olde," Matt furnished, "initial J — Juliet, though I have no idea what it stands for. Also known as Skipper. He's my age, twenty-seven."

"Was he into drugs back then?"

Matt shook his head. "Not that I know of. Mostly beer and whiskey, and a lot of it. He led Becca Benjamin, who's a couple years younger, down that path. Not that she maybe wouldn't have gone down it on her own. Just sure as hell not so far and so fast."

Harris nodded, then asked, "Is Olde the same as —"

"Yeah. Olde and Sons, the McMansion custom home builders. Philly, Palm Beach, Dallas. His old man J. Warren Olde, Sr."

"Oh boy."

Matt heard something in Harris's tone that suggested more than mere annoyance at the mention of another wealthy family name.

"What 'oh boy,' Tony?"

Harris didn't respond directly. He looked inside the motel room, and Payne followed his eyes.

"What in the hell happened here, Tony?" Payne then said, shaking his head in disbelief.

"On the assumption that that wasn't a rhetorical question, I thought I told you — a meth lab. They're volatile as hell."

"But is that all that this is about?"

Tony Harris shrugged, then said, "I don't know if it's 'all,' but it's certainly a large component."

Payne nodded. "So were those two crispy critters in the body bags running the lab, and selling to Skipper? Or was it Skipper's lab? Or had he come to throw them out of his motel? I cannot understand why he'd bring Becca, in Becca's Mercedes that screams everything that this place is not, here. . . ."

"Well, as you point out, there're a number of possible scenarios. My money's on the one that says your prep school pal —"

"He's *not* my pal," Payne interrupted. "Becca, however, I do like."

"— okay, this Skipper guy, then, was in the illicit drug manufacture and distribution trades, specifically crystal meth. Maybe the girl, too. But we won't know until we can talk to them. *If* we can talk to them. He was unconscious after he collapsed. And she was in and out of consciousness when the boys wheeled her out of here in the meat wagon." Harris heard what he'd just said. "Sorry, Matt. No offense."

Matt motioned with his hand in a gesture that said, *None taken.*

"Till then," Harris went on, "any other pieces to the puzzle you can fill in . . ."

Payne thought, *If anyone can figure this out, it's Tony.*

He then told him everything that Chad Nesbitt had said in the diner.

Harris finished writing that in his notes and said, "You were right. You're really close to this. Anything else?"

Matt Payne made eye contact with Tony Harris.

*In for a penny, in for a pound.*

"Yeah, there is, Tony. I want in on this job."

"And I'd like to have you. But I thought you were going —"

"No. That's not happening. I'm a cop."

"No, you're not," Harris said.

*What — ?* Payne thought.

Harris went on: "Matt, at the risk of inflating what already might be an oversize ego, you were a damn good detective. Now you're a sergeant — a supervisor. And I sure could use you on this job — if, that is, I get it."

Payne nodded once. "Thanks, Tony. That means a lot coming from you." He paused, then added, "Bari's going to get this job?"

Harris shrugged.

Harris then watched as Payne reached for his cellular phone, scrolled the list of names, then hit CALL.

"Good morning, Captain Hollaran," Matt said when the call was answered. "Matt Payne. How are you, sir?"

Captain Francis X. Hollaran was assistant to First Deputy Commissioner Dennis V. Coughlin, the second in command of all of the Philadelphia Police Department. Commissioner Coughlin had been the one to order the overworked and overstressed Sergeant Matthew M. Payne, who was his godson, "Matty, you're taking some time off. Thirty days. You've earned it, you deserve it — and you need it."

Payne said into his cell phone: "Thank you, Captain. I appreciate it. I do feel better. Would it be possible to speak with the commissioner when he gets in?"

He glanced at his wristwatch, then said: "He's in already? Then yes, please. Tell him I'm on my way to the Roundhouse, and I need ten minutes of his time."

Payne paused to listen, then, making eye contact with Tony Harris, added, "Of course you can give him a heads-up what it's about. Tell him my thirty-day R and R officially ended with a boom a few hours ago. I'm coming back to work."

## [THREE]
## Reading Terminal Market
## Center City, Philadelphia
## Wednesday, September 9,
## 7:45 A.M.

In a crush of rush-hour commuters, twenty-one-year-old Juan Paulo Delgado stepped off the Southeastern Pennsylvania Transportation Authority's R1 "Airport Line" railcar at the Market East Station. He followed a half-dozen of the commuters as they one by one passed through the Eleventh Street exit's revolving door. On the sidewalk, El Gato pulled up the hood of his sweatshirt, covering his head against the rain that was starting. Two women in business attire and sharing an umbrella walked past, and he trailed them to Filbert Street, then into the Reading Terminal Market.

El Gato had boarded the SEPTA regional railroad at the Thirtieth Street Station, which was about a mile to the west, just across the Schuylkill River. And it had been into that dark river, from the tree-lined eastern shore under the Thirty-fourth Street bridge, that thirty minutes earlier he'd unceremoniously dumped the headless body of Ana Maria Del Carmen Lopez.

In the back of the rusty white Plymouth minivan, he had put her remains into a fifty-gallon black plastic lawn care bag and tied to the outside, around her ankles, a pair of twenty-five-pound workout dumbbells. Then he had poked a few holes in the bag to vent any trapped air. Once in the water, the bag had floated half-submerged with the river current for less than a minute, air bubbling out the vent holes. Then, when the bag had sufficiently filled with water, it had slipped toward the river bottom, a final series of bubbles popping on the surface.

El Gato then had rinsed off the blood from his hands with river water and thrown his bloody black clothing into the brush, behind a cardboard box long ago vacated by a homeless person. He'd driven the half-mile to the Thirtieth Street Station, and there carried a backpack into the men's room. After cleaning up at a sink, he'd gone into a toilet stall. He had removed his gun from the backpack, run its sling over his right shoulder, then pulled on a clean hoodie sweatshirt and, over that, a cheap navy blue vinyl raincoat. Finally, he rolled up a Philadelphia Eagles ball cap and slipped it into his pants waistband at the small of his back.

The polymer-and-alloy weapon was a Belgian-made Fabrique Nationale submachine gun, Model P90, capable of firing nine hundred 5.7- × 28-mm rounds per minute, though its magazine held only fifty rounds. It was of a bullpup design, the action and magazine behind the trigger allowing for a shorter weapon with a barrel of equal length and accuracy as that of a longer gun. At just under twenty inches long, the P90's futuristic styling resembled something right out of a science-fiction movie.

He'd taken the gun off the hands, quite literally, so to speak, of a former business associate in Texas, who had acquired it in Nuevo Laredo from a low-level member of the Zetas, the paramilitary enforcement arm of the narco-trafficking Gulf cartel. Despite the P90 having been a prized possession, the former associate had had no further need of it. El Gato, in a crack house in South Dallas, agreed to the associate's offer of the weapon as collateral against the unpaid debt he owed El Gato for a kilogram brick of sticky black tar heroin. Then El Gato pulled his pistol and shot the associate dead. Or, more accurately, *shot up* the associate. First with the nine-millimeter pistol, then with the P90. The burst of forty rounds was meant to send a message to others who might consider shorting El Gato.

After he followed the businesswomen into the Reading Terminal Market, the heavy metal door slammed shut behind him.

Juan Paulo Delgado reached inside his raincoat and pulled up on the right side of his sweatshirt. He readied the P90 while keeping it concealed under the raincoat.

Tricia Hungerford Wynne — an attractive fair-skinned blonde of twenty-two years who stood a slender and athletic five-foot-ten — waited patiently in Reading Terminal Market. Tricia, whose family could trace their lineage back to Dr. Thomas Wynne, William Penn's personal physician and one of Philadelphia's settlers, was a Swarthmore College senior about to graduate early with a degree in education.

As a teacher-in-training at West Catholic High School, she had already begun what she considered a life of influencing future generations. And it was for that noble cause that she stood on line five back at the busy glass display counter of Beiler's Bakery. Beiler's sold homemade Amish delicacies only on Wednesdays through Saturdays (no later than five-thirty each day, three o'clock on Saturday), and she'd come to pick up the shoofly pie she'd ordered. Tricia taught a cultural diversity class for West Catholic freshmen, and today's emphasis was on the peaceful Amish of Lancaster County.

*I should bring some scrapple, too,* she thought, grinning mischievously.

*Just to watch the boys turn green as they read aloud all the parts of a pig listed in the ingredients.*

The Reading Terminal Market had opened in 1893 as a farmers' market. The massive riveted steelwork of the onetime Reading Railroad train shed now housed nearly a hundred merchants. The shops and restaurants were laid out on a grid, boxed in by Twelfth Street to the west, Eleventh to the east, Arch on the north, and Filbert to the south.

Like every day Tricia could remember, the

market was packed. Locals came regularly from their Center City offices; City Hall, with its statue of Willy Penn standing atop, was but blocks way. And tourists poured in from the nearby Marriott and Hilton Hotels and the Philadelphia Convention Center.

*And for very good reason,* Tricia thought.

She glanced around the market and marveled at the worldly mix it offered.

In addition to the dozen or so merchants representing the Pennsylvania Dutch communities, Reading Terminal Market had many others representing the four corners of the world. Up and down the aisles, hanging shingles advertised Little Thai Market, Kamal's Middle Eastern Specialties, Hershel's East Side Deli, Tokyo Sushi Bar. There were Greek souvlaki and gyros, French crepes, Italian hoagies, and the revered hometown favorite not to be forgotten, the Philly cheesesteak.

Then there was the market's mascot, Philbert the Pig, a life-size bronze pig that doubled as a giant piggy bank. Tricia smiled at the thought of the money that visitors donated to it being used to teach children healthy eating habits.

*Maybe next time I'll just arrange for a class field trip here.*

Because of the way that the line had bent

in the aisle, Tricia now stood almost exactly in front of the counter for the Mercado — *The Reading Market Market,* she thought, amused at the translation. She eyed the exotic variety it offered. Everything from homemade Mexican cheeses to burritos to even a chicken mole.

*Who knew a chicken dish could actually have chocolate in it?*

Behind a short wall that was the kitchen food-prep line, she noticed a black male of about twenty. He wore a white T-shirt and apron. He had his black hair in thick rope-like dreadlocks, a hairnet ridiculously over-stretched on them, and Tricia then realized that he was Jamaican.

*A Jamaican working in a Mexican café.*

*Now, that's really what you call a melting pot of worldly people.*

He smiled at her, and she returned it as she reached over to a display. She picked up a jar and began to casually inspect it. It was salsa, which she knew to be a spicy sauce of chopped tomatoes, onions, jalapeño peppers, and more. The festive red lettering of the label read HOLA! BRAND HOT & TASTY TEX-MEX SALSA, A TASTE OF OL' MEXICO VIA SAN ANTONE, TEXAS.

The line for Beiler's moved forward, and she returned the jar to the display, once

158

more smiling warmly. The thought of such a product — one having originated in a country so distinct and different — being readily available in the urban belly of a city like Philadelphia was wonderful.

(Her warm feeling would have been somewhat tempered had she turned the jar and read the tiny print on the back of the label: HOLA! BRAND IS A WHOLLY OWNED SUBSIDIARY OF NESFOODS INTERNATIONAL, INC., PHILA., PENNA.)

Tricia made brief eye contact with Kathleen Gingerich, who stood behind the counter at Beiler's. The shy and sweet sixteen-year-old was of slight build and light features, and of course, being Amish, wore absolutely no makeup. She was dressed in the traditional Amish conservative clothing — a simple ankle-length tan cotton dress, white cotton blouse, and a tan cotton head cover, its spaghetti straps tied in a tiny bow beneath her chin.

When Kathleen's light-brown eyes met Trish's blue ones, her gentle face glowed.

Kathleen pointed to say that the shoofly pie was waiting there on the glass display in a white cardboard box. Tricia nodded, then reached into her purse, a purple Pravda knockoff she'd bought the previous weekend from a sidewalk vendor in New York City's

Chinatown. She pulled out a twenty-dollar bill to have it ready when she got to the front of the line.

*That's so sweet of her.*

*If there's any place in Philly that better exemplifies its motto of the City of Brotherly Love than this market, I just don't know what it could be.*

Tricia Wynne then heard one of the heavy metal doors to Filbert Street slam shut. It was fifty or so feet down the aisle, beyond Beiler's. She looked there and saw two businesswomen. They turned and walked down a side aisle.

Then Tricia saw a young man in black jeans and boots and a navy blue raincoat standing at the door.

*A Latino,* Tricia noted approvingly.

She saw that the black hood of his sweatshirt was pulled over his head. It at first struck her as odd, but then she remembered the rain had just started and the chill it could cause when one entered an air-conditioned room.

The Latino began moving with a determined stride in her direction.

Then, behind her, Tricia heard a commotion at the food-prep counter of the Mercado.

She turned in time to see the Jamaican,

now with a stricken expression, quickly moving out from behind the short wall. He went to a table in the corner of the Mercado and pulled out from under it a brown paper grocery bag, its top folded over and stapled shut.

He began carrying the bag toward the Latino. He forced a smile as he came closer to him, holding out the bag in his left hand.

The next moment, everything happened so fast that Tricia could not comprehend it all.

The right side of the Latino's navy raincoat opened and out came what looked like some sort of firearm. It certainly had what looked like a barrel. Then the Jamaican threw the brown paper bag toward the Latino at the same time that he produced a small black semiautomatic pistol from the waistband behind his white apron.

She saw that the Jamaican held the pistol awkwardly, as if uncomfortable with it, and not in what one might call a traditional — or even natural — manner, which was to say with the grip of the pistol up and down, vertical. Instead, he held it sideways, the grip horizontal to the floor.

Then there came two series of deafening gunfire, the sound of which seemed to rattle around the heavy iron beams of the terminal.

One series, from the Latino's weapon, made a steady and pounding stream of *braaaaaps;* the other, from the pistol, of much slower and irregular *bang-bang-bangs.*

Tricia and those who'd been in line with her were on their knees, cowering, as the Latino strode past. He continued toward the Jamaican, who now lay on his right side on the concrete floor of the market with his pistol appearing empty. There were holes pierced in the upper part of his white apron, dark crimson stains spreading between them.

The brown paper bag had been shredded by bullets. Spread on the concrete near the Jamaican's feet were its contents, what looked to Tricia to be two bricklike objects wrapped in butcher paper and a lot of small sugar packets, maybe thirty or forty, all scattered.

With an amazing speed and grace, the Latino effortlessly bent and grabbed the butcher-paper-wrapped objects, then, ignoring the sugar packets, moved to a heavy steel door — and was gone.

Then there immediately came a woman's hysterical screams from behind the Beiler's Bakery counter.

And it wasn't until a woman beside Tricia wordlessly pointed to Tricia's bloody upper left sleeve that she first felt the burning sensation in her arm.

After exiting the steel door onto Filbert, El Gato began walking purposefully in an effort to blend in with the morning crowd moving along the rain-slickened sidewalk.

As he went, he peeled off the navy blue vinyl raincoat, balled it up, then stuffed it in the trash receptacle at the corner of Filbert and Twelfth. He pulled the hood of his sweatshirt from his head and put on the ball cap he'd tucked in his pants. Then, keeping his face down, he passed through the revolving door at the Market Street Station.

At the Thirtieth Street Station, El Gato disembarked the train and walked out to the lot where he'd left the white rusty Plymouth minivan. He drove it back to Hancock Street, then, exhausted, took his Tahoe home to Manayunk.

Police cars rocketed past him, headed toward Center City.

# [FOUR]
## Office of the First Deputy Commissioner
## Philadelphia Police Headquarters
## Race and North Eighth Streets, Philadelphia
## Wednesday, September 9, 7:50 A.M.

"Okay, gentlemen," First Deputy Commissioner Dennis V. Coughlin said, his ruddy face showing some displeasure. "So now we would seem to have two problems. Let's stick with the first one at hand, concerning His Honor the Mayor and Mr. James Henry Benjamin, president and chief executive officer of Benjamin Securities."

Coughlin, a tall and heavyset man, sat in the high-back black leather chair at his massive wooden desk and made a note on the leather-bound desk blotter. He was fifty-nine years old, still with all of his curly hair, though now silver, and all his teeth.

164

Standing beside him, and pouring coffee from a stainless-steel thermos, was his assistant, Captain Francis Xavier Hollaran. The forty-nine-year-old Hollaran was also a large Irishman who had all of his teeth. His luxurious mop of red hair, however, had thinned out long ago.

He was pouring into one of two heavy china coffee mugs he held. They bore the logotype of the Emerald Society. Both Hollaran and Coughlin belonged to the fraternal organization of police officers of Irish heritage. Denny Coughlin had joined "The Emerald" right out of the Police Academy. He had since served twice as its president, as the framed certificates behind him on the wall by the flat-screen television — which was muted and tuned to the local FOX newscast — attested.

Also in Coughlin's office on the third floor of the Police Administration Building were Chief Inspector Matthew Lowenstein, commanding officer of the Detective Bureau; Captain Henry Quaire, commander of the Homicide Unit, who reported to Lowenstein; and Lieutenant Jason Washington, whose immediate boss was Quaire.

They were all white shirts, though not one wore his police uniform; instead, all were in coats and ties or suits and ties. Denny

Coughlin had his well-tailored gray plaid double-breasted suit coat on a hanger on the peg on the back side of his office door, which now was closed.

And while this was a collection of department brass, a meeting of many of its best and brightest to handle a situation that had become a political hot potato, the air was at once serious and somewhat informal. The reason for the ease with which they worked was (a) that the men immensely respected one another and (b) that respect was the result of having a long history of working together.

In Coughlin's case, damn near forever — it had been thirty-seven years since he'd graduated from the Police Academy.

"My phone has been going off constantly all morning," Coughlin announced. "His Honor the Mayor is breathing down the neck of Commissioner Mariani, who of course has chosen to share said hot air."

Ralph J. Mariani, a natty, stocky, balding Italian, was the police commissioner. The image of the mayor leaning on the top cop triggered a couple of chuckles and a derisive snort.

"Ralph," Coughlin went on, "put it to me that His Honor had told him: 'Commissioner, I suggest you suggest to your deputy that he suggest . . .' " He paused to let that sink in. "So, you see where this is coming from. Short of a personal visit, it doesn't get much more direct than that."

Not that Coughlin was at all fearful of a personal visit from His Honor the Mayor of Philadelphia.

If it hadn't been for the Honorable Jerome H. "Jerry" Carlucci following protocol and passing orders down the chain of command, Coughlin knew he'd have damn sure seen Carlucci standing in his office — or, more likely, Coughlin called to the mayor's office.

Because before being elected to public office, Carlucci had, as he liked to brag, held every rank but that of policewoman in the Philadelphia Police Department. And during which time — as a captain, then on up through the ranks — Carlucci had been Coughlin's rabbi.

The purpose of a rabbi was to groom a young police officer, mentoring him in preparation for the greater responsibilities of the higher and higher ranks it was expected he would hold down the line.

His Honor also of course had had a rabbi, Augustus Wohl, who ultimately retired as a chief inspector, one step shy of deputy commissioner. Wohl's only son — who'd entered the Police Academy at age twenty, only two weeks after graduating from Temple University, and who'd at one point risen to be the department's youngest staff inspector — was now Inspector Peter Wohl.

Like his father, Peter Wohl was damn smart, damn honest, and a damn good cop. Which was why His Honor the Mayor had damn sure seen to it that Wohl had been made commander of the Special Operations Bureau, reporting directly to Coughlin.

And everyone in the room knew Inspector Wohl was the rabbi to one then-Detective and now-Seargeant Matthew Payne.

"Carlucci breathing on Mariani to breathe on you, Denny," Francis Hollaran, who had over the years followed Coughlin up through the ranks, said. "I believe that's called 'the shit flowing downhill.' "

The others in the room chuckled.

Coughlin glared at him. "Yes, it is, Frank. And would you care to wager a guess as to where, to use your crude phraseology, that shit's going to land next?"

"With any luck," Hollaran said, raising his Emerald Society mug to gesture toward the commander of the Detective Bureau, "right past me, and smack into Matt's lap."

Chief Inspector Matthew Lowenstein laughed out loud. He also was a large, stocky, ruddy-faced, barrel-chested man with a full head of curly silver hair. However, he did not belong to The Emerald. He was Jewish.

The very big and very black Jason Washington then intoned in his deep voice, "I pray that I am profoundly in error, but I suspect the flow of said fecal matter will wind up on my desk — thereon hitting the proverbial fan."

Denny Coughlin chuckled.

"Jason, your astute suspicions aside," Coughlin then said, "let's take it from the top. Beginning with what we know. Would you care to bring everyone up to speed?"

"Certainly. As I've shared with the captain and the chief inspector," he said, making eye contact with Quaire and Lowenstein as he said their ranks, "what we know is that at one-fifty this morning, there was an explosion at the Philly Inn on Frankford Avenue. Specifically, room fifty-two, which appears to have been actively used for the manufacture of the Schedule II controlled substance methamphetamine. We have two dead Hispanic males and two others, a white male and a white female, who suffered grave injury. The deceased were taken to the morgue, of course. The latter pair was transported to Temple Hospital, where they were admitted to the Intensive Care Unit, their conditions last listed as 'critical.' "

"Clearly the girl being Benjamin's daughter," Coughlin said.

Washington nodded.

"We're told," he went on, "but are awaiting positive ID, that the white male is one J. Warren Olde, Jr., of the custom homebuilder family. We're also told, but are awaiting verification, that he's the owner of the motel."

"And we're told this by whom?" Coughlin said. "A reliable source?"

Washington nodded again.

"Absolutely reliable," he said. "We have Anthony Harris on the scene, and after some initial confusion of the deskman on the Wheel, he now has the job —"

"Confusion?" Coughlin interrupted. "What's that all about?"

"Just an administrative matter that has been taken care of, sir."

Coughlin raised an eyebrow, nodded, then gestured for Washington to continue.

"Harris got the job in part because he's one of the best. But also because he has been on the scene since just about the time the motel blew up. He lives only seven, eight blocks away, and the blast rocked him out of bed."

"Jesus!" Denny Coughlin blurted.

"It was a significant explosion," Washington said.

"What do we know about the dead ones?" Coughlin said. "Anything yet?"

"Beyond the fact that one had his throat cut, not much. No IDs. They were severely burned, clearly. Practically everything in that room was consumed by the fire. The technician from the Medical Examiner's Office put their ages between twenty-five and thirty-five. The autopsy should narrow that."

Coughlin nodded in serious thought.

"Nothing else?" he then said.

Quaire grinned ever so slightly and made eye contact with his boss. Matt Lowenstein shrugged and grinned, too, his face saying *Why not?*

It wasn't lost on Coughlin, who barked, "What the hell is it?"

"The tech from the Medical Examiner's Office," Quaire said, and in his peripheral vision saw Washington cringe, "said that the critter making the meth got circumcised in the room."

"He got *what?*" Coughlin said incredulously, and wondered if he was having his chain pulled.

"It's true, Denny," Lowenstein offered. "But, I'm sorry, it's far beneath my dignified station to explain."

Coughlin looked at Quaire, who rose to the

challenge: "The tech said anybody involved in drugs was a dickhead, and so deserved to have his throat circumcised."

"Oh, Jesus Christ!" Coughlin blurted, but he was smiling.

"What we don't know," Washington went on, "among other things, is: Who cut his throat? That may be something we never learn, considering the conditions of the only other two people who were there."

After a moment, Quaire asked in a serious tone: "What I'm curious about is, how did Benjamin find out?"

"That's a good question, Henry," Hollaran said. "We wondered that, too. Turns out the vehicle Benjamin's daughter drives has one of those satellite systems. In the event of an accident, a crash sensor on the vehicle activates a communications module that uses the cellular telephone tower system — or maybe it's the global positioning system, or both — to triangulate the vehicle's location and then telephone an emergency number and pass along the details. Everything from whether the air bags deployed — how many of them, to determine the severity of the accident — down to the air pressure in the tires."

"I heard those calls go to some call center in Bombay, India," Washington offered.

"Making it an even more impressive system. Excuse me, that should be *Mumbai,* India. They changed it."

Hollaran nodded and a little disgustedly said, "That would not surprise me; Lord knows there's no one in Philadelphia — or Brooklyn or Iowa — who could be taken off the unemployment line and trained to do that. Why the hell keep jobs here? Anyway, this operator" — he glanced at Washington — "in Mumbai, India, could not get anyone in the Benjamin vehicle to respond when she or he dialed the vehicle's cellular telephone system connected to its high-fidelity sound system. So the operator then called the local 911 emergency number here. And, after that, started going down the list of emergency contacts that the owner of the vehicle had submitted when the vehicle was purchased."

"And the girl had her father as the first to contact in case of emergency, air bag deployment, et cetera," Washington said.

"Exactly," Hollaran said.

"And," Coughlin put in, "because her father has the mayor's personal cellular telephone number — it's my understanding that quite a few city bond-issuance programs have been managed by Benjamin Securities — His Honor knew all about whose SUV that was before we could even get there and run the plates or VIN."

"Ah, the miracles of modern technology!" Lieutenant Jason Washington intoned.

"In addition to the team of detectives Tony Harris is running," Matt Lowenstein offered, "we've got men sitting on the hospital in case either the Benjamin girl or the Olde boy is able to start talking. We've got a lot of manpower already on it, Denny. Unless you can think of something else?"

Coughlin considered that, then said, "No, not at this point. It sounds as if all the wheels are turning on this." He paused, then added, "I never doubted that, of course. It's just that this has become an extraordinary case."

He exhaled audibly.

"Okay, that was the first problem," Coughlin went on. "Now, as to Matty. I would like to hear everyone's thoughts on what we should do with Detective Matthew Payne."

He looked at Washington.

"I'm sorry, Jason. But it seems that proverbial fan you spoke of is attracting more for you. I'd like your opinion first, then Henry's, then Matt's, and then Frank's."

Everyone nodded, recognizing what Denny Coughlin was doing. It was the military method of beginning with the junior officer and working up to the most senior. It was an effective way of getting an opinion that was original — not something from someone who for self-preservation or other purposes simply agreed with what their boss had just said.

"Unequivocally, I think Detective Payne should stay on the case," Lieutenant Washington immediately said.

"What do you mean, 'stay on the case'?" Coughlin said.

"He's our absolutely reliable source. The one you asked about earlier?"

"How the hell is that?" Coughlin said. He looked at Hollaran. "Is that why he's on the way here, Frank?"

Hollaran shrugged. "He didn't get into that. He just said the heads-up was that he wanted to come back to work."

"Matthew went to school with the two in the hospital and is close to another who has a financial interest in the motel," Jason Washington explained, then went into the background he had on that from Tony Harris.

When Washington had finished with that a few minutes later, he added, "In summary, I believe Matthew would be indispensable. I welcome him back to Homicide with open arms."

"Okay," Coughlin said, stone-faced. "Thank you, Jason. Henry? Your piece of mind, please."

"Well," Quaire began, "it's no secret that I was not overly thrilled about Matt using The List and the mayor's top-five-scores-get-their-pick to come to Homicide."

About a month earlier, the department had released what was universally known as "The List."

Some twenty-five hundred police officers — corporals, detectives, and patrolmen with at least two years' service — had taken the examination for promotion. Those who passed and were promoted received a pay raise, a bump of four percent for the first two ranks, and fourteen percent for the patrolmen.

The List showed who had passed and how their scores had ranked them.

The exam was given in two parts, the first being written. Of the twenty-five hundred candidates, one in five had failed the written component. That washed them out, making them ineligible to move on to the exam's oral component.

Not everyone rushed to take the exam. Detectives could bring home more money in overtime than could sergeants, who clocked fewer hours. But because retirement pay was based on rank, they eventually would take it in hopes of being promoted and, then, retired as a lieutenant or captain.

The first hurdle, however, was passing. And not everyone did. And of those who did, not all were necessarily promoted right away.

After the names of those who passed the written exam were posted, the oral exams were given over the next four months.

In the Sergeant's Exam, nearly seven hundred detectives, corporals, and patrolmen had passed the oral component. That made them eligible for promotion, of course, but contingent on a number of factors. One was funding. There was money available for only ten percent of The List to be moved up immediately, in the next days or weeks.

The rest had to wait for attrition, a vacancy made by a sergeant who retired or was promoted.

Realistically, that meant if the score of one who passed the exam had them ranked no higher than the top one hundred or so, they would not get promoted. The List would expire after about two years, and the examination process would begin anew.

For those who did score very well, however, the mayor — in a moment of inspiration, thinking it would make for good public relations — had proclaimed that the five who scored the highest on The List would be given their choice of where in the department they wanted to serve.

And when The List had been recently posted, Number One on it was: PAYNE, MATTHEW M., PAYROLL NO. 231047, SPECIAL OPERATIONS.

And newly promoted Sergeant Payne had picked as his choice the Homicide Unit.

Captain Henry Quaire, commanding officer of the Homicide Unit, had not been thrilled with the news of the hotshot young sergeant's arrival. But putting two and two together, Quaire understood that there was more to it, more to Matt. He quickly had learned that Matt Payne, like his rabbi, Inspector Peter Wohl, was of the very smart sort. The bright ones destined for greater responsibilities and higher ranks.

Once, over drinks one night, Quaire even had heard Denny Coughlin offhandedly say that judging by the speed with which Payne was progressing in the department, Coughlin was worried that it wouldn't be long till Payne took his job.

Coughlin really hadn't been worried or serious, of course. No one would be prouder of his godson getting the job than the godfather himself. And, besides, realistically that just was not going to happen anytime soon. It was simply Coughlin's way of saying Payne was a rapidly rising star in the police department.

"And, Denny," Henry Quaire now went on, "I don't think it's any secret — I sure as hell hope it's not — that I now am in the camp of those who know Matt to be one helluva cop. I vote with Jason."

Coughlin looked at Lowenstein.

"I don't think you have to ask, Denny," Chief Inspector Matthew Lowenstein said simply. "But, officially, I concur."

"Ditto, Denny," Francis Hollaran said.

All eyes were now on Coughlin.

After a long moment that in the absolute quiet seemed much longer, he grunted and then said, "All right. I thank you for your thoughtful opinions. This, as I'm sure you know, is not an easy decision for me, and I appreciate your input. But, making such decisions is the reason that I'm paid the big bucks." He paused and grinned to show he was being facetious, then added, "*Both* of those big bucks."

There were the expected chuckles.

Coughlin glanced at each of them, then said, "Until I order otherwise, I do not —

repeat, do not — want Matty anywhere near the street."

The shocked silence in the room bordered on the awkward.

Coughlin went on, "I have my reasons. For one, he's had more than enough to deal with lately. Yes?"

There were a couple of agreeable nods.

Coughlin gestured toward the television with his right hand. "And he damn sure doesn't need to be in the news again anytime soon. What's it been? Not quite thirty days. The ink's still wet on the newspaper articles about his shooting at that Italian restaurant —"

"La Famiglia Ristorante," Hollaran furnished.

"That's it."

Hollaran said, "Matt's a good investigator, right, Jason?"

"A most excellent one," Washington said. "And supervisor."

"And I have absolutely no argument with that," Coughlin said reasonably. "So have him do it from the telephone. If I find out he's on the street, I'll put him on the goddamn midnight shift of the School Crossing Guard Unit."

Hollaran said, "There's no —"

"Of course there's not," Coughlin interrupted. "But I'll damn sure establish one, and man it with the rest of you. Do I make my point?"

There was a chorus of yessirs.

"All right, then. When he gets here, Henry, send him in. It's my order, so I'll break the news to him."

# IV

## [ONE]
## 826 Sears Street, Philadelphia
## Wednesday, September 9,
## 7:55 A.M.

Paco Esteban, a bloodstained gauze bandage on his forehead, walked swiftly toward his South Philly row house. The two-story flat-roofed structure — like the row houses on either side and many others up and down the street — had a façade of old red brick with dirty brown corrugated aluminum awnings above the door and windows.

In his left hand, Esteban carried two packed grocery bags, the sheer plastic stretching with the weight of their contents. He grabbed the black iron railing of the brick stoop and pulled himself along, quickly taking the three shallow steps up to the front door.

At the door, he nervously looked over his shoulder as he juggled the grocery bags and reached for his keys to open each of the door's three locks. About the time he got the second one unlocked, he heard the familiar metallic *clunk* that told him someone on the other side of the door was unlocking the third, a dead-bolt.

As he pulled out the key from the second lock, the door swung open.

Standing there in a dingy beige sleeveless cotton dress was his wife. As much as El Nariz's head hurt, he still managed to think: *My beautiful Salma. My Madonna. It is not fair that she should suffer such pain and worry. . . .*

Señora Salma Esteban was a swarthy black-haired twenty-nine-year-old who stood five-foot-four and weighed 160 pounds. Her face was puffy, the eyes somewhat swollen from crying. She clenched a wadded used tissue in her right hand.

On her left shoulder she held a toddler, the Estebans' three-year-old nephew, who had a thick mop of unruly black hair and wore only a diaper. He was sound asleep and snoring.

Señora Esteban, sniffling, motioned for El Nariz to quickly come inside. When he had, she pushed the door shut and rushed to relock the doors.

"How is she doing now?" El Nariz asked his wife in rapid-fire Spanish.

"Better," Salma Esteban said softly.

"*Bueno,*" El Nariz said, nodding thoughtfully.

He carried the bags into the cluttered kitchen. His wife followed.

She watched her husband, his coarse face still showing a mix of anger and fear, wordlessly unpack the bags with a heavy hand onto the counter. One bag held packs of flour tortillas, cans of *frijoles negros* and corn, and other staples of a heavy-starch diet. From the other he pulled out a pack of disposable diapers and handed them to his wife, then a box of gauze bandages, a bottle of hydrogen peroxide antiseptic, and a bottle of aspirin.

"While you were at the store," Salma Esteban said softly, "Rosario did say she wanted to tell us more."

Paco Esteban looked up from the bags. "More?" he said. "We know what she said about her being forced . . ."

He could not bring himself to repeat the sexual slavery part of her peonage.

He then shook his head and added, his tone incredulous, "There is more? *Madre de Dios.*"

"I will go and put the baby down," Salma Esteban said.

On the loading dock of the laundromat nearly two hours earlier, El Nariz had had to slap a wildly hysterical Rosario Flores twice across the face. Not that he necessarily felt that she was overreacting to the severed head and the shooting. He himself was in shock from that — and from his bloody forehead, which throbbed beyond belief. But he had made the immediate decision that anywhere else would be better for them to be than at the laundromat.

And her banshee screams were about to attract some unwanted attention, if the sound of the gunfire hadn't already accomplished that.

*At least I hear no sirens,* he'd thought.

*At least not yet.*

All of the other workers in his crew already had fled. He was not really worried about them. They knew how to take care of themselves, and for now that meant lying low, out of sight. He knew he would see some of them back in South Philly — particularly the ones who lived near his house, and especially the sister-in-law of his wife, who lived in his house with her husband and three-year-old son.

The others would at different times come out of the woodwork as they felt safer, as they collected information through their underground grapevine about what the hell had happened. And why. And how it did — or did not — directly threaten them.

The two slaps were enough to get Rosario's attention — and more important, to get her to shut up and listen to reason. He had then been able to convince her to get in the Ford minivan, and that it was safer for her in the backseat, lying on the floor under a pile of bedsheets.

El Nariz then had gone back inside the laundromat.

Considering what had just happened, he thought that the scene did not look that bad. Or certainly not as bad as it could have.

El Nariz looked at the arch of bullet holes in the brick wall.

*That crazy bastard!*

*What if he'd shot me — shot us all — instead of just leaving?*

The wire baskets between the walls of washer and dryer machines were scattered wildly, a few toppled on their side. The severed head lay where it had slid to a stop, down by the table along the wall used for folding. He walked to it, afraid he might throw up, and quickly covered it with a white bath towel. The bloody slime trail it had left was becoming more and more dry, and he grabbed a damp towel from a wire basket and quickly wiped up what he could.

Then he found a box of plastic garbage bags, pulled two from the roll, and went back to the towel-covered head.

*I still do not know who this is, may God rest her tortured soul.*

*Or how she is connected to Rosario.*

*But I do not question that she is.*

He crossed himself, then carefully gathered the white towel around the head, lifting it all at once. He placed the severed head and its towel in one of the plastic garbage bags, then placed that bag inside the other. He added the bloody towel that he had used to wipe the floor, then knotted the bags closed.

He scanned the room and shook his head in resignation.

*Nothing more to do right now.*

*Nothing but get the hell out of here.*

Then, carrying the bag, he quickly moved to the steel double doors of the loading dock. He pulled them closed from the outside, locked them, then went to the minivan.

As the rear door of the minivan swung upward, he could hear the muffled sobbing coming from under the small pile of bed-sheets.

"It is okay, Rosario," he said softly. "It is only me."

El Nariz carefully placed the garbage bag inside the rear storage area of the minivan — *If she knows this is here, it will not be good for either of us; but it is not right to just leave it* — and pulled the door down and closed it as gently as he could.

Rosario had sobbed uncontrollably on the drive to the South Philly row house.

And she was still inconsolable after Señora Esteban sat with both arms around her on the well-worn couch in the back-room parlor.

El Nariz had gone to clean up his head wound. He then took the double-bagged head down to the basement and, not sure what the hell else could immediately be done with it, he put it in the Deepfreeze, buried under plastic zipper-top bags of frozen vegetables.

Back upstairs, he'd stood watching from the doorway to the kitchen, taking an occasional pull from a liter bottle of agave liquor he held by his hip.

As Rosario continued sobbing, he'd finally gone back into the kitchen and poured two fingers of the tequila into a plastic cup. He'd then added twice as much orange juice to that and taken the drink into the parlor. With some effort, they got the girl to drink it.

After a short while, the alcohol had the desired effect. Rosario became somewhat calmer. She still trembled at times, but at least she no longer wailed.

Rosario now sat on the back-room parlor couch as Paco and Salma Esteban came back into the room. She had her knees pressed to her breasts and both arms wrapped tightly around the outside of her knees. She slowly rocked to and fro as she tried to hold back the sobs that seemed to rise from deep down inside.

"Rosario," Salma Esteban began softly, "you do not have to do this thing now. You have been through very much."

She shook her head vigorously.

"No," she said. "It must be done."

She sobbed.

"And I must go to church," she added, "to confession."

Paco and Salma Esteban exchanged glances.

Paco Esteban said, "Who's the girl?"

His wife glared at him for asking such a question at such a delicate time.

He shrugged, in effect saying, *What did I say?*

Rosario buried her face in her knees and breasts. Then she looked up and between them.

She wailed, "I killed my cousin!"

Paco and Salma Esteban again exchanged glances, this time ones of deep shock.

## [TWO]
## The Roundhouse
## Eighth and Race Streets,
## Philadelphia
## Wednesday, September 9,
## 8:15 A.M.

Lieutenant Jason Washington was in his glass-walled office in the Homicide Unit. Minutes earlier, he had decided to deal with the matter of Detective Bari at a later time, if not date, and felt a twinge of guilt for having more or less brushed off Denny Coughlin's question by saying the "administrative problem" had been taken care of.

Now he turned to reviewing the notes Tony Harris had taken so far in the Philly Inn job. He noticed the sound of voices growing louder in the outer office.

Washington looked up and saw Sergeant Matthew M. Payne being welcomed by a small crowd of detectives. They shook Payne's hand and patted him on the back as he slowly but certainly moved through them and toward Washington's office.

Washington heard Payne say, "I'd better check in with the boss." A moment later, Payne rapped a knuckle on the edge of the doorway.

"Matthew," Jason Washington said warmly. "I had heard a rumor that you were on your way back to the Roundhouse."

"How are you, Jason?"

They shook hands.

"Very well, Matthew. Thank you for asking."

"Mind if I ask where you came across this rumor? I was really afraid that the rumor circulating was the one that painted me as having turned in my gun and badge and gone off to take art classes in the south of France."

Washington chuckled. He motioned with his hand, waving Payne into one of the two metal-framed chairs across from his desk.

"Oh, no," Washington said, smiling. "*That* rumor — and it had you in Gay Paree, emphasis on the *Gay* — died a slow death weeks ago. This new one I got from far up the chain of command."

Payne figured that one out — *From my call to Hollaran* — right when Washington confirmed it.

"I just enjoyed a visit to Commissioner Coughlin's office," Washington said.

Payne nodded but didn't say anything, waiting for him to continue.

"The commissioner had brought me and my boss and his boss in," Washington went on, "to discuss the situation of the Philly Inn."

Payne nodded. "I was just out there at the scene."

"So I understand." He pointed at the notes on his desk. "I've been speaking with Tony."

Payne nodded again. "Does that mean Tony's got the job? And not Bari?"

Washington considered his reply for a long moment, then said, "It's now Tony's. The answer to the other part of your query is — how do I put this? — that it's on the back burner for now."

"As long as Tony's got it, I don't care about the how or why. I want in on this, too, Jason. It's important to me."

Washington's eyebrows went up.

"Matthew, it would never cross my mind

that you had anything other than a strictly professional interest in this case." He paused. "Would it?"

"My interest is to find out — professionally — what the hell happened out there. And why."

Washington did not immediately reply. He looked at the notes on his desk. "Tony tells me you have a history with" — he glanced at the notes to refresh his memory — "with this Warren Olde and Rebecca Benjamin."

"And with Chad Nesbitt," Payne said, then went on and gave Washington all the background he'd given Tony Harris.

"Matthew, you didn't hear this from me."

"Yessir," Payne said, but it was more of a question.

"Denny Coughlin is of course going to welcome you back with open arms —"

"Great! I didn't want this to be difficult."

Washington gave him a hard look. "Kindly allow me to complete my thoughts, Matthew."

"Sorry."

"Thank you. And what the commissioner has in mind — and, again, you did not hear it from me — is that you're welcome back to your desk." He nodded to the outer office of Homicide. "You'll work out of here."

"I'm tied to a desk? What is that about, Jason?"

"He's concerned for you, Matthew. We all are. You went through a lot."

"Which was why I took the thirty days. Now I'm back. I'm well. And I want to work."

Both Lieutenant Jason Washington and Sergeant Matt Payne knew there never was any real chance that Payne would be denied his job if and when he said that he wanted it.

After all, it was a fact that the shooting had been declared a good one; thus, the department could not use that against him. And it was a fact that the psychiatrist, Dr. Aaron Stein, had said that Payne had suffered only from emotional exhaustion — "The treatment is rest," Stein said, "and don't push yourself so hard again" — which sure as hell was not cause for suspension or termination.

Finally, while it had been the Number Two man in the police department hierarchy, Denny Coughlin, who'd strongly suggested to Payne that he take off the deserved time, it also was a fact that it had been exactly that — a suggestion.

*And now Uncle Denny is probably going to throw Dr. Stein's "Don't push yourself so hard again" line in my face.*

*Which translates to running in low gear while driving a goddamn desk.*

Had anyone hinted at denying Sergeant Payne his job, Payne knew that technically he could have created one helluva stink. Starting with the Fraternal Order of Police getting its lawyers to file grievances against the department to reinstate Sergeant Payne, and on up to a team of big-gun litigators from the prestigious firm of Mawson, Payne, Stockton, McAdoo & Lester dragging the City of Philadelphia to the Supreme Court of the United States of America for whatever unlawful action they could muster.

But that was technically. Realistically, of course, no one wanted it to come to blows. And it wouldn't, because that would not have served either side's best interests.

"I don't agree with the order, Matthew, but the commissioner has his reasons. And he's the boss. I'll make it as best I can for you. You know that."

Payne nodded thoughtfully.

*And Jason will.*

*But it'll still be a personal purgatory.*

Payne then said, "Thank you, Jason."

"You should go upstairs and make your manners. The sooner you start to meet whatever threshold the commissioner has in

194

mind, the sooner everything will be back the way you want it."

A detective walked up to Washington's office.

"Sorry to interrupt, Lieutenant."

"No interruption. Sergeant Payne here was just leaving. What is it?"

"Just got word of a shooting at the Reading Terminal Market. At least two dead."

"What the hell is going on with today?" Washington said disgustedly.

First Deputy Commissioner Dennis V. Coughlin was leaning back in his high-back leather chair, feet on the desk, and in deep thought, when Captain Francis X. Hollaran stuck his head in the half-open doorway.

"Chief, Matt's here. And more info is coming in on the market shooting."

Coughlin nodded, then slid his feet off the desk and onto the floor.

"Thanks, Frank. Give it to me when it's solid. And send him on in, please."

The door opened more and Payne came through it.

"Matty!" Coughlin said, his tone genuinely pleased.

Coughlin stood and came around the desk. He affectionately put his arms around Payne and patted him on the back as Payne

195

returned the gesture.

"Have a seat, Matty," he said, pointing to one of the pair of upholstered armchairs.

As Payne did, he watched Coughlin go back to his leather chair. Coughlin wasn't wearing the double-breasted jacket of his suit, and Payne noticed that he also wasn't wearing his Smith & Wesson snub-nosed .38 Special revolver. Nor did he have the well-worn holster threaded on his belt on the right side.

Coughlin had slipped the five-shot revolver, butt forward, into that same holster every morning for thirty-seven years, since the day he reported on the job as a rookie detective. Payne knew that it was the same standard sidearm that Philadelphia Police Department cops had carried for damn near forever, including his father and his uncle when they were killed.

Then Payne saw, sitting on top of a copy of *The Peace Officer,* the official publication of the Fraternal Order of Police Lodge #5, a new black molded plastic clamshell box. It had the logotype GLOCK — the big G circling the smaller LOCK — molded into its top and bottom.

"That's not a new pistol, is it, Uncle Denny?"

Coughlin looked at it with a sour face.

"Yours?" Payne pursued.

"Mariani insisted."

Payne raised his eyebrows at the mention of the police commissioner.

"Since the department now is issuing the Glock 17," Coughlin went on in explanation, "he said that I needed to set an example."

Payne nodded, then said, "Why not one of the other Glocks, the optional models?"

Police Commissioner Mariani had lobbied — and, remarkably, won the battle — for the city to allow the police to carry more firepower. The Philadelphia Police Department issued to every officer on the force a Glock Model 17 — at no cost, after they of course had qualified with the weapon at the department gun range. The 17 was a semi-automatic pistol chambered for the nine-millimeter round. It could hold eighteen rounds, one in the throat and seventeen in the magazine.

The commissioner, even more remarkably, had also lobbied for and, beyond belief, gotten approval for four Alternative Service Weapons. These were also Glock models, two of the models chambered in .40-caliber and two in .45-caliber.

It had been remarkable because there were those of the mind-set — said mind-set more often than not being of one's head being deeply stuck in the sand, or firmly up one's ass — that it was a danger to the very public they were sworn to protect for the police to carry such powerful weapons.

All sorts of wild-eyed hysteria surfaced during the debates as to just how powerful a firearm a police officer should have. There had even been a troop of protesters who — perhaps coincidentally, perhaps not — looked like they might rob a bank at any moment. They had marched on City Hall carrying posters bearing a red circle with a diagonal bar across photos of Clint Eastwood as "Dirty Harry," the movie character cop who'd terrorized the sensibilities of San Franciscans.

But in the streets of Philly, as more and more gun battles with bad guys — and gun battles between the bad guys themselves — showed that damn near none of the thugs carried a .38-caliber or similar-size weapon, cooler heads successfully argued that the cops were being outgunned.

For a Philly cop to carry one of the larger-caliber pistols as his duty weapon, there were rules, of course. Chief among them: The officer had to buy the larger-caliber gun with personal funds. The department would issue only the Model 17 at no cost. Second, the alternative weapon had to be inspected.

Which meant undergoing a mandatory inspection by a department armorist at the police department firing range.

Then there was the actual qualification test. If the officer successfully completed this, she or he was given a certification card that had to be carried on their person at all times. There was also the rule that the pistols could be loaded only with department-issued ammunition — 165-grain tactical rounds in .40-caliber and 230-grain tactical rounds in .45-caliber. That ammo had to be used exclusively, whether the officer was on duty or off duty. Finally, upon meeting all the requirements to carry one of the larger-bore Glocks, the officer had to give the department-issued Model 17 back to the department.

There were absolutely no exceptions to the rules — except, of course, one.

The Special Operations Bureau was tasked, as its name suggested, to perform particularly extraordinary ops. Emphasis on *extraordinary*. And it was in that environment that Matt Payne, before the police force even began issuing Glocks, began carrying his Colt Officer's Model .45-caliber semiautomatic. Even after leaving Special Operations (and its commander, Peter Wohl, his rabbi) for Homicide, he continued carrying it, having successfully argued that (a) it had been grandfathered in as an approved weapon, and (b) it could be considered not as powerful as the Glock .45 because it held fewer of the 230-grain tactical rounds that he fed it.

Payne devoutly believed that his Colt, a smaller version of the dependable John Browning–designed Model 1911 semiautomatic that many argued damn near single-handedly won the Second World War, was superior to the Glock in almost every way. And its size sure as hell made it better for concealed carry.

Matt motioned toward the pistol box. "May I?"

Coughlin snorted. "Go ahead. But be damned careful, Matty. When you're around guns, they tend to go off."

Matt looked quickly at him and saw that Coughlin was smiling.

Matt unsnapped the two silver latches, opened the box, and removed the weapon. He automatically took care to keep the muzzle pointed down, then ejected the magazine and pulled back the slide enough to see that no round was in the chamber.

"Nice," he said.

"Damn thing's a monster compared to my .38." He paused. "Which, I might add, served me just fine."

"You never had to use it, Uncle Denny."

"Precisely."

"So why the nine-millimeter?"

"You're not listening, Matty. I'm supposed to be setting an example. Besides, my .38 was fine. Why carry around an elephant gun? And I sure as hell didn't want to have to buy a damned gun. If Mariani is forcing me to take one, it'd damn well better be a free one."

Payne put the pistol back in the box, closed the lid, and snapped the latches shut.

"You know what they say about a nine-millimeter, don't you, Uncle Denny?"

"I'm sure you'll tell me."

"It's a .45 set to 'stun.' "

Coughlin grunted.

"Thank you for that educational ballistic tip, Marshal Earp."

Payne shrugged and smiled.

" 'If an injury has to be done to a man, it should be so severe that his vengeance need not be feared,' " Payne quoted.

Coughlin's Irish temper flared: "Jesus H. Christ, Matty!"

Payne put his hands up, palms out. "Hey, Niccolo Machiavelli said that, not me. Early 1500s, I believe it was."

"If you think that kind of talk's going to help with your case . . ." He paused, shaking his head. "Well, I suppose we actually should get into that, into why you're here."

"I heard —" Payne began just as the intercom speaker on the phone buzzed.

"Hold that thought, Matty."

Coughlin pushed a button. "Yeah? What is it, Frank?"

"Call for you holding on line four, Chief," Hollaran's voice came over the speaker. "Sorry to interrupt, but I think you want this one. Could be educational for Sergeant Payne to listen in on."

Coughlin looked to the bottom edge of the phone and saw the blinking red light under one of the row of five buttons, three of which were regular phone lines and two of which were secure lines.

He punched the SPEAKERPHONE button on the phone base, then punched the button above the blinking light and said, "Commissioner Coughlin."

"How's my favorite small-town police chief?" a soft feminine voice inquired.

Coughlin's face lit up and Payne smiled at the sound of the voice.

Coughlin then glanced beyond Payne. Across the room was his I Love Me wall, and there he saw the picture of him standing beside the diminutive Liz Justice. The photograph had been taken two years earlier, when the Philadelphia Executive Women's League had given her their annual Benjamin Franklin Leader of the Year Award.

She was a petite thirty-five-year-old with a bright face and deeply intelligent dark eyes who wore her shoulder-length brunette hair parted on the right. In the picture she wore a navy blue woolen business suit with a double row of brass buttons down the front, navy silk stockings, black leather shoes with low heels — and a dazzling smile.

"How the hell are you, Liz?" Coughlin said, his voice also showing his pleasure.

"Plodding ahead in the never-ending war against crime, Denny."

"Indeed. Welcome to the club."

"I need a favor, Denny."

"You got it."

"I need some doors opened for a friend of mine."

"They're wide open, Liz. Who is he?"

"A Texas Ranger. The youngest one. Reminds me of Peter Wohl. Or maybe Matt Payne —"

Coughlin glanced at Payne, who was somewhat glowing in the praise.

"His name is Jim Byrth," she went on. "He's after a charming guy who likes to cut girls' heads off. He heard the bastard's in Philadelphia."

"We sure as hell can do without any of that. This Byrth will be doing us a favor. When's he coming?"

"He'll be on the Continental flight arriving at three twenty-two."

"He'll be met. If he's a friend of yours, I'll meet him myself."

"That would probably get the word out that the doors are open. He wants to nab this critter quietly."

Liz Justice had been a chief inspector of the Philadelphia Police Department running Internal Affairs when the City Fathers of Houston, Texas, had decided that their troubled police department needed a new chief. One with lots of experience in internal affairs. To say that the Houston PD was having more than a little problem with corrupt cops was akin to calling the mafia a misunderstood boys' club. "You can beat the rap, but you can't beat the ride" had become such common knowledge it may as well have been painted on the fenders of every squad car. And everything they'd tried thus far had failed to effect any significant change.

When the search of the nation's major police departments came up with Chief Inspector Justice's name, the only thing against her was her gender.

But the mayor had solved that in genuine

Texas fashion: "Who better to break up the Old Boy Network than a lady who's a fourth-generation cop?"

Not only did Liz still have friends on Philly's force, she still had family. Including a cousin in South Detectives, Lieutenant Daniel "Danny the Judge" Justice, Jr. He was reputedly the smallest and without question the most delicate-looking white shirt in all of the Philadelphia Police Department.

Two weeks after the Houston mayor made the decision to hire Chief Inspector Liz Justice, she had been sworn in as the United States' first female chief of a major city police department. The historic news put her on the cover of *Time* magazine.

"I do appreciate it, Denny. Please give my love to your far better half."

He chuckled. "Will do, Liz. Take care of yourself down there in the Wild West."

She laughed appreciatively.

He punched the SPEAKERPHONE button, breaking the connection.

Coughlin looked at the I Love Me wall again. Payne could almost see the gears turning in his mind.

And Coughlin was indeed thinking.

*The reason Hollaran said that Matty overhearing that conversation would be educational was because (a) he'd had a nice talk with*

*Liz before sending her call in here and knew what she wanted and because (b) he believed that sitting on this Texas Ranger would solve our problem of what to do with Matty.*

*That's what you call a good assistant — one who solves problems for his boss.*

"That's one terrific woman," Payne said with genuine praise.

Coughlin turned to Payne.

"Yeah, and one terrific cop." He paused. "And you, Matty, are one lucky one. Guess where you'll be at three twenty-two this afternoon?"

# [THREE]
# 826 Sears Street, Philadelphia
# Wednesday, September 9,
# 8:16 A.M.

Sitting on the well-worn parlor couch, her legs crossed beneath her, Rosario Flores sipped from a can of Coca-Cola.

Across from her, Paco and Salma Esteban each sat in a stackable molded plastic chair, of the type commonly found on backyard patios.

"Are you sure?" Salma Esteban said softly,

leaning toward her.

Rosario nodded. "It is all my fault. I could have stopped it, or at least been smarter, when we met El Gato in Matamoros . . ."

She then explained herself.

It had been no accident that Ana and Rosario had crossed paths with Juan Paulo Delgado just over the border from Brownsville, Texas.

On that late afternoon in March, he had lain in wait, carefully watching the pedestrian traffic crossing the Gateway International Bridge into Matamoros, Mexico. He again was ready to cull from the crowd.

Ana and Rosario, wearing jeans, T-shirts, and dirty sneakers, were walking off the bridge in a group of twenty others. They had been officially declared by United States immigration officials to be unaccompanied minors. They had no way of knowing, of course, but they had joined some 35,000 other immigrant children who in a given year were so declared and, accordingly, lawfully deported.

This afternoon's group was a mix of teenagers and younger children. One was a six-year-old, being carried by another teenager, whose mother was said to be missing in the desert. And Rosario held the hand of a sad-eyed ten-year-old boy whom she'd met only an hour earlier, when the group had been gathered. He'd warmed to her and taken her hand.

Two days earlier, Ana and Rosario had been in another group, one of a dozen Latino women and children, when they were caught illegally attempting to enter the United States of America.

They had come from Honduras, setting out weeks earlier by foot, then crossing Guatemala and Mexico by truck and train. When they had reached the Rio Grande, the "Great River" that was the United States border, their coyotes waited with them in the foliage until night, then secretly ferried the group the thirty-yard distance across in three small rubber rowboats.

Then bright portable floodlights had popped on. And they were almost immediately apprehended — following a futile attempt at fleeing — by the green-uniformed officers of the United States Border Patrol.

At that point, of course, their coyotes were nowhere to be found north of the border.

The American government's processing of unaccompanied minors was similar at all southern U.S. points of entry. Within twenty-four hours of the declaration, with the detainees held in secure rooms, the usual telephone call was made to the local Mexican consulate. For Ana and Rosario, that meant the one in Brownsville. It was located on Mexico Boulevard, adjacent to the Amigoland Shopping Mall, not quite a mile's walk to two of the three bridges there that crossed into Mexico.

The Mexican consulate in Brownsville then arranged for an official in Matamoros with the more or less Mexican equivalent of child protective services to meet the group of unaccompanied minors. The children then would be repatriated to Mexico and, the Mexican government hoped, swiftly returned to their families.

The cold damn reality of that, however, was that in all likelihood their immediate family was still in the United States (parent and child having gotten separated during a crossing, for example). Or, worse, that their immediate family no longer existed for one of any number of tragic reasons, including a mother being lost and presumed dead in the desert.

And the task of (a) finding the child's extended family and then (b) getting them to agree to take custody (and with it the financial burden) of the minor was daunting — if not damn impossible.

Thus, most of the unaccompanied minors

had of course absolutely no desire to be returned home. Certainly not Ana Maria Del Carmen Lopez or Rosario Flores, who had struggled — had very much risked their lives for six weeks along dangerous smuggling routes — to reach the opportunities that awaited them in America.

Yet now, Ana and Rosario — having been processed by the American immigration system and given the status of unaccompanied minors — found themselves in the late-afternoon confusion of the crowd on the international bridge.

And out of that mix of tourists taking quick trips into Mexico to shop or eat and Mexican nationals returning home from working in Brownsville, a handsome young man suddenly appeared before the pair.

He had been exceedingly charming. With a calculated manner, so that the girls would come with him not only willingly but enthusiastically, he immediately began appealing to their desires.

And he began by saying he could get the pretty senoritas back to the United States.

Rosario was charmed.

Ana was wary.

*How does he know what we want?* Ana thought.

That was quickly replaced with: *Is it not*

*obvious? We were just thrown out. Everyone sees it.*

*And I don't want to be stuck in cells here.*

When caught at the river, they'd first been in the custody of the U.S. Department of Homeland Security's Border Patrol. That agency had then turned them over to the Customs and Border Protection, also under DHS, which in turn had delivered them to the Mexican officials. They'd thus just suffered through the United States' bureaucratic system, killing time in cold and sterile holding areas for what seemed like a month. It had actually been four days, and they were told it had taken longer than the standard twenty-four hours thanks to the delay of the weekend.

Neither Ana nor Rosario liked the idea of going through any of that again. Especially in Mexico, which without question would be a worse system with even fewer resources than those of the United States.

As Ana eyed the handsome young man, she thought, *And we can't get sent all the way back to Tegucigalpa.*

So far, Ana and Rosario had avoided that by lying to the U.S. Border Patrol *policía*. They'd stated that they were Mexican nationals, which was what their coyotes had coached them to do if caught.

Neither had any official papers — no birth certificate, certainly no driver's license, no passport, nothing — proving that they were or were not Mexican.

But they also did not have anything that stated they were from Honduras or Guatemala or Nicaragua or any other country. The Americans called that "OTM," any country Other Than Mexico. If the illegal aliens admitted to being from a particular country OTM, American law required that they be sent back to that particular OTM country.

If, however, they proclaimed Mexico was their home, the *norteamericanos* — Customs and Border Protection, to be precise, but it made no difference to the girls which official agency — would expedite their repatriation via the nearest port of entry.

Even Ana Lopez and Rosario Flores — with very little formal education, barely able to read or write beyond basics in their mother language, let alone the least bit literate in English — had the street smarts to figure out that game. And walking across the international bridge and winding up in Matamoros was a helluva lot closer to getting back into America than being trucked or bused or whatever all the way back to Honduras.

Of course, conveniently, repatriation via

the nearest port also happened to be the most expeditious option for the U.S. government and its agents.

The Mexican official who was meeting the group of unaccompanied minors was an overweight gray-haired Latina woman in an ill-fitting pantsuit. She held up a clipboard and looked more than a little weary, if not overwhelmed.

Standing with Ana and Rosario at the edge of the bridge, the handsome young man gently applied pressure: "You must decide now! Quickly!"

He looked at the official, then added, "Before you are taken into her custody!"

And before, the girls knew, the long — and what would turn out to be futile — process of finding their families began.

Rosario and Ana exchanged glances, then Rosario handed off the ten-year-old boy to another in the group.

The two teenage girls disappeared with the handsome young man into the lengthening shadows of a trash-strewn side street.

If the female Mexican official had noticed the two teenage girls leaving the group, she certainly did not show it.

Almost immediately — within two blocks — the handsome young man stopped and turned to the girls. When he told him that his name was El Gato, Rosario giggled. He smiled back, then said that if they wanted to get back to the United States, they would have to trust El Gato.

"We have little money," Ana had said, looking at Rosario, knowing that that was a lie.

They had absolutely no money.

Most of what they'd had had gone to the coyotes for their failed first illegal crossing. The rest, little more than a hundred dollars, had been on a prepaid debit money card. On the back of the card, they had written the U.S. phone number of Rosario's cousin, whom they'd planned to call once in America. But during the rough rowboat ride, unbeknownst to Rosario, the card had slipped free from the back pocket of her jeans. Both card and phone number were somewhere on the bottom of the Rio Grande.

"We can discuss that later," El Gato had said agreeably, then held out his right hand and cocked his head. "And you are . . . ?"

"Rosario Flores," Rosario said, grabbing his hand. She nodded toward her cousin and added, "Ana Lopez."

"Well, *Ana* and *Rosario*," he'd said charmingly as he shook their hands in turn, "can you trust El Gato?"

"Who does not trust a kitten?" Rosario had quickly answered — Ana thought a little too quickly.

Ana then pressed for details — who was he, where would he take them, how much would it cost?

El Gato smiled at her. He commented that she would do well in America.

"You have such a wise and questioning mind," he said.

Then he'd told them of the great many jobs that America offered pretty girls like themselves. Ones that paid cash to work as a waitress in restaurants, to clean houses and offices, even to watch over young children, jobs that the gringos called "nannies" and "au pairs."

More money than they could believe, he'd said, more than enough to live on in great comfort and still send plenty back home to their families.

Juan Paulo Delgado said that once the girls were across the border he would introduce them to some of the others he'd helped. They were ones he called his "growing family," he said with a smile. Then he said he'd set up Ana and Rosario, as he had the other girls, with work. He'd even help show them how to wire their extra money home.

*Extra money!* Rosario had heard.

*Not just money, but extra!*

Rosario — who people often confusedly assumed was Ana's older, wiser sister despite the fact that Ana was far more grounded — leaned over and whispered in Ana's ear: "Juanita!"

Juanita Sanchez, Ana knew, was a cousin on the other side of Rosario's family, the one whose telephone number they had lost in the river. Juanita had been sending money home to Honduras, first from Dallas in Texas. Then it had come from the *ciudad* called Newark, in Nuevo Jersey, where the cousin now worked — though Rosario was not sure for whom — as a *criada,* a maidservant.

Rosario had told Ana that she knew that was true because she'd gone once with Juanita's mother to collect the money — five hundred dollars, which came out to be more in Honduran *lempiras* than the aunt earned in half a year. Juanita had wired the money from the United States to the bright yellow-and-black Western Union office nearest their Tegucigalpa barrio.

And that, in fact, had been what encouraged Ana and Rosario to start on their journey north.

Standing on the side street near the international bridge, Ana looked her cousin in the eyes and anxiously considered their options.

That had taken no time whatsoever. They had no money and no other place to go save for the streets of Matamoros or the Mexican system of child protective services.

"*Bueno,* El Gato," Ana had said. "What do we do?"

El Gato smiled, then motioned with his hand over his head. He said that if they trusted him, they would also trust his friend Hector — who on cue suddenly came around a corner. As he approached them, Ana and Rosario saw that he was younger than El Gato, maybe even the age of Ana and Rosario, but far coarser-looking, with an acne-pocked face and bad teeth.

El Gato introduced them. Then he looked from one girl to the other and promised them (a) that they should have no worries with Hector, (b) that Hector would be their coyote and see that they safely got across the Rio Grande, and (c) that he himself would see them shortly on the U.S. side.

And then El Gato said his goodbyes.

Hector led Ana and Rosario around the dirty street corner to a battered and rusty yellow Toyota compact pickup. They all squeezed into its cab, with Rosario sliding across the torn fabric of the bench seat to sit in the middle. After about an hour's drive on paved highway — during which an increasingly disgusted Rosario didn't think Hector's hand brushing her knees as he worked the gearshift was exactly an accident — the truck turned onto a narrow, bumpier macadam road.

Just past the corner, they passed a police car that was parked on the side of the small road. The officer made no effort to stop them. Ana even thought that she saw the man smile and nod.

Minutes later, the truck turned off the macadam road and drove a short distance down a tree-lined rutted dirt road. It then slowed and made an abrupt turn through some brush between the trees. The surprise turn caused Rosario to squeal, then laugh a little nervously.

Limbs scraped the side of the truck. One bough popped through the open passenger-door window. It struck Ana on the ear but caused no injury.

The Toyota pickup stopped fifty feet later, and Hector got out and motioned for the girls to do likewise.

They were upstream of Matamoros and standing alone on a small rise above the riverbank. The meander of the river made a tight bend here, almost turning back onto itself. The Mexico side was thick with scrub trees and brush, the low sun causing long dark shadows. The immediate area of the bank stank and was littered with trash — empty plastic bottles of fruit drink, empty snack bags, and dirty ragged discarded clothing, both men's and women's.

Ana then caught herself suddenly inhaling deeply. She nudged Rosario to look. Rosario followed her gaze and saw the tree with a dozen or more pairs of women's panties dangling from its limbs. She thought she heard Hector chuckle.

They looked toward him and saw him reaching into a big cardboard box in the back of the pickup. Hector brought out some clothes, then gave them to the girls.

They held them up and saw that they were uniforms: tan cotton dresses with brown piping and off-white cotton blouses with frilled collars. Each had a plastic name tag pinned to the lapel. The tags were a darker brown color with etched white letters at the top — RGG&RC — and one reading ANGEL, one ROSA.

Hector then said that they were to change into the clothes. Right there.

Reluctantly, the girls stepped to the far side of the pickup for some privacy, and stripped to their panties and bras. Hector pretended not to watch, but it was clear that he seemed to enjoy every moment of it.

When they were done, Hector pulled out of the cardboard box three small tan backpacks with a Nike logotype stitched on them. He slipped one over his shoulder and gave the girls the others. It took Hector's help for them to shoulder the bags, the contents of each weighing exactly ten kilos — just over twenty pounds.

Hector motioned for the girls to follow. They began walking along the shoreline, within the line of trees and out of sight of the other shore. They came to a small rapid where the river bottom was exposed and the murky green-brown river rushed over it.

*Walk across?* Ana thought.

*Why didn't we do this the first time? Instead of those stupid rowboats!*

*Could the policeman in the car have something to do with this? Maybe control this part of the river?*

Hector pulled out a cellular telephone. In a flurry of finger movements, he typed then sent a very short text message.

Almost immediately on the U.S. side of the river border, not a hundred meters away, there was movement at the top of the rise above the river's edge. It was some sort of small cartlike vehicle. It stopped, and a man got out of it. He was heavyset, like a larger version of Hector, and wore a uniform that was the same tan and brown as the outfits that the girls wore. He then started down toward the river, walking awkwardly under the weight of a .long black bag he carried with both hands.

Hector started across the river shoal. The girls looked at each other, then followed.

Wading the shallows was uneventful save for Ana at one point snagging her foot on something underwater. She stumbled, and Rosario laughed. But when Ana went to free her foot and found it stuck in yet another pair of women's underwear — this pair snagged on a submerged tree limb — Rosario's smile quickly disappeared.

Once they reached the U.S. side of the river border, the heavyset man nodded a greeting but said nothing.

The girls watched as he and Hector exchanged the backpack for the long black canvas duffle. Hector grunted under the big bag's weight, and when he slung its web handles over his right shoulder, the girls heard what sounded like metal pipe and dense plastic clunking against each other inside it.

Hector then said, "José, he will take you the next step."

And, without another word, he struggled with the long bag and went back across the river.

José led the girls with their backpacks to the cartlike vehicle they had never seen before. It had four small tires, a dull scratched dark green body, and not much more than a steering wheel and a black vinyl-covered bench seat that could accommodate no more than the three of them. There was lettering on the front of the cart — though neither girl could translate it, recognizing only the same logotype that was on the badges of their outfits — that read RGG&RC MAIN-TENANCE.

José smiled warmly but said nothing as he drove them down a narrow asphalt-paved path that Ana thought looked as if it had been made expressly for this vehicle.

They came to an automobile parking lot, where José pulled to a stop. A sign there announced RGG&RC VALET PARKING ONLY. They were beside a dusty white Chrysler Town & Country minivan, which a very long time ago had had its sides professionally lettered KIDDIE KASTLE PRE-SCHOOL in a glistening red. They all got in it and wordlessly drove off, passing a grand sign at the entrance reading RIO GRANDE GOLF & RACQUET CLUB.

A half hour later, they turned into a neat neighborhood of nice-looking one-story houses. When José pulled the minivan to a stop on the street before one of them with a single scrawny tree in the middle of its yard, he announced with no emotion whatever that their trip was over.

Elated, Ana and Rosario looked at each other and smiled.

Ana then shook her head in wonder. The whole trip back into the United States had taken no time compared to what they'd just gone through from the time they'd been caught by the *policía Americano* to when they'd been sent back across the bridge to Mexico.

José relieved the girls of their backpacks, then showed them the two bedrooms where they'd be staying. The girls beamed when shown a closet full of girls' clothing in various sizes. They were told to pick their outfits from the closet and return the brown uniforms they were wearing to him.

After they had gotten cleaned up and were getting dressed, they heard the front door open and close, and then voices speaking in English. They pulled back the thin curtain and looked out the window. Out by the KIDDIE KASTLE PRE-SCHOOL minivan was parked a bigger vehicle, a

Chevrolet Suburban.

Then they thought they recognized one of the voices, and when they went out into the living room, they found El Gato and another young Latin male drinking beers on the couch. The tan Nike backpacks that they had carried across the river were on the coffee table.

The girls were nervous at first, even somewhat scared, but Juan Paulo Delgado, switching back to Spanish, had been all charm. He played up the friendly El Gato, and introduced the newcomer wearing black jeans and T-shirt as "El Cheque." The Check was no bigger than either Ana or Rosario, but looked meaner than a snake. He was twenty-five with dark features and had a scar on his cheek in the shape of a check mark.

El Cheque, El Gato said, as he and the girls later shared a dinner of delivered pizzas, soon would be driving Ana and Rosario north. He explained how they would be permitted to find their family while they were working to repay the costs of their passage. He said it was not uncommon for that to happen quickly.

He saw them smile. "If that pleases you, then we must celebrate your arrival and new lives!"

He went into the kitchen and brought out

a bottle of tequila, three squat shot glasses, and a small teabag-size cellophane packet containing a fine white powder.

The girls took a sip of the alcohol and made a face. El Gato laughed loudly and shot his down in a single swallow.

El Gato then playfully introduced the cocaine to them. First he rubbed some on his lips, smiled, then reached over and rubbed some on their full lips. After they smiled awkwardly at the funny tingling feeling it caused, he rubbed some of the white powder between the inside of his upper lip and gums — and then on theirs.

It was not long before he had dumped another cellophane packet on the table and they had decided to follow his lead and sniff a little line of it through a short straw.

They all became very comfortable and relaxed. There was much laughter.

The next day, El Gato told the girls he had a special surprise: He took them shopping for new clothes. "For looking nice when you start to work," he said. And that night he produced more packets of coke. The girls needed no further formal introduction.

After these were consumed and they had the desired effect, and there was more laughter, the doorbell rang. El Gato then announced that he had one very special surprise.

He went to the front door and opened it. There stood an older white man carrying a black hard-plastic box resembling a small suitcase. As El Gato embraced the older man, the girls noticed that he had his long graying black hair pulled back in a ponytail — and that his hands and arms, from fingers on up into his shirtsleeves, were covered in tattoos. The body art even extended onto his neck.

El Gato introduced the man simply as *"mi amigo,"* and moments later his friend had opened the box on the kitchen table and was pulling from it what turned out to be a tattoo machine.

Not an hour later, both Ana Lopez and Rosario Flores were enjoying another cellophane packet of the white powder. It was to celebrate their newest gift from El Gato: a tiny tattoo, no larger than their smallest fingernail, at the hairline behind the left ear. It was of a gothic black letter D with three short black lines shooting out on either side.

"The whiskers of El Gato," he said with pride.

Later, after they had all retired to bed, Ana had been grateful for the very numbing sensation caused by the white powder.

Particularly when El Gato had come into her bedroom, said that he loved her — then torn off her new panties and forced himself inside her.

The next night, Juan Paulo Delgado had his way with Rosario Flores, too. But without the numbing benefit of the coke, she suffered. Earlier, she'd turned down the drug for fear it would lead to what Ana said had happened to her.

The next night, when the girls thought they might have the power and control to spurn his advances, he beat them. And had his way with them again.

If they weren't getting the message, he spelled it out for them: They now bore his mark and were his until they repaid him for their passage.

Then, confusing them even more, El Gato went repeatedly to each girl individually, telling her that while the beating had been "necessary," he was still very sorry, that in fact he loved them both.

The proof of that, he said, was that the next day they would leave with El Cheque to go north. And he, El Gato, would see them at the end of their trip.

El Gato was gone the next morning when El Cheque arrived at the house driving a four-year-old Chevy Suburban with deeply tinted windows.

The three of them loaded up the SUV, including the tan Nike backpacks the girls had brought across the river. These went into hidden compartments in the back.

They drove U.S. Highway 281 the 250-plus miles from Brownsville to San Antonio, then continued on it north another 250 miles through the rolling terrain of the Texas Hill Country.

Over the many miles and hours, the girls tried to engage El Cheque in discussions about something, anything. Except for answering their questions about where they were going — someplace they could not pronounce called "Philadelphia"; it may as well have been the moon — he had no personality and said absolutely nothing. Not even on his cellular telephone, which he used exclusively for sending and receiving text messages.

He simply played the radio and drove.

They hit Fort Worth, then turned east toward Dallas. On the far side of downtown Dallas, they went through an area where the billboards — advertising radio stations, beers, and more — were all in Spanish. They stopped overnight at an East Dallas house. It was surrounded by chain-link fencing and the backyard held a half-dozen utility trailers loaded with lawn care equipment beside a wooden garage.

El Cheque delivered one of the backpacks to a young Latino who came out of the back of the house to greet them.

The next morning, El Cheque went to the wooden garage. It stood separately from the house, freestanding, and looked much newer. He backed out of it another late-model Suburban, nearly identical to the one in which they'd driven up from Brownsville. The only differences were its color, silver, and its Tennessee tag. After transferring their luggage and the two remaining backpacks, he put the Suburban bearing the Texas tags inside the garage, then closed and locked the garage doors.

Just before they left, the young Latino came out with a long black duffle. The girls noticed that it not only looked similar to the one Hector had carried across the Rio Grande into Mexico, but made the same metal-and-heavy-plastic clunking sounds when its contents were jostled.

The spare tire under the rear deck of the Suburban was lowered on its cable hoist. That revealed a sealed compartment that had been added under the far-back flooring. The bag was placed in there, and the spare tire cranked back into place.

They drove Interstate Highway 30 to Little Rock, Arkansas, then I-40 into Tennessee, first passing Memphis, then going on to Nashville. El Cheque covered the six hundred–odd miles — coldly ignoring the girls' pleas for more bathroom breaks — in just under ten hours.

Outside Nashville, the same thing happened as in Dallas: They stopped overnight at a house in an area that was heavily Latino, then swapped vehicles. This time the garage held a late-model Dodge Durango with darkly tinted windows and Pennsylvania plates.

The next day, down to one backpack and the big black duffle — all secreted in various parts of the vehicle — they drove on eastward, passed Knoxville, then picked up Interstate Highway 81. They took it in a northeast direction, following along the western side of the Smoky Mountains.

The girls marveled at how they had gone from the dusty desert of south Texas to this place with verdant green cloud-topped mountains — all within a couple days' drive.

Just shy of the Pennsylvania border, they got off on U.S. 15 and drove to Gettysburg. El Cheque always recalled the first time he and El Gato had made this same trip —

particularly when El Gato out of nowhere suddenly started dramatically reciting the Gettysburg Address.

*"Four score and seven years ago our fathers brought forth on this continent a new nation, conceived in Liberty, and dedicated to the proposition that all men are created equal . . ."* Then El Gato laughed and said, "Thank you, North Dallas High, for forcing me to memorize that. Ol' President Lincoln — I wonder what Honest Abe the Great Emancipator would think of El Gato's little operation?"

From Gettysburg, they took the Dodge Durango up U.S. 15 the hundred or so miles right into Philadelphia.

It was just after dark when El Cheque pulled to a stop before what looked like an old city warehouse near a river. He killed the headlights. The warehouse had a corrugated overhead door, and after El Cheque sent a text message on his phone, the door began rolling upward with a clunking sound. The warehouse was darkened, and once the Durango had rolled inside, the overhead door clunked shut.

Interior mercury lights then began to come on with a glow.

And there Ana and Rosario saw a smiling El Gato.

El Cheque delivered the girls and hidden goods, then loaded the Durango's secret compartments with bricklike objects wrapped in black plastic. He got back in the Durango, the overhead lights were killed, the overhead door opened — and he drove off.

El Gato had welcomed Ana and Rosario to what he said was his home. It was an old warehouse that had been converted to a very nice living space, clean and comfortable and spacious. It had a view of a river and city lights and was much nicer than any place he had had them stay before.

He kept up the act that he loved the beautiful girls. But that did not last long.

There were nights — or early mornings — he would come home, often either drunk or high or both, looking for a sexual release. First it had been himself alone; later, he would bring a friend and allow him his choice of girls.

When they complained, El Gato finally said it was time for them to begin earning money to repay their passage. He took Ana and Rosario to the run-down row house on Hancock Street and coldly explained what they would be doing. They protested that it was nothing like what he'd promised. And he beat them.

Thus, they'd been turned over to El Gato's men who ran the house, and joined the other girls held there. And the next day, the men had taken Ana and Rosario by van to various convenience stores, where they'd been treated like any of the store's other commodities — first to be sampled by the store managers, then put on display and made available to customers.

Neither Ana nor Rosario had any idea how much they owed or earned. El Gato simply showed them sheets of paper on which he said he kept track. Yet no matter how much they worked, they never seemed to make any progress.

And one day in a spontaneous act that surprised even Rosario, at the Gas & Go on Frankford she had fled her bondage, leaving behind that awful life.

And leaving Ana to suffer the consequences.

Señora Esteban now sat on the couch with Rosario Flores's head resting on her lap. She soothingly stroked Rosario's hair.

"It will be okay," Señora Esteban said softly in Spanish.

"He did the same thing with Jorgina and Alicia and the other girls!" Rosario sobbed.

Then she suddenly sat upright and wailed.

"And if it wasn't for me," she cried out, beating her fists on the sides of her head, "Ana would be alive!"

She sobbed.

"I got Ana to leave Guatemala! I got her to believe El Gato! And then I was the one who ran away from him, leaving her to . . ."

She crossed herself.

"I got Ana killed! It is all my fault!"

Crying, she lowered her head back onto Señora Esteban's lap.

*Madre de Dios,* El Nariz thought.

He said a silent prayer for her.

*I cannot let this monster continue — but what can I do?*

*Something, anything . . .*

El Nariz put the tequila back on the high shelf above the kitchen sink, then went to his wife. When she looked up to him, he gently kissed her on the forehead.

"I must go," he said.

She acknowledged that by closing her eyes and nodding.

And he turned and went out the door.

# [FOUR]
# Cup O'Joe's Internet Café
# 4309 Main Street, Philadelphia
# Wednesday, September 9,
# 9:30 A.M.

When Juan Paulo Delgado looked through the windows of the coffeehouse, he saw that the morning rush of business types was gone. The small café had a well-worn painted concrete floor and held ten round wooden tables, each with a pair of wooden chairs. There was a stainless-steel lip wide enough to hold a cup — and not much more — that was four feet off the floor and ran the length of the front picture windows. The windows overlooked the chairs on the sidewalk and, a block farther, offered a glimpse of the Schuylkill River. A wide wooden bar, with a dozen wooden stools, ran the length of the right wall to the rear of the café. And there, at the back, were four cubicles, each containing a desktop computer and flat-screen monitor that the café rented to customers in fifteen-minute increments of

235

Internet online time.

Juan Paulo Delgado strode in through the wood-framed glass front door. A tan backpack was loosely slung over his right shoulder by one of its two straps. He wore sandals, desert camouflage pants with the lower legs off, making them into shorts, and a black T-shirt. The frames of his dark sunglasses wrapped so close to his face that they completely hid his eyes. The tight-fitting T-shirt accentuated his defined muscles and looked to be brand new. On the back across the shoulders, it was emblazoned with bold white type that read GET SLOSHED AT SUDSIE'S, and under that was a cartoon drawing of foam spewing from an oversize beer mug and a clothes-washing machine.

Delgado quickly but carefully scanned the coffeehouse.

A smattering of students and stay-at-home moms, chatting while their babies snoozed in strollers parked nearby, sat sipping lattes and iced coffees. Some clicked away at their laptop computers, using the wireless connection to the Internet. A paunchy middle-aged man wearing dark blue slacks, work boots, and a baby blue shirt embroidered with PETE'S PEST EXTERMINATORS was getting up from the far right of the four rental computers. He grabbed his paper cup of coffee and stepped out the back door, which led to a parking lot.

Two black teenagers, one male and one female, were working behind the counter. The male, who was six feet tall and rail thin to the point of being bony, took orders and ran the cash register while the girl, slightly overweight with a very round face, prepared the drinks.

There was no one in line, and Delgado walked right up to the register. As he did, he slid off his backpack and put it on the counter.

"Hey, brother," Delgado said to the young man.

He unzipped an outer pocket on the backpack and pulled out a white fiberboard document-mailer envelope. It had FEDEX LETTER printed on it. Its top flap was sealed and there was an obvious bulge, indicating that it contained something other than a flat stack of papers.

The bony black clerk said, "What up, Cat? What can we brew for you? Maybe some trouble?"

He smiled, showing a mouthful of bright white teeth.

Delgado looked at the girl and said, "Usual, please."

She nodded, and the coffee machine almost immediately began making the high-pressure hissing of steam being released.

As she worked, Delgado slipped the Federal Express envelope to the clerk. He took it and casually placed it under the counter. He then came back up with a brown paper sack the size of a lunch bag. Imprinted on it was FIND YOUR WORLD AT CUP O'JOE'S INTERNET CAFÉ. The sacks were provided to customers who bought muffins and sandwiches for takeout.

This bag was packed full, its top stapled shut.

"Our specialty sandwich," the clerk said with another smile, this one suggesting it was an inside joke. "With our compliments."

Delgado did not return the smile. Without a word, he simply placed the brown sack in his backpack and again slung the backpack over his shoulder.

The pudgy girl delivered his double espresso. Delgado took it, put four single dollar bills on the counter and one in the tip jar, then turned and walked toward the back of the café. In the middle of the room, he came upon an attractive olive-skinned brunette. She sat alone at a round table with her laptop and a coffee in a stoneware mug. She glanced up and smiled, her eyes catching his.

Delgado looked at her, then slowed his

steps, as if he was going to stop. After a moment, he smiled back at her and picked up his pace, continuing toward the back of the room.

She cocked her head as she watched him walk away. Then she shrugged and returned her attention to her laptop screen — blissfully unaware of how close she'd just come to having her life turned tragically upside down.

Delgado put the backpack on the floor beside the chair in front of the far left computer. It was the computer nearest the wall and had a courtesy panel dividing it from the other monitors, affording the most privacy. He turned the monitor so its flat screen was completely out of sight of anyone else. Then he turned his chair so that he had a clear view of the front door.

He pulled out his cellular telephone and placed it beside the computer keyboard. He put his sunglasses there, too.

Then he reached into a pocket of his cut-off camo shorts and pulled out a computer memory device that was half the size of a stick of gum. The USB flash drive held a single file that was a computer program. The program could create a mirror image of the contents of a computer — everything from applications to data files — to use on any other similar computer. It was akin to carrying one's computer around in the palm of one's hand.

Delgado had set up the program on his flash drive to mirror a laptop that he kept locked in a safe at his converted-warehouse loft.

He also had the flash drive tethered with a plastic zip tie to a high-intensity butane cigar lighter, of the type advertised as "NASA Space Age Technology Windproof to 100 MPH!" If necessary, he could torch the chip into a molten — and unreadable — mass in seconds.

He inserted the flash drive into one of the two USB slots on the side of the flat-screen monitor, then hit the CONTROL, ALT, and DELETE keys all at once. That briefly shut down the computer, and its screen went black. Then he held the CONTROL and Z keys simultaneously as the computer re-started so it would load the program from the flash drive.

After a moment, the LCD screen lit up. He was looking at the same desktop image and icons that were on the laptop locked away in his loft safe.

He clicked on the icon for the Firefox Internet browser. In his computer cod-ing class in high school, he'd learned that

Firefox was a very intuitive and clean interface, far better than the crappy ubiquitous Internet Explorer. All those gee-whiz self-congratulatory messages — "IE Just Denied an Unknown Program Unauthorized Access!" or "IE Just Successfully Sold You Yet Another Program You Don't Need!" — along with the other annoying inflated features made the program more sizzle than steak.

More important for Delgado, Firefox also had a far more complex code for security. Between the flash drive and Firefox, he could encode and decode — then wipe absolutely clean — anything he did on the computer.

He typed PHILLYBULLETIN.COM and hit the RETURN key.

A second later, the screen was awash with articles and photos, updated on the quarter hour, of the day's news.

The biggest and brightest image was that of a motel in glorious flames. It was surrounded by various emergency vehicles, their lights flashing. Delgado grinned. Then his eye caught the red text of a ticker across the top of the page, the words crawling from right to left: *Breaking News . . . 2 Dead & 4 Injured in Shooting at Reading Terminal Market. Police Said to Release More Details Shortly. . . .*

Delgado nodded knowingly.

*Don't fuck with me,* he thought, *and these things won't happen.*

*Assholes. They all think they can rip me off and get away with it. . . .*

His cellular phone vibrated for a second, indicating a received text message. He picked it up. The tiny LCD screen, beginning with the sender's cellular phone number, read:

609-555-4901

ALL CREWS WORKING

WHAT U WANT DONE 2 VAN??

Delgado picked up the phone. Using his thumbs on the tiny keypad, he punched out:

TELL OMAR 2 FILL TANK, PARK IN KENSINGTON W/ ANY 2 OTHERS & LIGHT 3 TIGERTAILS

Delgado grinned at the mental image that came with "tigertails." It had been a tigertail that had got him sent for his brief first and only visit to the Dallas County Jail in Texas.

He'd just turned eighteen years old and had started to move a lot more product on his own. He needed some help. In order to trust the help, he put the guys through some tests. And one of those tests was torching the cars of some of their East Dallas neighbors. The damn picky people were making louder and louder noises about traffic — both foot traffic and the lawn care trucks and trailers — in and out of Delgado's house and property.

The term "tigertail" came from a gasoline company and its cartoon tiger mascot. One of the company's giveaway promotions was a foot-long fake furry black-striped orange tail to tie to the gas tanks.

For a while, judging by all the tails flapping from gas caps, it seemed cars everywhere had "a tiger in their tank."

Delgado had stolen that idea, but there *were* a couple of critical differences with his. He had taken a wire coat hanger, straightened it out, then wrapped it with a gas-soaked strip of bedsheeting, bending a hook in the wire's end to secure the fabric. The sheet-covered wire was then stuck down a target vehicle's gas tank. Then the "fuse" was set afire.

The neighbors' cars became blackened hulks in minutes.

As a message sender, the tigertail had been an effective tool. Too much of one, in fact, because Delgado's boys began torching enough vehicles that the Dallas Police Department had decided it necessary to put together a small task force. And the first night out, the cops caught one of Delgado's boys — a fifteen-year-old who shit his pants the moment the cuffs were slapped on.

And he quickly fingered Delgado.

Delgado's lawyer had been able to convince the prosecutor that discrediting the kid's word would be effortless — "He shit his pants, for chrissake! He'd roll over on his own grandmother if it got him out of this. No one's going to believe him!" — and that resulted in the charges against Delgado being dismissed.

Delgado never saw that kid again. That, of course, did not stop the unfortunate event that followed — the car belonging to the fifteen-year-old's mother being tiger-tailed.

Delgado's cellular phone vibrated again, and he read the screen:

```
609-555-4901

OK U GOT IT
```

Delgado then thumbed:

```
& U GO 2 TEMPLE LIKE WE TALKED . . .
DO IT NOW
```

A second later, the incoming reply vibrated
Delgado's phone:

```
609-555-4901

SI . . . SI
```

Delgado put down the phone and turned to
the computer monitor.

Going to the website for Southwest Airlines, he punched in PHL and DAL, checking
for flights out of Philadelphia International
Airport going into Dallas Love Field.

"Shit!" he said, seeing he'd missed the
nine-thirty departure that morning.

He clicked on the next-most-direct routing, Southwest Flight 55, and booked it, paying for the ticket with a Visa credit card. The bill would go to a post office mail drop in a shopping strip center in East Dallas.

Then he picked up the cellular phone and sent another text to a different cellular phone number:

> PLAN 2 PICK ME UP @ 730PM @ LOVE, SW#55

As he went to put down his phone, he saw a kid enter the coffee shop.

Delgado guessed that the short boy, who was black and overweight, could not be more than fifteen and was very likely closer to twelve. And that extra weight was probably baby fat. He had on very baggy blue jeans that were hanging loosely, a white T-shirt with a silk-screened image of a hip-hop singer, white sneakers, and a solid white ball cap with the bill turned sideways.

He looked awkward — and not exactly what Delgado would have considered a regular coffee drinker.

After entering the café slowly, the boy made a beeline for the register at the counter.

He kept his head down as he went, looking mostly at his feet with an occasional glance around the room.

The short fat kid dug deep into his jeans pocket and produced a folded paper bill. He slapped the money on the counter. The bony male clerk then pulled two coffee cups from a tall stack upside down on the counter, and quickly but casually reached under the counter. It was near where he had put Delgado's FedEx envelope. He came back up with the cups, but now one was inserted in the other. The clerk turned to the sink behind him, then filled the top cup with tap water and snapped a lid on it.

Delgado glanced at his own coffee sitting beside the computer monitor. The steam-hot double espresso had been given to him in only a single cup.

Delgado looked back to the counter as the clerk was handing the stacked cups to the kid. The boy took them, then, without waiting for change, turned and went out the door somewhat quicker than he'd entered.

Once outside the door, the boy pulled the top cup out and tossed it in the trash receptacle next to the outside seating, then took off down the sidewalk in a trot.

Delgado made eye contact with the clerk, who smiled knowingly back.

The phone vibrated in his hand, and he read the incoming reply:

> 214-555-7636
>
> C U THEN . . .

Delgado thumbed back:

> GET SUBURBAN READY 4 TRIP SOUTH

His screen then read:

> 214-5-155-7636
>
> ITS IN GARAGE N READY NOW

Delgado thumbed:

> BUENO . . . C U 2NITE

He put the phone back down, then looked

back at the computer monitor.

A link under the photograph of the burning Philly Inn went to the article. He clicked on it and waded through screen ads for a King of Prussia Chevy automobile dealer, casinos in Atlantic City, New Jersey, and a Center City brew pub.

## MASSIVE EXPLOSION, FIRE ENGULFS MOTEL

**At least two known dead and two injured after the Philly Inn blew up and burned early Thursday morning**

By Jim Striegelvich
Bulletin Staff Writer
Photographs by Jack Weinberg
Bulletin Photographer
Posted Online 09/09 at 8:45 a.m.

Philadelphia — A violent explosion at the Philly Inn on Frankford Avenue in Northeast Philadelphia blew out at least one motel room this morning just before two o'clock.

The cause of the blast, and subsequent fire, said a spokesman for the Philadelphia

Police Department, has yet to be positively determined. Initial reports, however, suggest that an illegal ad hoc laboratory for the manufacture of crystal methamphetamine was involved.

The fire displaced more than 150 people who were staying at the motel, including a twenty-five-year-old who identified himself as Demetrius Xavier "X-J" Johnson.

"It's gotta be meth, man," said Johnson. "This place has stunk of cat piss for months! And ain't nobody done nothing about it."

The police spokesman said that two men, as yet to be identified, have been confirmed as dead in the motel room. Two others were injured and transported by ambulance to Temple Burn Center; no details on them or their condition have been made available at this time.

*Check back for updates as they become available.*

COMMENTS (3)

From **Independent1inPhilly (9:01 a.m.):**

*Those druggie slimeballs. Can't think of a better way for them to depart this world.*

Recommend [ 6 ] <u>Click Here to Report Abuse</u>

From **WhatWouldBenFranklinDo (9:22 a.m.):**

*I'm with you, Indy1. Too bad they ruin so many lives first, however.*

Recommend [ 4 ] <u>Click Here to Report Abuse</u>

From **Hung.Up.Badge.But.Not.Gun (9:50 a.m.):**

*Amen to both of you, Indy1 & WWBFD. I spent enough time walking the beat to see everything at least once. And nothing is as insidious as what these drugs do to families of every walk of life. I say, Shoot 'em all and let the Good Lord sort 'em out.*

Recommend [ 4 ] <u>Click Here to Report Abuse</u>

Delgado shook his head.
*Fuck you people!*
*I'm not forcing anyone to buy and swallow*

*anything they don't want.*

*They want it bad.*

*Hell, even the kids.*

*And look at those ads — booze, gambling, hookers.*

*Everyone's got a habit.*

*What the hell's the difference with drugs?*

He clicked on the part of the page to leave a comment, then pounded out the message on the keyboard and clicked the SEND button.

After a moment, his message appeared on-screen, last on the comment list:

---

From **Death.Before.Dishonor (9:52 a.m.):**

*F\*\*k you pendejos! Dudes sell drugs because people (are you paying attention?) because people want to buy them! Look at the ads on this page — booze, gambling (and where there's gambling there's hookers) . . . Something for everyone. What's the difference with drugs? And you know what? Sometimes we even clean up the rats from the gutters — like those in this motel!*

Recommend [ 0 ] <u>Click Here to Report Abuse</u>

---

# V

## [ONE]
## Temple Burn Center
## Temple University Hospital
## North Broad and West Tioga
## Streets, Philadelphia
## Wednesday, September 9,
## 10:10 A.M.

The third-floor Intensive Care Unit was ringed by a corridor that went around the entire floor by the exterior windows. Chad Nesbitt stood leaning against the north-west corner window, which looked out onto Broad and Tioga and, across the street, the Shriners Children's Hospital. The two medical facilities were connected by an enclosed sky bridge.

Inside, Nesbitt had a view down the north and west corridors. Near the ends of each were pairs of swinging doors that led into the Intensive Care Unit sterile areas. The ICU room at the end of the corridor to Nesbitt's left was where the doctors had put the burn victim initially admitted as "John Doe." Sitting in a chrome-framed plastic chair across from it was Skipper Olde's father.

Joseph Warren Olde, Sr., had his head in his hands and was staring at the highly polished tile floor, seemingly frozen. He was tall and lanky, with thin, patrician features.

Nesbitt knew that he was a graduate of Harvard, and even now he had on the school's unofficial uniform. He wore it damn near every day — a Brooks Brothers two-piece striped woolen suit (summer weight now, the cuff of the pants barely covering his ankles) with blood-and-blue rep necktie, white button-down shirt, and Alden black leather shoes.

*It's on twenty-four/seven,* Chad thought.

*I've even seen him in it in Florida. He looked like Richard Nixon walking down the beach. Ridiculous.*

*It's like he hides behind that suit.*

*Skipper said he'd overhead his grandfather once say, "Joey never really excelled at anything, except perhaps being arrogant."*

Sitting in another chrome-framed plastic chair beside him was a blue shirt Philadelphia Police Department patrol officer.

Police Officer Stephanie Kowenski was twenty-five years old, five-foot-four, and 150 pounds. She more than filled out her uniform, and her bulletproof vest served only to accentuate her bulk. In the molded polymer holster on her right hip she carried a Glock Model 17 nine-millimeter semiautomatic pistol with a fully charged magazine of seventeen rounds and one round in the chamber. Two additional fully charged magazines were on her kit.

Police Officer Kowenski's orders were to keep watch on the door. She had a police radio on her belt, its coiled cord snaking up to her shoulder mic — the microphone pinned to her right shoulder epaulet. The orders further said to immediately report any news of any kind concerning J. Warren Olde, Jr. She was reading for the third time a *People* magazine she'd taken from the dog-eared stack on the coffee table next to her chair, and was attempting not to notice the anguished father of the victim.

At the end of the corridor to the right was the ICU room in which they'd put Becca Benjamin. There, a male version of Police Officer Kowenski — short, squat, bored, but reading a paperback novel — guarded the door.

Pacing in front of the swinging doors was Mr. James Henry Benjamin. The fifty-year-old president and chief executive officer of

Benjamin Securities, who was five-eleven and 160 with a striking resemblance to the actor Pierce Brosnan, kept shaking his head and muttering, "I don't understand this. I just don't understand. . . ."

His wife, Andrea, who also was fifty and a very attractive older version of her daughter Becca, sat in one of three chrome-framed plastic chairs against the wall of windows. She held a cellular phone in one hand, a white linen handkerchief in the other. After every third or fourth pass of her husband, she tried to calm him, and added, "Honey, please sit down."

Nesbitt pulled out his phone and hit the key that speed-dialed Matt Payne's mobile. It rang only once before he heard Payne's voice.

"Hey, Chad. What's up? Where're you?"

"At Temple. The Burn Center? I felt it best to be here . . ."

His voice trailed off.

Matt Payne knew the hospital. And he knew why Becca and Skipper had been taken there, and not to Nazareth Hospital, even though it was only blocks away from the Philly Inn.

Tony Harris had explained to him that the "Where do we take 'em?" decision for the medics on the scene had been a no-brainer.

"The medics followed the trauma triage protocol," Harris had told Payne. "The first thing, they measured for vital signs and level of consciousness. Then came other immediate steps, including establishing an airway, immobilizing the spine, beginning a high flow of oh-two — maintaining an oxygen saturation of at least eighty or ninety percent — controlling the hemorrhaging, attempting to determine the level of injury. Then there's a long list of criteria that, if a patient meets any one of them and certainly more than one, the medics contact the Level One Trauma Center. And because both of these victims were pretty fucked up, and 'trauma with burns' is one criterion, it was a simple call. Temple has (a) the only Level One Trauma Center, and (b) it has the Burn Center."

"Matt," Nesbitt then went on, "any chance you can swing by? You know the Benjamins better than I do. They could use a friendly face to maybe answer any questions."

"What kind of questions, Chad?"

"Hell, I don't know. What kind of fucking questions go through a parent's mind when their daughter's just suffered through an explosion and now lies in a burn unit ICU? And the parent has no idea what's happened and what may happen." He paused.

"I'd guess *those* kinds of fucking questions. Maybe if you were a parent, Matt, you'd understand."

Nesbitt saw that Police Officer Kowenski had looked up from her magazine, and he realized how loud he'd been. He looked down the other corridor; luckily, it appeared that the Benjamins hadn't overheard him.

"Sorry, Matt," he said more quietly. "Can you come?"

"I'm maybe ten minutes out. Just coming up on Broad and Race now. See you shortly."

"Thanks, pal."

Omar Quintanilla was at the wheel of the rusty white Plymouth minivan as it drove up Broad Street. The Temple Burn Center was no more than a fifteen-minute drive from the row house on Hancock Street and about a dozen blocks north of Susquehanna, where Juan Paulo Delgado had delivered Ana's head at the laundromat. Quintanilla made a right turn onto West Tiago Street and pulled to the curb just shy of Germantown Avenue.

Jesús Jiménez opened the front passenger door, stepped out, and slammed the door shut without any formalities.

The minivan drove off.

Jiménez was nineteen years old, stood five-feet-one, and weighed just over a hundred pounds. He kept his dark hair cut somewhat short, and his attempt at growing a mustache left it looking a bit ragged. On occasion, El Gato called him "El Gigante" — but always from a distance and always with a smile. Jiménez could have a vicious temper.

He wore a top and bottom of royal blue cotton hospital scrubs over a pair of blue jeans and a white T-shirt. A black nine-millimeter Beretta Model 92 was hidden inside the front of his waistband. The 92 was the civilian variant of the M9 semiautomatic pistol that was standard U.S. military issue.

Jiménez started back toward Broad Street, setting a slow pace until he saw a clump of four others in hospital scrubs moving toward the Temple Burn Clinic entrance. He quickened his pace so that he more or less joined their flow. The group of men and women entered the building.

Once inside, he headed for the bank of elevators and there joined a mix of visitors in street clothing and others in various colored scrubs.

In the elevator, one of the female visitors pushed the button for the third floor, then quickly corrected herself and pushed the one for four. He slipped to the back of the car.

At the second floor, all but two visitors got off.

The elevator doors closed, and it rose to the third floor.

When the doors next opened, the visitors did not move. But then they realized there was a hospital worker behind them and stepped aside.

He squeezed through the closing doors and stepped off the elevator. He turned a corner and found himself looking down a corridor. Halfway down it, he saw an empty gurney along the wall and went to it.

He pushed the gurney to a nurse's stand. There, an obviously overworked, and overweight, white female nurse with a puffy face and thin brown hair sat behind the counter, looking at a chart.

"Excuse me?" Jesús Jiménez said, using a meek tone. "They call for this. For the burned one, the man?"

The overworked nurse looked up from the chart and made no effort at all to conceal the fact that she was annoyed (a) by the interruption and (b) by an orderly's interruption.

Then that look changed to one of confusion.

"Why," she said, "would they call for a gurney for him? There're gurneys everywhere."

Jesús Jiménez shrugged, his facial expression saying, *I just do as I'm told.*

Then she answered her own question, muttering: "Unless they're preparing for the inevitable. If he ain't dead yet, it's only a matter of time."

Jesús Jiménez looked at her with a blank face.

He thought, *If you only knew. . . .*

The nurse then pointed. "ICU 303. Around the corner, at the end. Can't miss it. Look for the woman cop."

*Woman cop?* Jesús Jiménez thought.

*Shit!*

But he simply said, "Gracias," and began pushing the gurney in the direction she'd pointed.


"It's so good of you to come by, Matt," Mrs. Andrea Benjamin said after she had given him a big hug. "It's such a terrible time. Did you see Chad?" She looked down the corridor. "He was just here. . . ."

"Yes, ma'am, earlier," Payne said. "He sent me a text message saying he got a call and had to run an errand."

James Benjamin was not in the mood for niceties.

"Matt, this situation has all the makings of that goddamn Skipper Olde. You know he's

261

a no-good sonofabitch. Had to be his drug deal gone bad. And he dragged in my girl." He paused. "You can't charge her with anything for just sitting in her car in a damned parking lot!"

Payne, out of the corner of his eye, saw the blue shirt look up from his paperback.

*Well, that got the bored guy's attention.*

"James!" Mrs. Benjamin said softly. "Please."

"Mr. Benjamin," Payne replied, "I'm not charging anyone with anything. That will be someone else's call, most likely a white shirt at the Roundhouse. There're a lot of questions yet to be answered."

*And that really got his attention.*

Then one of the swinging doors to the ICU beside the cop opened.

"Dr. Law!" James Benjamin said. "Any news?"

Matt Payne turned to see an absolutely beautiful blond woman in the white coat of a doctor step out into the corridor. She pulled a powder-blue surgical mask down from her face. She looked to be not quite thirty, five-feet-five and maybe 110 pounds, her golden hair pulled back in a short ponytail under a surgical cap. She had the lean look of a runner, and an air about her of complete confidence.

*Jesus!* Payne thought. *Now, that is a gorgeous woman!*

*Bright, intelligent face and eyes.*

*And the body of a goddess.*

She walked up to them, a clipboard under her left arm.

Payne's eye went to the left patch pocket of her white lab coat. There, enhanced by a magnificent mound of bosom beneath the fabric, was stitched in blue: *Amanda Law, M.D., F.A.C.S., F.C.C.M.*

Payne mentally translated the alphabet soup:

*A medical doctor who's a Fellow of the American College of Surgeons and the American College of Critical Care Medicine.*

*Correction: An absolutely stunning Fellow.*

Payne decided he must have been staring, because Dr. Law suddenly turned and looked at him questioningly.

"Doctor," Mrs. Benjamin then said, "this is an old friend of the family. And of course Becca's. Matthew Payne, Dr. Law."

Dr. Amanda Law looked at him again, curtly nodded once, then turned back to the Benjamins.

She pulled the clipboard out and flipped pages.

"As we discussed briefly, the trauma is significant, worse than the burns, which are about three percent TBSA —"

"Would you mind going over that for me?" Payne said.

She made a face of annoyance at the interruption. She looked to the Benjamins for permission.

They nodded their assent.

"Total Body Surface Area," Dr. Law said. "A specialized burn center is required for any injury over five percent TBSA, or a burn of the face or hands or one that encircles an extremity. Third-degree — what do you know about burns, Mr. Payne?"

He held up his right hand about ear high. The palm faced her, the thumb holding down the pinky to leave the middle three fingers extended together.

"Everything! I'm an Eagle Scout! And, please, call me Matt."

She looked at him incredulously.

"First-degree burns," he went on, lowering his Scout sign, "are mildest. Only the skin's outer layer is damaged. Second-degrees are worse — deep and very painful. Usually blisters. And third-degree burns, also called full-thickness burns because all skin layers have been affected, are the worst. Very deep and serious. And there may be no pain in the burn because of destroyed nerve endings."

"Not bad," Dr. Law said with a serious face. "That is, for a Boy Scout. But there is a fourth-degree. They extend down to the muscle, sometimes to the bone. Fourth-degree is rare."

Payne nodded. "The pair who died in the explosion had fourth-degree. I just assumed those were categorized as severe third-degree burns. Which, now that I say it, would appear redundant."

Payne then wondered if Skipper had fourth-degree burns.

Tony Harris also had told him that when Skipper bolted out of the burning motel room, he thought that the staggering man had been damn lucky to get out alive with only his clothes blown to shreds. Then Harris had realized the man was naked. What he'd thought were strips of clothing actually had been his flesh blown into strips.

"You were at the motel, Matt?" Mrs. Benjamin said with great interest.

"Yes, ma'am. Afterward. After the firefighters finished."

"And you saw the ones who died?" Dr. Law asked.

Payne nodded. "The tech from the Medical Examiner's Office showed me."

"May I ask what you were doing there?" Dr. Law asked.

"I'm with the Homicide Unit." He reached into his front pants pocket and pulled out a wad of cash folded under a silver money clip. From the middle of the bills he slipped out one of the three or four business cards he kept there. He held out one to her. "Sergeant Matt Payne. My information, in case you can think of something I should know later."

*And with that statement the blue shirt now has figured me out.*

She looked at it, then wordlessly — and perfunctorily — took it. She stuck it on her clipboard, then looked him in the eyes.

*Do I detect, my dear doctor, something more than idle interest?*

*Please? You're certainly Law. I would like to study . . .*

"Matt," Mr. Benjamin injected, "do you mind if we get back to Becca?"

Dr. Law said: "My apology, Mr. Benjamin. Your daughter is now heavily sedated and immobilized. The windshield that hit her actually did her a bit of a favor. That is to say, what hurt her also helped her."

"I don't understand," Mrs. Benjamin said.

"It served to protect her from worse injury. Her burns are limited to her upper scalp and her right hand. The glass protected the rest of her body."

"Thank God!" Andrea Benjamin said, then audibly sighed with relief.

"Unfortunately," Dr. Law continued, "the blunt-force trauma of the windshield has caused intracranial hypertension —"

"Becca's brain is swelling?" Payne interrupted.

Dr. Law nodded. And it was clear by the look on her face she was impressed Payne even knew the term "intracranial hypertension."

She looked between the Benjamins and went on: "We are going to try some first steps, ones that could correct the problem. But, Mr. and Mrs. Benjamin, I must caution you to be prepared that it may come to us having to induce a coma."

"A coma!" James Benjamin said.

Andrea Benjamin put the handkerchief to her face and sniffled.

"We may not," Dr. Law said, her tone soft yet reassuring. "I will of course be conferring with colleagues, specialists, before deciding. And of course with you."

James Benjamin shook his head in disbelief. "Jesus!"

Payne could see that Benjamin's muscles were now even more tense.

"Can you tell us what is going to happen

now?" Andrea Benjamin said.

"Yes, of course," Dr. Law said. "As I said, we have your daughter as comfortable as possible. She is in what might be described as a plastic tent. It creates an absolute sterile environment. There is a HEPA filter system hooked up to it that removes dust, dirt, and other particles from the air inside the tent to reduce the chances of infection of the patient."

"What about the burns?" Andrea Benjamin said. "Will she require . . . oh, what's the word?"

"Grafts?" Payne offered.

That earned him the glare of Dr. Law.

"Mrs. Benjamin," she then said calmly, "I do not think skin grafts will be necessary. We have come a long way with specialized treatments. There are, for example, enzymatic agents. These dissolve the burn's dead tissue on the surface. The process then lets the tissue underneath heal. Also, we have the option of artificial skin, with which we have had significant positive results."

"Oh, that is all such wonderful information," Andrea Benjamin said, her tone somewhat hopeful. "Thank you, Doctor."

Dr. Law nodded and said, "But please remember: We're very early in this process. There's much work" — there was a perceptible pause as her eyes looked down the corridor — "to do."

Payne looked to where she'd glanced. Joseph Olde was walking toward them.

"Good morning," Olde called as he saw them looking at him.

"What the hell is good about it?" James Benjamin blurted.

"James . . ." Andrea said reprovingly. She looked at Olde. "Any news on Skipper, Joseph?"

"Nothing new yet." He stared at Payne. "You're Matt Payne, aren't you?"

*You didn't have the decency to return the courtesy?* Payne thought.

*You could've at least asked Mrs. Benjamin about Becca.*

*Even if apparently you don't give a damn.*

Matt looked at James Benjamin.

*And that's not lost on her father. . . .*

*No wonder Skipper can be such a prick.*

*Clearly, the nut didn't fall far from the fucking tree.*

"That's right, Mr. Olde," Payne replied.

"You still playing cop?" Olde said, but didn't wait for a response before looking at James Benjamin. "Listen, Jim, I'm prepared to let bygones be bygones, but this time, this meth —"

"What the hell are you talking about?"

Benjamin snapped.

Payne could see the veins in Benjamin's temples pulsing.

Olde arrogantly went on: "Well, clearly this girl of yours has an established long pattern of substance abuse —"

"Why, you son . . . of . . . a . . . bitch!" James Benjamin shouted, furiously drawing out his declaration of *sonofabitch*.

What happened next transpired so quickly that Payne did not have time to even try to stop it.

Benjamin balled his right fist and swung. His punch hit Olde square in the left cheek, causing Olde to stagger back two steps. But remarkably Olde quickly recovered, and practically launched his lanky body at Benjamin, knocking them both to the floor.

"Stop it, you two!" Andrea Benjamin demanded.

The blue shirt sitting by the swinging doors dropped his paperback book. He reached up to his right epaulet, where the microphone of his radio was pinned.

He keyed the mic, and barked, "Kowenski! Get your ass down here!"

Then he jumped out of the chair and moved toward the brawl to break it up.

As Payne also moved that way, he saw a gurney come around the corner and into the corridor. It was being pushed by an orderly in blue scrubs.

# [TWO]
# 1344 W. Susquehanna Avenue, Philadelphia
# Wednesday, September 9, 10:40 A.M.

Chad Nesbitt weaved his cobalt-blue BMW M3 coupe through the slower traffic headed down Broad Street. He idly wondered if he was about to walk into some kind of setup, but the anguished voice on the phone sounded painfully genuine.

It had been that of a man. He spoke reasonably good English, but it was clearly with a Spanish accent. And when he said he was trying to find "Meester Skeeper," Nesbitt knew that that was just too coincidental. He had to grant the man's request for a meeting.

"How did you get my number?" Nesbitt had asked.

"From Meester Skeeper."

"I don't understand."

"He give me his old cell phone. One day,

I make mistake when I push a button. I thought the phone call Meester Skeeper. But it had all Meester Skeeper's numbers, and it call you, your voice mail. I hang up. When I tell Meester Skeeper this, he say it is no problem. That you are his best friend. That you are partner in his business."

"But why are you calling me now?"

"Because there is a problem with the business. Very bad. And I cannot reach him. He does not answer his cell phone."

"What sort of bad problem?"

There had been a long silence before the man spoke. "I cannot say."

"You cannot tell me? Or cannot tell me on the phone."

"On the phone. Is better that I tell Meester Skeeper in person."

And there had been a long silence before Nesbitt spoke. "That won't be possible for some time. He's badly hurt, and in the hospital."

Nesbitt heard the man mutter, *"Madre de Dios!"* Then he said, "Is Meester Skeeper going to be okay?"

Nesbitt did not know how to answer at first, then said, "We don't know. I can tell you that it will be some time before he's able to speak with you."

The man then said, "Then, please, I must

272

speak with you. His best amigo and partner in business."

Six blocks after crossing Lehigh Avenue — which almost didn't happen because he nearly got sideswiped by a damn rusty white Plymouth minivan that ran the red and then flew down Lehigh — Nesbitt approached the intersection of Dauphin and Broad. This was the outer edge of the neighborhood where Temple University served as somewhat of an anchor.

The light at Dauphin turned red. As he waited for it, he looked down the street. On the left he saw a series of retail chains — a McDonald's fast-food restaurant, a Rite-Price pharmacy — and some mom-and-pop shops.

The man on the phone had said the laundromat was there, but he could not make it out.

*And that's another coincidence.*

*A laundromat. And Skipper.*

*Who is this guy?*

*He absolutely would not tell me what he wanted.*

*Except that it was "mucho important."*

The traffic light cycled. He crossed Dauphin and started scanning for the laundromat. At the next corner, which was Susquehanna, he saw a convenience store's signage — TEMPLE GAS & GO. Next door to that, sharing a wall, was a brick-faced building that looked as if it recently had been renovated.

The brick was clean and bright, as if freshly sandblasted. There was a glistening glass door set in shiny aluminum framing. On either side of the new door were six large plate-glass windows, also similarly framed in aluminum, that were covered from the inside with what looked like brown wrapping paper.

As Nesbitt slowed the car, he read the announcement that was painted on the paper in bright festive colors:

COMING SOON! ANOTHER NEW SUDSIE'S!

Under that, with lots of cartoonish foam overflowing from an oversize beer mug and a washing machine, was Sudsie's' marketing slogan:

GET SLOSHED WITH US!

Nesbitt groaned audibly.
*What were you thinking, Skipper?*
*About that and everything else?*

He then pulled the M3 coupe into an empty parking spot at the curb around the corner.

When Chad Nesbitt got to the new front door of Sudsie's, he saw that someone had posted a sign that read CLOSED — PLEASE COME AGAIN and an emergency contact telephone number. He didn't recognize the number.

He hammered the door with a balled fist, but there was no answer.

He then pulled out his phone from the left front pocket of his pants. He thumbed keys to reach the RECENT CALLS menu, then highlighted the first call on the list. He hit the CALL key.

When the man answered, he said, "This is Chad Nesbitt. You asked to see me? I'm at the door."

There was silence on the phone for a moment. Then Nesbitt saw the brown paper on the glass of the door pull back just enough for someone to peer out. There then came the sound of the front door being unlocked.

Nesbitt hit the END key, put the phone back in his pocket, and scanned the area. About all he saw were students coming from the Southeast Philadelphia Transportation Authority's Susquehanna-Dauphin Metro stop. Some of them crossed the street, headed for McDonald's before class.

The door, its hinges squeaking, opened not quite halfway.

Nesbitt saw standing there a five-foot-two Hispanic male. He was heavyset, with an enormously wide, flat nose. He looked to be maybe thirty.

"Come, come!" the man anxiously told Nesbitt, waving him in.

Nesbitt did. The man looked nervously up and down the sidewalk before closing and locking the door.

Chad Nesbitt looked around the brightly lit, newly renovated laundromat. It was obvious to him that this was Skipper Olde's work, that this was one of the locations they had acquired in the package deal. There were lines of brand-new commercial-quality washers and dryers in the walls, and positioned neatly against the back of the room at a long tan linoleum counter were waist-high thick-wire baskets on heavy-duty casters.

The man walked up to him and held out his hand.

"Señor Nesbitt, *mucho gusto.* I am Paco Esteban."

"Paco," Nesbitt said shaking his hand, "you want to tell me now what the hell's going on here?"

"Here?"

Nesbitt looked around the room. "Okay. Start with that. Why are we here?"

El Nariz looked him in the eyes, then nodded.

"*Sí.* I have agreement with Meester Skeeper," he began, "to use his machines for my laundry service . . ."

". . . And as the evil man was leaving, he shot holes," Paco Esteban said, as he finished his five-minute explanation. "And so everyone, all of my crew, they run for their lives. I come back here to clean up the place. I could not leave it the way it was."

"This evil man shot holes?" Nesbitt repeated.

"*Sí.* Come. I show you."

El Nariz led Nesbitt to the rear room. He pointed to the arch that was the bullet-riddled masonry wall.

"My God!" Nesbitt exclaimed.

"*Sí.*"

"Why did he do that? I mean, to scare you?"

El Nariz nodded. "*Sí. Muy* scary."

"And you have a head in your freezer?"

"*Sí.*"

Chad Nesbitt could not believe what he was seeing and hearing.

The gunfire was bad enough — gunfire in a business he partly owned.

*But the barbarism?*

*Jesus!*

*That's the kind of thing you hear about those animals committing in faraway backward countries!*

He pulled out his cellular phone and hit the speed-dial number of Matt Payne. The phone beeped in his ear, and when he looked at the screen, he saw:

```
NO SERVICE
```

Then he saw that the signal bars were low.

"Shit!"

Nesbitt typed out a text message to Matt and sent it:

```
CALL ME WHEN YOU GET THIS . . .
MORE TROUBLE
```

"Paco," Chad Nesbitt said anxiously, "you must not tell anyone about this! Understand? Not until I figure out what to do."

He nodded, and said, *"Sí. Muchas gracias."*

# [THREE]
## Temple Burn Unit
## Temple University Hospital
## North Broad and West Tioga
## Streets, Philadelphia
## Wednesday, September 9,
## 10:43 A.M.

Police Officer Stephanie Kowenski came pounding down the third-floor corridor, her hands on either side of her ample hips. One held her police radio and the other her Glock pistol, both in their respective holsters, in an attempt to keep them from banging against her as she ran.

She turned the corner. Just as she glimpsed what looked like a scuffle at the southeast end of the corridor, she ran smack into a gurney that was being pushed up the corridor. When she hit it, both she and the gurney went flying.

The Hispanic orderly who had been pushing the gurney got knocked on his ass.

After a second, Police Officer Stephanie

Kowenski regained her footing. Ignoring the gurney, and not saying a word to the Hispanic orderly, she rushed toward the two men scuffling. She recognized now that one was Joseph Olde.

The orderly righted the gurney, then calmly continued pushing it up the corridor. He got to the corner and made the turn.

About the time that Police Officer Stephanie Kowenski reached the end of the corridor and the altercation, the other uniform and a young male civilian had managed to pull apart Olde and the other older man, who were on the ground. The young male civilian now stood between them as they started to regain their composure and get up.

"That, Benjamin," Joseph Olde said indignantly as he attempted to straighten his necktie, "was completely uncalled —"

From far down the corridor, there suddenly came the sound of a rapid series of shots. At least ten of them.

"What the hell?" Payne said as he automatically pulled out his black Officer's Model Colt .45.

"You can't use that in here!" Dr. Law said.

Payne looked at her incredulously. "What would you have me use, Doc, a fucking tongue depressor?"

"Drop the gun!" Police Officer Stephanie Kowenski ordered as she reached for her Glock. She did not yet have it drawn from her holster.

Payne blurted, "Three-six-nine!" using the old Philadelphia Police Radio code for police officer. He pulled back his shirt to show his badge on his belt.

Police Officer Stephanie Kowenski, finally with her weapon out, looked at the male blue shirt, who nodded. He already had his gun drawn. And he had his left hand on the police radio microphone on his shoulder, his head cocked toward it, calling for backup — "Assist officer! Shots fired! Temple Burn Unit. Third floor. Broad and Tioga." Then he repeated it.

"You four!" Payne ordered, herding Dr. Law, the Benjamins, and Jason Olde toward the swing doors. "In there and get down. Bolt the doors if you can!"

He pointed to the blue shirts. "You two cover this door! No one gets in after the Benjamin girl or anyone else!"

Then Payne ran up the corridor, stopped at the corner, and carefully checked down that corridor. All he saw was the empty gurney. It was standing by the stairwell exit door.

He turned the corner and ran in a crouch, holding his pistol up and ready. His elbows were bent, the gun close to his chest.

He was halfway down the corridor when the left swinging door to Skipper Olde's ICU flew open. Out ran the Hispanic male orderly in the blue scrubs. He had a black semiautomatic in his hand.

*Did he pop Skipper? Shit!*

"Police!" Payne yelled. "Drop the goddamn gun!"

The orderly did not slow. And he damn sure did not drop the gun. In a flash, he ran right to the steel door of the stairwell, leaning his shoulder into it as his hip smacked the horizontal bar that unlatched its lock.

The door flew open. And the Hispanic male went through the doorway.

"Shit!" Payne said.

He took off after him.

The steel door was starting to swing closed when Payne reached it. Payne kicked it open, his right foot slamming the horizontal bar. He stopped and checked to see if it was clear to continue, then heard the fast footfalls echoing down the concrete stairwell. He could see the man's left hand sliding down the inside handrail as he went.

Payne looked down the stairwell to see if there would be an opportunity to get a clear shot. There wasn't.

"Shit, shit, shit!" he muttered as he started

down the steps, taking two at time.

As he passed the steel door to the second floor, he saw that he was gaining a little on the man, whose hand was sliding on the handrail only half a floor below him.

Payne tried to take three steps at time and damn near rolled his ankle. It twisted, a flare of fire burning deep in his muscle. He went back to taking only two steps at a time.

He heard the metallic *bang* of the horizontal bar getting hit on the first floor's steel door.

"Police!" he yelled again. "Stop!"

*Maybe he doesn't understand English?*

*"Police" is — what? — something like "policía"?*

*But what the hell is "stop" in Spanish?*

*Shit. Who's kidding who?*

*He knows what the hell I want. . . .*

Payne reached the door and kicked it open. The door swung open onto the sidewalk on Tioga. The Shriners Children's Hospital was across the street. He looked left and saw people running away, clearly in fear. He started to look around the leading edge of the open door when he heard two shots being fired — and the unmistakable sound of bullets impacting metal.

Payne dropped to his knees.

A glance up the door revealed two exit

holes, the thin sheet metal with two ragged holes roughly resembling a king's crown.

"You sonofabitch!" Payne said.

He quickly stuck his head around the edge of the door and back again.

His split-second view had shown him the man running down the middle of the street, holding his right hand up as he fed the pistol a fresh magazine of ammunition.

Payne popped to his feet and gave chase, running along the sidewalk to use the cars parked at the curb for cover and concealment.

The man cut the corner at Germantown Avenue and started running up it. Payne started to cross Tioga to follow, but the loud horn of a taxicab he hadn't seen coming forced him back on the sidewalk. He checked again for any traffic, then bolted up Germantown Avenue.

Payne kept looking for an opportunity to shoot. But there were people on the sidewalks and vehicles beyond the running Hispanic male, all of them in what would be the field of fire.

As the man approached the intersection of Germantown and Venango, the traffic light changed. The vehicles started moving east and west, effectively blocking the male's path. At the corner, he made a right onto Venango, and Payne, looking over his shoulder, crossed over Germantown Avenue to follow.

Two blocks later, at Camac Street, the man again got caught by the changing of the traffic light. This time he cut down an alleyway behind the row houses there.

Payne, breathing heavily, turned down the alley. But when he got there, he saw that the only row houses there were the ones facing Venango Street. Behind them, the alleyway opened up for more than half a block. The other row houses had been torn down, leaving a huge vacant area.

And the man was running right down the middle of it, wide open.

Payne could hear the sirens of squad cars in the direction of the burn center. But he had no way of directing them to his location.

Payne once more shouted, "Stop! Police!"

Surprising him, the man did stop — only to turn and fire off two shots.

The shots struck the pavement near Payne. He dropped to one knee and, trying not to let his heaving chest botch his aim, squeezed off one round, then a second one.

The second shot found the Hispanic male. He went down, rolling as he hit the ground, holding his left thigh with his left hand.

Payne stood and started toward him cautiously, shouting, "Drop the goddamn weapon! Now, goddammit!"

From where he lay, the Hispanic male rolled and fired another round at Payne, causing Payne to seek cover behind a tree. Then the man popped up and took off, running with a bit of a limp.

"Sonofabitch!" Payne muttered to himself. "The fucker just won't quit."

Up ahead, Payne saw that vehicles were again stopped at a traffic light, this time at Old York Street. And the light was about to cycle from red to green.

*Good! I can close the gap again.*

But then Payne watched in surprise as, just before the lights changed, the man ran up to the first car in line. It was an older silver Chevrolet Caprice sedan — *The Whale Car,* Payne thought, for whatever reason remembering its nickname. The man grabbed the handle to the driver's door, flung it open before the driver — a fat middle-aged black male — even knew that anyone was there, put the muzzle of the pistol to the driver's left cheek, and started shouting at him.

Payne could not hear what he was saying, but it was obvious what was happening. And the fat driver clearly understood he was being carjacked. He was frantically rushing to undo his seat belt.

Payne ran with what energy he had left.

The Hispanic male grabbed the fat driver by the shirt collar and yanked him to the street. The Chevy Caprice, having been in gear, started to roll on its own, and the man then ran alongside and jumped in, hitting the accelerator. There was a squeal of tires and then the driver's door slammed shut.

Payne ran over to the man on the ground, who appeared dazed as he tried to sit up.

"Are you okay?" Payne said.

"Don't shoot me!" the terrified black man said.

Payne shook his head. "It's okay. I'm police."

He then looked down Tioga and saw the tail of the Caprice disappear in the distance. He shook his head.

His mind wandered back to the Platoon Leader's Program at Marine Base, Quantico.

*What'd that wise guy crack in the tactical course at Quantico?*

*"When in doubt, empty the fucking magazine!"*

# [FOUR]
## Executive Command Center
## The Roundhouse
## Eighth and Race Streets,
## Philadelphia
## Wednesday, September 9,
## 11:30 A.M.

"Okay," Police Commissioner Ralph Mariani said to First Deputy Police Commissioner Denny Coughlin. "Who wants to get me up to speed on where we stand? The mayor is screaming bloody murder, if you will pardon the phrase."

Coughlin made a motion with his hand, effectively passing the request on to Deputy Commissioner Howard Walker, the two-star Chief of Science & Technology. Walker had not been Denny Coughlin's first choice to work directly under him, but Mariani had said he'd had his reasons for installing him in the job.

Walker was a very tall and slender black man of fifty. He had a cleanly shaven head, a long thin nose, and wore tiny round Ben Franklin glasses. He spoke with a soft intelligent voice like that of a cleric, with a somewhat pious air about him. His domain of Science & Technology included the Forensic Sciences, Communications, and Information Systems Divisions — the latter two, of course, with oversight of the Executive Command Center.

The ECC was the nerve center of the Philadelphia Police Department Headquarters. It was situated between the offices of the police commissioner and the first deputy police commissioner, in an area that had once been another office and a large conference room, the wall between them now torn down.

Also present in the ECC were Chief Inspector Matt Lowenstein, commanding officer of the Detective Bureau; Captain Henry Quaire, Chief of the Homicide Unit; Homicide Lieutenant Jason Washington; and Corporal Kerry Rapier, an impossibly small white man with soft features who looked far younger than his twenty-five years. All wore coats and ties, except Rapier, who was in his police uniform, a pair of silver-outlined blue chevrons on each sleeve.

The cost of the ECC had been paid in large part with federal dollars. It had been built just before the City of Philadelphia hosted the Democratic National Convention. The politicians coming from Washington, D.C., fearing a terrorist attack with so many of them being present in one place at once, wanted proper protection in the City of Brotherly Love. And they were more than happy to let taxpayers from Boise, Idaho, to Tupelo, Mississippi, help pay for the best technology that Philadelphia could acquire.

The room was carpeted in a charcoal-colored industrial carpet, in the center of which were two T-shaped, dark gray, Formica-topped conference tables. Each table seated twenty-six and had accommodations for that many notebook computers beside a small forest of black stalk microphones and the multiline telephone consoles. Gray leather office chairs on casters ringed the table, and forty black armless leather chairs along two walls formed somewhat of a long couch.

On the ten-foot-tall walls opposite the line of armless chairs were banks of sixty-inch high-definition LCD flat-screen TVs, frameless and mounted edge to edge. One bank of nine created a single giant image. Two other banks of nine TVs had different images on each, or eighteen different picture feeds.

These consisted of live video. Broadcasts of local and cable news shows were on a half-dozen. Another half-dozen cycled feeds from the cameras of the Pennsylvania Department of Transportation. These somewhat grainy black-and-white DOT shots showed traffic on major arteries — such as Interstate Highway 95 along the Delaware River and the Schuylkill Expressway along that river — and on heavily traveled secondary streets. If the Philadelphia Police Department's Long Rangers were flying, the DOT images would rotate with those of the thermal and standard color videos sent from the Aviation Unit's Bell 206 L-4 helicopters.

In addition to the network of telephones, the Executive Command Center had secure communications networks with other city and state police departments, as well as the federal law enforcement agencies, including the Federal Bureau of Investigation, the United States Secret Service, and all those agencies under the Department of Homeland Security. There was even assigned seating for the liaisons from those agencies.

It was indeed an impressive mass of high technology. So much so that Police Commissioner Mariani was prone to hold all of his press conferences in the ECC just for the gee-whiz backdrop it provided for photo ops.

While it was true that the Executive Command Center served to aid in the collection, assimilation, and analysis of information, not everyone blindly believed the great wizardry of the room to be all that magical in the catching of criminals.

Denny Coughlin, for example, was a devout believer that nothing beat the basics for gathering intel — and the basics meant shoe leather pounding the streets, cops talking with citizens. Or what was in many circles now called "humint," short for human intelligence.

But Coughlin and his peers were willing to admit that the eyes in the sky (and everywhere else) of the ECC did serve a purpose. Pulling together so many different things in one place did manage to communicate the information of people and places and events in an effective manner. And the ECC also met a political component, that of interagency cooperation. Despite the fact that many felt the term "interagency cooperation" more often than not was an oxymoron akin to jumbo shrimp, working with the feds was necessary, and the ECC provided an appropriate environment for that.

"We shall begin, Commissioner Mariani," Howard Walker said, "with the Philly Inn."

He turned to Corporal Rapier. "Kerry,

please punch up number thirteen on the main screen."

All of the TVs were serially numbered, starting with the main bank of nine TVs that showed the one enormous video feed. It was number one. The second bank had numbers two through ten, and the third eleven through nineteen. (In the event the main bank became nine individual images, its screen numbering went to 1a, 1b, 1c, and through to 1i.)

On the lower right-hand corner of each TV was a digitally produced numeral in a circle, either a black or a white orb, depending on which provided the best contrast to the main image. TV number thirteen was, of course, in the third bank of TVs.

TV number one, the big one, was showing a real-time feed of the front façade of City Hall.

When Corporal Rapier manipulated his console, his fingers flying across the keyboard, the image that was on TV number thirteen suddenly was duplicated — but much bigger — as the image on the main bank of TVs, replacing City Hall.

It was a color shot of the crime scene at the Philly Inn. It was made by a high-definition camera mounted to the crime-scene lab truck at the back of the motel. The yellow tape was still strung up, but there was no noticeable activity, even when Corporal Rapier used the console joystick to pan and zoom the area.

In the bottom right-hand corner was:

---

**Philly Inn**
**7004 Frankford Avenue**
**1135 hours, 09 Sept**

---

"As you can see," Walker said, "there is not much going on at the scene."

*No shit,* Denny Coughlin thought. *Thank God for gee-whiz gizmos. I don't know how we would've learned this otherwise.*

But he saw that his boss was nodding thoughtfully, impressed with the crisp imagery. And Coughlin did have to admit that the huge screen and its clarity made one at least feel like they were indeed on the scene.

*But isn't that just an artificial sense of accomplishment?*

"Kerry," Walker said, "transpose number fourteen on that."

A second later, a box appeared in the lower right, just above the text there. It was a list of data:

> **Cause: Explosion. Ninety percent probability from a methamphetamine lab.**
>
> **Known Dead: Two Hispanic males, approximate age mid-20s, no known history. Both suffered fourth-degree burns. One of the deceased suffered a cut to the throat. Jagged flesh of cut thought to be made by serrated blade of knife found at scene.**
>
> **Known Injured: Two, a White male and a White female. Male is one J. Warren Olde, age 27. Female is one Rebecca Benjamin, age 25. Olde suffered extreme burns, possibly/probably fourth-degree. Benjamin suffered lesser burns but serious blunt-force trauma. Both now in Temple Burn Ward ICU.**

"That data," Walker then added, "is due at any moment to be updated. As we know, Olde is now dead."

"Yes, we do," Police Commissioner Mariani said dryly.

"So let's go to that," Walker said almost excitedly.

"Why not the scene of the shooting at the Reading Terminal Market?" Mariani asked.

Coughlin thought he saw Walker wince.

"It would appear that the security camera system there has been neglected," he said, looking a bit embarrassed.

"Meaning what exactly?" Mariani snapped.

"Compromised," Walker said carefully. "Rendered inoperative."

"Then we have nothing from this morning's shooting."

Walker shook his head. "No, sir. Nothing yet."

"Jesus Christ!"

"We do have this," Walker said. "Corporal Rapier, number fifteen, please, and put sixteen on it."

The image of the Philly Inn disappeared and was replaced with a static shot of the Reading Terminal Market. The image even had text across it, reading, *Visit Historic Reading Terminal Market!*

Coughlin, despite great effort to hold it back, snorted.

Matt Lowenstein, Henry Quaire, and Jason Washington were showing rapt interest in their shoes' tips and the color and texture of the carpet — anything not to make eye contact with one another.

"What in the hell is that?" Mariani said incredulously.

"Well, sir," Walker said, "because we have no live feeds from the market, we pulled a stock image off the Internet to serve as a placeholder."

"Jesus H. Christ!" Mariani sighed disgustedly. "What's in here — a million bucks' worth of gadgets? Two million? — and we've got a goddamn Chamber of Commerce promo picture of a crime scene!"

"We are working on a live feed, sir." He waved his hand at the bank of TVs showing newscasts. "And we do have an image of the market via the FOX 29 news cameras, but it's not a steady real-time feed."

TV number sixteen popped up in a corner of the big image as an inset. It read:

---

**Cause: Shooting. One hundred percent probability drug-related. Heroin-based product recovered at the scene, also 42 5.7- x 28-mm shell casings and 10 9-mm shell casings, and a Ruger P89 9-mm semi-auto pistol.**

**Known Dead: Two. One a Hispanic male, one Devon A. Desmond, age 22. Dual U.S.-Jamaican citizenship. Last Known Address 1805 E Boston St, Phila. Employed by the Mexican Mercado. One**

---

a White female juvenile, age 16, name of Kathleen Gingerich. Last Known Address a rural route in Lancaster County, Penna. Family owns Beiler's Bakery.

Known Injured: Three, a White male and two White females. Male is one John Todd, of Phila. Two females are Japanese Nationals, approximate age 30, attending a convention of clothes designers at the Phila. Convention Center. Local address the Marriott Hotel at Filbert & 12th. All suffered bullet wounds believed to be from the 9-mm Ruger firearm. None life-threatening. Transported to Hahnemann Hospital.

"Kerry," Walker then said. "Let's go to seventeen."

The main screen showed a crisp, clear, full-color image of the Temple University Hospital. There was a mix of unmarked Crown Victoria Interceptors and marked police cars, all with their lights flashing, lining the curbs.

The text in the lower right-hand corner read:

"And here we have a real-time feed of the hospital," Walker said. He turned and looked at Corporal Rapier. "Eighteen, please, Kerry."

The color image was replaced with a somewhat grainy black-and-white exterior shot of the Temple University Hospital. There were cars in the street and people on the sidewalk. But none moved. The image was frozen. The text read:

"You might find this one interesting," Walker said. "Run it, Kerry."

A second later, the cars began rolling and the people walking.

Then, at street level, an exit door to the hospital flew open. It almost struck two pedestrians. A Hispanic male wearing blue

299

scrubs and holding a gun came out of the doorway. He immediately turned right and, as the steel exit door began to shut, ran down the sidewalk toward Germantown Avenue. The pedestrians started fleeing in the opposite direction.

"Jesus!" Mariani blurted. "There's our doer!"

"Yes, sir!" Walker said a little too proudly.

The steel exit door then flew open again. Sergeant Matt Payne in plainclothes slowly came out in a crouch.

The Hispanic male, running down the center of Tioga, then turned and shot back at the exit door.

The camera clearly showed Matt Payne drop to his knees, then glance up at the door. After taking a quick look around the door edge, he took off after the doer, keeping to the sidewalk. The doer turned left on Germantown Avenue. When Payne went to follow, everyone in the room saw what he hadn't — the taxicab flying down Tioga.

"Oh shit!" Henry Quaire blurted.

But then they saw Payne freeze and the cab swerve.

Payne then disappeared around the corner, headed up Germantown Avenue. And the black-and-white image froze again.

"We're working," Walker announced, "on

getting any surveillance camera imagery along the route that Sergeant Payne stated he took in pursuit of the doer. Also, we have men reviewing the last two days of imagery from this same camera. They're looking for foot and auto traffic anomalies or patterns on that sidewalk in case the victim was targeted, but randomly —"

"What about images from cameras inside the Burn Unit?" Matt Lowenstein asked, wondering why Walker would waste time with that.

"Those belong to the school," Walker said with clear disdain. "They're being cooperative, but due to technical compatibility problems, we're having to use their equipment on site to review the very limited material they actually have. And I'm afraid it's rather inferior to anything that we have here. Budgetary, you know. Someone had to decide whether to buy the latest scalpel or security camera. . . ."

"Well, the good news," said Henry Quaire, "is that what we just saw shows without a doubt that the doer shot at Matt. He had every right to shoot back."

"Commissioner Coughlin," Lieutenant Jason Washington said, "what about Matt? What do we — or I — do with him now?"

Coughlin looked at ease. "Nothing."

"Nothing?" Mariani repeated.

Coughlin nodded. "There was the discharge of his firearm. So until Internal Affairs officially clears him on that, he's on administrative duty. Which works out fine, because I pretty much had him assigned to that already. He's due out at the airport" — he looked at this wristwatch — "in about three hours."

"Your call, Denny," Mariani said.

"I would suggest one thing, Commissioner," Coughlin said.

He pointed to the main screen. The video had started to loop, and now showed the critter kicking open the exit door and scattering the pedestrians.

When Mariani's eyes went to it, the Hispanic was taking shots at the door and Payne was dropping to his knees.

"I wouldn't let His Honor the Mayor see that," Denny Coughlin went on. "He's liable to slip it to the media. I think he likes that Wyatt Earp persona of Payne's. Makes folks see that his administration stands with the police and isn't afraid to boldly go after the bad guys."

There were chuckles.

"Commissioner Walker," Corporal Rapier suddenly said. "Some fresh imagery coming in. Shall I put it up on the main screen?"

"Yes, of course, Kerry. Punch it up."

All eyes turned to the big screen.

The black-and-white shot of Payne running down the sidewalk with his pistol raised disappeared. In its place, up popped a new full-color video feed. It was an aerial shot, somewhat shaky and at times pixilated, the image turning momentarily to colored dots and squares. That suggested it was being shot by one of the Aviation Unit's Bell helicopter Long Rangers.

When the image became stable, it clearly showed a Philadelphia Police Marine Unit boat making a slow circle on a river. The vessel was a twenty-four-foot-long Boston Whaler, its fiberglass hull silver with the department's blue-and-yellow-stripe color scheme. It had a two-hundred-horsepower Evinrude outboard. The light bar atop the aluminum tower was pulsing red and blue.

In the lower right-hand part of the screen, text popped up:

---

**Schuylkill River at Grays Ferry Avenue Bridge**
**1158 hours, 24 Sept**

---

"What the hell are we looking at?" Mariani

said. "Some sort of fishing expedition?"

Walker looked at Corporal Rapier.

"Well, Kerry, anything on it?"

Corporal Rapier shook his head. "No, sir. All we just got was a call from the Marine Unit stating that they just recovered a body that was bobbing in the Schuylkill."

# VI

## [ONE]
## Mall de Mejico
## 1118 South Sixth Street, Philadelphia
## Wednesday, September 9, 12:16 P.M.

The Mall of Mexico carried on in much the same South Philly tradition as that of the nearby historic Ninth Street Market. Dating back to the turn of the twentieth century, the storefronts and open-air vendors of the Ninth Street Market — roughly the area along Ninth that covered the five blocks between Washington Avenue and Christian Street — served the great masses of immigrants of its neighborhoods. At one time or another — and most often overlapping — there were merchants catering to the tastes of the city's immigrant families from Italy and Ireland and Germany and Israel and Africa.

The flat-roofed one-story concrete-block building that housed the Mall of Mexico had originally been built for Unity Frankford Stores, one of Philly's longtime grocery store chains. (And if one looked beyond the gaudy paint, the original signage was still there, painted over countless times.) Each of the Unity Frankford Stores had been individually owned, and got their goods wholesale from the Frankford Grocery Company warehouse at Griscom and Unity Streets.

Then along came the corporate giants, the Great Atlantic & Pacific Tea Company (the "A&P") among them. These eventually squeezed out Philly's Unity Frankford and another grocer, American Stores. American did eventually become Acme, and there was in fact an Acme down around the corner from Mall de Mejico, on Washington.

Unity Frankford, however, was long dead and buried, and a vibrant Latin American marketplace its latest incarnation there on Sixth at Washington.

The Mall of Mexico merchants were arranged on a grid, much like those in the

Reading Terminal Market. They offered South Philly's immigrants the foods and more of Mexico, of course, but also of Guatemala, Honduras, El Salvador, Nicaragua, even Cuba.

The mall's front windows and doors overlooked a small asphalt parking lot. Its cinder-block walls were brightly painted in yellows and blues and reds. There was graffiti tagged at the rear. It had been spray-painted along the Sixth Street sidewalk by the beat-up pay telephone that was lag-bolted to the cinder-block wall. One large yellow section of that wall had a listing of mall merchants and the services that they offered. The lettering was done in black paint by what someone might kindly suggest was a shaky hand holding the brush.

Pacing the sidewalk along Sixth Street were thirty-odd Hispanic males of nearly all ages, starting around twelve and on up to sixty, the majority in their twenties. They were itinerant day laborers, many having just arrived in the city. They watched the passing traffic on Sixth, their interest piquing when a pickup or other work truck approached and slowed.

One or two of the laborers were selected by the others as their representative, mostly for the ability to speak English. The representatives went to the truck and spoke with the driver. After being told the type of work that needed to be done and negotiating a cash price, the representatives then consulted in Spanish with the other laborers. Workers were selected according to various criteria — for example, younger ones for hard labor requiring a strong back — and these workers then jumped in the back of the pickup.

And the rest went back to waiting for another truck to arrive.

On the sidewalk in front of the mall, an elderly Hispanic woman stood under the umbrella bolted to her food vendor cart. She was heavyset, and despite the shade of the umbrella was sweating in the heat of the September sun. The rubber-tired steamer cart was small, its diamond-patterned stainless steel battered. A handwritten menu taped to the front advertised tamales in pork, chicken, or cheese for one dollar each. A can of Coke or Sprite from the plastic cooler she used for a seat between sales also sold for a dollar.

As Juan Paulo Delgado drove into the parking lot in his Chevrolet Tahoe, the meat and corn smells of the tamales came into his vehicle through the open sunroof. He saw the elderly Hispanic woman pulling four aluminum-foiled wrapped tamales from her steamer. She handed them to two stout Hispanic women who appeared to be only a little younger than she was.

To Delgado, the scene had the same third-world feeling he'd found in so many other U.S. cities.

*It's like this just off Calle Ocho in Miami's Little Havana.*

*And in East L.A., East Dallas, Fort Worth's Northside.*

*And now here.*

*It could be Calle Nueve at the Mercado Matamoros.*

*All that's missing is the damn chickens and goats running wild.*

Delgado still wore what he'd had on earlier — the sandals, camo cutoffs, black Sudsie's T-shirt, and dark sunglasses. As he put the SUV in park and shut off the engine, his cellular telephone vibrated.

He looked at its screen. Omar Quintanilla had sent:

---

609-555-1904

JESUS WENT 2 TEMPLE . . . DEAL DONE . . . BUT HE GOT SHOT

---

"What?" Delgado said aloud.

He punched the keypad with his thumbs and sent the text:

```
HOW BAD?
```

The phone vibrated, and the screen read:

```
609-555-1904

BULLET WENT IN ABOVE LEFT KNEE &
OUT FRONT OF LEG . . .
```

Delgado replied:

```
THAT ALL?
```

There was a long moment before the cellular vibrated. He read:

609-555-1904

THAT ALL??

HE WONT STOP YELLING!!!!

BUT SI . . . THAT ALL . . . JUST STILL
BLEEDING

Delgado exhaled audibly.
*Bueno.*
*That could have been worse . . . especially
if the bullet had hit bone. Or a big vein.*
He had a mental image of the self-styled
tough guy Jesús Jiménez.
*The badass is being a crybaby.*
Delgado thumbed:

CALM DOWN . . .

TELL EL GIGANTE HE WILL LIVE

PUT CLEAN SOCK OVER HOLES &
WRAP W/TAPE

GET ANGEL 2 FIX HIM

Delgado then had a mental image of the frail-looking Angel Hernandez in his West Kensington "clinic."

The gray-haired sixty-year-old had been confined to a wheelchair for the last twenty-two years. He had been a medical technician working for an ambulance company. On his last call, he had been working on a car wreck victim in the back of an ambulance en route to University of Pennsylvania Hospital. The ambulance itself had been broadsided by a stolen Lincoln Town Car.

There had been a twelve-year-old African-American male at the wheel of the swiped Lincoln. He was fleeing at a high rate of speed from a Philadelphia Police Department squad car, its siren screaming and lights flashing. The investigators at the scene of the accident found it practically impossible to estimate accurately the Lincoln's speed at impact. There had been no skid marks going into the intersection — the kid never braked.

The collision had been spectacular. The Lincoln opened up the box-shaped back of the ambulance. The car wreck victim inside had been ejected and thrown against the side of a building. He died instantly.

Angel Hernandez had not been ejected, but

he had been trapped in the mangled metal of the wreckage. He had suffered a spinal cord injury, one that left him paralyzed from the waist down. The kid — who could barely see over the dashboard — split his head open like a ripe melon on the steering wheel. He died at the scene.

The ambulance company paid for Hernandez's doctors and subsequent rehabilitation therapy. But he would never walk again, and as he could no longer perform his duties from a wheelchair, the company eventually let him go.

There were suits against anybody and everybody, including the cops for carelessness. The claim was that their hot pursuit of a juvenile had made a more or less harmless situation go from bad to worse. That lawsuit, of course, had done nothing but enrich Hernandez's lawyers. They made off with most of the out-of-court settlement that the city had paid out to Hernandez.

All of which had left Hernandez with a bitter outlook, particularly toward the city and the cops — never mind that it had been the lawyers who'd made out like bandits.

Regardless, the end result was that Hernandez found himself trying to find a way to earn a living somehow. He did still have a fine skill set, even if he was stuck in a goddamn wheelchair.

And as there were plenty of brothers in Philly too quick to settle their disagreements with fists and knives and guns, and as hospitals crawled with cops looking for homeys showing up in the ER with some bullshit story about their wounds being accidentally self-inflicted, Angel Hernandez became the man for someone to get patched up on the QT.

Juan Paulo Delgado had Hernandez take care of his girls when there were problems with them, from a flu to the rare occasion some john got abusive. (El Gato ensured that the johns never made that mistake again — nor any others henceforth.) Getting prescription drugs, though very expensive, was no problem; someone was always willing to rob a pharmacy for the right price.

For that matter, everything about Hernandez was pricy. Delgado knew that it was going to cost him at least five hundred bucks for Angel's services to mend Jesús Jiménez in his West Kensington living room that he'd converted to a makeshift clinic.

But he also knew that that was the price of doing business.

*At least that fucking thief Skipper finally got what was coming to him.*

Delgado's phone vibrated just as West Kensington made him think about the van getting tigertailed.

He read the text:

609-555-1904

OK . . . WE GO 2 ANGEL NOW

Then he sent to Quintanilla:

WHAT ABOUT MINIVAN?

Quintanilla replied:

609-555-1904

GONE . . . IT & CHEVY

*What Chevy?*
Delgado thumbed and sent:

> CHEVY?

Delgado sat staring at his cellular phone screen. And waited.

*What the hell is he —*

The phone vibrated, and he read:

> 609-555-1904
>
> SORRY . . . WAS TAPING LEG
>
> JESUS JACKED A CHEVY . . . AFTER COP SHOT HIM

Delgado said, "Cop?"

He wrote:

> COP? U SURE? HOW U KNOW IT WAS A COP?

There was another long delay.

This time when Delgado finally got the reply, he decided the delay had been because Quintanilla had been trying to figure out what to say.

The text read:

> 609-555-1904
>
> MAYBE CAUSE THATS WHAT JESUS SAID THE FUCKING COP YELLED AT HIM??

*Shit.*

Delgado thumbed and sent:

> OK . . . OK . . . LET ME KNOW IF ANYTHING ELSE COMES UP

After he hit SEND, he stared at the phone for a long moment.

*What else can go wrong?*

Then he thumbed a text and sent it to Jorge — El Cheque's name was Jorge Ernesto Aguilar — in Dallas:

> STILL COMING 2NITE . . . ANY WORD ON THE KID?

El Cheque replied:

214-555-7636

NOTHING . . . GETTING CALLS FROM
HIS STOPS ASKING WHEN HE COMES

U THINK ZETAS?

*Zetas! Shit! I hope not.*
*Maybe he just took off?*
*I thought he could be trusted.*
He replied:

NOT ZS

PROBABLY NOTHING . . . C U 2NITE . . .

Delgado's phone vibrated with El Cheque's
reply:

214-555-7636

OK . . . HOPE U R RITE

Delgado then put the phone in his pocket, reached down and grabbed the tan backpack with the Nike logotype from the passenger-side floorboard, then got out of the Tahoe.

Inside the front door of the Mall of Mexico, Juan Paulo Delgado found that he had to step around two long lines of Latino men and women in order to get deeper in the building. He'd never seen it this busy.

The lines almost wound out the front doors. He started walking, following the lines to the right and down around the corner. He saw that they led to a yellow-and-black Western Union counter.

There were two teller windows there, and next to them a couple dozen yellow fiberglass bucket chairs bolted to an iron rail painted a glossy black. At least half of these were filled with more Latinos, people either waiting for a cell phone call to say that their money had been sent and they could join the queue to collect it, or those who had just sent or collected their funds.

As Delgado continued toward the back of the mall, he noticed that few of these people were making much effort to conceal from anyone the fact that they were handling wads of cash, in some cases hundreds of dollars each.

*Might have to get someone to check this out.*

*Figure out what day and time the line's the longest.*

*Why send all that remittance money south when it can go in El Gato's pockets?*

Delgado passed a vendor selling pay-as-you-go, no-long-term-contract cellular telephones featuring inexpensive calling rates to Central America. Then he reached the back of the mall. He stopped at a storefront with a wooden sign etched with TITO'S TORTILLA FÁBRICA.

He went inside the "factory," then to the stand with the register in the right corner.

A teenage Latino perked up when he saw Delgado coming his way. He had a white fiberboard box imprinted with TITO'S TORTILLAS already on the stand when Delgado got there.

"Hola, El Gato," the teenager said.

*"Hola,"* he replied as he pulled a bulging FedEx envelope from the outside pocket of the tan backpack.

*"Gracias,"* the teenager said as he took it.

Delgado nodded once and grabbed the box of corn tortillas.

As he walked purposefully back to the Tahoe, he scanned the mall for anyone who might have an interest in his unleavened pancakes, ones covering U.S. Federal Reserve notes.

He also made one last inspection of the lines for the Western Union.

*Got to be an easy way to get a piece of that. . . .*

Then he got in the Tahoe, picked up I-95 south, and drove along the Delaware River the five or so miles to the Philadelphia International Airport.


# [TWO]
## Terminal D
## Philadelphia International Airport
## Wednesday, September 9, 3:01 P.M.


"Yeah, Jason, I do understand that I'm really to keep a low profile and that this time Coughlin really means it," Sergeant Matt Payne said into his cell phone. He was walking down the airport's D/E Connector. "I will bring this Texas Ranger by the Roundhouse, and we will work out of Homicide. I got it."

Due to construction work at Terminal D,

which served United and Continental Airlines and others, Payne had had to park his rental Ford near Terminal E, which served Northwest and Southwest Airlines.

He left the car in one of the three parking spaces at Terminal E that were marked OFFICIAL POLICE USE ONLY, and put one of his business cards on the dash. He realized that the rental Ford easily could be ID'd as such — a simple running of the plates would show the name of its corporate owner, never mind the thumbnail-size tracking sticker with the corporate logo in the corner of the rear window. He further realized that an airport traffic cop could jump to the conclusion that it was a rental by some idiot who thought he could get away with parking in a cop's spot — Philly wasn't about to run out of idiots anytime soon — who would then call for a Tow Squad wrecker and have it hauled off.

So Payne had taken a black permanent marker and redacted everything on the business card except SERGEANT M.M. PAYNE, PHILADELPHIA POLICE DEPARTMENT, HOMICIDE UNIT, and his cell phone number. If any airport cop questioned the validity of the vehicle being there, a simple call to the Roundhouse or to Payne — or both — would answer that.

■ ■ ■ ■

The Philadelphia International Airport's D/E Connector was a wide mall-like passage that, as its name suggested, linked Terminal D and Terminal E. It was lined with towering white columns flying flags. And it had a marketplace that offered air travelers quite a few of the conveniences of the retail world, everything from newsstands and bookstores to well-known national chains selling clothing, jewelry, computer accessories, and more.

In the center of the highly polished tile floor were kiosks for smaller vendors. One of the kiosks that Payne approached sold what it called "specialty" pretzels. He thought that they were outrageously priced even if one were traveling on an expense account. Another kiosk was home to an Internet access provider called the Road Warrior Connection. Its signage advertised that it offered PHILLY'S FASTEST, CHEAPEST INTERNET.

Something familiar caught his eye as he passed, and he glanced inside. Then he found it, and shook his head as he kept walking.

*Maybe Skipper was onto something.*

In the kiosk he had seen a guy working

on one of the rental laptop computers. He'd had his back to Payne, but on his back was a black Sudsie's T-shirt. And just as Chad Nesbitt had said, this guy looked to be about the right demographic for a place like that — a clean-cut, decent-looking Hispanic male in his early twenties.

He got to Terminal D, to the point where the passengers from the airline gates in the secure Concourse D came out to go to Baggage Claim D or, if they hadn't checked any luggage, simply made a straight exit of the airport.

Payne took a seat so that he had a clear view of the area. He sighed audibly, then realized he was somewhat tired.

And that caused him to begin thinking about all he'd been through in the course of the day.

*It's been surreal . . . and I'm far from being done.*

He looked at his watch. It showed it was quarter after three.

*Jesus! In the course of — what?*

*Chad called me at quarter of five this morning. So that makes it right at eight and a half hours.*

*And in that time I've gone from being on nearly thirty days' R & R and shopping for a Porsche to being back on the cops to a shoot-*

*out with a critter to being put back on ice.*

*And, now, to whatever happens with this guy from Texas.*

*Liz Justice — wearing the hat of Houston Chief of Police Justice — said he was tracking some critter who cut off girls' heads?*

He shook his head.

*Un-fucking-believable.*

*Talk about an animal. That's inhuman. . . .*

He watched a clump of people flowing out of Concourse D. He had no idea which flight they had come in on, but not one of them looked like his idea of a Texan, let alone of a Texas Ranger law-enforcement officer. There were only two males in the group, neither close to resembling an active LEO. One wasn't old enough to shave. The other, in a crouch, walked with a cane.

His mind went on:

*And in the course of those same eight and a half hours, five people in Philly — three of whom I more or less crossed paths with — are no longer among the living.*

*And the fate of another is not looking damn good at all.*

An image of a laughing, full-of-life Becca Benjamin flashed in his memory.

*Godspeed, Becca. . . .*

*And what about those two Hispanics killed in the motel?*

324

*I'd hoped Skipper would've told us some-
thing about how that one guy got his throat
slit.*

*But now all the witnesses are dead.*

*Unless Becca knows something . . . but
that's a long shot, both (a) on the chance that
she knew what was going on in the motel room
and (b) if she actually survives and can tell us
that she does.*

*Or doesn't. Then we're back to square one.*

*And that crazy sonofabitch coming into the
hospital and pumping thirteen nine-millimeter
rounds into Skipper.*

*What if he came back?*

*Thank God we beefed up the cops sitting on
her.*

*Jesus! What next?*

A big group of air travelers, easily thirty
of them, came out from Concourse D. They
were mostly teenagers. They had a handful
of chaperones. All wore the same bright
blue style of T-shirt. Payne could read some
part of what had been silk-screened on the
shirts, something about a church mission
trip.

*I do know what I'd like to happen next.*

*I'd like another shot at that sonofabitch who
popped Skipper.*

*Not a gunshot . . . just a chance to bring him
in.*

*First, because he doesn't need to be on the street.*

*And second, because he damn sure knows something.*

*That's obvious because he knows Skipper knew something. Why else target him for assassination? That's what they were calling it at the scene in the ICU.*

*And that's exactly what it was — thirteen rounds' worth of nine-millimeter assassination.*

*Which means that the sonofabitch may very well know what went on in that motel room. Or, if not what went on in there in the last few minutes, hours, whatever, then who the players in there were.*

*And it's damn sure no coincidence that the guy I shot and the two crispy critters from the motel are all Hispanic males.*

Payne heard the rhythmic *thump, thump, thump* of hard rubber wheels rolling over an expansion joint in the tile floor. He turned to find a heavy-duty polymer custodial cart moving in his direction. It had two twenty-gallon plastic garbage cans on either end and the handles of a broom and feather dusters poking up between them. Pushing the cart was a hollow-faced Hispanic female. She looked to be maybe thirty. She stopped at a trash receptacle, and there went about her cleaning job quietly and effortlessly and, Payne noted, more or less completely unnoticed by anyone.

Then he was struck by the fact that that had been the exact same response he'd had to the Hispanic "orderly" at the Burn Unit when he saw him pushing the gurney into the corridor.

*I didn't give him a second thought.*

*Why is that? And is it good or bad?*

*I have no idea. But I know there's something there I can't put my finger on.*

*Where is that sonofabitch now?*

*How badly did I wound him?*

*There hadn't been hardly any blood at the scene, either where he went down or where he carjacked that Chevy Caprice.*

*But maybe that one round did enough damage to get the critter to find an ER.*

Payne knew that it did not matter which hospital emergency room. As long as it wasn't, say, ten states away. But even ten states away there was a chance of catching the guy. It just would take longer.

And the hospitals did report, either officially or quietly, someone coming in with a gunshot wound. Even if — for whatever reason, say, some sanctimonious bastard at the intake desk took offense at the release of the scum's "personal and privileged information" to the cops — not right away. There were others on staff who knew that almost all gunshot wounds were dirty and eventually would leak the info to the authorities. Not to mention the ones working security, who were either once cops or were cops moonlighting; they didn't have to be convinced that keeping a critter off the street was all-important. They would call it in right then and there, damn any consequences.

Already the Philly Homicide detectives had begun distributing an Armed and Dangerous Alert to all of the hospital ERs within a fifty-mile radius. The single-page alert had a grainy black-and-white snapshot of the doer that had been pulled from the city-owned surveillance camera video on the exterior of the Temple University Hospital wall. (There had been as yet no luck with the hospital's interior video equipment.)

The Armed and Dangerous Alert also contained, of course, a description of the Hispanic male, including the detail that his wound had been inflicted by a .45-caliber bullet to the left leg at a point believed to be somewhere above the knee. And, of course, there was the directive to first call 911 in the event anyone requesting medical attention came even remotely close to the description on the alert. Then the hospital could contact the Philadelphia Police Department Homicide Unit at the Roundhouse via the information provided, or the responding cops could do so.

Payne then thought about Skipper Olde.

When Payne had gone back into the Temple Burn Unit, he had been surprised at his own reaction to the news that the doer had indeed pumped thirteen rounds into Skipper.

*It didn't really bother me one bit.*

*Knowing his chance of survival, maybe I had already dealt with the fact he probably wasn't — what did Tony Harris tell me he thought? — that Skipper wasn't going to make it to lunch.*

*And he sure as hell didn't.*

*But my being unaffected . . . something weird about that.*

*I need to call Amy and ask her.*

Amy was Amelia A. Payne, MD. His sister was the Joseph L. Otterby Professor of Psychiatry at the University of Pennsylvania.

*If she doesn't have an opinion, which would be the first time that ever happened, then she'll find me someone who does.*

Then another mental image flashed up, and Payne suddenly grinned.

*That and see if someone in Amy's medical circles can give me background on that gorgeous Dr. Amanda Law.*

His mind wandered to the Texas Ranger. He checked his wristwatch. It showed three thirty. The airplane had been due in at three twenty-two.

*Flight's late. Nothing new there.*

Payne had taken fifteen or so minutes at the Roundhouse to do a fast Internet search on the Rangers. And what little he'd found had been fascinating.

*Real Wild Wild West stuff,* he'd thought.

He'd copied the information into an e-mail and sent it to himself. Then he'd taken his cellular telephone and used it to check his e-mail, downloading a copy of the file to his phone.

He pulled out his phone now and opened the e-mail:

---

From: SGT M.M. Payne <payne.m@ppd.philadelphia.gov>
Date: 09SEPT 1201
To: MMP (Mobile Email) <w.earp.45@gmail.com>
Subject: Tx Rangers Notes

Texas Rangers Sergeant Jim Byrth, Continental flight from IAH arriving PHL at 1522 hours, terminal D.

---

Snippets on Texas Rangers . . .

>>> Began in its first form in 1823.
Stephen F. Austin, developing settlements
in the Mexican province of Tejas, called for
men to "Range" the frontier to protect its
people. Officially became Texas Rangers
in 1835.

>>> Austin recruited settlers from Europe
and U.S. with the promise of land. Settlers
agreed to become Mexican citizens, join
the Catholic faith, speak Spanish.

>>> Mexican law authorized Austin to
form militia to protect settlements. The
Rangers were formed to ward off raids
by Tonkawa and Comanche Indians
and others, to capture criminals, and to
"range" against intruders.

>>> "A Ranger is an officer able to handle
any given situation without definite
instructions from his commanding officer,
or higher authority. This ability must be
proven before a man becomes a Ranger."

>>> "One Riot, One Ranger" — In 1896,
Texas Ranger Captain Bill McDonald sent

to Dallas to stop an illegal prize-fight. The Dallas mayor met McDonald at Union Station, and said, "Where're the other Rangers?"

McDonald replied, "There's only one fight. Hell, ain't I enough?"

>>> Early Texas Ranger badges hammered out of silver Mexican five-peso coins. Badge is a five-point star within a ring engraved with oak leaves and an olive branch borrowed from the Texas Great Seal to represent strength (oak leaves) and peace (olive branch).

>>> Senior Ranger Captain Frank H. Hamer — commissioned as a Texas Highway Patrolman — went after Clyde Barrow and Bonnie Parker. Tracked Bonnie and Clyde for more than three months before finding them in Louisiana. The outlaws fired — and were killed in the ensuing shoot-out on 23 May 1934.

>>> Present Day: Rangers are a division of the Texas Department of Public Safety. The 134 Texas Rangers (as authorized by

Texas Legislature) are posted in seven companies: Waco (headquarters), Garland (Dallas/Fort Worth), Houston, Lubbock, Midland, San Antonio, and McAllen. Administrative office in Austin.

>>> Has been called one of the most effective investigative law-enforcement agencies in the world.

>>> Texas Rangers wear, as living symbols of a unique heritage, boots, white hats, and pistol belts of their predecessors.

Payne noticed movement and looked up from his phone.

There was another group coming out of Concourse D. But all Payne really noticed was a white Stetson cowboy hat seemingly floating down the concourse. It looked to be made of finely woven straw. Its crown was huge. The portion of the round brim over his ears spread out to resemble wide wings.

*The Hat,* Payne labeled it.

There were, of course, other passengers exiting ahead of and behind The Hat, but all Matt Payne could see of the Texas Ranger was The Hat.

*And, boy, does it stand out.*

*Especially here in the Philly airport.*

*Should be interesting to see it in Center City. . . .*

Payne was standing with five others who were watching the passengers coming out of Concourse D and going their different directions. He saw The Hat make a slow sweep of the terminal as Byrth scanned the area, no doubt looking for him. Then Byrth made eye contact with him and walked purposefully toward him.

With the exception of The Hat and his pointy-toed western boots, James O. Byrth did not look unlike Matthew M. Payne.

Byrth, who appeared to be about thirty years old, stood right at six feet tall and weighed 170 pounds. He was lithely muscled. He had dark, intelligent eyes and kept his dark, thick hair trimmed conservatively short. He wore gray slacks that actually had cuffs and a sharp crease, a stiffly starched white button-down collared shirt, and a single-breasted navy blue blazer with gold buttons.

The Hat stepped up to Matt Payne.

"Marshal Earp, I presume," Jim Byrth said with utter confidence. His distinct Texas drawl made it only more so.

"That's interesting," Payne replied dryly. "I was about to say the same to you. You forget your horse in the plane's overhead bin?"

Byrth grinned. "No. I checked it. Should be waiting at the baggage claim."

*Wait,* Payne thought. *How the hell did he pick me out so quickly?*

*And confidently?*

*Liz Justice probably gave him a basic description.*

*But he knew without question that it was me.*

"Okay, how'd you make me?" Payne said, holding out his right hand.

Byrth didn't reply immediately, as if he was considering whether he would.

"Penatekas," Byrth finally said, powerfully squeezing Payne's hand as he looked him right in the eyes. He added: "Sergeant Jim Byrth, Texas Rangers, Company A." He nodded once, and The Hat moved with great drama. "Pleasure to meet you."

"Sergeant Matt Payne, Philadelphia Police Department, Homicide."

"I know."

" 'Penatekas'?" Payne repeated, stumbling over the pronunciation.

Byrth nodded again, and again The Hat accentuated the movement.

"One of the warrior bands of the fierce

Comanches," Byrth explained solemnly. "Back when Texas was the Mexican province of Tejas, early Rangers learned from them their various methods of how to tell everything about a person simply by knowing what to look for."

Payne stared at him.

*He's pulling my chain.*

*Or is he?*

*That "Mexican province of Tejas" stuff I read about. And those Comanches were ruthless.*

"Fascinating," Payne said. "What sort of methods?"

"Well," Byrth began, stone-faced, "they were nomads, and roaming the plains. When they hunted down a buffalo, they had a spiritual ceremony and prayed for its soul. They honored the great animal by letting no part of it go to waste. The flesh they cured for food. The skins became blankets and clothing and other protection. Even the *cojones* were used for special purposes. The *cojones* were dried and ground and consumed for the powers to observe. In particular, to observe people, and even more in particular, to observe enemies."

"Co-what?"

"Co-hone-ees," Byrth repeated, this time phonetically. "That's actually the Spanish word. The Indians had their own, which

336

varied from band to band."

"And that's how you knew it was me? With these co-hone-ees?"

Still stone-faced, Byrth stared Payne in the eyes. Payne felt that he was reading him. Then Byrth nodded once. The Hat mimicked the motion.

"Co-hone-ees is Spanish?" Payne said. "For what?"

" 'Testicles.' "

Byrth grinned.

"Actually, it translates closer to 'balls.' "

Then Byrth wordlessly pulled out his cell phone and punched at its touchscreen.

"That, and then there's this."

He held it out to Payne, showing him a big bright glass screen that filled the whole face of the device.

There was a digitized photograph on the screen.

Payne grunted.

He immediately recognized it as one that four years before had run on the front page of *The Philadelphia Bulletin.* It showed a bloody-faced Officer Matthew M. Payne, pistol in hand, standing over a fatally wounded felon in an alleyway. And it had had the screaming headline: "Officer M.M. Payne, 23, The Wyatt Earp of the Main Line."

"Your reputation precedes you, Marshal.

And, I might add, lives online for all to see."

Homicide Sergeant Matthew Payne's eyes went between the phone and Byrth's face. He shook his head.

*Shit. He got me. And good.*

Then he burst out laughing.

*I think we're going to get along just fine.*

"Nice job, Jim."

Byrth smiled.

Payne added: "But just remember that payback is hell."

Now Byrth laughed aloud and said, "Liz Justice said you were a good sport. I'll deal with the payback."

# [THREE]
## D/E Connector
## Philadelphia International
## Airport
## Wednesday, September 9,
## 3:10 P.M.

Juan Paulo Delgado sat at a rental Dell laptop computer inside the Road Warrior Connection kiosk.

He reached into his camo shorts and pulled

out the flash drive. He stuck it in a USB slot on the side of the laptop, and simultaneously hit the CONTROL, ALT, and DELETE keys. When the screen went blank, he held the CONTROL and Z keys simultaneously. The computer restarted, loading the secure program from the flash drive that mirrored his laptop in the safe of his converted warehouse loft.

As the computer booted up, he wondered if there actually was something to what Jorge Aguilar had suggested in his text message.

*Did Los Zetas have anything to do with the kid's disappearance?*

The Zetas, led by Heriberto "The Executioner" Lazcano, were mercenaries working as the enforcement arm of the narco-trafficking Gulf Cartel. They numbered some five hundred men, and were heavily armed and well-trained. The majority of them had been commandos in the Mexican Army's Grupo Aeromóvil de Fuerzas Especiales, which, ironically, went after members of the drug cartels. They were ruthless and fearless. And what they could not or would not do — assassinations inside the United States, for example — they hired others, most notably gangbangers, to carry out for them.

The Gulf Cartel — if not the biggest of the Mexican drug-trafficking organizations

(MDTOs), then one of the richest — was based due south of Brownsville, Texas, on the Gulf of Mexico, thus the source of the cartel's name. Since the 1970s, the Gulf Cartel had trafficked pot, coke, meth, and smack into the United States. And they taxed anyone who used their "plazas," or smuggling routes. The Zetas acted as their lethal collection agency for slow- or no-payers.

Thus, Juan Paulo Delgado knew that the Zetas were not to be fucked with.

He also knew that, compared to the gangs to whom the cartel wholesaled drugs for re-sale in the United States, he was a very, very small player. He operated on the fringes of what to the cartels was a multibillion-dollar-per-year enterprise. As long as he kept paying the plaza taxes that the Gulf Cartel levied on him, and he didn't step on their toes, and he didn't try to become a bigger player, he would more or less be left alone with his crumbs.

Which meant that it had been a damned dumb move to pump forty-two rounds — two of 9-millimeter and forty of 5.7-millimeter — into his former business associate in that South Dallas crack house. Not because it was wrong to take out the bastard who owed him for the kilo of black tar smack.

But because that property had also been an occasional stash house for the Zetas.

Not long afterward, he'd learned on the street that they were not exactly pleased that El Gato (a) had drawn unwanted attention to the stash/crack house and (b) had made the mess with what once had been their P90 Fabrique Nationale submachine gun.

Like toothpaste from a tube, there of course was no way to put fired bullets back in a gun. The damage was done. But Delgado had a hard time believing that any of that actually warranted the anger of the Zetas.

*You never know, though, what sets those fuckers off.*

*Or whom they'll hire to pull the trigger.*

*They could've grabbed the kid — or had him grabbed — to send a message.*

*Or it could be the kid's just out getting laid. . . .*

*For two days?*

He shook his head, then clicked on the Firefox browser icon to connect to the Internet.

He signed in to his Gmail account. There was nothing new to read except junk mail. He deleted that. He then decided that while he was signed in, he would just send an e-mail to Jorge Aguilar. Typing took less effort than thumbing and, like text messages, the e-mails also went to Jorge's cellular phone. He opened a new window and wrote:

---

From: jjd <4.n.dallas.high@gmail.com>
Date: 09SEPT 1520
To: jorge <cowboys_fan_16@yahoo.com>
Subject: the kid

send someone (maybe Gomez?) to A&M to see if he can find out anything.

we need to know if something's happened.

---

Then he clicked to send it, and logged out of Gmail.

He typed PHILLYBULLETIN.COM and hit the RETURN key.

A second later, the screen loaded.

He saw that the image of the Philly Inn ablaze had moved farther down the screen. Now the main image was that of emergency vehicles at the Reading Terminal Market. And below that was a photograph of the Temple University Hospital surrounded by Philadelphia Police Department squad cars and what looked to Delgado to be very likely unmarked police cars.

The red text of the ticker crawling from right to left across the top of the page read: *BREAKING NEWS . . . Police Investigating Suspicious Burning of 2 Vehicles Parked in West Kensington . . . BREAKING NEWS . . .*

Delgado saw that under the photograph of Reading Terminal Market there was a caption:

---

**Gunfire killed two people and injured four others this morning at Reading Terminal Market in Center City Philadelphia. Click here for full story. (Photograph by Jimmy Bell / Bulletin Photographer)**

---

And under the image of Temple University Hospital was also a caption. It read:

---

**Temple University Hospital on North Broad Street was the scene of a shooting late this morning, Philly's second of the day. (See related story by clicking here.) Police said that they were withholding details pending the initial investigation. Witnesses, however, stated that police pursued an armed gunman running**

---

from a hospital exit. The gunman fired at the officer chasing him. Click <u>here</u> for full story. (Photograph by Phan Hoang / Bulletin Photographer)

*That gunman was El Gigante.*
*And so it was a cop who chased him . . . and shot him.*

Delgado clicked on the link to read the story:

## ARMED MAN MURDERS BURN VICTIM BEFORE FLEEING HOSPITAL, FIRING AT POLICE

**While police remain mum on details of the murder, witnesses claim gunman fired shots at man who shouted "Police!" while chasing gunman from hospital.**

By A.A. O'Reilly
Bulletin Staff Writer
Posted Online 09/09 at 11:30 a.m.

Philadelphia — A critically burned man who had just been admitted to the Intensive Care Unit of the Temple

University Hospital was shot multiple times by an unknown assailant this morning, according to a source inside the hospital who asked to remain anonymous.

Witnesses on the sidewalk outside the hospital said that about 10:50 a.m. the gunman ran out of the hospital from an exit door at street level. He then fled eastward down Tioga Street. When the exit door opened again, witnesses said, the gunman fired back at it, narrowly missing a man who identified himself by shouting "Police! Stop!"

"It was absolute chaos," said Sylvia Morris, who was returning to her job at the hospital. "Everyone on the sidewalk was running for their lives."

As the gunman ran toward Germantown Avenue, witnesses said, he reloaded his pistol. The man who identified himself as police then pursued him.

A short time later, witnesses said that they heard at least four more gunshots in the direction that the two had run, but that they could not see them at that point.

The gunman was described as being a Hispanic male of tiny stature, no older than a teenager. He wore royal blue hospital scrubs and carried in his right hand a black semiautomatic pistol. He remains at large.

A spokesman for the Philadelphia Police Department confirmed that a sergeant from the department had been the one who had chased the shooter. But the spokesman would neither identify the sergeant nor give any details on what happened in the hospital prior to the street chase.

*Check back for updates as they become available.*

COMMENTS (3)

From **PutGodbackinPhilly (1:48 p.m.):**

*How on earth can something like this be possible? Is there no place in our city of brotherly love that's not safe? This is what happens when we stop teaching The Bible. What part of "Thou Shalt Not Kill!" do these people not understand?*

Recommend [ 12 ] Click Here to Report Abuse

From **PhillyEaglesFan (2:34 p.m.):**

*Amen, sister. And thank God for our men in blue.*

Recommend [ 14 ] <u>Click Here to Report Abuse</u>

From **Hung.Up.Badge.But.Not.Gun (2:56 p.m.):**

*I talked to an inside source, too, and was told that this was a hit job. Maybe not a professional one, but the burn victim (there's more to that story that I cannot share) was targeted. So sad to see this happening in Philly. I'll say it again: Shoot 'em all and let the Good Lord sort 'em out.*

Recommend [ 6 ] <u>Click Here to Report Abuse</u>

*What bullshit!* Delgado thought.

He clicked on the page to leave a comment, then typed one and clicked SEND.

After a moment, his message appeared last on the list of comments:

From **Death.Before.Dishonor (3:20 p.m.):**

*What about "Thou Shalt Not Steal"?? The only sad thing about what happened is the gun didn't empty all of its bullets into that pendejo! Skipper deserved every damn bullet!*

Recommend [ 0 ] <u>Click Here to Report Abuse</u>

Delgado shook his head disgustedly, then shut down the Dell rental lap top. He pulled out his USB flash drive. And then he walked out of the kiosk, headed to the Transportation Security Administration checkpoint for Concourse E.

# [FOUR]
## Delaware Expressway
## (I-95 North), Philadelphia
## Wednesday, September 9,
## 3:45 P.M.

Philadelphia Police Department Sergeant
Matt Payne was behind the wheel of his
white Ford rental sedan. Texas Rangers Sergeant Jim Byrth was in the front passenger
bucket seat looking out the window at the
Delaware River and, on the other side of
that, New Jersey. The Hat was sitting upside
down on the backseat.

When Payne's cellular telephone started
ringing, he had to do some juggling in order
to answer it.

And the first thing he did was toss his
"specialty" pretzel onto the dashboard.

As Payne and Byrth had headed for Baggage Claim D, the Texan had suddenly said,
"Hey, look! Soft pretzels! I didn't eat a damn
thing on that lousy flight. C'mon. The Great
State of Texas is treating."

The pretzels had been huge, each weighing at least a pound. Payne had been impressed, but not to the point where he'd have paid for one.

The two cops had chewed on theirs while waiting for Byrth's one leather suitcase to show up on the baggage carousel. And then chewed on them on the walk to Terminal E. And then after that during the drive up I-95.

When they had walked up to the rental car where Payne had left it in the Terminal E OFFICIAL POLICE USE ONLY parking spot, Payne had pushed the button on his key fob that remotely unlocked the trunk. Byrth tossed his leather suitcase inside, then put down his pretzel and went about opening the suitcase.

Payne had watched with curiosity as Byrth then removed from it a pair of Smith & Wesson chrome handcuffs.

Byrth felt him watching and said, "I left the standard-issue leg irons and transport belt in my truck at the airport in Houston. Figured you'd have some I could borrow if necessary."

"I think we can find something suitable. Maybe even rope."

Byrth slipped the cuffs into the right patch pocket of his blazer, then pulled from the suitcase two hard-plastic clamshell boxes. He put them side by side on the carpeted floor of the trunk. They were identical. Payne thought they looked like the case that had been on Denny Coughlin's desk, the one containing the police department–issued Glock 17 pistol. Except these boxes were smooth-sided, with no markings whatever. There was only a combination lock and a luggage name tag on each.

Wordlessly, Byrth spun the dials of one combination lock, then the other, and removed them. Next he slid open the latches of the box on the right and opened up the box.

Now, Payne saw, the box did look like the one on Coughlin's desk. It held a black semiautomatic pistol in a dense black foam cushioning that was customized to fit the exact contours of the gun.

Payne smiled.

*A Colt Combat Commander.*

*Customized and engraved with a Texas Ranger badge.*

*Very nice gun.*

When Byrth opened the other clamshell, Payne saw that it also had the black foam cushioning, but this one had been custom-fitted to securely hold five magazines, a polymer box labeled .45ACP TACTICAL JHP, 230-GRAIN, 50 ROUNDS, and a black leather skeleton holster.

*Tactical jacketed hollow points.*

*Same rounds we use.*

Byrth took out one of the magazines. He snapped back the top of the polymer box to reveal the shiny brass bullets inside.

"This'll take just a second, if you don't mind," he said.

"No problem," Payne replied. He added, "So you like the .45, too?"

Byrth clenched a magazine in his right hand and was pulling rounds from the box and using his thumb to feed them one by one into the top of the magazine.

"Too?" Byrth repeated. "I take it you're a fan, then."

Payne said, "You ever hear the story of the pacifist who got in the cop's face and whined, 'How come you carry a .45, tough guy?' "

Byrth grinned and made a soft grunt.

"Yeah," he said. "And the cop replied, 'Because they don't make a fucking .46.' "

"That was no story," Payne said. "That was me."

Byrth chuckled.

Payne then discreetly reached inside his shirt and brought out his Colt Officer's Model, taking care to keep it concealed from passersby.

Byrth nodded appreciatively. "I sometimes carry an Officer's as my backup."

He fed the eighth round to the magazine he'd been charging, then took a single round from the polymer box. He picked up the pistol, pulled back its slide, slipped the single round into the throat, and let the slide go forward. The moving of the slide backward caused the hammer to go into the cocked position. He then used his right thumb to throw the lever on the left rear of the slide, thereby leaving the pistol "cocked and locked." And he slid the charged magazine into its place in the grip of the pistol.

He reached back into the clamshell box and took out the black leather skeleton holster. He unbuckled his belt and threaded the holster onto it so that it rode on his right hip inside his navy blazer. He secured the pistol in it. Finally, he loaded a second magazine, then a third. These he slipped into the front pockets of his pants, one magazine in each pocket.

He looked at Payne with what Payne thought was a look of satisfaction.

"Okay," Byrth said with a smile. "I feel whole."

"I know what you mean," Payne said, securing his Officer's Model back under his waistband.

■ ■ ■ ■

"Excuse me, Jim," Payne said motioning with the phone as they drove up I-95. "This won't take a second."

Jim Byrth shook his head in a gesture that said, *No problem,* then casually took in the river view.

Payne noticed motion at Byrth's left hand, which he rested on his left thigh. He looked more closely and saw that Byrth had a small dry white bean on the top of his fingers. He manipulated the bean by moving the fingers in series — tumbling it end over end from his pointing finger to his middle finger to his ring finger to his pinky, then tumbling it back to the pointing finger.

He moved the bean quickly. It was evident that Byrth had had plenty of practice.

*Some kind of nervous energy going on there, Jim?*

Payne turned his attention to the highway. Into his cell phone he said, "Hi, Amy. Can I call you back in a bit?"

He listened for a moment.

"Yeah, that's what I want to talk with you about." He paused. "No, Amy, I didn't 'kill another one.' I could do without your attempt at sarcasm."

That caused Jim Byrth to twitch his head

in interest.

"So then do you want to meet someplace later?" He paused. "Okay. That works. See you then." He was about to push END but had an afterthought. "Amy? You still there?"

He pulled the phone from his ear and looked at the screen. It showed that the call was dead.

*Dammit! If she'd just been talking to someone at Temple's Burn Unit, she might know something about that Dr. Amanda Law.*

He put down the phone, then retrieved his pretzel. He glanced at Byrth, who was still looking out the window, still tumbling the bean.

*The guy looks tough as nails.*

*I can just see him riding the range, then single-handedly driving off a mob of marauding Injuns.*

*But how's he going to do here in the big city?*

*Then again, he did just come in from Houston.*

With Byrth sitting, the cuffs of his pants rode higher, and Payne could see the upper parts of the western boots. They appeared to cover the complete calf. They had some intricate patterns of stitching and there was another representation of the Texas Ranger badge, this one in silver leather, and the red leather initials J.O.B.

Payne then looked at the pointed-toe part. The material that made up the part covering the foot was a high-gloss black, textured with a grid of little bumps every half-inch or so the size of BBs.

"Mind if I ask what kind of leather that is on your boots?" Payne said.

Byrth glanced down at his boots as he lifted the flap of the left patch pocket of his blazer and slipped the dry white bean inside.

"Skin," Byrth corrected.

"What?"

"We say 'skin.' "

"Oh. Okay, what kind of *skin* is that? All those bumps. They look like tiny nipples."

There was a moment's pause as Byrth considered that.

"Do they really?" he said.

*Oh shit!*

*He's taking offense to "tiny nipples"?*

"No offense."

Byrth laughed. "None taken. I'd just never seen my boot skins in that light. But I believe I will from this point forward. So is that what they call Freudian?"

Payne grinned.

"Quite possibly," he said. "I'll ask my sister. She's a shrink. That was her on the

356

phone just now."

Byrth nodded.

Payne pursued, "So, what are they? What skin?"

"Ostrich. Ugly damn bird. But pretty skin. Soft, too."

"Is that common?"

"Not as much as cowhide. But more than some snake skins. And eel or lizard. There's a pretty long list."

Payne shook his head.

"I had no idea," he said.

"Let's talk about why I'm here," Byrth said suddenly.

Homicide Detective Matt Payne raised his eyebrows, surprised at the ninety-degree change of subject. He said, "Sure."

"By the way," Byrth said, "where're we headed?"

"The Roundhouse. It's Philly's police headquarters. You'll understand why we call it that when you see it. We're maybe fifteen minutes out."

Byrth nodded.

"So," Payne said, taking the last bite of pretzel, "what did bring you here?"

"Texas government code section four one one dot zero two two," he rattled off. "Authority of Texas Rangers." He paused and looked at Payne chewing his pretzel. "It even covers your chewy there."

Payne glanced at him with a curious look.

"Subsection (b)," Byrth went on, "and I quote: An officer of the Texas Rangers who arrests a person charged with a criminal offense shall immediately convey the person to the proper officer of the county where the person is charged and shall obtain a receipt. The state shall pay all necessary expenses incurred under this subsection."

"What about the bad guy Liz Justice mentioned?" Payne replied. "The one who cuts off heads? What the hell is that all about?"

"That's only part of it. It's my personal opinion that this guy is a ticking time bomb. He's a psychopath with one helluva temper." Then, surprising Payne, he made the sounds *"Tick, tick, tick . . . BOOM!"*

"This guy got a name?"

"El Gato."

"What?"

"The Cat. That's his street name."

"What about a real name?"

Byrth shook his head. "Nope. Not yet, anyways. But his MO's pretty consistent. Won't be hard to track him down. As far as we can determine, he's not MDTO. He just has connections with them."

Payne of course recognized MO — the short version of the Latin *modus operandi,* the critter's "method." But the other acronym was new to him.

"MDTO?"

"Mexican drug-trafficking organization."

Payne nodded. Then he said, "You just quoted 'a person charged with a criminal offense.' How does the name on this guy's — this El Gato's — warrant read?"

Payne glanced over at Byrth, who looked back and said, "What warrant?"

*What? No warrant?*

*No wonder Liz Justice asked for doors to be opened in Philly.*

*But she would not have done that unless this guy's a straight shooter.*

"How did you track him to here?" Payne said.

"Night before last night, we bagged one of his runners in College Station." He looked at Payne. "Where Texas A and M University is?"

Payne nodded. "Yeah. And home of the Presidential Library, Bush 41's. Its recent chancellor, like old man Bush, used to be DCI. He left A and M to be secretary of defense."

Byrth stared at Payne.

"Secretary of defense?" Byrth repeated. "Director of the Central Intelligence Agency? If that bit of Texas Connection trivia was

359

meant to impress, it worked. About all I can recite about Philly is that there's a broken bell here somewhere."

Payne made a face. "No, not to impress. It's actually information I'd really rather be blissfully ignorant of. At least the Bush Library part. But let's get off this tangent."

"If you don't mind, I'd really like to hear what all that's about."

"Sorry. Maybe later. You were saying about the runner?"

Byrth raised his eyebrows in a sort of surrender.

"Okay," he then went on, "we tracked this runner while he was en route to Houston. One Ramos Manuel Cachón, just turned age seventeen. He's got the usual list of priors, mostly petty stuff like truancy and assaults. He'd made a stop in College Station to service his retailers —"

"Explain that," Payne interrupted as he changed lanes to pick up the Vine Street Expressway.

"Convenience stores, places that he wholesaled to. Some cocaine. But mostly blue cheese."

"Blue cheese?" Payne said with some enthusiasm. "I love blue cheese. But something tells me we're not talking about Roquefort."

"Unfortunately, no. It's a snortable combination of diphenhydramine and heroin —"

"*Die*-what-dramine?"

"Die is right. It's a killer. Smack mixed with cold medicine."

Payne nodded.

Byrth went on: "This cheese crap all started in Dallas, and grew quickly. The dealers began targeting inner-city kids, mostly Hispanics. That's where this El Gato got involved. He marketed it with a friendly look and name — 'Queso Azul.' The coloring comes from a blue sugar candy he mixes in it. But the smack in the mix makes it highly addictive. Right from the first hit."

"How much does it cost? Heroin isn't cheap."

"Ain't none of it cheap. But here's the math. A kilo of coke costs from fifteen to twenty grand. A key of smack from Mexico — which tends to be the cheaper black tar stuff but still is every bit as deadly as any from, say, Afghanistan — can be had for about that much, and on up to fifty, sixty grand a key. All depending on supply and demand, of course."

"Of course," Payne said darkly.

"So, understanding the target demographic — kids — they take the cheapest black tar they can get and make the cheese. Then they sell it at an affordable two bucks a bump."

*"Target demographic"?*
*Sounds like Chad's buzzwords.*
*And probably Skipper's. . . .*

"Cheese is about ten percent heroin," Byrth went on. "Get them hooked on that, then when their body craves more, move them up to the real thing. And once they've had a good taste of the lovely effects of withdrawal, they're up to a hundred- or two-hundred-a-day habit."

"Jesus! That's insidious. Snorting smack makes it easiser to get hooked. I've always thought that most people stayed away from heroin because of its difficulty. Especially the needle part."

*Although that needle phobia didn't stop my lovely Penny Detweiler from doing herself in with that shit.*

"Yeah, Matt, it is insidious. El Gato and his ilk started out supplying inner-city convenience stores. Ones close to middle schools and high schools. Next thing we knew, the nonprofit and state-funded rehab clinics and the halfway houses were maxed out. They were overrun with young Hispanic kids who had nowhere else to go. Their families, often single moms, were already on some type of government program — things like Emergency Assistance to Needy Families with Children, Section Eight Housing, et cetera.

And it got worse because these rehab clinics and halfway houses are geared for teenagers, college kids, adults. Not for middle-schoolers. So that became a problem — first keeping the age groups separated, and then protecting the youngest from being preyed on."

"I'm afraid to ask, but in what way?"

"Free smack. It wasn't unusual at all for the girls to be bribed. They either were lured away from the overfilled facilities, or they ran away. And after they turned that first trick, they found they'd do anything for their next high. And some boys were no better."

"Jesus! Middle-schoolers? What is that, twelve, thirteen years old?"

"Yeah. And sadly, it really wasn't considered a 'problem' until cheese became chic in the suburbs, until kids there started getting strung out — and dying. And suddenly it was a problem. The difference was that the families in suburbia could by and large afford to send their kids off to a decent rehab. And having your golden straight-A teenager in drug rehab simply became a soccer mom's dirty little secret."

"What drove the kids to do that?"

"The usual. Peer pressure. The desire to fit a clique. That cute little blonde with the ponytail? The one trying to keep the weight off to make the cheerleader or gymnastics squad? The cheese works like cocaine to suppress the appetite — plus the added benefit of a great high."

Payne shook his head. He drove along in silence.

*Is that what happened, ultimately, with Becca?*

*Did Skipper do that to her?*

"So," Payne finally said as he exited off the expressway, "getting back to the runner you collared at A and M."

"The punk had tried to throw away his cell phone during the chase; actually did toss it, but we recovered it. It was a pay-as-you-go one, paid for with cash. But the call list on the phone's internal memory had a steady string of calls to the area codes here. And I'm betting that the phone records we subpoenaed from the cellular service provider will have more of them."

"What about the cache of texts?"

Byrth nodded. "The text messages could have been a mini gold mine. But because this punk wasn't very far up the ladder, there wasn't much detail. When our computer forensic people worked on the memory chip, they uncovered a few new names and numbers and data that had been 'deleted.' So we're working on connecting those dots."

Payne made the turn off Race onto Eighth, then just down the block made a left into the asphalt parking lot behind the Philadelphia Police Department headquarters.

"Ah," Byrth said. "So this is the famous Roundhouse."

Payne pulled into a slot marked HOMI-CIDE. He shut off the car and turned to Byrth. "So does that cover all of this El Gato's MO?"

Byrth shook his head. "Oh, hell no. Wait till you hear the good stuff. Starting with the sexual assault bordering on torture."

# VII

## [ONE]
## 826 Sears Street, Philadelphia
## Wednesday, September 9,
## 3:51 P.M.

Paco Esteban could hear the sounds of the crowd even before he unlocked and opened the front door of his home.

Inside, he was not surprised to find that the voices belonged to eight members of his extended family, all women and all of whom had been in the laundromat that morning. Most filled the parlor in the back, sitting on the couch and in the stackable plastic chairs. Almost all were fingering a rosary. There was a Bible in one's lap.

All but one, who was sobbing into her hands, glanced at Esteban as he entered. They nodded, then went back to their noisy conversations.

Paco Esteban walked into the kitchen, where he found Señora Salma Esteban. He smiled warmly at his wife as she approached him. He saw that her face was still puffy from crying. It was all the more evident as she'd pulled her dark hair back and pinned it into a bun. She wore the same dingy beige sleeveless cotton dress that she'd had on earlier.

"What did you find out?" she asked in Spanish. "Did you find out who this evil man really is?"

Paco Esteban went to his wife. He wrapped his arms around her and squeezed affectionately. Then he kissed her softly on the cheek.

"How is Rosario?" he said.

She nodded. "*Bueno.* She is sleeping upstairs. What did you learn?"

He kissed her cheek again.

"My love, I went and met with Señor Nesbitt, the man who is the business partner of Señor Skipper."

"And?" she said anxiously.

"And he said it will be all right. That I am not to do anything until he says."

"What!" Señora Salma Esteban almost screeched. She grabbed her husband's sleeve and pulled him to the doorway leading to the parlor.

She then said in rapid-fire Spanish: "Look at this! Our family! And their families! Everyone is terrified for their lives!"

Paco Esteban saw some of the women look his way. And their eyes did indeed look terrified.

He moved back into the kitchen, almost tugging along his wife with him.

"My love, there is only so much that I can do. . . ."

"Paco! We cannot live this way! We cannot be so fearful that we do not know what will happen to us the next minute."

"My love, it is not that I disagree with you. I would like answers, too. And peace. But Señor Nesbitt said that he would call me." He pulled out the cell phone that Skipper Olde had given him. "He said for me not to do anything until he called."

"Where is Señor Skipper?" Salma Esteban said. "Why can he not help?"

Paco Esteban shook his head. "He is in hospital, Señor Nesbitt said. He is unable to speak with me for now."

"*Madre de Dios!*" Salma Esteban exclaimed, looking at the ceiling.

She looked back at her husband and said, "And now we have your sister's daughter coming here!"

The look of shock was apparent on Paco Esteban's face.

"You have forgotten this!" Salma Esteban said.

He did not know what to say.

*"Maybe: My love, it has been a bad day"?*

Meekly, he nodded. "*Sí*. I am sorry. But it will be okay."

She began pacing the kitchen. She walked with her arms crossed, her hands nervously rubbing her upper arms.

Paco Esteban tried to stop her and wrap his arms around her. This time she would not allow him to do so. Her tears had started again.

"Paco! You must do something. You have always been able to do something when we've had difficulty. We cannot sit and wait like this. Please? You must go and do something . . . anything!"

*Yes, I have always thought that I could do something.*

*But this is something very bad. Very evil.*
*What could I possibly do?*

He heard wailing coming from the other room.

Then he saw his wife's face, her eyes darting in the direction of the parlor as she nodded sharply toward it.

*She's saying, "There! See!"*
*And she's right. I must go.*

There was another wail.

*If only because I cannot stand much more of this here.*

"My love, you are right. I go now."

She went to him and hugged him. He felt her sobbing on his chest.

When she finally pushed back, he saw her tears flowing down her cheek. They caused him to tear. He kissed the tears on her left check.

Then he went to the kitchen drawer and removed the keys to the minivan.

As a matter of habit — and because he could not immediately think of any other place to drive — he headed in the general direction of the laundromat.

Along the way, he tried to think what his options were.

*Not many.*

He said prayers to God. He said prayers

to every saint he could think of. Anyone who could help him think of how he could begin to find this evil man.

And still he came up with nothing.

As he drove north on Broad Street and came closer to the laundromat on Susquehanna, the knot in his stomach became bigger and tighter.

He was not sure if that was because he was getting closer to the scene of where the evil man had turned their lives upside down, or because he was getting farther from finding any solution.

Then he saw the sign for the business that shared a wall with Sudsie's — the Temple Gas & Go.

And he suddenly realized that Rosario had already given him the answer.

*Praise God!*

He continued driving up Broad Street. He made a right on Erie Avenue, headed for Castor Avenue.


Paco "El Nariz" Esteban pulled the minivan up to the island of gas pumps at the Gas & Go in the 3900 block of Castor Avenue.

It was the same convenience store, of course, where the previous Thursday Rosario had run for her life. And had jumped into Paco's minivan.

Later, when Rosario had told Paco and Salma Esteban her stories, she had described how she and Ana had been kept at an old row house somewhere in the city. She did not know where in Philadelphia. Nor did she have a good idea of where in the city she and Rosario and the other girls were taken to work. Only that they were all some type of convenience store with regular customers.

But Paco Esteban knew the exact location of this particular Gas & Go. And he had decided that all he had to do was wait for the car or van — *Rosario said they used a van* — to pick up the girls. Then he could follow it back to that prison of a row house.

And that would lead him to the evil man who Rosario said called himself El Gato.

*What I will do then, I do not know.*

*But first I must find him.*

*God help me . . .*

El Nariz turned off the vehicle, opened the door, and got out. He reached into his wallet and pulled out a twenty-dollar bill to prepay for his gasoline.

Then he walked to the door of the convenience store.

As he grabbed the metal handle, he suddenly realized he was not only scared. He was terrified. He was sweating, and it wasn't because of the hot late-afternoon sun. This sweat, he noticed with some unpleasantness, had a foul smell to it.

He understood why he was terrified.

*It was only early this morning that the evil man almost shot me.*

*What would happen if it is him inside this store?*

He shook his head and tried to be reasonable.

*But what chances are there of that?*

*I do not know.*

*And that also scares me.*

He pulled open the door and walked in with all the confidence he could muster. He found that he was forcing himself to focus looking ahead, on the counter with the cash register. He did not want to look to the right, to the corner. The last time, that was where, under a sign with an arrow to the XXX video room, the Hispanic male in his mid-twenties stood, keeping an intense watch on the door he just came in.

The pungent kimchee and garlic smells still hung heavily in the air. But the arrogant young Asian man wasn't behind the register. Now there was an older Asian who looked to be maybe forty. And not so arrogant, like the other one, who acted as if he had something to prove.

As El Nariz stood at the counter, he had the sensation that he was being stared at. The feeling did not help ease his nerves.

He gave the man at the register the twenty-dollar bill and said, "Unleaded." '

The man nodded, then put the bill under a clip on the wall behind him that was labeled UNLEADED. Next to it was a similar clip, labeled SUPREME. Then the man punched buttons on the machine connected to the gas pumps that would allow El Nariz to pump twenty bucks' worth of fuel.

*Maybe he will not try cheating me of my money this time.*

*The arrogant young one last time did not use those clips.*

As Paco Esteban turned from the register, he tried to scan the store casually. He kept his head down so as not to make any eye contact.

But there they were: a pair of impossibly young Latinas who looked somewhat like Rosario.

*They cannot be fourteen!*

*I pray for you. . . .*

They sat at the same folding table, absently flipping through old magazines.

And there in the corner was a Hispanic male keeping watch.

*Not El Gato.*

*But I think not the one from last week, either.*

Paco Esteban, head down, went quickly to the door and outside.

As he worked the gas pump, removing the hose handle and turning the lever, he tried to calm himself. His heart was beating heavily. His hands were clammy.

*Okay, so they are there.*

*Now what?*

*I pump my twenty dollars and leave?*

*Then what?*

He scanned the area, trying desperately to decide what to do next.

*And Señor Nesbitt said to do nothing.*

*Maybe that is what a smart man would do.*

*Señor Nesbitt is a smart man.*

*Maybe if I could show him what is happening here . . .*

*Pictures!*

*If only I could get a picture of the young girls and their guard.*

*Then I show them to Rosario. If she knows the girls or the guard, then I tell Señor Nesbitt.*

*Such a smart man could get the pictures to someone who could help them.*

*But how do I get pictures?*

*And how do I go back inside if the man does*

*not try to cheat me?*

*I would be expected to put in twenty dollars,*
*then leave.*

He heard his cell phone ringing. He glanced
inside the minivan. The phone was where
he'd left it in the cup holder on the dash.

He let go of the pump handle and opened
the driver's side door. He grabbed the phone,
but the call had already gone into voice mail.
He looked at the phone, waiting to read who
had called.

Then he noticed the tiny glass circle on the
phone's back.

*The camera lens!*

*I can use the camera of the phone!*

*But how do I go back in the store? To buy a*
*Coke? A beer?*

*That may not look good. . . .*

The screen lit up, and he read that it was
his wife who had called.

*She I can call back.*

*She is probably asking what I have done.*

*With luck, soon I have something to tell her.*

He slipped the phone into his pocket and
went back to the pump handle. He looked at
the register on the pump. It read $14.50.

*That is it! I overpay. And now I must go back*
*in for my change.*

Paco Esteban had his cell phone to his

ear as he walked back through the Gas & Go's door. He had it up to his right ear, his right thumb on the button that triggered the camera to capture an image. At the pump island, he had gone through the camera menu to ensure that the camera sounds were muted. Now he casually spoke to no one on the phone while thumbing the camera button repeatedly as he crossed the floor.

At the register, he held the phone to his chest so that there was no chance the Asian would see the screen with a photograph of the store.

When he had explained he'd had more gas in the minivan than he'd thought because the gas gauge never worked, the Asian man nodded. The man pulled the twenty from the clip marked UNLEADED and made change.

El Nariz moved his phone to his left hand. Then he took his six-fifty and stuffed it into his left front pants pocket.

*"Gracias,"* he said.

He put the phone to his left ear, put his thumb to the camera button, then snapped away as he walked casually to the front door.

And went out it — smiling for the first time in a long time.

■ ■ ■ ■

Five minutes later, after parking down the street just out of sight of the Gas & Go, he walked to the alleyway behind the shopping strip.

Each of the steel doors along the back side of the shopping strip had some sort of signage. A few read NO DELIVERIES FROM 11 TO 2. Others read NO PARKING! DO NOT BLOCK! And almost all had the name of the business that they belonged to.

El Nariz found the one that read GAS & GO. Then, keeping what he thought was a safe distance, he found a spot to sit between three big trash Dumpsters. It was smelly there. But he already reeked from the nervous sweating. And this spot provided him with a good view of the back doors to the Gas & Go. There was even a cracked mop bucket that, turned upside down, he could use for a seat.

*With luck, tonight I see something.*

*Maybe get a picture of what van they drive.*

*Maybe get the license plate.*

He smiled.

*Maybe even follow them to the row house.*

Then he started looking through the photographs he'd just taken with the phone to see how they had come out.

# [TWO]
## Philadelphia Police Headquarters
## Eighth and Race Streets, Philadelphia
## Wednesday, September 9, 4:04 P.M.

"On behalf of the department, Sergeant Byrth, allow me to say that it's an honor for us to be able to help out our Texas brethren in any way," Lieutenant Jason Washington intoned as he shook the Texas Ranger's hand. "Any friend of Liz Justice, et cetera, et cetera. And I have the utmost confidence that Sergeant Payne here will see to it that you have everything you need during your visit to the City of Brotherly Love."

Payne, as he'd promised Washington on the phone, had brought Byrth to the Homicide Unit on the second floor of the Roundhouse. The three were in Washington's glass-walled office.

"I appreciate that very much, Lieutenant," Jim Byrth replied.

"And, please, call me Jason," Washington said, waving them both into chairs.

Byrth nodded once. "Only if you'll call me Jim."

"Very well, Jim." Washington paused, and looked to be gathering his thoughts. "I have some understanding as to why you're here."

"Yes, sir," Byrth said, but his inflection made it more of a question.

"And I'm afraid you may have arrived a little late," Washington went on.

"I don't follow you."

"Just shy of noon today, one of our Marine Unit vessels recovered the headless body of a young Hispanic female from the Schuylkill River."

"Fuck!" Byrth angrily blurted. His face was clearly furious — his squinted eyes cold and hard, his brow furrowed.

"Sonofabitch," Payne added with his own look of disgust.

Byrth then relaxed somewhat and said, "Jason, please forgive that outburst, it's just —"

Washington motioned with his right hand in a gesture that said, *No apology necessary.* "That word has been thrown around here once or twice. Even I, in a fit of anger or frustration, have been known to make use of it."

"I'm not apologizing," Payne said. "That's just despicable. What animal does that? And to a young girl?"

"I want this guy bad," Byrth said.

Washington looked Byrth in the eyes a long moment, then said, "As unsettling as the thought is, there's always the possibility that it's another doer. But whoever did it, I agree with you, Jim. We both, as you say, want him bad."

"Any details on the victim yet?" Payne said.

"Very little, Matthew," Washington said. "Only that she was found in a black garbage bag weighted with dumbbells. Apparently, the current had pushed her onto a shoal in the river."

"Jesus!" Payne said, shaking his head. Then he said, "Has the media got its hands on the story?"

Washington shook his head. "We've squashed it."

"Story like that is going to get out," Payne said. "It's too sensational."

"Agreed," Byrth said. "And it's just what we don't want. It'd be better if the doer thinks she's still at the bottom of the river."

"Jason," Payne then said, "I've been giving Jim background on what a typical boring day it's been around here today —"

Washington grunted.

"— and," Payne went on, "I'd planned on giving him an overview of what we have in the way of working cases and of assets he might find helpful. I thought that part of that would be showing him the Executive Command Center. Now, with this news, that seems essential. You see any problem with us using the ECC?"

Washington was quiet a moment as he considered that.

Then he picked up the phone and punched a short string of numbers.

"Commissioner Walker? Jason Washington. Sorry to bother you, sir, but I have what I fear may be an unusual request." He paused to listen. "Yes, sir. I do appreciate that. But I thought it best to ask, if only to give you a heads-up. Commissioner Coughlin has Sergeant Matthew Payne —" He paused again, having apparently been interrupted. Washington's eyes glanced at Matt as he went on: "Yes, sir, that Payne. As I was saying, the commissioner has Payne working a special project. And Payne has requested access to the ECC." He paused to listen, then added, "Understood, sir. He would of course relinquish control if it were needed by the police commissioner or others." He listened, then finished by saying, "I will indeed tell him, sir. Thank you for your time and your help."

Washington hung up the phone and looked at Payne.

"Okay, Matthew, the ECC's laid on for you. All you need to do is call up there first to make sure that either Corporal Rapier or his assistant is available to run the machines. And in the event something comes up, you're to relinquish use to whoever needs access."

"Got it," Payne said as he began to stand. "Thank you, Jason."

"Just stay out of trouble, Matthew." He looked at Byrth. "You do realize you're running with dangerous company, Jim?"

Byrth smiled.

"I'll take my chances," he said as he stood up. "Thanks again for your hospitality, Jason."

Washington leaned back in his chair as he watched Payne lead the Texas Ranger across Homicide. Payne stopped at an unoccupied desk and used the phone to call Corporal Rapier.

*That Byrth is an interesting man,* Washington thought.

*But there was something in his eyes when he said, "I want this guy bad."*

*What could that be about?*

*Or am I projecting something on him that's not really there?*

*Because I also really want this doer bad.*

Corporal Kerry Rapier was at his electronic control console when Sergeant Payne and Sergeant Byrth entered the Executive Command Center on the third floor.

"Hey, Matt!" Rapier said. "So you're coming to play with my toys?"

"I'll let you play with them, Kerry. We'll just watch." He looked to Byrth. "Sergeant Jim Byrth, this is Corporal Kerry Rapier."

The big Texan held The Hat in the crook of his left arm as he nearly crushed the right paw of the tiny blue shirt.

"Pleasure," Byrth said with a nod.

When they had finished, and Rapier was flexing his hand to get the blood flowing again, Rapier said, "You're not from around here, are you, Sergeant?"

Payne said, "Jim's a sergeant with the Texas Rangers."

Byrth shifted The Hat under his arm and looked around the room. "Nothing gets past you, does it, Corporal?"

Rapier grinned.

"Glad you noticed," he said. Then, with a tone that showed professional pride, he began: "We have one of the finest command centers in the country —"

"For which we have you in part to thank, Jim," Payne interrupted.

"How so?"

"Your tax dollars. The fine folks in Washington sent us all kinds of federal funds to ramp up for the protection of the Democrats' national convention here."

"How damned kind of them," Byrth said dryly.

Rapier went on officiously: "We have approximately four million dollars invested in all of the electronics. That is just in this room and what's on the roof. There's another couple million worth of commo equipment — cameras to radios — in the field. We can accommodate fifty-two officers at these conference tables, and another forty in the seating along the walls."

"That's one helluva crowd," Byrth said.

Rapier nodded. "That's capacity, from Philly cops to the feds. We generally run with maybe half that many people, all Philly cops. The Secret Service, FBI, and DHS have their own war rooms in Philly, of course."

"Of course," Byrth said, shaking his head.

Rapier waved at the banks of frameless flat-screen TVs. They were dark.

"Sixty-inch high-definition LCDs, nine to a bank, with the capability of up to twenty-seven unique video feeds. We can have live feeds from all sorts of unclassified and classified sources, everything from our helos in the sky down to the bomb squad robots. All absolutely secure."

He moved his hands over the control console.

"Let me show you the various live video feeds," he said.

He threw a bank of switches. The darkened flat-screen TVs all blinked to life.

When the main screen of nine flat panels lit up with a single huge image, Payne could not help but let out a laugh. He thought he was going to wet his pants.

Rapier looked up from the console — and his face lost all color.

"Dammit!" Corporal Kerry Rapier said. "I'm, uh, I'm really sorry about that, Sergeant Payne. Particularly it happening in front of a Texas Ranger."

"What is that?" Byrth said.

Rapier looked somewhat nervously at Payne.

Payne grinned. He turned to Byrth and said, "Looks to me like an episode of *It's Always Sunny in Philadelphia*. Right, Kerry?"

"Yeah," Rapier said, clearly embarrassed.

He gestured to a notebook computer on the console. "I've got the series saved on my personal laptop's hard drive. It's wired to the console here. When you called just now, I was on my afternoon break and watching. . . ."

"No harm done, Kerry," Payne said, still grinning. "I'm actually a fan, too. Especially of Sweet Dee."

The sitcom revolved around a boneheaded crew of schemers trying to run an Irish bar called Paddy's Pub — the worst bar in South Philly, if not all of Philly. Corporal Kerry Rapier glowed at Payne's mention of the name of the white-hot but dim-witted blond main character.

Payne described her to Byrth.

"Ah," Byrth said. "She'd be what a buddy of mine would call 'a radio station.'"

"A what?"

"One anyone can pick up, especially at night," Byrth said with a grin. "You know, naturally horizontal."

Payne and Rapier chuckled.

Rapier punched a button on the console and the main bank of TVs with the show on it went dark.

Payne then said: "How about punching up whatever you have on the girl they pulled out of the Schuylkill."

"So, you heard about that?" Rapier said. "They've put that case on a need-to-know basis."

"I know," Payne said. "And we're on that need-to-know list."

Rapier considered that a moment, then nodded. There was no need to call and have it confirmed. Everyone knew Sergeant Payne was Homicide — and with friends in high places. Even if he wasn't on the list, Rapier figured he'd probably have quietly honored Payne's request anyway.

Rapier then manipulated switches on the console, and the aerial image of the river with the Marine Unit's Boston Whaler came up. The shot was frozen.

In the lower right-hand corner of the screen, a block of text popped up:

---

**Schuylkill River at Grays Ferry Avenue Bridge**
**1158 hours, 24 Sept**

---

"As you can see by the time stamp," Rapier said, "this is from earlier, during the recovery of the body."

He threw another switch, and the image went into motion. The silver twenty-four-foot-long Boston Whaler, its light bar flashing red and blue, slowly moved backward. A shoal in the river became visible. The vessel then turned. The camera captured images of the officers onboard the boat pulling in a very full and very large black trash bag.

"Jesus!" Payne said.

"Yeah," Rapier said. "Disgusting, huh? Toss away a human being like so much trash."

"Is there anything else, any other details, on this case besides what's on the text block?" Byrth said.

"Very little," Rapier replied. "There are some shots of the medical examiner coming on the scene, but nothing of note. Javier told me . . ." He paused and looked at Payne.

Payne said, "Javier Iglesia. I know him." He looked at Byrth. "He's a technician in the Medical Examiner's Office. Good guy, even though his humor runs on the really dark side."

Rapier then went on: "Javier told me the body is that of a Hispanic female. He said he's guessing that she can't be even twenty years old. They haven't done the autopsy yet. But they did take her fingerprints, and ran them." He looked at his wristwatch. "That was almost two hours ago, so we should know at any time if we got a match on IAFIS."

The Integrated Automated Fingerprint Identification System was run by the FBI. With more than 55 million subjects — voluntarily submitted by local, state, and federal law-enforcement agencies — it was the largest biometric database in the world. Accessible twenty-four/seven year-round, it could on a good day provide a response to the submission of a criminal ten-print fingerprint within a couple hours.

"With any luck, we'll get a hit," Corporal Rapier said. "Then it's 'In God We Trust — everyone else we run through NCIC.' "

Byrth chuckled.

"Amen to that," he said.

Like IAFIS, the National Crime Information Center also was maintained by the FBI and available to law enforcement at any time. Its database contained critical records on criminals, including fugitives, as well as stolen property and missing persons. The data was provided by the same sources as those feeding IAFIS, plus whatever courts were authorized to contribute and some foreign law-enforcement agencies.

Then Byrth said, "If the doer is who I think it is, I wouldn't hold your breath on getting that hit, Corporal."

"Can I ask why?" Rapier said.

"The guy I'm hunting likes to lop off the heads of undocumented aliens. My money is on the real possibility that this poor girl has no paper trail."

Rapier looked at him but didn't know what to say. He looked to Payne.

"There was one other thing Javier did say," Rapier added.

"What?" Byrth immediately said.

Rapier looked to Payne, who made a face that said, *Well?*

"He noticed something unusual as he casually inspected the body before putting it in the body bag," Rapier said.

"What?" Byrth repeated.

"Grass clippings. Javier told me that it was weird but there were some grass clippings, you know, where her head had been."

"That is weird," Payne said. "Maybe she was dragged through grass at some point? Or they were in the garbage bag?"

"No, not loose clippings," Rapier said. "More like deep in the bone. Like what cut her was a tool that had had grass on the blade. And that grass got embedded."

Payne looked at Byrth, who raised his eyebrows and made a face that said, *Hell if I know . . .*

They were all silent a moment. They looked absently at the other two banks of

TVs. These showed the local and cable news show broadcasts, and the DOT highway and city traffic shots. Payne scanned the feeds. He found the ones of the Philly Inn, the Reading Terminal Market, and the Temple University Hospital. Their imagery was frozen.

"Anything else in particular you wanted to see?" Corporal Rapier said.

"Panel eighteen," Payne said. "Is that what I think it is?"

Rapier punched a button on his console and the image on panel eighteen was replicated on the main bank of TVs, taking the place of the body recovery by the Marine Unit on the Schuylkill River. And Rapier punched another button, unfreezing the somewhat grainy black-and-white exterior shot of the Temple University Hospital.

Payne turned to Byrth as the cars and people began moving.

"This is the hospital I told you about," Payne said.

Then the Hispanic assassin in royal blue scrubs kicked open the exit door and ran down the street.

"And that's the sonofabitch I shot this morning!"

They watched the scene unfold.

When it was over, and started to loop,

Byrth whistled.

"Pretty impressive, Marshal Earp. And that was a nice dodge of that taxi."

"Not really," Payne said. "I mean, I didn't get the sonofabitch off the street."

"Internal Affairs came and got a copy of that," Corporal Rapier said. "I don't know squat about how they do their job — I've heard some good stories, some horror ones — but that loop should get you cleared quickly."

"Thanks, Kerry. I certainly hope so." He looked back at the other banks of screens. "Can you put up the Philly Inn?"

Rapier did. And then for Byrth's benefit, Payne went over the main facts of that scene. Rapier filled in any gaps. Then they did the same with the Reading Terminal Market scene.

When they had finished, Byrth grunted. "Almost as busy as one of our days just on the south side of Houston."

"Still no surveillance imagery from the Reading Terminal Market," Rapier then said. "But there are new images of evidence from the scene."

"Such as?" Payne said.

"Still digital photos of the spent shell casings. And the drugs. Let me punch it up."

Rapier manipulated the console and the main image replicated the smaller one from panel number sixteen. The image of the Reading Terminal Market on-screen now was updated with a still shot taken at the crime scene. It even included rubber-gloved investigators working it.

The text box popped up in the right-hand corner, and Payne's eyes went to the text, which read:

> **Cause: Shooting. one hundred percent probability drug-related. heroin-based product recovered at the scene. also 42 5.7- x 28-mm shell casings and 10 9-mm shell casings, and a Rwuger P89 9-mm semi-auto pistol.**

Payne noticed that the underlines looked like they were hyperlinks. Rapier was manipulating an on-screen cursor over them.

"Those are hyperlinks?" Payne said. .

"Yeah. As the information is added to the master case file, the links are added. These links weren't there earlier. This is sweet. Watch."

He clicked on RUGER P89 and an image of the pistol popped up as an inset. Along the bottom of the image frame was a series of digitized buttons.

The pistol was on a concrete floor, an inverted V plastic marker beside it bearing a black numeral 44. The pistol's slide was in the full-back locked position, indicating the semiautomatic had fired all of its bullets.

"They shoot these with digital cameras, taking four overlapping angles so we can construct on the computer a three-dimensional rendering. Watch."

He worked the joystick on the console. The pistol practically spun on the screen, allowing almost all angles of view.

Payne said, "Now, that's pretty cool."

"Yeah," Rapier said proudly. "And if there's detail on the evidence, you can drill down. Like this . . ."

He moved the cursor to the series of digitized buttons. He clicked on the one with a question mark on it. A text box popped up over the image of the pistol. It was translucent; they could still see the pistol. The text read:

---

**Ruger P89 9-mm semiautomatic pistol.**

**Serial Number R34561234**

**Sold 02 JUN**

---

Seller: Philadelphia Archery and Gun Shop, 831-833 Ellsworth Street, Phila., Penna.

Buyer: Harold Thompson, 1201 Allendale St, Phila., Penna.

Notes: Owner Thompson Reported Weapon Stolen 15 AUG from Owner's Personal Vehicle Parked in Front of Allendale St. Residence.

"Jesus," Payne said somewhat disgustedly. "Another careless owner lets his gun get stolen, and not two weeks later it kills innocent people. Another reason why citizens probably shouldn't be allowed to have guns."

Byrth raised an eyebrow. "I take it you don't believe in the Second Amendment, Matt?"

"To a degree. But with all the illegal guns and shootings in this city? Are you kidding me?"

Rapier said, "Matt —"

Byrth interrupted him. "That didn't answer my question. So you're telling me that the guns are the problem? You just said 'it' killed."

Payne looked at him a long moment.

"You're telling me," Byrth pursued, "that if a law were passed that miraculously made every gun go away — *poof!* — all the problems would disappear, too?"

"It wouldn't hurt," Payne said more than a little lamely. He motioned toward the TV. "This gun wouldn't have been on the street."

"Matt —" Rapier began again.

"Let me see if I can finish that thought," Byrth interrupted him again. "Only cops should have guns, right? Because only they can use and care for them reasonably. Because cops never make mistakes." He paused. "I guess you missed that little anecdote from the Super Bowl. The FBI boys at the Holiday Inn?"

Matt shook his head.

Byrth explained: "The hotshots left their cache in the van in the parking lot. Long about oh-dark-thirty, while they were having sweet G-man dreams of their hero J. Edgar Hoover, their van got burgled. The thief made off with four .308-caliber sniper rifles, a pair of fully auto M4 carbines, and — you'll appreciate this, Marshal — a pair of Springfield .45s. The thief then sold 'em all to his cousin the drug dealer."

"Jim, I'm not suggesting that that doesn't —"

"Wait," Byrth interrupted, putting up his hand, palm out, "I'm on a roll here. And maybe you missed that hilarious video clip of the DEA agent with the dreadlocks. He's in a classroom setting, wearing the obligatory T-shirt with the big D-E-A lettering in case anyone should forget who they are. And he's warning the students how dangerous guns are, that only the select few should have access to them. Then, to demonstrate, he pulls out his Glock — and promptly puts a round through his foot. Then he commences with what we real professionals call the I-Just-Shot-Myself Silly Dance."

"Hey, I've got that on my laptop, attached to an e-mail," Corporal Rapier said. "It is pretty funny. Want me to punch it up on-screen?"

He immediately regretted speaking when he saw Payne's expression.

"Matt," Byrth said, "I'd suggest you do a little research. Take a look, for example, at our friends in England. They passed a law that pretty much turned every citizen's gun into scrap metal. And you know what then happened? Crime went up. So now the brilliant political minds in Parliament that brought gun control are tinkering with a law banning the carrying of pocketknives. Why? Because that's become the punks' new assault weapon of choice."

"That's a bit of comparing apples and oranges."

"Is it really? And when they ban pocketknives, what next? Cardboard box cutters? Those came in pretty handy on the aircraft that the terrorists hijacked on 9/11. The problem is not the weapon."

"Look, Jim, I take your point," Payne said. "I still maintain, however, that this Ruger would not —"

"Matt," Rapier now interrupted, "I've been trying to tell you that Harold Thompson is a Twenty-fourth District blue shirt."

Payne did not say anything for a very long moment. Then he laughed.

"Okay, okay. I surrender."

Jim Byrth sighed, then said, "Matt, I apologize for all that. I'm the guest here."

"No apology necessary. I guess I deserved that," Payne said. He smiled. "Besides, I've been known to let loose with some strong opinions myself. Political correctness be damned."

He looked at Rapier. "Let's get back to the images."

"You got it," Rapier said, and clicked on 5.7- X 28-MM SHELL CASINGS.

An image of scattered spent shell casings popped up in another inset.

"That 5.7-millimeter round was developed by FN to pierce body armor," Rapier said. "You don't see many of them."

"That's because there're only about five weapons chambered for the five-point-seven round," Byrth said. "If we find one, odds are those casings will belong to it. Click on the smack link, would you?"

They watched as Rapier moved the cursor to HEROIN-BASED PRODUCT. The image of the white packets scattered on the concrete floor appeared.

"Is that the best shot?" Byrth said. "Can you do what you did with the three-dimensional shot of the Ruger?"

Rapier clicked on a button that had a plus sign on it. The image zoomed in on one of the white packets. Then he used the joystick to turn the packet so that they had a better view of it.

The packet had a rubber stamp imprint in light blue ink of a cartoonish block of Swiss cheese. To either side of the cheese block were three lines that shot outward. Above the cheese was a legend in blue ink.

"*Queso azul,*" Payne read, then said, "That's the blue cheese you told me about."

"Bingo," Byrth said.

"What's blue cheese?" Rapier said.

"Cold medicine mixed with black tar heroin and sold to kids at two bucks a bump," Payne said. He looked at Byrth and asked, "What's with the three lines on either side? They look like cartoon sun rays."

"Whiskers."

"Whiskers?"

Byrth nodded. "El Gato. Cat whiskers. That's his product. So it's here. But where the hell is he?"

"Jesus," Payne said. He added, "You think he shot up the market?"

"Could've been anyone," Byrth said. "Anyone with a five-point-seven weapon. It's certainly not outside the scope of what the bastard is capable of doing."

Payne was looking back at the bank of screens with the various TV news broadcasts. The feed from the local FOX News channel showed images of the Philadelphia Fire Department at work. Firemen were battling extraordinarily large flames from two vehicles ablaze in a vacant lot adjacent to run-down row houses. Between the roaring fires and the wall of water being pumped at them, it was difficult to distinguish what type of vehicles they were.

Text along the bottom of the screen read:

EARLIER TODAY IN WEST KENSINGTON, FIREFIGHTERS FOUGHT TO EXTINGUISH THE FLAMES FROM TWO VEHICLES. AUTHORITIES SAY ARSON WAS THE CAUSE.

Matt felt a vibration in the front pocket of his pants. He pulled out his cellular phone and saw that he had a text message. The color LCD screen read: AMY PAYNE — 1 TXT MSG TODAY @ 1730.

He went to it:

---

AMY PAYNE

We still on for Liberties . . . 6ISH?

---

Payne looked again at the time stamp.
*Five thirty.*
*That's right. She said meet at six.*
*We can still beat her there.*
He typed and then sent:

---

see u @ 6

---

"I think we're finished here for now, Kerry," Payne said, slipping the phone back into his pocket. "Thanks for your help."

"Anytime."

Payne looked at Jim Byrth.

"How about we go get a few fingers poured of your choice of adult intoxicants? If we get to Homicide's unofficial favorite spot early enough, we can enjoy our beverages before She Who Is Always Right arrives. Then we can bounce some of this off her."

Byrth nodded appreciatively. "I could use a little something to cut the dust, Marshal."

# [THREE]
## 3900 Block of Castor Avenue, Philadelphia
## Wednesday, September 9, 5:54 P.M.

Sitting in the shadows of the trash Dumpsters in the alleyway, Paco "El Nariz" Esteban twice had had to move. The first time was because the big garbage truck had come to empty the three Dumpsters serving as his cover. That had stirred up the trash and caused the receptacles to really reek.

The second time was because a Philadelphia Police Department squad car came rolling down the alley.

That had caused Paco Nariz too many thoughts. And they came practically all at once.

The immediate one was the thought that always came first: *Are they looking for me?*

Then he thought: *I can tell them about the girls in the store!*

*I can show them pictures!*

*But would they believe me?*

*And would they do anything if they did?*

*If the police went in and made an arrest, then El Gato would lose those girls and their guard.*

*But he would be free.*

*And then I would have to find another way to get to him.*

He had glanced at the cruiser rolling nearer.

*Here they are! Decide, dammit!*

El Nariz had avoided any interaction with the police. He quickly but calmly picked up his mop bucket makeshift seat, then started shaking it in the side door of the Dumpster, pretending to be emptying it.

When he'd glanced at the cruiser rolling past, the cops hadn't even bothered looking back at him.

And he figured that that was logical. Who would waste time to question a dirty Hispanic male who clearly was carrying out his janitorial tasks? They probably could guess at his biggest crime: smelling like shit.

That had been about a half hour ago.

Now El Nariz, back on his bucket between the Dumpsters, heard the sound of another vehicle coming down the alleyway. He looked around the corner of the Dumpsters. He saw a big dirty tan Ford panel van. It had no windows other than the windshield and those on the front driver and passenger doors.

Paco Esteban heard its brakes squeak. It slowed to a stop beside the back door to the Gas & Go. He could not see from his angle but could hear a large sliding door on the van opening. Then he heard a Hispanic male's voice. Looking under the van, he could see black boots on the far side of the van, where the sliding door would be.

El Nariz started to get his camera ready, then decided it wasn't a good idea with so much daylight still. Whoever was behind the wheel of the van might see him.

He looked at the bumper and saw the Pennsylvania tag there. It read GSY-696. He thought that he could write down the license plate number — until he realized he'd left his pen in the minivan.

*Dammit!*

There was more movement on the far side of the van. Visible beside the black boots were two more pairs of shoes. They were very small and low-heeled. Then the back door of the Gas & Go opened. The boots moved in its direction first, and the two pairs of shoes followed.

For a split second, El Nariz had a clear view of the three people — two young girls, one in a black dress and one in a schoolgirl skirt and top, and a very thin young Hispanic male in jeans, black boots, and a T-shirt.

*I need to get back to my minivan if I am to follow them. . . .*

Then El Nariz had an inspiration.

*The phone!*

He scrolled through its menu. He reached the screen that asked if he wanted to add a new telephone number. He clicked the key for OK, then keyed in GSY696.

Then he picked up the mop bucket. He put it on his right shoulder so that it would block his view of the dirty tan Ford van — and block his head from the view of whoever was driving the van. He started walking across the alleyway until he was out of sight of the van, then trotted back to the minivan.

It was ten minutes before Paco Esteban heard the sound of the Ford panel van accelerating down the alley. He started the engine of his minivan — and just in time, as the Ford van flew out of the alley.

*I do not know if the girls are in there.*

*And I do not know where they go next.*

*But what else do I do?*

He put the minivan in drive, checked for traffic, then followed the tan Ford van down Castor Avenue. He tried to maintain a safe distance back. But not so far as to lose sight of the van.

The Ford van made the turn onto Erie Avenue, headed toward Broad Street. At Broad, it went south.

*This is the way I just came, but backward.*

About a mile later, he thought, *Are they going where I think?*

A block later, at Susquehanna, the van made a left, driving past the Temple Gas & Go and the adjoining Sudsie's. At the next corner, which was North Park, it turned right.

*Yes!*

*They are going to that Gas & Go!*

*And using the alley.*

El Nariz knew that that alley gave access to both the Gas & Go's back door and the loading dock of the laundromat. He also knew it was a dead end; the way in was the only way out.

He drove straight through the intersection where the van had turned right, then eased up to the curb and stopped. He put the minivan in park and adjusted the mirror on the windshield so that he could see the alley entrance behind him.

Fifteen minutes passed before the dirty tan Ford panel van came roaring out the alley. It made a right turn.

*Damn!*

Paco Esteban quickly put the minivan in drive and spun the steering wheel counterclockwise. He glanced over his shoulder as he started his U-turn. A blaring horn caused him to slam on the brakes. A pickup truck blew past, the driver angrily pumping his right fist at El Nariz.

El Nariz looked over his left shoulder again and hit the gas.

He made the turn onto Park, and as he passed the alley he saw the dirty tan Ford panel van far ahead. It approached the next intersection, which was Diamond Street, and went left.

El Nariz pressed harder on the accelerator, then braked heavily at the intersection. He blew through the stop sign, turning left onto Diamond. Then he smashed the accelerator, the aged minivan's engine bucking.

*Don't quit on me.*

A dozen blocks later, crossing Germantown Avenue, El Nariz could see he was closing fast on the Ford van. He eased up on the accelerator.

After another dozen or so blocks, the brake lights of the Ford van lit up for a moment. The van turned left in front of a small park.

As El Nariz followed, he saw that the street was marked HANCOCK.

The Ford van crossed over Susquehanna, then three blocks later its brake lights lit up. And stayed lit.

Paco Esteban saw that it had pulled to a stop along the right curb. A block back, he did the same. Then he watched as a Hispanic male jumped from the front passenger door, slammed it shut, and trotted across the street.

The man went to the gate of a wooden-slat fence that surrounded a lot next to an old row house. A heavy chain was looped on the gate, with a lock on it. The man unlocked the gate, then slid it open.

Paco Esteban suddenly got a knot in his stomach.

*The fence that Rosario described!*

From his angle and distance, Paco Esteban could just make out that the lot was paved with gravel.

*Another thing that Rosario described — tires on rocks!*

The dirty tan Ford van then rolled through the open gate. The man swung the gate closed after it. Then it looked as if the chain was being locked on the inside of the enclosure.

Paco Esteban took his foot off the brake. The minivan rolled forward. He slowly drove up to the house.

Except for what he'd just witnessed, there were no other visible signs of activity. No motion. And no lights. It took some effort, but he finally saw numbers on the wall beside the front door: 2505.

*Hancock Street. 2505.*

*Keep driving!*

*2505 Hancock . . .*

A few blocks north, he again pulled to the curb. He was just shy of Lehigh Avenue. His heart was pounding against his chest. He had to force himself to inhale, then to exhale.

He crossed himself.

*Dear God!*

*To be so close to such evil!*

El Nariz reached for the ink pen that was wedged into the vent on the dashboard. He found a scrap of paper.

He started to write "2505 Hancock Street"

but found that his hands shook so badly he could barely read his own handwriting.

*Does not matter.*

*I will always remember where that house is.*

He reached for his cellular telephone and pushed the key that speed-dialed his wife's phone.

When Señora Salma Esteban answered, he said with a shaky voice: "My love, please do not ask me any questions right now. Just listen —"

He paused at the interruption.

"Salma, please! Listen to me! Tell Rosario that I will be there in about twenty minutes. Tell her I will pick her up —"

He paused again.

"Yes, it is good. Now, please see that she is ready when I get there."

# [FOUR]
# 705 North Second Street, Philadelphia
# Wednesday, September 9, 5:55 P.M.

As the bird flew, the distance from the Roundhouse to Liberties was about four thousand feet. During the very short drive in Matt Payne's rental Ford sedan, Jim Byrth had said: "Two questions, Matt."

"Shoot."

"One, this is a rental, right?"

"Yeah. The insurance company is paying for it. Because my car got shot up?"

Earlier, Payne had related to Byrth the story of his shoot-out in the Italian restaurant parking lot. The one that had left his Porsche blasted by shotgun fire and sent into some sort of insurance adjustor hell. Which at more than one point had caused him to wonder:

*It's been a month. How damn long does it take to determine if it's fixable or if they're going to write me a check for a total wreck?*

*A check that no doubt will be as small as they can possibly make it.*

*Maybe that's it. The older the car, the less it's worth. So the longer they wait . . . But that's absurd. I put no miles on it. And Porsches, particularly Carreras and Turbos, hold their value.*

*So then they probably don't know what to do with it. Or with me.*

*Jesus, do I hate insurance companies.*

"Right," Byrth said. "But why are you using your personal vehicle on the job? None of my business; just idle curiosity how it's done here."

*Good point,* Payne thought. *I hadn't given it much thought.*

*Maybe because there hadn't been time to think about it.*

*I've only been back on the job this one day.*

"I hadn't given it much thought," Payne said. "I guess since the insurance company is footing the bill, it's not coming out of my pocket. I could put in for reimbursement. Not that that's going to be any big wad of cash."

"They won't issue you a Police Interceptor?"

"We have the Crown Vics. They're just hard to come by. There's a shortage. But if you need one, I'm sure we could get a loaner. Or something close. Maybe an undercover car from the pool at Special Operations. I've got a connection there."

Matt Payne had been in Special Operations when he'd made the top five list for promotion to sergeant, and had then to go to Homicide. The commanding officer of Special Operations was one Inspector Peter Wohl, who of course was Payne's rabbi. There also was another connection: Payne's sister and Peter Wohl sometimes considered themselves a couple.

Byrth shook his head. "No. Thanks. Like I said, just curious."

Payne glanced at him and nodded, then made the turn onto Second.

Then he said, "Shit! She beat us here. So much for our drink in peace."

Byrth saw only two vehicles parked in the angled spaces. Payne pulled in next to the nearest vehicle, a nearly new black Honda Accord coupe with deeply tinted windows. On the other side of it was a two-year-old, somewhat battered, GMC Yukon XL. Its right rear tire was up on the curb, causing the massive SUV to sit at an awkward pitch, like a ship that had run aground.

"She?" Byrth repeated.

"Amy. That's her Yukon."

"Back home, that and its twin, the Suburban, is called the National Truck of Texas. Damn near every elementary and middle-school drop-off/pickup lane is packed bumper to bumper with those twice a day."

"Not Amy. No kids."

"That's a late-model Yukon," Byrth said. "What the hell happened with all those dents and scratches? A Demolition Derby? And was it parked there — or deserted?"

Payne looked at it and chuckled at the observation.

The SUV had originally belonged to Brewster Payne. He had made it a gift to his daughter, Amelia Payne, MD. It wasn't that she needed it for its large size. She had yet to marry and, appropriately, she had no children. Which may have been fortuitous in and of itself, as any husband or child would have been terrified to be a passenger of a motor vehicle operated by Amy Payne.

Amy Payne had many fine qualities. For whatever reason, being a decent driver was not among them. And it baffled everyone why she even bothered getting behind the wheel. Her mishaps with her various motor vehicles on (and occasionally off) the roads of the Commonwealth of Pennsylvania bordered on the legendary. No curb, street sign, light pole, or other vehicle in her path was safe.

And knowing all this, Brewster Payne passed his Yukon to her in the hope that the big truck just might keep her alive.

Matt Payne put the rental Ford in park, turned off the engine, and looked at Jim Byrth. "You know, if you're feeling brave, I'll let you ask its owner. My sister just loves nothing more than to talk cars."

"Why do I suspect you're setting me up?" Byrth replied.

Payne's cellular phone started ringing.

"Excuse me."

He pulled it from his pants pocket and saw from the screen who was calling. He pushed the key to answer. "Yes, sir?" he said into it. There was a pause. Then he said: "No, Jason, no problems in the ECC. Thanks for asking. We left it not twenty minutes ago. I'm about to introduce Jim to the stubby Statue of Liberty —" He paused again.

Byrth grinned as he looked out the windshield. On the sidewalk in front of the bar's window was a scale model of the Statue of Liberty. It was green and stood about five feet tall. The bar itself was a narrow three-story brick-faced structure that was at the end of a block-long building. Its wooden front door was on the left, under a half-circle canvas awning.

Payne went on: "Right. And he's about to meet our favorite family shrink. I thought we could combine a welcome party with some shop talk. Care to join us?" Payne listened a moment. "Great. See you shortly."

Payne ended the call and looked at Byrth. "Good news. The Black Buddha is going to join us."

Byrth laughed aloud at that.

"You've got the *cojones* to call him that behind his back?"

Payne, now that he knew the translation, grinned at the term.

"I've got the co-hone-ees to call him that to his face," Payne said. "It doesn't offend him. He once told me that he believed Buddha to be a very wise man. Then he added, 'And, Good Lord, there's no denying I'm black.' "

Byrth chuckled. "He strikes me as a good man."

Payne, his tone serious, said, "Yeah, a very good man. He's one of my favorite people. And one of the best homicide detectives anywhere. I'm glad he's joining us."

They got out of the car. As they started for the door to the bar, Payne motioned at the stubby Statue of Liberty.

"Meet Miss Liberty," he said formally. "And welcome to Liberties, sometimes referred to as the preferred watering hole of Philly's Homicide Unit."

Inside Liberties, Matt found the place was maybe a third full. Along the left wall were wooden tables with booths. They all were taken by patrons. A large wooden bar ran a good part of the opposite wall, from the front window almost back to the wooden stairs leading upstairs. It was mostly empty. In the middle were more tables and chairs. There, Matt saw Amy sitting at a table, her head down. She apparently was reading the screen of her cellular telephone.

"There she is," Payne said to Byrth.

Byrth followed him across the room. He saw that Amy Payne looked to be about thirty years old, petite and intense, her brown hair snipped short. She wasn't necessarily pretty, but was an attractive, natural-looking young woman.

As they approached Amy's table, she looked up from her cell phone. Byrth was removing The Hat from his head, and she was unable to hide her surprise.

"Hi, Amy," Matt said. "I want you to meet a friend of Liz Justice's."

Amy Payne well knew the family and police connections with the Justice family. She recovered from her initial shock and smiled warmly.

"Jim Byrth, this is my sister, Amy Payne. Amy, Jim."

"It's a pleasure," Byrth said, offering his hand.

Amy took it.

"Jim is a sergeant with the Texas Rangers."

"Really? I'm not sure what that is, but it sounds impressive."

"It is," Matt said, then added, "The Black Buddha is going to join us."

"The more the merrier," Amy said without much conviction.

*Jesus Christ. Is she in one of her moods?*

417

*It's been too long a day for that.*

Matt looked at her. "Everything okay?"

"Should I be asking the same of you, Wyatt Earp?"

"You two want to be alone?" Byrth asked.

Matt made a face. "No, Jim. You're fine."

"Sorry about that, Jim," Amy said. "Didn't mean to put you on the spot."

"No apology. I'm a big boy. I just thought you might want some privacy for when you punched Matt."

She looked at him and smiled. It was a genuine one.

"C'mon, Amy," Matt said. "That was a good shooting. For Christ's sake, that sonofabitch pumped thirteen rounds into Skipper. It was an assassination. And there's video that proves I got shot at."

He stared at her.

After a moment, he said, "Can we not get into this right now? It's been one helluva day, and Jim and I could use a drink. Or three."

He looked at the table. All that was there was the usual centerpiece. It held salt and pepper shakers and a container with packets of sugar and sugar substitute. But there was no drink, not even water.

"You're not drinking, Amy?"

"We haven't ordered. We just got here."

*We?* Matt thought.

She glanced toward the back of the bar, where the steps led to the second-floor dining area and, beyond the steps, the men's and ladies' rooms.

Matt's eyes followed hers back there — and he thought he was going to have a heart attack.

Coming out from the very back, by the restrooms, was an absolutely gorgeous blonde who was running the fingers of her right hand through her thick, luxurious hair.

*Good God! Amanda Law!*
*In Liberties!*
*Be still, my heart!*

# VIII

## [ONE]
## 705 North Second Street, Philadelphia
## Wednesday, September 9, 6:05 P.M.

Sergeant Matt Payne watched the gorgeous Dr. Amanda Law as she walked across the well-worn wooden floor of Liberties. He saw that she no longer had her doctor's lab coat.

Now she wore jeans that fit her toned body remarkably snugly, gold metallic leather flat-soled espadrilles, and a clingy white linen top that was cut to reveal just a suggestion of cleavage.

He had a hard time believing that this goddess was in one of his favorite bars.

*Look at that stride,* he thought. *She just seems to float across the room.*

Matt turned to his sister.

"You *know* Dr. Law?" he said.

"Yeah," Dr. Amelia Payne replied. "So do you."

"I do? I just met her this morning, at the hospital."

Amy stared at her brother.

After a moment, she said, "You really don't remember?"

Matt broke the stare, then glanced at Jim Byrth.

Byrth smiled and said, "Don't look at me, Marshal. I just rode into town."

Amy then said, "Her father was a cop, Matt. In Northeast Detectives."

Matt shook his head. "Sorry. Doesn't ring a bell."

"He had twenty years in when he got shot on duty. Took a bullet to the hip. So they gave him disability and he retired. And Amanda and I were suitemates our fresh-

420

man year at UP."

"Suitemates?"

Amy shook her head disappointedly, as if she were speaking to a five-year-old.

"Yeah," Amy said. "She and her roommate had one bedroom, my roommate and I had the other, and we shared a bath. Don't be so dense."

"I know what a suitemate is. I just forgot she'd been yours."

*If I ever knew.*

*I was still at the academy — blame it on my being preoccupied with whatever girlfriend I had at the time.*

Amy went on: "When I heard about Becca, I called Amanda. It's no small wonder it turned out that Becca's her patient; Amanda's the best. She wanted to meet me for drinks, but I told her you and I were doing that. And so I asked if she wanted to join us. I hope you don't mind."

Matt glanced at the approaching Amanda.

*Mind?*

*Me mind?*

*Never.*

"This Becca is the one who was injured in the motel explosion?" Jim Byrth said. "And this woman is her doctor?"

"Yeah," Amy said. "Becca Benjamin. We've

known the family for years. And Amanda is Becca's doctor."

Byrth nodded and said, "Matt told me that. I was just making sure I had it straight."

Dr. Amanda Law walked up to the table. She smiled and said, "Hello again, Matt."

He felt his pulse start to race.

Matt held out his hand and said, "We're going to have to stop meeting, or people are going to start talking."

*Now, that was lame!*

*I'm just making all sorts of great impressions on her today.*

*God, she even smells heavenly!*

She raised her eyebrows. "It has been an interesting day. At least these circumstances are more civil."

Matt said, "Amy tells me we met a long time ago."

"Amy told me the same. I don't doubt it. But I'm sorry. I'm afraid I don't remember."

*What? I'm crushed!*

Amanda went on: "When you gave me your card this morning, I thought the 'Payne' was familiar. But then I didn't know if the connection was because of Amy having the same name or because of my dad knowing cops."

"Speaking of cops," she said, and reached into her purse, "I brought you something."

She pulled out a tongue depressor and held it out to him.

*Damn!*

"Amanda, I do owe you an apology . . ."

"What's that about?" Amy said. "An apology?"

Matt ignored his sister.

He took the flat wooden stick, looked at it a second, then said, "I'm really sorry, Amanda. Really. It was an extraordinary moment."

"Yes, it was. Apology accepted."

Matt smiled.

*Thank God.*

"Thank you," he said, slipping the depressor into his pocket.

He motioned toward Byrth.

"Now that that's all straightened out, Dr. Amanda Law, this is Sergeant Jim Byrth."

"How are you, Sergeant?" Amanda said.

"It's 'Jim.' And I'm fine, thank you, ma'am. Pleasure to meet you."

Payne pulled out a chair for Amanda.

"Thank you," she said as she sat down.

Payne then waved his hand above his head to get the attention of the waitress. She was at the end of the bar, putting an order of drinks on a round tray. When she saw him, he motioned with his fist to mime drinking, then pointed at their table. The waitress

423

smiled and nodded.

Jim Byrth was about to sit down.

"You can't sit there," Payne said.

"What're you going to do," Amy said sharply, "have your guest stand all night?"

Matt raised his eyebrows. "And I thought that I had a bad day."

He stepped over to the adjacent table, put his hands on opposite ends of the tabletop, and began sliding it toward the table where Amy and Amanda sat. Jim Byrth saw that the chair that he'd been about to sit in was in the way. He moved it. When the tables had been pushed together, he and Matt rearranged the empty chairs.

The new arrangement had Amanda sitting at one end and Amy on the corner to her left. Matt sat down in the chair on the corner to Amanda's right, which gave him a clear view of the front door. Byrth then sat to the right of Matt. The Hat went into the empty chair at the end of the table, the one opposite Amanda Law.

The bar's wooden front door squeaked open.

Matt Payne automatically glanced at it — and saw that Byrth did the same. It was obviously no accident that the Texas Ranger had also made sure he had a view of the door — and of everyone who entered or left.

In came Jason Washington. On his heels was Tony Harris. Both were in plainclothes. Washington was in a tailored tan poplin suit that even after the long, hard day looked crisp. Harris had on dark slacks, a white knit shirt, and his usual well-worn blue blazer.

Matt waved and got their attention.

As they came up to the table, Washington lit up like a kid at Christmas.

"That *is* you, Amanda!" he exclaimed. "How are you, sweetheart?"

*Jesus H. Christ!* Payne thought as he watched him move around the table to reach her. *Does everyone know this woman except me?*

*And, clearly, love her?*

*Has she been right there in front of me all these years?*

*Reminds me of that saying . . . how's it go? Oh, yeah.*

*"If you want to find something, stop looking for it."*

Payne felt Byrth looking at him as Matt stared at Amanda. Payne turned to Byrth, then shrugged and raised his eyebrows to say, *Who knew?*

"I'm well, Jason, thank you very much," Amanda Law was saying.

She turned her head slightly, holding up her left cheek. Washington gently kissed it.

"And your father?" Washington went on. "How is he?"

"Doing very well. I'm sure if he knew I was here, he would have sent his regards."

"Please give him mine. It's been a long time."

"I will. This is a nice surprise. How is Martha? Please tell her I said hello."

*I'll be damned!* Matt thought. *And she's friendly with Martha Washington, too.*

*That's as good as being family!*

*How the hell have I missed out on this goddess?*

*A goddess who's not only obviously very bright and skilled — but one who knows about cops.*

*I won't have to try to explain what it is that I do.*

*And, maybe more important,* why *it is that I do it.*

*Unbelievable. . . .*

Jason Washington was saying, "My beautiful bride is doing marvelously. She'll be even more so when I tell her you said hello."

The Black Buddha turned to Amy Payne and said warmly, "Nice to see you, too, Amy. How are you?"

"Doing pretty good, Jason. Thank you," she replied pleasantly, then looked at Harris. "Hello, Tony."

"Hi, Amy." Harris waved. "Good to see you."

"Tony," Jason Washington said, gesturing toward Amanda, "this is Charley Law's daughter, Amanda. *Dr.* Amanda Law."

Harris stepped over and shook her hand.

"Good to meet you, Doctor. I never met your father, but I do know his reputation. He was one helluva detective."

Amanda Law made a small smile. "That's kind of you to say."

"And," Washington went on, "this is Jim Byrth."

Byrth stood. Harris held out his hand.

"Tony Harris, Jim. Have heard a bit about you, too. Good to meet you."

"And you," Byrth said gripping the hand.

The waitress appeared.

"Impeccable timing!" Jason Washington said, and with his arms extended and his huge hands open, he made the exaggerated fanning motion of a minister telling his congregation to be seated in the pews. "Everyone sit so we can order."

# [TWO]
## 705 North Second Street, Philadelphia
## Wednesday, September 9, 6:30 P.M.

"When we got word from our informants that this El Gato had gone ballistic and was whacking drug runners who were in arrears to him," Byrth was saying to his attentive audience at the table, "we scrambled. But unfortunately not before the psychopath lopped off the heads of two girls, one in Fort Worth's Northside and one near downtown Houston, last week. Both heads were thrown into packed barrio bars where their family members were known to hang out. The bodies are still missing. Then I figured out that El Gato had fled to Philadelphia. And here I am."

He drained his Jack Black on the rocks and sighed.

"And now it's maybe three girls he's killed."

He slid the glass on the table. It stopped

beside a large bowl of cashews. Another bowl next to it was almost empty of its stick pretzels. Also on the table was a collection of glasses and bottles, the latter consisting of one each Old Bushmills Irish Whiskey, Famous Grouse, Jack Daniel's, and Concho y Toro Shiraz wine.

"We don't automatically jump at the term 'psychopath,'" Dr. Amelia Payne said.

"I do," Byrth said. "Among other choice words that my manners do not allow to be repeated in such polite company."

Amy, holding a half-full glass of red wine, said, "The reason we don't is because psychopathy is the most severe condition. It's found in only one percent of the population."

Byrth said, "Doc, with all respect — if it walks like a duck and talks like a duck, it's a damned duck."

Amy stared at the Texas Ranger, clearly considering her next words.

Before she could speak, he added, "That, or it's *la folie raisonnante*."

"What the hell is that?" Matt Payne said, reaching for the bottle of wine.

"Impressive," Amy said, nodding appreciatively.

She smiled at Byrth.

Holding the bottle by its bottom, Matt

poured more of the Chilean Shiraz into Dr. Amanda Law's glass.

Amanda silently mouthed the words "Thank you." It was somewhat exaggerated, and Matt saw that it caused the tip of her tongue to linger between her lips for a long moment. His pulse raced.

*How do I get a taste of that particular fine vintage?*

After a moment, Payne heard his sister clearing her throat, each time more noisily. When he looked in her direction, he saw that she had her arm stretched out and was impatiently rocking her now-empty glass at him.

The Black Buddha, holding in his ball mitt of a hand a golden-colored Bushmills martini, chuckled deeply at the sight.

Matt reached over and refilled his sister's stem.

Jim Byrth explained, "In 1801, Phillippe Pinel described his patients as *la folie raisonnante.*"

"Okay, and that means . . . ?" Matt said, returning the bottle to the table and picking up his glass of Famous Grouse.

"'Insane without delirium,'" Byrth explained, looking at him. "Pinel found his patients were not necessarily impaired mentally. Yet they still committed impulsive acts that were harmful to themselves. So he called it 'insane without delirium.' "

Byrth looked at Amy.

"We had a serial killer loose in Texas a few years back. He traveled around by hopping trains, killing near tracks all across the state. I did some research on psychopaths during that, and afterward. Fascinating stuff." He paused. "I know just enough to be dangerous, Doc."

He smiled.

She smiled back.

Then she asked, "Would you like me to give you my version?"

"I certainly would," Detective Anthony Harris said. "But please try to use little words for young Matthew's sake."

Dr. Amanda Law laughed out loud.

Matt mock-glared at Tony. With the glass resting in his right palm, he held up his drink in a salute — the middle finger and thumb extended — and said, "Et tu, Brute?"

Harris grinned when he saw that Payne was giving him the bird.

Payne then took a healthy sip and put down the glass.

Amanda reached over and squeezed Matt's left wrist. "I'm sorry. I really wasn't laughing at you."

"Apology accepted," Matt said, looking in her eyes and smiling.

*And as long as you keep touching me, any and every other of your transgressions shall be immediately forgiven.*

She pulled back her hand.

*Damn!*

Amy said, "I'm afraid that's going to be difficult, Tony, but I'll try."

She looked at Matt and feigned a sweet smile. Then she made a toasting motion toward him with her glass, and sipped from it.

Matt felt a vibration in his pants pocket. He pulled out his cell phone and saw that he'd received a text message from Chad Nesbitt.

It read:

---

SOUP KING

U GET MY TXT?? U DIDNT REPLY

---

*Not now, Chad!*
*What text?*
He replied:

---

can it wait till later?

---

Then almost immediately after he hit SEND, his phone vibrated again.

The text message read:

```
SOUP KING

WHENS L8R??
```

Then Matt's phone started to ring. Its screen flashed: SOUP KING — 1 CALL TODAY @ 1848.

*Later is not now, dammit.*

Matt pushed and held the 0/1 button.

*Oh, look, Chad — my phone just "died."*

His phone screen went dark and then the phone turned off.

"Okay," Dr. Amelia Payne was saying, "what often is confused with psychopathy is what's called dissocial personality disorder. In concept, the two share the same criteria. But in reality there are distinct differences, ones that determine who truly is a psychopath."

"What are these shared criteria?" Jim Byrth said.

"Behavior that is delinquent and criminal."

"Well, our boy meets that criterion in

spades. As my grandfather used to say, he's meaner than a rattlesnake in a red-hot skillet."

The Black Buddha chuckled.

"Furthermore," Amy said, "prison studies have found that up to eighty percent of those incarcerated meet the criteria for dissocial personality disorder. But of those, only ten or so percent are in fact true psychopaths."

"To borrow Jim's word, that is fascinating, Amy," Washington said. "Are there any precursors to the condition?"

She nodded, then took a drink of her wine.

"In the early 1960s," Dr. Payne explained, "J. M. Macdonald came up with three indicators that pinpointed psychopathy in children. Those are bedwetting, starting fires, and torturing animals."

"The Macdonald triad," Jim Byrth said.

"Exactly," Amy Payne said, her face showing she was again impressed.

Byrth then said, "Well, I can't speak to whether or not El Gato wets his bed. But he clearly has a history of torching and torturing."

Everyone was quiet for a moment.

"Perhaps worse," Amy then added, "it's been found that a psychopath is untreatable."

Byrth nodded. "The best you can do is incarcerate them — in solitary confinement, away from the general population, unless you want more deaths — and throw away the key."

"I'll drink to that," Matt said, and did.

The Black Buddha sipped thoughtfully at his Bushmills martini, then said, "Amy, it's been some time — I won't date myself — since I sat in a Psychology 101 class. Would you mind going over what causes such a sickness? What makes them different than any of us?"

Matt looked at Tony Harris. "Don't even *think* of saying what you're thinking, Tony."

Harris grinned, then downed his Bushmills on the rocks and reached for the bottle for a refill.

Amy looked at Matt and shook her head.

She then said, "Of course, Jason. It's fairly familiar ground for all of us. It goes back to what Freud said. He wrote of *das Es, das Ich,* and *das Über-Ich.*"

She took a sip of her wine, then said, "As you'll recall, that translates, respectively, as the It, the I, and the Over-I — or the Id, the Ego, and the Superego.

"The Id is the part of our personality that acts on pleasure, on immediate gratification. It is absolutely unashamedly amoral."

Byrth saw Payne and Harris exchange glances. The three of them then grinned at the thought of what the other might be thinking.

It was not lost on Amy.

"The classic example," she said pointedly, looking at Matt, "is that of an infant. A baby has been described as an alimentary tract exhibiting no sense of responsibility at either end." She paused, sipped her wine, then added, "So, not surprisingly, the Id is all about our basic drives, from food to sex."

"And I'll damn sure drink to that," Matt said.

That earned him a glare from Amy.

She snapped, "Jesus, little brother. How about reining in *your* Id! This sophomoric behavior is ridiculous!"

Matt looked at her, about to bark back. Then he realized that he'd heard some genuine disgust in her tone.

*Shit. Maybe she's right.*

*Hope I didn't just embarrass myself in front of Amanda.*

*And I don't know if it's because I'm exhausted or what, but I'm starting to feel this booze.*

*It has been an absolutely incredible day . . . in every way.*

Payne looked at Amanda.

*Especially now that I think I've found the per-*

436

*fect woman.*

He felt a warm sensation, and was not convinced it was not from the scotch.

*Crank up the violins.*

*Looks like it's time to think about winding up living happily-ever-after in that vine-covered cottage by the side of the road.*

Amanda felt his attention.

When she looked at him, he quickly averted his eyes.

Then he looked back.

She was still looking at him.

*Am I hoping beyond hope?*

She made a slight smile, and turned her attention to Amy.

*I devoutly hope not. . . .*

Amy was saying, "The Ego, Freud said, represents reason and common sense. It's our reality for the long term. And being in the middle, it tries to balance the extremities of the Id and Superego. The Superego being the opposite of the Id. It's our conscience. It understands what's wrong and right — and wants perfection. It triggers our guilt."

Byrth grunted. "And it's what the psychopath is missing."

"In a broad stroke," Amy said, "yes, it is. Would you care to hear details on defining a psychopath? Or am I boring everyone to tears?"

"No, please do, Amy," the Black Buddha said.

"Yes, continue," Tony Harris put in.

Amanda Law and Jim Byrth were nodding their assent. Matt made a grand motion with his hand that said, *Carry on.*

Amy looked at him, then at her wine stem. She held it out toward Matt, who refilled it with the Sharaz.

"Okay," she began, "a psychopath is defined as one with chronic immoral and antisocial behavior. Someone whose gratification is found in criminal and sexual and aggressive impulses. And they are not able to learn from past mistakes.

"There is a standard instrument used by researchers and clinicians worldwide that's called the Hare Psychopathy Checklist–Revised. The PCL-R has proven to be reliable. And very much valid. It was named for Dr. Robert D. Hare, a well-known researcher in the field of criminal psychology.

"The PCL-R separates behavior into two categories: aggressive narcissism and socially deviant lifestyle."

She paused to look between Matt and Tony. But there was no more of their sophomoric humor. They were paying rapt attention.

She went on: "Within these two categories, Hare lists separate character traits that the patient may or may not have. For each, he assigns a grade between zero and two. The higher the sum, the more severe the patient's pathology."

She paused and looked around the table.

"Everyone still with me?"

There were nods. Matt grunted an "Uh-huh."

"All right," she continued, "under aggressive narcissism are: superficial charm, a grand sense of self-worth, pathological lying, being cunning and manipulative, no remorse or guilt, shallowness, a cold lack of empathy, and inability to take responsibility for his own actions."

Matt Payne perked up. "Well, hell, that pretty much paints the perfect picture of most bad guys."

Amy nodded. "Right. But there's also Hare's other component. Under socially deviant lifestyle are these traits: a need to be stimulated; can't handle being bored; a lifestyle that's parasitic; can't control own behavior; promiscuity; no long-term goals, at least ones that are realistic; being impulsive; irresponsibility; juvenile delinquency; childhood behavior problems. And one or two others I can't recall just now."

She paused and drained her glass.

"And that ends my speech," she said. "You

add all those up, and you have your psycho-path."

Byrth grunted. "I do indeed wish we did have our psychopath. He needs to be off the streets."

Matt Payne looked at Amanda Law and said, "While we're on topics that are uncomfortable, Amanda, am I allowed to ask about Becca?"

She looked at Matt and could see his concern was genuine.

"There's more than professional curiosity, isn't there? You do care about her, don't you?"

Amy said to Amanda, "At Episcopal Academy, Matt used to have a crush on her." Amy looked at him. "Didn't you, Matt?"

"A crush?" Amanda repeated. "How sweet!"

Payne shot his sister a glare.

"You're Episcopalian?" Byrth said.

Payne nodded. "Not exactly a practicing one, but I've kept the faith, so to speak."

"So am I. Remarkable. But then, in this crowd, I guess not." He paused. "And I understand your disappointment with the church and its politics these days. Me, I'm with whoever said that going to church no more makes you holy than standing in a Porsche showroom makes you a sports car."

Everyone at the table laughed.

Matt said, "Let's not get started on religion tonight, too."

"Sorry," Byrth said, shrugging.

"Amanda," Matt said, first looking at Amy then turning to Amanda, "for the record, Becca and I never had a relationship. But, yeah, we were kind of close growing up. And I cared about her. Enough to be disgusted with her getting involved with that goddamn Skipper Olde."

"Matthew," Jason Washington said solemnly, "I know your mother taught you not to speak ill of the departed."

"There's exceptions to every rule, Jason. And I'm still pissed off at Skipper — RIP, ol' buddy — for putting Becca in this situation."

Dr. Law smiled warmly at his explanation.

"Your concern is sweet," she said with sincerity. "But, I'm sorry, I just can't discuss a patient. It wouldn't be ethical."

Matt could tell from the way she said it that she truly was sorry.

"She's worse, Matt," Amy blurted. "That intracranial hypertension has not subsided. It's looking more and more like Amanda will have to induce the coma."

Dr. Law looked at Dr. Payne and said, "Amy!"

"For the record, Matt," Dr. Amy Payne said, "that information I got directly from Mrs. Benjamin. She shared with me what Becca's attending physician" — she glanced at Amanda Law, who now looked less horrified — "had told to Mr. and Mrs. Benjamin."

Matt made a face, then drained his drink.

He looked at Dr. Law and was again amazed by her air of complete confidence.

*She oozes it.*

*What a woman. . . .*

He said, "Amanda, can you describe in broad terms — just hypothetically, nothing patient-specific — what inducing a coma involves?"

Dr. Amanda Law considered that a moment.

Then she nodded and said, "Sure. With a brain injury, fluids collect in the brain and cause it to swell. The skull, however, does not expand to allow for the fluids, so that basically causes the brain to be compacted, and blood, and the oxygen in it, is prevented from reaching all of its parts. That can cause brain damage, even death."

Matt shook his head.

She took a sip of her wine, then went on: "When conventional therapy fails, and we are unable to surgically open the skull to

442

drain the fluids, we carefully consider the barbiturate-induced coma. The coma reduces brain activity, but that has to be balanced against the side effects of the drug."

"What side effects?" Matt said.

"It could stress the cardiovascular system to the point where it causes more harm. And there can be complications — from infections, deep blood clots — leading to death."

"Jesus!" Matt said, sighed, and refilled his glass with more Famous Grouse.

"The positive part," Dr. Law went on, "is that the barbiturates act to reverse all that. They reduce the brain tissue's metabolic rate and the flow of cerebral blood, causing the brain's blood vessels to narrow, which decreases the swelling."

"But even if all that works," Dr. Amy Payne added, "there's still a long recovery period. Becca's not out of the woods by a long shot."

Matt looked at Amanda. She nodded her agreement with Amy. "Hypothetically, of course."

She checked her wristwatch, then pushed back her chair.

"I hate to be rude and run," she said, "but I'm going to have to be rude and run right after I visit the little girls' room."

She stood, and Matt popped to his feet to

help with her chair.

She smiled her thanks, then added, "Tomorrow is going to come too quickly. And I don't usually get out like this. It's been delightful."

Jason Washington checked his watch.

"I concur," he said. "No rest for the weary. Matthew, what about the tab?"

"It's taken care of," Jim Byrth said. "The great state of Texas appreciates those who help her Texas Rangers."

Washington grinned. "And yet another reason to like the legendary lawmen of the West."

As Matt watched Amanda walk toward the ladies' room, he felt an elbow in his right side.

He turned to see Byrth handing him a napkin.

"What's this for?" Matt said.

"Traditionally, for wiping food from one's lips. You, however, might want to try your chin. You're drooling."

"That bad, huh?"

Byrth shook his head. But he was grinning.

"More like disgusting," Amy Payne put in.

As they were leaving, Sergeant Matt Payne intercepted Dr. Amanda Law.

"I, uh, I wanted to say thank you for this," Payne said, waving the tongue depressor.

She grinned, but her eyes showed she didn't believe one damn word of that.

"And," he said, "I wanted to ask if maybe we could do this again, but without all those annoying people at our table and the depressing talk."

Matt saw her face turn sad. Then she made a weak attempt at a smile. He saw that there now was pain in her eyes.

"Matt, that's very sweet of you to offer —"

"Please don't let there be a 'but' . . ."

She made a thin-lipped smile.

He thought her pain was practically touchable.

"But," she said, "can I think about it? I'm a slave to my work, as you may have noticed. I haven't seen anyone in, well, quite some time. And I'm not sure there's time for . . . for any relationship."

*There's something more to the "but" than work.*

*She's been hurt!*

*And deeply!*

*What sonofabitch would do that to such a goddess?*

He nodded slowly . . . numbly.

She could tell he was disappointed, and

said, "I am flattered that you asked."

Not knowing what to say, he just looked at her. Then he mumbled, " 'Besides that, Mrs. Lincoln, how was the play?' "

He saw her grin at that. And he saw it was genuine.

She said, "Good night, Matt."

And she was out the door.

He just stared at it.

*"Think about it"?*

*That ache I just felt in my chest?*

*And that deafening crack?*

*That was the unmistakable sound of a heart breaking. . . .*

*Shit!*


# [THREE]
# Love Field, Dallas
# Wednesday, September 9,
# 7:34 P.M.
# Texas Standard Time


Juan Paulo Delgado had collected his large black duffle bag at baggage claim and was waiting impatiently on the curb for El Cheque to show up. The Southwest Airlines flight had landed ten minutes early, and

Delgado had sent him a text message telling him to step on it. El Gato hated waiting for anything.

There were two cast bronze plaques mounted on the exterior of a nearby wall, each plaque illuminated by a pair of bright halogen floodlights.

Bored, Delgado stepped over to read them.

On the first was:

⭐

**TEXAS HISTORICAL SOCIETY
"The Lone Star State Presents . . ."
LOVE FIELD**

*This airport was named in honor of First Lieutenant Moss Lee Love (1879–1913), Eleventh Cavalry, by the United States Army on October 19, 1917.*

*Love was killed on September 4, 1913, when his Type C Wright pusher biplane crashed at North Island, San Diego, California.*

*He had been flying for his Military Aviator Test.*

*Born in Fairfax, Virginia, Love was appointed to the U.S. Army in 1910. In April*

*1913, he was ordered to Texas City, Texas, and there detailed for aviation duty with the Signal Corps and the 1st Aero Squadron. He was with the Signal Corps Aviation School at the time of his death.*

*Love Field opened for civilian use in 1927, and remained the major aviation hub for Dallas and its citizens until being joined by the Dallas–Fort Worth Regional (now International) Airport in 1974.*

✯

Delgado shook his head disgustedly.

*Who gives a shit?*

*Just another dead gringo.*

*Damn land-grabbers.*

Delgado looked at the other cast bronze plaque. It had a replica of a Texas lawman. He wore a big Stetson hat, a gun belt with a Colt revolver, a Western-style shirt bearing a badge that was a five-pointed star within a circle, Western-style pants, and pointed-toe boots.

The sign read:

## TEXAS HISTORICAL SOCIETY
## "The Lone Star State Presents . . ."
## ONE RANGER, ONE RIOT

*While developing settlements in what then was the Mexican province of Tejas, Stephen F. Austin called for men to "range" the frontier to protect its people. These "Rangers" in 1835 officially became the legendary policing force known as the Texas Rangers.*

*In 1896, Texas Ranger Captain William McDonald was sent here to Dallas to shut down a planned illegal heavyweight prize fight.*

*Dallas Mayor F. P. Holland met Captain McDonald as he disembarked his train at Union Station downtown.*

*Mayor Holland looked at Captain McDonald and in great shock said, "Where are the other Rangers?"*

*"There's only one fight," McDonald said. "Hell, ain't I enough?"*

*McDonald's legendary reply became known as "One Ranger, One Riot."*

*The phrase embodies the toughness and*

*determination of all those who have sworn the oath to uphold the laws as a Texas Ranger.*

*One creed of the Texas Rangers is also from Captain McDonald:*

*"No man in the wrong can stand up against a fellow that's in the right and keeps on a-comin'."*

*(Sculpture created by Waldine Tauch, and gifted by Mr. and Mrs. Earle Wyatt on the occasion of the dedication of Love Field's new terminal, 1961.)*

★

*More gringo bullshit.*

*And this should still be the "Mexican province of Tejas."*

Delgado's phone vibrated, announcing a received text message.

He pulled out the phone and read its screen:

214-555-7636

TURNING INTO AIRPORT NOW

*About damn time.*

He looked at the clock on the phone's display. It showed seven forty-five. The cellular service in Dallas had automatically set back the time on the phone; Texas Standard Time was an hour behind Eastern Standard Time.

*That makes it eight forty-five in Philly.*

While he had the phone out, he typed and sent a text to Omar Quintanilla:

---

JESUS OK? FIXED?

---

A moment later, his phone vibrated. Quintanilla had replied:

---

609-555-1904

SI . . . BUENO . . . NOW SLEEPING

---

Delgado snorted. *Poor little El Gigante.*
Another text then came from Quintanilla:

---

609-555-1904

ANGEL TOOK THE 9S

---

Delgado nodded.

He had told Quintanilla to settle Jiménez's bill with two of the TEC-9 pistols that they had stolen from the Fort Worth gun store last month. The store was on the south side of town, and they had carefully cased it over time.

He grinned at the memory of that morning.

El Gato, El Cheque, and Paco Gomez had taken the Chevy Suburban to a salvage yard on the western edge of Dallas, where they'd swapped the plates with ones they'd taken off a just-totaled pickup. They'd also helped themselves to a twenty-foot length of rusty heavy-duty chain from one of the tow trucks there.

At two the next morning, El Gato, El Cheque, and Gomez had driven the SUV to the gun store in South Fort Worth.

The store was in a deteriorating shopping strip two blocks east of Interstate 35, and its storefront was covered with large signs advertising the guns and accessories inside. It had surveillance cameras, and wrought-iron bars bolted over the windows and the aluminum-framed glass door.

El Gato and Crew had a can of black spray

paint, a length of chain, and a half-ton Suburban.

Delgado had let Gomez out at the corner. Gomez, who stood six-one, wore a black hoodie, its top up. He carried the can of spray paint along the side of his leg, attached to the end of a four-foot-long extension arm they'd bought at Home Depot for ten bucks. He trotted down the sidewalk of the strip center, keeping his face concealed from the cameras. When he got to the gun store, he simply extended the aerosol can to the camera lenses and squeezed the extension arm's grip. The lenses were quickly covered in a coating of black paint.

Moments later, El Gato was backing up the Suburban to the front door. Then El Cheque, the chain coiled over his shoulder, jumped out the right rear passenger door.

He dropped the chain at the foot of the gun store's front door, grabbed one end with his leather-gloved hands, and began threading it through the wrought-iron bars. Then he wrapped the chain around the heavy metal support bar bolted across the center.

Gomez, also wearing leather gloves, took the chain's other end and doubled it around the trailer ball of the receiver hitch that was affixed to the Suburban's rear frame. Then, with an open palm, he pounded twice on the big SUV's rear window . . . and ran.

El Cheque got out of the way just as the accelerating truck took up all the slack in the chain — and popped the bars and the door off the face of the storefront. It made an enormous noise. There was mangled metal and broken glass everywhere and, inside, an alarm blared angrily.

El Cheque ran inside the store and spray-painted the cameras there, while Gomez went to the Suburban, unwrapped the chain from the hitch, and pulled the door frame and twisted wrought iron to the side. El Gato then backed up the Suburban to the doorway, and Gomez threw open the SUV's rear hatch, removed a pair of bolt cutters, and went into the store to cut the steel cable the store owner had strung through the trigger guards of all the shotguns and rifles on the racks. El Cheque was already coming out with an armful of the TEC-9s.

They'd had the back of the Suburban, its rear seats all folded flat, covered with guns and ammo in five minutes.

And two minutes after that, they were on the interstate and getting far away from the scene and its blaring alarm.

Juan Paulo Delgado was not surprised that Angel Hernandez had agreed to the barter.

The TEC-9, a more or less cheap knockoff of a fine Swiss submachine pistol, was a coveted weapon. Early semiautomatic TEC-9s had an open bolt design and could be converted to fully automatic. They even had a fifty-round box magazine, which made for one lethal weapon.

The newer models that El Gato and Crew had stolen were of a slightly different design and could not be converted, and their mags held only twenty bullets. But they still resembled the older fully auto TEC-9s that Hollywood had glorified by having all the badass movie drug-runners shooting them. And that was enough to give the gun "street cred" — credibility in the ghetto. So much so that homeys even shot one another just to get their hands on any variant of the TEC-9. They even mimicked that moronic pose they saw in the shoot-'em-up flicks: holding the guns sideways while they fired.

There was also a strong irony about bartering the guns for stitching up Jesús Jiménez, and it was not lost on Juan Paulo Delgado.

Not only was Angel Hernandez going to flip the pistols for a helluva lot more money than if he'd just been paid in cash for his services — but he was also likely going to get more business from whomever those TEC-9s shot up.

A horn honked.

Delgado looked up from the phone and saw Jorge Ernesto Aguilar at the wheel of Aguilar's ten-year-old dark brown Ford Expedition.

He could not help but notice that the SUV had brand-new twenty-two-inch chrome wheels and low-profile high-performance tires.

Delgado shook his head as he slipped the phone into his pocket.

*They must've cost more than the damn truck is worth.*

*What a waste of money.*

*But . . . he's not the only homeboy with them.*

The Expedition pulled to a stop at his feet. Delgado opened the back passenger door and threw his duffle on the bench seat. Then he went to the front passenger door and got in.

*"Hola,"* El Cheque said.

"What took so long?"

El Cheque made a face, which caused his cheek scar, the check that gave  him his name, to distort. Then he looked out the driver's-door window, scanning his mirror for a gap in the traffic. He saw one and accelerated the Expedition into the flow.

Delgado knew that it bothered the twenty-five-year-old Aguilar that his boss — Delgado — was only twenty-one. That Delgado was also physically much bigger did not help with Aguilar's inferiority complex. Nor did it help when Delgado went out of his way to remind Aguilar exactly who was his El Jefe, in subtle and, occasionally, not-so-subtle ways.

Delgado said, "And what's with those new wheels on here? It's not good to draw attention."

El Cheque remained silent. Delgado could see that Aguilar's eyes were moving quickly, as if he were considering saying what was on the tip of his tongue. Then El Cheque just shrugged.

They drove in silence as Aguilar steered the Expedition off the airport property and made a right turn onto Mockingbird Lane.

Two blocks later, at Maple Avenue, he hit his left-turn signal.

"Where're we going?" Delgado challenged.

"Umberto's. He's got the Suburban. When I went to get it out of the garage, it would not start. So he put a temporary battery in it, then brought it here to put a good one in it for the trip."

"I thought that I told you —"

"*Sí!*" El Cheque interrupted, his temper about to flare. He then spoke carefully: "And I did do as you said. That is why we are here. Now it *is* ready for the trip."

Delgado looked out the window and grinned to himself in the dark.

"What're we going south for?" El Cheque said.

"The usual. And we need a new girl or two."

El Cheque nodded.

"Any news on the kid?" Delgado said.

El Cheque shook his head. "Gomez is in College Station trying to follow his trail. What if it is Los Zetas?"

The mention of the Zetas caused Delgado to think of them with guns.

And that made him remember that he was unarmed.

Delgado glanced quickly around the dark SUV and said, "We got guns in here?"

El Cheque opened the top of the console that was between their bucket seats. He punched the overhead map light. Delgado looked inside. There were three handguns, butts up, one a TEC-9.

El Cheque said, "And there's a twelve-gauge pump in the back."

Delgado saw that one of the other pistols

was a black Beretta Model 92, the same model Jesús Jiménez used to shoot Skipper Olde.

He pulled the semiautomatic nine-millimeter out and closed the top of the console. In the beam of the map light, he removed the magazine, then worked the slide. *No round in the chamber.* He pushed on the top round in the magazine. No movement downward, which meant the magazine was full. *Good.* He reinserted the magazine in the pistol's grip, racked the slide, decocked the hammer, then slipped the pistol into his waistband beneath the tail of his T-shirt.

As Aguilar drove down Maple Avenue, Delgado took in the sights of the familiar neighborhood. Most of the signage and billboards were in Spanish, and it reminded him of that plaque at the airport.

*"Mexican province of Tejas."*

*With places like Little Mexico here, it may as well still be.*

*Or will be again. . . .*

They passed Maria Luna Park and approached Arroyo Avenue.

Up ahead on the southeast corner of Arroyo was a brightly lit convenience store. Taped to the inside of the plate-glass window beside the door was a handwritten sign reading:

At the covered island of fuel pumps was a somewhat battered white Dodge van. The chipped and faded black lettering on its side read FIRST UNITED CHURCH OF THE REDEEMER, BURKBURNETT, TEXAS. It was a Ram 3500 with seating for fifteen, and each row had a window, all painted over in white except for those on the doors of the driver and front passenger. The driver's door was open.

A short, very grimy-looking Latino was walking away from the van. He'd left the pump handle in the van's gas tank.

"Turn around," Delgado said forcefully, looking over his shoulder as the man walked to the side of the convenience store. "Now!"

"What?" Aguilar said. But he was already spinning the steering wheel so fast that the tires screeched.

He made the U-turn on Maple and accelerated.

"Pull in to that store," Delgado said, pointing. "To that side. Not in front."

Aguilar looked where he pointed, hit his

left signal, then found a gap in the line of headlights. He turned into the convenience store parking lot.

When the Expedition slowly rolled past the fuel pump island, Delgado surprised Aguilar by opening the passenger door and leaping out.

Aguilar, pulling to a stop, followed Delgado in his mirror.

El Gato moved with speed and grace. He went quickly to the fuel pump island, then to the open driver's door of the white church van there. He stepped up on the running board and put his head inside the van, looking toward the rear of the vehicle.

Then he hopped down from the running board, shut the van door, and damn near flew to the side of the convenience store where the grimy Latino had gone.

El Cheque lost sight of El Gato just as he was going behind some shrubbery — and just as he was pulling the Beretta from his waistband.

# [FOUR]
# 7701 Brocklehurst Street, Philadelphia
# Wednesday, September 9, 8:56 P.M.

Stanley Dowbrowski took a sip of his bourbon, then cocked his head as he looked at his computer screen.

*Something there's not right,* he thought.

Stanley Dowbrowski was sixty-five years old and in March had become a widower. He stood five-foot-eight, weighed 225 pounds, and kept his salt-and-pepper hair closely cropped; it looked almost like the three days' growth of his white beard. He wore thick bifocal eyeglasses and, for their comfort and ease of care, a two-piece athletic warm-up suit with a white cotton sleeveless T-shirt.

Stanley Dowbrowski had once been more or less physically fit. He'd worked out regularly. Now, however, he was in failing health, mostly due to having spent nearly the last half-century burning through pack after pack of cigarettes. The resulting scar tissue on his lungs had reduced their capacity to only thirty percent, which meant that getting around took him great effort, and when he did get around, it was with the aid of an aluminum walker, and with an asthma inhaler in his pocket.

Consequently, Stanley Dowbrowski rarely left the nice comfortable four-bedroom house just off Roosevelt Avenue in Northeast Philly. It was where he and his Betty had reared their two children.

He now, of course, was what people called an empty-nester. The kids were adults with young kids of their own, and living in nearby suburbs. He was grateful that over the years Betty had been able to win most of her many battles against the different cancers. Not only had she been able to spend time with her kids' kids, but the grandchildren had gotten to know — and have memories of — their wonderful "Grandmama."

Since Betty's passing six months before, Stanley Dowbrowski's kids had begun regularly dropping by to check on Grandpapa. Once a week they brought him food from the grocery and precooked dishes that had been frozen so all he had to do was thaw and warm them.

And they brought their pleas that he sell

the old house and come out to live with them in suburbia.

But Stanley Dowbrowski wouldn't hear of it. He told them that he was far too set in his ways. He was not going to become a bother to them. They had their families, and he had his home and all its dear memories.

"I'll leave when the boys from the Philly ME's office tie a tag on my big toe," Stanley Dowbrowski dramatically announced more than once, "and carry me out in a body bag."

Which, of course, always triggered the desired reaction.

"Dammit, Dad!" his daughter yelled. "Don't talk like that — especially in front of the kids!"

Stanley Dowbrowski still knew some of the people at the Medical Examiner's Office. (He also knew they wouldn't tie a toe tag on him; he just liked the black humor of the metaphor . . . and the response it elicited.) But not as many people as he used to.

He had retired from the Philadelphia Police Department fifteen years earlier.

Yet he'd never really left the police department. He kept up with old friends from there, also retired or, like the one in Homicide who lived by the middle school a few blocks away, still on the force. And he read cop books and watched cop movies. He lived and breathed — albeit sometimes on an oxygen tank now — everything about being a law-enforcement officer.

And high on his list of proud cop-related moments involved his sister's daughter. Police Officer Stephanie Kowenski had joined the cops six years before — after telling him she'd first gotten the idea of going out for the police department from listening to "Uncle Stan's cop stories."

Stanley Dowbrowski had many memories. Even the bedroom that he'd converted from his oldest child's bedroom into an office occasionally triggered one.

It had damn near taken an act of Congress for the conversion to happen. His beloved Betty had practically turned the boy's bedroom into a shrine to her son — who was now married, he and his bride happily living on their own. It had taken his son's help to convince Betty that it was fine if his father moved his office from the small corner of the basement into the old bedroom.

The office soon became packed with all of the stuff that Stanley Dowbrowski had collected over the course of his service to the citizens of Philadelphia. On the walls he'd hung black wooden frames holding diplomas and commendations and uniform patches and old photographs and newspaper clippings. He had added a wall of bookshelves, and on these were all his cherished books, arranged alphabetically by author, and a healthy collection of movies. Most were on VHS videotape, but he had a growing number of DVDs, too. His kids brought him a lot of movies with the weekly food deliveries.

The one thing that Stanley Dowbrowski considered the real gem of his office, however, was his desktop computer. It was a brand-new tower model, and he'd bought it with all the bells and whistles. These included a lightning-fast processor, more memory than he could believe, a home-theater audio system, and a pair of twenty-four-inch LCD monitors.

Of the latter, he used one LCD panel for his main screen. The other held all the different screens of whatever he was working on — an Internet browser window, say, showing a police scanner website, another with his e-mail in-box, and so on. He had even started watching some of the DVDs on the computer.

Stanley Dowbrowski used his mouse to scroll back up the browser window that had caused him to look askance at the screen.

Since Betty's passing, Dowbrowski had established a daily routine. Most of it was centered in this room and around the computer.

It was something he knew Betty would have frowned upon had she still been alive. But she wasn't there. And he had decided his life — at least what was left of it — was his to live in any way that he wanted. Or, considering his failing health, any way that he could manage.

*And if the ME boys have to pull my cold body out of this office chair to tie on that toe tag, so be it.*

*Metaphorically speaking . . .*

Every night around nine o'clock, Stanley Dowbrowski poured himself his usual nightcap of a double Buffalo Trace bourbon over three ice cubes. Sometimes, he might even slip and pour three shots. Then he would bring the cocktail into the office and make one last check of his e-mail. He also usually clicked on the website of his local newspaper to see what the forecast was for the next day's weather. And he'd run the program that backed up the files on his computer's internal hard drive to an external drive that he kept in his fireproof safe.

Then he would grab a book from the bookshelf — tonight he was excited about a new novel by a Florida cop named James O. Born — then take it and his bourbon down the hall to his bedroom. And there he'd climb in between the sheets and read till the nightcap kicked in.

He stared at the screen now, which showed the news story on the hospital shooting:

---

**ARMED MAN MURDERS BURN VICTIM BEFORE FLEEING HOSPITAL, FIRING AT POLICE**

**While police remain mum on details of the murder, witnesses claim gunman fired shots at man who shouted "Police!" while chasing gunman from hospital.**

---

He scrolled down to see if the story had been updated.

And he found that there was something new. It was a single-sentence paragraph at the end of the article:

---

*Update (5:44 p.m.):* **According to the anonymous source inside the hospital, the patient who was shot to death was J. Warren Olde, Jr.**

---

Then Dowbrowski scrolled down to the comments section. His comment was there, of course:

From **Hung.Up.Badge.But.Not.Gun (2:56 p.m.):**

*I talked to an inside source, too, and was told that this was a hit job. Maybe not a professional one, but the burn victim (there's more to that story that I cannot share) was targeted. So sad to see this happening in Philly. I'll say it again: Shoot 'em all and let the Good Lord sort 'em out.*

And below it there were five new postings, including one that seemed vaguely familiar:

From **Death.Before.Dishonor (3:20 p.m.):**

*What about "Thou Shalt Not Steal"?? The only sad thing about what happened is the gun didn't empty all of its bullets into that pendejo! Skipper deserved every damn bullet!*

Recommend [ 0 ] <u>Click Here to Report Abuse</u>

And he repeated to himself: "Something there's not right."

*At three twenty, that article had not ID'd who got shot.*

*And it sure as hell hadn't said "Skipper."*

*I only know the guy's name was Skipper Olde because Stephanie told me. And that he was the son of that McMansion builder.*

He glanced over at the secondary LCD screen, where he could see the e-mail in-box. The list of e-mails included Stephanie's.

*Maybe this guy knew him, too?*

*But how did he find out?*

*And that screen name, "Death.Before.Dishonor," rings a bell.*

*Where the hell else I have seen it?*

He sipped his bourbon, then clicked around the newspaper site, trying to remember.

He saw a link in the box that read TODAY'S MOST READ ARTICLES.

In the box was: 2 DEAD AFTER METH LAB EXPLODES, BURNS PHILLY INN MOTEL.

He felt the hair stand up on the back of his neck.

*That's it!*

*Death.Before.Dishonor had posted a comment at the end of that article that said, "Fuck you!" and something else.*

*It was listed right after mine.*

He clicked on the link, then scrolled down. He found his comment and the one after it:

---

From **Hung.Up.Badge.But.Not.Gun (9:50 a.m.):**

*Amen to both of you, Indy1 & WWBFD. I spent enough time walking the beat to see everything at least once. And nothing is as insidious as what these drugs do to families of every walk of life. I say, Shoot 'em all and let the Good Lord sort 'em out.*

Recommend [ 4 ] <u>Click Here to Report Abuse</u>

From **HowYouseGuysDoin' (9:22 a.m.):**

*And amen to that! I'll provide the ammo! This nonsense has got to stop. The inmates are running the asylum!*

Recommend [ 1 ] <u>Click Here to Report Abuse</u>

---

He scrolled farther down the list. There were four other comments.
*But not one from Death.Before.Dishonor.*

*And clearly not the one that ranted about "fuck you!" — oh, and said that drugs were no different from booze and hookers.*

*It's gone now.*

*Huh. Guess someone reported it as abuse, and they pulled it off.*

Stanley Dowbrowski quickly clicked back to the article on the Temple University Hospital murder.

He scrolled down and saw that the Death. Before.Dishonor comment was still there.

He clicked on the printer icon, and in a minute his color printer was spitting out sheets with the article and all of its comments on it.

Then he reached over and picked up the phone. He punched in a number.

*Great.*

*Got his answering machine.*

"Yo, Tony," he said to the answering machine. "Stanley Dowbrowski here. Sorry to bother you this late at home. But I got something weird here. Not sure what. Or even if it's really anything. But it made the hair stand up on the back of my neck. It's about that shooting at the hospital. And the motel that blew up over on Frankford. *That* damn thing rattled the hell out of my windows this morning. Thought the world was coming to an end. Anyway, give me a call when you can. 555-1840. Later."

Stanley Dowbrowski then picked up his James O. Born cop novel and wheezed his way down the hall to the bedroom.

# IX

## [ONE]
## 140 South Broad Street, Philadelphia
## Wednesday, September 9, 8:45 P.M.

Captain Francis X. Hollaran pointed to his wristwatch and said to First Deputy Police Commissioner Dennis V. Coughlin, "You're on in fifteen, boss." Both were wearing suits and ties.

Coughlin nodded.

From the corner of the room, he looked around at the audience. People were beginning to fill the fifty seats set up around the ten round tables in the western wing of the Grant Room of the Union League of Philadelphia. The room, thirty-seven feet square with ten-foot-high ceilings, was elegantly decorated with stunning chandeliers, dark wood-paneled walls, rich burgundy drapery, and thick deep-red-patterned woolen carpeting. A waitstaff in understated black outfits served light hors d'oeuvres and drinks, the latter being mostly coffee and water and soft drinks but also a fair number of cocktails.

The crowd was composed mostly of men. All were well-dressed and well-groomed.

And well-connected.

The Union League of Philadelphia was founded as a patriotic society in 1862, during the Civil War, by men of the upper middle class. They supported the Union side in the war and, of course, President Lincoln's policies. In keeping with its motto of "Love of Country Leads," the League fiercely supported the military of the United States of America. Its building, listed on the National Historic Register, occupied a whole block of Center City.

Coughlin regularly came and spoke to the Union League's members and guests as an outreach of the police department. The gathering had evolved — which was to say, had grown far beyond his expectations — from smaller informal chats over drinks in the League's bar down the corridor. Still, he tried to keep the tone of the larger gathering the same as that of those earlier ones — that of a more or less casual get-together.

The outreach was a self-appointed task, one he felt neither the mayor nor the police commissioner could do effectively because of their high profiles. And they both agreed with Coughlin; as first deputy police commissioner, he was the top cop who really had his hand in the everyday business of all the varied departments.

Coughlin considered it highly important that the city's heavy hitters had a better understanding of what the department was doing — and what the men on the street were up against. If they did, he figured, then they would be more prone to defend and support the police department. And, failing that, at least not be of a limited mind-set to rush to judgment and damn the department for the slightest infraction.

Denny Coughlin quickly patted his suit coat at chest level, first one side then the other. He felt relief when he found that the half-dozen index cards bearing his notes for the evening discussion were still in the inside left pocket.

Coughlin then looked at Hollaran and said, "Frank, Jason Washington told me that that Texas Ranger is with Matty."

"That's right, Denny."

"Put out the arm for them, would you,

please? For one, I'd like to meet the man. Liz Justice spoke highly of him. For another, he might be able to contribute to tonight's topic. Meantime, I'm going to visit the gentlemen's facility before this thing gets started."

Hollaran nodded, then stepped into the corridor. He pulled out his cell phone from his suit jacket's inside pocket. But then he remembered that by the door was a chrome-plated four-foot-tall pole on a round chrome base that displayed a sign:

---

**CELLULAR TELEPHONE CONVERSATIONS PROHIBITED! PER STRICT LEAGUE POLICY 0654-1. KINDLY *TURN OFF* ALL SUCH DEVICES. THANK YOU.**

---

Hollaran walked down the corridor and went to a bank of telephones. He picked up the receiver of one that had a small sign beside it that read LOCAL CALLS. He looked at his cell phone. He scrolled down its phone book list until he found PAYNE MATT HOME, then PAYNE MATT CELL. He punched a key to show the number, then he punched the number into the landline

476

phone's keypad.

"Matt," Hollaran said when Payne answered. "Frank Hollaran. Commissioner Coughlin would like you and your guest to join us at the Union League. How soon can you get here?"

"We just left the ME's office," Payne said.

"Anything new?"

"Yeah. And it doesn't look good. I think we can be there directly. 'We' being Jim Byrth and Tony Harris."

*Harris?* Hollaran thought. *He's a damned good cop.*

*But he'd be out of his league here in, well, the League. Would that make him uncomfortable?*

"I have no problem with Tony, Matt. But would he be comfortable?"

"A helluva lot more comfortable than where we just were and witnessed."

Hollaran heard a strange tone in Payne's voice. *Anger maybe?*

"Okay," he said. "I leave the decision in your capable hands, Sergeant. See you shortly."

Forty-five minutes earlier, Philadelphia Homicide Detective Tony Harris and Philadelphia Homicide Sergeant Matt Payne

477

and Texas Rangers Sergeant Jim Byrth had walked out of Liberties feeling no pain. The questions had arisen as to where they were going to have dinner and where Byrth was going to rent a room for the duration of his stay in the City of Brotherly Love.

Payne had said, "I'd offer you the guest room in my apartment —"

"Thanks, but no way could I accept your offer," Byrth had interrupted.

"And you're exactly correct," Payne had replied. "Because I'm not."

Byrth turned to him with a look that said, *Then why the hell did you offer it?*

Tony Harris explained, "It's because he doesn't have one. His apartment is tiny."

Payne's stomach growled.

"Excuse me. Obviously, I am in need of sustenance," he said. Then he added, "Jim, that was what's known as a *hypothetical* statement. Because if I did have one, it'd be all yours. That's where I was going with that train of thought."

Byrth smiled, then shook his head. The Hat on top accentuated the motion.

Harris added, "You're welcome to stay at my house. I do have a guest room."

"Thank you, Tony. But, really, I couldn't impose. Besides, I'm not spending my money."

Then Harris's phone had started ringing. That reminded Payne he'd turned his off, and he pushed the 0/1 button till his screen lit up. He cleared out the MISSED CALLS list — all from Chad Nesbitt, who within a twenty-minute period had called a dozen times, then had gotten the message and given up.

*I told you, ol' buddy, I'll deal with that later.*

Harris answered his phone.

After a moment, he said, "Okay, thanks." And ended the call.

"Dr. Mitchell's finishing up with the girl they fished out of the river," Harris said. "I asked him to call me when he did. I wanted to swing by. You guys don't need to go."

"Am I allowed to ask, 'Who's Dr. Mitchell'?"

Payne said, "Sure. Feel free to ask anything. He's the medical examiner."

"As strange as it might sound, I'd like to go," Byrth said. "You always learn something. Even if it's only a little thing that triggers a thought later."

"The Black Buddha calls that 'Looking under the rock under the rock,' " Payne said. "I'm in, too, Tony. I figure I've got enough liquid encouragement in me to get through it."

"Won't take but a moment," Harris said.

479

Harris had been wrong. It had taken longer than he had thought. They'd had more to discuss than just the young Hispanic woman.

The Medical Examiner's Office, just across the Schuylkill River, was next door to the University of Pennsylvania and, somewhat appropriately, just up University Avenue from Woodlands Cemetery.

The medical examiner's job was to investigate all "non-natural and unattended natural deaths."

The Medical Examiner's Office was open round-the-clock. In a city like Philly, that was an absolute necessity. Its investigators handled some six thousand cases each year — which averaged out to be a staggering sixteen a day. They worked long hours to determine what caused a person's violent or suspicious death, particularly all homicides and suicides and any deaths that were drug-related.

And they were good at it. They more or less quickly determined the manner of death in about half of the cases; the remainder required an autopsy. The ME's office then wrote up a report of the autopsy for use in the criminal justice system, and the ME himself often appeared in court and provided expert testimony.

tigators held weekly meetings with police detectives. They updated the policemen on cases, reviewing new information and reminding them which bodies remained unidentified and held at the morgue. One such recent case had been the bullet-riddled body of a black male. The victim had been pulled from the Delaware River at the foot of the Benjamin Franklin Bridge that connected Philly to Camden, New Jersey.

Dr. Mitchell had explained to Payne the "washerwoman effect" — the term in modern society of course being the complete opposite of politically correct. But "washerperson" just didn't seem to carry the same descriptive impact.

The ME had said that the wrinkles on the body were caused by its having been immersed in water for an extended period of time. They were particularly pronounced on the flesh of the feet and, of course, of the hands. The condition was consistent with that of a woman who spent a lot of time washing with her hands. Thus, its name.

Harris then said, "Anything unusual jump out at you, Doc?"

Mitchell shook his head. "You mean, except for not being able to do a cranial exam? Not that I'm complaining; that saved me a good half hour off the usual two-hour process."

"Yeah."

"Define 'unusual' in this business, Detective," he said dryly. He then added, "Nothing beyond the grass particles embedded in the bone of the spinal column."

"Tell us about that," Payne said.

"Well, it's clear that whatever was used to cut through the flesh and bone had previously been used in someone's yard."

*Kerry Rapier told us in the command center that Javier Iglesia had mentioned he'd seen the grass embedded on the body.*

"Like a pair of those long-handled shears?" Payne said.

Mitchell shook his head. "No, these weren't leaf particles. These were fibers of grass. I could show you in the microscope, but that's not necessary. It's pretty clear to the naked eye. Here, look."

He waved them over to the end of the table where the neck wound remained open. He pointed.

"Jesus!" Payne said when he saw the hacked bone and flesh. "She was whacked at — look at all those chunks taken out. Shears would have made a cleaner cut. I mean, *cuts*. From two sides."

"Are those also metal fragments?" Byrth said.

484

"Good eyes," Mitchell said. "Blade fragments, I'd say. I believe the severing was caused by either a very sharp blade from, say, a lawn mower or, more likely, a more brittle blade, such as a machete."

"Well, now, that's good news!" Payne said, the sarcasm evident in his tone. "There can only be — what? — ten, twenty thousand machetes out there? Or one particular one rusting on the bottom of the Schuylkill."

Byrth raised his eyebrows. "Yeah, but it's consistent with what happened to the two in Texas."

Payne and Harris turned and looked at Byrth.

"They used machetes?" Payne said.

Byrth nodded. "It's a common tool used by the Latino lawn-mowing crews in Texas. You'll see them pruning bushes and tree limbs with them. Apparently they use them on tall grass, too. If you think about it, it's a pretty efficient bush tool. By 'bush' I mean jungle. They used it wherever they came from in Central America; why not here?"

The three stood in a shocked silence as they watched the ME go back to suturing the body of the young Hispanic female.

Payne had a mental image of some Latino towering over young girls and flailing with the long-bladed machete, just hacking away at their necks.

*What sort of animal does that?* he thought.

*Certainly a godless one . . .*

Harris finally broke their silence.

"What happens next, Doc?" he said. "We got nothing back from the FBI on her fingerprints. No records, nothing."

"The examiners will make the usual calls, trying to see if she's a runaway or similar. But unless someone comes forward, I guess she'll just go on the list with the other two."

He nodded at a clipboard hanging on a hook by the door.

Dr. Mitchell explained: "We went ahead and wrote up the two Hispanic males from the motel explosion."

The ME's office had a Forensic Investigative Unit. Among other tasks, the FIU worked to identify human remains. Then, if successful, it contacted the next of kin.

Most unidentified bodies brought to the ME were identified within a matter of hours. This was accomplished by matching fingerprints to FBI database records. Folks who died violent deaths of a suspicious nature tended to have an arrest record, which of course included a full set of fingerprints. For those who didn't have a rap sheet the size of a phone book, the identification sometimes was made using dental records or DNA matching, both of which tended to be more difficult than matches by prints. But, like the prints, these matches were indisputable.

There were those victims, however, who just could not be so matched. Decomposition and charring of the body topped the list of reasons why no records could be found on a John or Jane Doe. And so the ME's office published a list of these non-name victims available for public review.

Payne walked over and collected the clipboard. He read the top sheet:

---

**City of Philadelphia**
**Medical Examiner's Office**
**Forensic Investigative Unit**
**Howard H. Mitchell, MD**
**Medical Examiner**

To date, using current methods, the Forensic Investigative Unit of the Medical Examiner's Office has been unable to identify the following persons. It is hoped that this listing of unknown individuals and their description being made public will aid in our identifying them.

Anyone having any information that may

---

help the FIU identify these person or persons is asked to contract the Forensic Services Manager at 215-685-7445.

CASE NUMBER: 09-4087

RACE: Hispanic

GENDER: Male

ESTIMATE AGE: 25–30 years

ESTIMATE HEIGHT AND WEIGHT: 5'4", 140 pounds

DATE BODY FOUND: 09 September

LOCATION OF BODY: Philly Inn, 7004 Frankford Avenue, Philadelphia

DISTINGUISHING MARKS: tattoo of a tear drop at corner of right eye; tear drop incomplete, only bottom inked in

PERSONAL EFFECTS: gold earring stud right lobe.

CLOTHING: LUCKY brand jeans size

34x32, [unknown] brand T-shirt size medium, NIKE athletic shoes size 10

BRIEF DESCRIPTION: Charred remains. The decedent was killed in the explosion of a meth lab. Clothing mostly burned. The decedent can be identified by dental record or DNA.

CASE NUMBER: 09-4087

RACE: Hispanic

GENDER: Male

ESTIMATE AGE: 20–25 years

ESTIMATE HEIGHT AND WEIGHT: 5'0", 100 pounds

DATE BODY FOUND: 09 September

LOCATION OF BODY: Philly Inn, 7004 Frankford Avenue, Philadelphia

DISTINGUISHING MARKS: None

PERSONAL EFFECTS: Timex wristwatch

CLOTHING: Notorious BIG brand jeans size 34x32, [unknown] brand T-shirt size medium, NIKE athletic shoes size 10

BRIEF DESCRIPTION: Charred remains. The decedent was in an explosion of a meth lab but may have died from a cut to the throat. Clothing almost completely burned. Timex wristwatch melted to wrist. The decedent can be identified by dental record or DNA.

Matt Payne snorted as he read.

He handed the clipboard to Tony Harris.

Payne said, "Get a load of the brand names of their jeans. 'Notorious BIG' and, irony of ironies, 'Lucky.'"

Harris took the sheet and looked. He grunted as he handed the board to Byrth.

"Jim, any idea what's with the older, bigger guy's tattoo?" Payne then said.

"Hard to say," Byrth replied as he scanned the sheet, "because the gangbangers have bastardized it so much. A teardrop originally was basically a symbol of someone crying over a lost one, either incarcerated or murdered — a display of closure. Then it came to be a badge of honor, or warning, especially in prison, indicating that the bearer had murdered someone in or out of prison."

"What about the one on this guy? A tear with an empty top and a full bottom."

"Could mean he avenged the murder of a loved one."

Payne looked at Tony Harris.

"The other guy had the slit throat," Payne said.

Harris nodded. "Could be something. Maybe suggests he wasn't shy about taking someone out?"

"Certainly fitting," Byrth said. He then added, "You don't want to walk around with one in Australia."

"Why?" Payne said.

"There, convicts who're accused as being child molesters basically get branded with a teardrop."

Payne shook his head. "Hell, I don't want to walk around with one anywhere." He sighed as he glanced again at the abused corpse. "No offense, Doc, but I'm getting the hell out of here."

"None taken, Matt. This particular job even depresses a callous veteran such as myself. Good luck catching the sonofabitch."

Harris and Byrth said their thanks and goodbyes, and followed.

And as they stepped outside, Payne's cell phone began ringing.

He looked at the screen. It read: UNION LEAGUE OF PHILA — 1 CALL @ 2045.

"Wonder who this is?" he said, and a moment later heard Hollaran's voice.

# [TWO]
## 2480 Arroyo Avenue, Dallas
## Wednesday, September 9,
## 7:56 P.M.
## Texas Standard Time

Juan Paulo Delgado stepped carefully as he went through the six-foot-tall wall of red-tip photinias that grew thickly beside the convenience store. He had his Beretta semiautomatic nine-millimeter pistol out, and slowly thumbed back its hammer.

He heard and smelled the grimy man before he saw him in the shadows.

The coyote was humming as he took one helluva piss on the bare dirt.

*He's dirty and he stinks!*

El Gato pounced.

His right arm outstretched, he brought up his pistol to shoulder level and smoothly closed on his target. Just as the muzzle of the weapon touched the back of the man's skull — and the man suddenly realized that he was not alone — El Gato squeezed the trigger.

The hollow-point copper-jacketed lead bullet made a neat entrance hole and mushroomed. It traveled through the soft gray matter, then made an exit wound that fractured so much bone it tore off the flesh of the man's right cheek.

He immediately fell forward, making a soft splash as he landed in his own pool of urine. Blood drained from the head wounds, mixing with the pool.

*Shit!* Delgado thought, wiping at the blood spatter on his hands.

*And I don't want to have to dig around in that mess!*

Then he saw light reflecting off something metallic in the man's left hand.

*The keys!*

He grabbed them. Then he ran a finger through the right back pocket of the man's blue jeans. He pulled out a wallet and stuck it in his left front pants pocket.

He kicked the man, checking for any sign of life.

The man's body responded with an extraordinarily long final act of flatulence.

El Gato began stepping back to the wall of bushes. As he went though the bushes, he decocked the Beretta and slipped it back in his waistband. The barrel was still warm, almost uncomfortably so against the sensitive skin of his groin.

He looked around. No one seemed to be paying any attention to him or to the side of the convenience store.

Delgado walked up to the driver's door of the Expedition. He motioned for El Cheque to roll down his window.

"What the hell was that about?" El Cheque said.

Delgado didn't reply. He was pulling the dead man's wallet from his pocket. He thumbed through it. He found a state of Texas driver's license with the man's picture on it. On the license was the name Salvador Zamora.

He handed it to El Cheque.

"That coyote won't be needing this anymore. Hang on to it. We might be able to use it for a fake, if it's not already a fake. Or sell it."

El Cheque took it.

"Follow me to the house," Delgado then said. "We can send someone for the Suburban later. Anyone at the house?"

"Sí. Miguel."

"Get on the phone and call him. Tell him to be ready to open the gate when he sees that van. Describe it to him, okay?"

El Cheque began, "Okay. But what — ?"

El Gato was already on the way to the fuel pump island.

El Cheque put the Expedition in reverse. He backed up, then stopped and waited, watching Delgado return the pump handle to the pump then get in the driver's seat of the van.

"Good evening, everyone!" Juan Paulo Delgado said cheerfully in Spanish as he sat in the driver's seat of the white Dodge van and closed the door. The front passenger seat was unoccupied.

Hoping to project an air of comfortable confidence, he went on, "I am El Gato! And I'll be taking you to the final stop."

He pulled on his seat belt. Then he slipped the key in the ignition and turned it. The engine turned over very slowly, then finally rumbled to life.

He looked into the rearview mirror on the windshield. A sea of surprised and curious faces looked back at him. He counted eighteen heads. There were only two males, both older than maybe fifteen. The age range seemed to go from a couple of toddlers with their young mothers to one of the males who looked to be in his forties. The majority were in their teens and twenties.

*And the old guy right behind me looks angry as hell.*

They all also looked road-weary. The van reeked of human sweat and greasy fast food.

Juan Paulo Delgado turned on the charm.

"Señor Zamora asked me to remind you that he would catch up at the next stop. He told you I would be helping, yes?" He didn't wait for a reply. But he could tell they were not convinced. "Where we are going is only ten, maybe fifteen minutes away. Very close. You will see him soon. Meantime, I'll start helping you get in touch with your families."

Delgado smiled broadly into the mirror.

*Mentioning family brought smiles to those younger faces.*

*So there's no question they're illegal — and tired from that long trip.*

*There's also no question not everyone is convinced I'm their new friend.*

*But they're also not trying to run.*

*Maybe because they are exhausted.*

As he reached for the gearshift, he glanced at the instrument cluster. The needle of the fuel gauge showed full. The engine temperature needle was in the red but just starting to move back toward the green. The odometer read 218,990.

*Not its first trip.*

*Hope it makes it to the other side of downtown.*

He put the van in gear and drove away from the convenience store fuel pump island.

Juan Paulo Delgado, with Jorge Ernesto Aguilar following two car lengths back in the brown Ford Expedition, followed all the laws of the road as he drove the Dodge Ram passenger van. He did not go faster than the speed limit — as best he could tell, because the needle of the worn-out speedometer tended to bounce occasionally — and he faithfully used the blinker when changing lanes and making turns.

He knew that that was not a guarantee he would not get pulled over by the police. They could stop a vehicle for damn near anything if they wanted. But it was better than being careless and stupid by drawing their attention.

He pulled onto Stemmons Freeway and took it south, skirting the shiny tall buildings of downtown Dallas. He picked up Thornton Freeway eastbound. A mile later, he took the exit that went past Fair Park — or what he called Gringo Park. It had the nice open-air concert shell where the rock bands and country music singers performed, mostly on weekend nights. It also had the football stadium that every New Year's featured the Cotton Bowl college championship game and every October, during the Texas State Fair, hosted the Texas–Oklahoma college rivalry game.

Delgado knew that all kinds of gringos gravitated to this part of town for those events. And then, when the events ended, promptly got the hell out of the rough neighborhood.

A half-mile later, he turned off Hatcher Street into the driveway of an older one-story house.

Across the street from the house was Juanita Craft Park. It was what Delgado thought of as a more representative park for those who lived in these parts. The football games played there used a soccer ball, not the pigskin kicked around in the Cotton Bowl. Spanish-language billboards advertised fast-food restaurants, Latino radio stations, various brands of booze. And Juanita Craft Park abutted a stream, one that was more of a rancid drainage ditch and flowed under the train track trestle two blocks south.

The one-story older house sat by itself well back from Hatcher Street. Its wooden siding had white paint that was chipped and peeling. It was surrounded by chain-link fencing that blocked any view of the backyard.

In the backyard were usually a half-dozen utility trailers loaded with lawn care equipment, as well as a detached wooden garage. Beyond the back fence, a thick tree line separated the house and its property from a children's playground, on the far side of which was another line of trees and thick shrubbery, which grew along the train track.

All of which served to further isolate the house, though there were some houses far across the four lanes of Hatcher.

The headlights of the Dodge Ram van lit up the chain-link gate.

Out of the shadows there suddenly appeared a man.

*Good man, Miguel. You're here.*

*Now get the damned gate open.*

Miguel Guilar physically looked a lot like Delgado. He wore black jeans, a dark T-shirt, and black athletic shoes. They had grown up together and graduated from North Dallas High School, which was across the freeway and a couple miles away. At almost ninety years old, the school had outgrown its name. Realistically, present-day North Dallas was the sprawl of suburbia much farther north.

Guilar pushed on the chain-link gate and it swung inward. Delgado eased the van through the gap and into the dark, unlit backyard. When he looked toward Guilar, he saw that Miguel held a black pump shotgun, its butt on his hip. Then Guilar stepped back into the shadows. El Cheque rolled the Expedition in behind the van, and Guilar closed the gate.

Except for one of the toddlers repeatedly saying, "Mama, Mama, Mama," it was deafeningly quiet in the van. Delgado thought he could feel the tension, if not some terror.

"Welcome!" he said cheerfully in Spanish as he pulled the van to a stop and shut off the engine. "You have made it! Your journey is over! My associates will help you bring your things into the house. And then we can get you on your way."

He opened the driver's door and hopped to the ground.

Miguel Guilar was walking up to him with the gun. Delgado saw that it was his black Remington Model 1300 pump-action twelve-gauge. He knew that Guilar kept his "Defender" loaded with six rounds of double-ought buckshot.

Delgado said, "You have the zip ties?"

Guilar reached into the back pocket of his black jeans and pulled out the two-foot-long plastic strips that were generally used to quickly and securely bind damn near anything they would fit around. There were at least twenty in the bundle, held together with a rubber band. Delgado stripped two from the bundle and slipped them into his pants pocket.

"We separate the women from the men first, okay?" Delgado said in English as he pulled the Beretta from the waistband of his pants. "Just follow my lead."

"Okay," Guilar said, then walked with Delgado to the large sliding door on the other side of the van.

Guilar and Delgado were standing in front of the sliding door when Aguilar walked up to them, holding the TEC-9 that had been in the Expedition's console with his Beretta.

*No surprise that he would like that gun.*

*He likes looks.*

Delgado said to him, "El Cheque, you take the females into the house."

"*Sí,*" he replied. "One minute."

He trotted to the back door of the house and opened it. The lights from inside backlit him. Then he trotted back to the van.

"Okay," El Cheque said.

Delgado, keeping his Beretta along his right thigh, opened the sliding door with his left hand.

"Women and children first!" Delgado said in Spanish, his tone upbeat. "Come, come!

Follow El Cheque. He will show you to the house."

Delgado looked at the woman sitting at the end of the second-row bench seat nearest the door. She was at least forty, overweight, and wholly unattractive. Slowly, hesitantly, she slid to the edge of the seat and stepped to the ground. She pulled a dirt-smudged silver backpack out from under the seat.

*That is all of her possessions,* Delgado thought.

*Amazing.*

Then El Cheque gestured toward the open back door of the house.

The woman did not move. She looked in the van to the dark-haired girl of about eight who'd been sitting beside her. The woman waited until the girl exited the van and collected her small vinyl overnight bag. The girl walked to the woman and took her hand. And they stood there.

The angry man Delgado had seen in the rearview mirror was the last one on that bench seat. He started sliding across the seat toward the door.

*"Alto!"* Delgado said forcefully, holding up his left hand palm outward.

The man stopped. He made an angry face.

"That is my family," he said, gesturing toward the woman and child.

*You poor bastard,* Delgado thought, glancing at the woman.

*Love is blind.*

"Women and children first," Delgado said again. He looked to the next row back, which held four teenage girls. "Come, ladies. You're next."

As they stepped off, Delgado caught El Cheque out of the corner of his eye. El Cheque was watching with growing interest as the teenage girls exited.

*Taking your pick, are you?*

*Your pick of one?*

*Or of which one first?*

Three of the four were about fifteen and somewhat attractive. The third was maybe eighteen and, Delgado thought, not exactly unattractive. But she was a bit pudgy, and had badly bleached streaks in her hair. There were tattoos on her arms. They were not gang symbols, as far as he could tell.

Delgado looked back inside the van. He decided he wouldn't have trouble with the other male. He looked to be about seventeen, and sat on the last bench, up against the window. He naturally would be the last off. Sitting next to him was a very attractive girl wearing a pink lace blouse. She looked a little younger than the boy, maybe sixteen. By their body language, they appeared to be more than just seatmates.

He motioned for Aguilar to come over.

"When you get them in there, collect all their phones and whatever address books or papers they have. Strip them of everything, especially any weapons or anything that could be used as a weapon. If they're difficult, use that TEC-9 if necessary. Then let me know when it's done."

Delgado waited until Aguilar had herded all the women into the house before he let the two males in the van even move.

They had of course protested. But Delgado quelled that by raising his pistol. He said in Spanish, "I can use this now, or you can do as I say — and find out if I let you live later. Right now, I don't need either of you or this van."

Then Delgado said, "What you're going to do to stay alive is step out of the van one at a time." He pointed the pistol at the teenage boy in back. "You first."

The boy slowly worked his way from the back of the van to the open sliding door.

"Okay," Delgado said, "now step out and lean against the van's hood, hands on your neck."

Delgado had had some experience with

504

this series of motions. However, he'd been the one taking orders from the police.

Delgado then pulled one of the zip ties from his pocket. He looked at Miguel Guilar and said, "Get my back."

Guilar nodded, and aimed the shotgun at the van, the muzzle pointing between the boy on the hood and the man inside.

Delgado then decocked his Beretta and put it in his waistband. He stepped over to the teenager and with his right hand grabbed the boy's right wrist. He brought it down to the small of the boy's back and held it there. Then he started to do the same with the left. But when he grabbed the teenager's left wrist, the kid spun on him, striking Delgado in the cheekbone with his elbow.

"Motherfucker!" Delgado yelled in pain, and wrestled the teenager to the ground.

Guilar stepped in closer, swinging the muzzle of the shotgun toward the two, trying to get an aim that didn't include Delgado.

Then he saw the man in the van start to move. Guilar quickly pointed the shotgun at him, and the man cowered back in his seat.

Guilar looked back down at Delgado.

He saw that Delgado now had the teenager on his belly, a knee on the back of his neck that forced his face into the grass. Delgado's other knee pinned the teenager's right arm against his back. With some effort, he got the boy's wrists crossed. He pulled out the other zip tie from his pocket and looped it around the wrists. He threaded the tag end of the tie into the box end and pulled tight. The kid screamed as the plastic banding cut into his flesh.

Delgado stood — and kicked the kid in the face.

The teenager's nose began bleeding profusely.

"*Pendejo!*" Delgado said, gently touching his injured cheek. He spat on the boy's back. "Try that again and you're dead!"

Delgado then turned to the man in the van. His eyes were wide, and he had his hands up, palms out, in surrender.

Delgado went to the mirror on the door of the van and tried to inspect his injury. In the dim light, he could not see anything obvious. But it hurt like hell.

He looked at the teenager, who was trying to sit up.

"I'm not through with you," Delgado said.

The teenager glared back defiantly.

El Cheque then stuck his head out the back door of the house.

"Done!" he called to Delgado.

After the older male had been zip-tied without incident, Delgado looked at Guilar.

"Okay," he said, "now put the van in the garage, then get some chain and locks off the lawn trailers and bring them inside."

When Delgado approached the back door of the house, he held the two zip-tied males by the back of their shirt collars. He pushed them through the open doorway and into the kitchen.

The women and children were sitting in mismatched chairs, some old broken ones made of wood, but the majority white molded plastic.

The girl in the pink lace shirt saw the teenage boy's bloodied face and began screaming. She ran to the boy.

She looked back at El Gato, her eyes wide with fear.

"Why did you do this?" she wailed.

"He is a very lucky boy," Delgado said in Spanish. "He could be dead right now."

Guilar came in with the chains and locks that normally were used to secure the lawn mowers and other tools to the trailers.

"Okay," Delgado said in English, looking between Guilar and El Cheque, "you know what to do next." He nodded at the teenage boy and the girl in the pink lace shirt. "I'll handle these two."

# [THREE]
## 140 South Broad Street, Philadelphia
## Wednesday, September 9, 8:58 P.M.

It was only a little more than a mile from the Medical Examiner's Office on University Avenue to South Broad Street. Payne got on Chestnut Street, and planned on taking it the whole way, passing within a couple blocks of his place on Rittenhouse Square.

After Payne had explained what Hollaran had said, Byrth had said, "What's a Union League? Texas is a right-to-work state; not many unions."

Payne had then clarified. He gave him the organization's background, ending with, "It's still a strong supporter of our military services, and it's played host forever to world leaders, business chieftains, celebrities. Nothing like a union hall at all. It drips with Old World Philadelphia of 1862."

"Another thirty years, it'd be as old as the Rangers," Byrth said.

That caused Payne to look at him curiously. But he saw that Byrth wasn't bragging. He was, instead, making a statement that showed his appreciation of the long history of both institutions.

Payne said, "It also solves the problem of your lodging. My family's been members for generations. I'll sponsor you so you can stay in The Inn at the League. The room will not only cost less than any lousy Marriott or Hilton you'll find, it'll be a helluva lot better."

Byrth shrugged. "When in Rome . . ."

Payne then explained the background of the function they were about to attend. And the reasoning behind why the second-highest-ranking officer in the Philadelphia Police Department held it.

Payne pulled to the curb on Broad Street in front of the Union League property.

Byrth observed that the building, with its brick and brownstone façade, was very well-preserved for being some 150 years old. Its design certainly stood out from the modern surroundings, all the tall shiny office buildings around it. At the front, two dramatic circular staircases led up to the main entrance on the second level. Bronze statues stood dramatically beside each of the staircases. And Old Glory, spectacularly lit by a bright floodlight, slowly flapped atop a twenty-foot-tall flagpole mounted to the fore of the flat roof.

Inside, Byrth found that Payne was right. The Union League did indeed drip with Old World Philadelphia.

The ambience oozed old school luxury — polished marble floors with exotic rugs, rich wood paneling, magnificent leather-upholstered furniture that you could actually smell. On the walls hung handsome works of art, from old warships sailing far out at sea to portraits of presidents of the United States of America. Along the walls were distinguished displays featuring bronze and marble busts and sculptures.

Byrth watched Payne as he walked up to a marble-topped oak desk, behind which sat a somewhat distinguished old man with a full head of silver hair.

Byrth saw that the geezer wore a dark pin-striped suit with a silver silk tie — and an incredible air of snootiness.

The geezer looked up from the appointment book he had been reviewing.

"Ah, good evening, Young Mr. Payne," the geezer said with a nasal tone. "So good to see you again."

The geezer's eyes studied their small party.

Payne said, "Good evening, Baxter. We're here for Commissioner Coughlin's regular group."

"That would be in the Grant Room. All the way down, on the right."

"Thank you, Baxter. I do believe I remember where it is. And I have two guests tonight, one of whom is in town on business." He gestured toward Byrth. "Mr. Byrth will require a room."

The geezer said nothing. He stood.

"Mr. Payne, I'll call down to the Inn and alert the deskman."

The geezer surveyed Harris. Then he surveyed Byrth, his dull gaze lingering on The Hat in the crook of his arm.

Then he looked back at Payne.

Payne said, "Is there some problem?"

*Oh, boy,* Jim Byrth thought.

*This is where I get us all thrown out to the curb of this snooty joint.*

"If you will excuse me a moment," the geezer said nasally.

He wordlessly disappeared into the cloakroom.

Payne looked between Harris and Byrth, his eyebrows raised to say, *Wonder what the hell this is all about?*

Moments later, the geezer reappeared with an old navy blazer. It had two gold buttons on the front and three on the right sleeve. But there were only two on the left sleeve.

"So sorry, Mr. Payne," he said, but he didn't sound at all sincere. "This is the only jacket we have available at this time."

Then the man held it out to Payne as he repositioned a small framed sign that was on the desk.

Payne glanced down at it and shook his head.

"Sorry, Baxter," he said as he took the jacket. "I'm really tired. I forgot."

Byrth read the sign:

---

**MEN'S DRESS CODE POLICY**
(Strictly Enforced)

*The League requires a jacket be worn by men. Jeans, denim wear, athletic attire, T-shirts, shorts, baseball caps, sneakers, or tattered clothes are never permitted on the first or second floor of the League house.*

---

"Again," the geezer said with some emphasis. "Which of course is why we keep jackets for you, Mr. Payne."

Payne slipped it on.

*This damn thing feels two sizes too small.*

*I could walk the five blocks to my apartment, but then we'd really be late.*

Tony Harris chuckled.

"House rules, sir," the geezer said snootily.

Payne's stomach growled again as he glanced down the hall. He could see the entrance to the Grant Room, and saw people still milling in the corridor.

He looked at his watch: one minute to nine.

"Oh, to hell with it. These things never start on time." He looked between Byrth and Harris. "After what we just went through, we deserve some more liquid courage undisturbed. Maybe a bite to eat, too. Let's go in the bar, then we can go down to the Grant. With luck we can sneak in and no one will even notice."

"I'm with you, Marshal," Byrth said. "But I'm afraid I have to tell you: No amount of booze will flush the mental image of that girl, or the anger at her murder."

Payne nodded. "Doesn't mean I can't give it the old college try."

Byrth and Harris followed Payne the twenty or so feet down the hall. They entered the bar through a doorway on the right.

■ ■ ■ ■

The first person Sergeant Matthew M. Payne saw at the bar as he entered was First Deputy Police Commissioner Dennis V. Coughlin.

Coughlin had his head back so that he could drain the last drop of his double Bushmills Malt 21. He caught Payne — and The Hat — out of the corner of his eye.

After lowering his head and putting the glass on the bar, Coughlin turned toward them. He looked a little guilty, as if he'd be caught. But only a little guilty.

"Waste not, want not," he then said with a twinkle in his Irish eyes. "Glad you gentlemen made it."

"Commissioner Coughlin," Payne said formally, "I'd like to introduce Sergeant Jim Byrth of the Texas Rangers. Jim, Commissioner Coughlin."

"Pleased to meet you, sir," Byrth said, offering his hand.

"My pleasure, Jim," Coughlin replied, meeting his firm grip. "Liz Justice speaks highly of you. That goes a long way in my book."

"Thank you, sir."

Payne waved for the bartender to come over.

"Uncle Denny," Payne said, "do you want another double Bushmills 21?"

Byrth caught the "uncle" and looked to see how the commissioner of police was going to respond.

"No, thank you, Matty. I don't need to start slurring in there."

Byrth then decided that Payne and Coughlin had to be uncle and nephew.

"Jim," Coughlin said, "I'm going to put you on the spot here."

"Yes, sir?"

"I'm speaking tonight about what's been going on recently, particularly today. I know you'll find this hard to believe, but today's murders weren't our fair city's first. But it might be a first for them to happen at almost the same time. I plan to go over that and the illegal drugs behind it. I'm hoping you might speak to the crowd about your perspective of it."

Byrth nodded once. "Absolutely. It would be my honor."

Payne passed out the bourbons to Byrth and Harris, then held up his glass. "To our health — and to our catching that bastard who killed that poor girl. And all the other bastards."

The four of them touched glasses and drank to that. Denny Coughlin wound up chewing on an ice cube.

"What happened at the morgue?" Coughlin then said. "What'd you find out?"

Payne told him.

Coughlin shook his head slowly in disgust. Then he checked his watch and said, "These things never start on time. But we need to get the show going. Bring those drinks with you."

Then First Deputy Police Commissioner Dennis V. Coughin marched out of the bar and through the doorway.

When Matt Payne, Jim Byrth, and Tony Harris entered the Grant Room, Commissioner Coughlin was already standing beside the dark wood lectern at the front of the room. He was talking to Captain Frank Hollaran, who stood in front of a flag of the United States of America. The flag was on a wooden staff that was held upright on the floor by a round golden stand.

All the tables were full except the one at the back of the room. Payne, Byrth, and Harris got to three of its five empty seats just as Hollaran stepped up to the lectern.

Exactly at the time that they sat down, Hollaran used his left hand to pull the microphone from the lectern.

He said, "Good evening, all. As most of you know, I'm Captain Frank Hollaran of the

Philadelphia Police Department. Thank you for being here tonight. Now, if you'll please stand and join me, we'll get the formalities of tonight's meeting out of the way."

The room rose to its feet en masse. Everyone faced the American flag and placed their right hands over their hearts.

Hollaran, microphone to his lips, then surprised the hell out of Byrth by belting out in a rich baritone voice "The Star-Spangled Banner."

Everyone near Byrth, including Matt Payne and Tony Harris, sang along with gusto. But none in harmony. Nor in tune. And all seemed oblivious to that fact.

As they all sang, ". . . the land of the free and the home of the brave!" Byrth couldn't help but glance and grin at Payne.

*Matt must be tone-fucking-deaf.*

Everyone took their seats.

*Still, I liked that.*

Byrth looked around at the people. They were as Payne had described in the car, upper-middle-class types who were clearly of comfortable means.

*And it's good to be among people who actually know all the words to our national anthem.*

*And are respectful of it.*

*Hand over heart. No talking during its singing.*

*No yelling "play ball!" at its end.*
*A real class act.*

Hollaran now said, "If you'll please join me in welcoming First Deputy Police Commissioner Denny Coughlin. . . ."

The room filled with polite applause as Hollaran handed the microphone to Coughlin.

"Hear, hear, Denny!" a dashing gentleman seated at a table closer to the lectern called out as he pounded the tablecloth with an open hand.

Byrth saw Payne make eye contact with the gentleman. He looked to be about fifty. He wore a crisp seersucker suit and red bow tie. He was enjoying a cigar the size of a small baseball bat. He nodded politely at Payne.

Payne saw that Byrth was watching and leaned over.

"D. H. Rendolok," Payne whispered as he nodded in Rendolok's direction. "Can usually be found at the bar lost in his thoughts and an enormous cloud of Honduran cigar smoke. His father-in-law was one of our finest police commissioners, under a previous mayor. His wife gave up a lucrative law practice to become one of the most respected judges in Eastern Pennsylvania, if not the entire Eastern Seaboard. D.H. won't tell you himself, but he volunteers time as a consultant in building structure analysis in a highly classified homeland security project. Good people."

Byrth nodded. He then looked at Coughlin.

The big Irishman smiled warmly. He held up his hand to get them to stop. "Thank you. That's quite kind of you."

The crowd became quiet.

Coughlin said: "As usual, I must begin by saying that this session is off the record. What's said here in the Grant Room stays in the Grant Room." He grinned. "My old pal Ulysses would want it that way."

He got the expected chuckles.

"That said, I want to repeat Frank's sincere thanks for all of you taking time to be here. It tells me that not only do we have fine citizens who care about our great city, we also have people who care about what their police department is doing."

Byrth saw more than a few heads nodding. But he also heard behind him what sounded like a derisive grunt. And some mumbling.

He turned and saw two men right behind him, at the next table.

Byrth did not hear exactly what had been said. But the tone and body language — and knowing smirks — clearly suggested that it had been derogatory.

The two men were murmuring between themselves. They looked to be between thirty-five and forty — and terribly smug. One had what could be described as a three-day growth of beard. It was what in some circles passed for a fashion statement and in certain other circles qualified for insubordination. The other was skinny and frail, appearing almost sickly.

*"Inbred" comes to mind,* Byrth thought.

*Or "professorial."*

*Well, at least the bearded one looks like he could be a college teacher.*

*One tenured or someone still living on Daddy's Money — same difference.*

When the bearded one noticed Byrth looking at him, he made a face that was at once condescending and disdainful. Then the bearded one looked at Payne in his undersized loaner blazer and at Harris in his wrinkled well-worn blazer. He made a similar look of condescending disdain.

*He's clearly decided that we're all interlopers.*

*I'm surprised he hasn't called for security to have us booted out.*

Byrth turned his attention back to Coughlin. But out of the corner of his eye, he saw that Payne had not missed any of that exchange.

Byrth looked at Payne, who shook his head just perceptibly in a gesture of mild disgust.

"It's been another challenging day in our fair city," Coughlin was saying. "You very likely have seen part of it on tonight's newscasts. We had two deaths at the motel on Frankford that blew up around two o'clock this morning. We believe the explosion was caused by a lab manufacturing illegal drugs. Two other people were injured in the blast and taken to Temple University Hospital's Burn Unit ICU. Then, later in the morning, there was a shooting at the Reading Terminal Market. It was a multiple murder, including that of innocent bystanders. Our detectives and investigators found evidence that that shooting was also drug-related. Then, just before noon, an assassin disguised as a hospital orderly snuck into the Burn Unit's ICU and murdered one of the victims from the motel explosion. The assassin —"

He pulled the microphone away and cleared his throat.

"Excuse me."

Hollaran brought him a glass of water from their table.

"Thank you, Frank. As I was saying, that assassin was pursued through the streets of Philly on foot by one of our Homicide sergeants. The assassin shot at the sergeant.

521

Just before he unfortunately got away, the sergeant, we believe, wounded him. The shot was made to his leg in an effort to stop him, not cause fatal injury."

*My ass,* Payne thought. *I wanted that sonofabitch dead.*

*I was aiming for a chest shot, hoping it might turn into a head shot.*

*Breathing so hard, it knocked my aim off — that's why I only winged the sonofabitch!*

Byrth looked at him and smiled conspiratorially.

Payne thought, *He just read my mind!*

He grinned back.

"Finally," Coughlin went on, "about the time of that foot chase, the Marine Unit of the Philly PD recovered from the Schuylkill River the body of a young Hispanic woman."

One of the few females in the audience gasped audibly.

"Yes," Coughlin said softly. "And I'm saddened to say that that story gets worse. Before this poor young woman was put in a black trash bag and weighted and tossed in the river, she had been beheaded."

"My God!" the woman now said loudly and forcefully.

"And within the last hour, we have additional information that gives us reason to believe beyond any doubt that we know who her killer is. We are applying our full resources in apprehending him. As well as the others."

There was a wave of appreciative murmuring though the audience.

Then Byrth heard the bearded one's voice say in a stage whisper: "These Keystone Kops couldn't catch a cold barefoot in a December snowstorm."

His inbred pal chuckled.

"And with that information," Coughlin went on at the front of the Grant Room, "we now have a common thread between all these crimes I've mentioned: illicit drugs."

Another audible wave went through the audience.

Coughin nodded. "Now, tonight I'm going to depart from the usual focus on Philly. I've given you just now an idea of what problems our city faces today. And I mean today." He looked to the table in the back of the room with Payne, Harris, and Byrth. He gestured. "I am privileged to introduce some of our finest members of law enforcement who are with us tonight. The first is a guest, Sergeant James Byrth of the Texas Rangers."

Byrth half-stood, waved once, then glanced at the two men behind him as he backed down. The audience applauded politely.

*Their body language is saying, "Oh, so you're cops. That's how the riffraff gets in the Union League."*

Coughlin went on: "Just like those Texas Rangers of fame and legend who have proceeded him, Sergeant Byrth is on the trail of the fellow who we now believe killed this girl and, last week, two others in Texas. Beside him is Homicide Detective Anthony Harris" — a somewhat shy Harris half-stood and gestured to the crowd, then sat down — "who this morning was among the first on the scene of the motel explosion. Tony has had a very long day."

There was another smattering of polite applause.

"And finally, Sergeant Matthew Payne, also of our Homicide Unit. Many of you, I'm sure, are familiar with the Payne name, if not with Matthew personally. Sergeant Payne is a legacy member of this fine society, his great-grandfather having been among the founders of the Union League."

Payne smiled nicely at the bearded one and his inbred pal. The manner in which he held his glass in his palm, with his right hand's middle finger and thumb extended, was not lost on them.

"Sergeant Byrth, would you please come forward?"

# [FOUR]
## 140 South Broad Street, Philadelphia
## Wednesday, September 9, 9:45 P.M.

"Good evening," Byrth said as he held the microphone and began addressing the audience. "It's an honor to be in your city and here at the Union League. I hesitate to use the word 'pleasure.' If you had been with Sergeant Payne and Detective Harris and me an hour ago, I know you would understand my reluctance.

"So I will start with that. I came here hunting an evil man. We do know that he's a drug trafficker. And that he's Hispanic, preying mostly on illegal immigrants. He knows they fear the police and other authority due to their being in America illegally. And, among his other heinous acts, he has the horrific habit of cutting off the heads of family members of those who in some way have crossed him."

He gestured to the table at the back of the

room. "Sergeant Payne, Detective Harris, and I just came from the Medical Examiner's Office. The autopsy had just been performed on the young Hispanic woman who had been beheaded. As horrible as the description sounds, I am here to tell you that witnessing such horrific abuse of a human being is manifoldly worse. It affects one in ways unimaginable. Even Dr. Mitchell, who in the course of his duties I'm sure has witnessed more than most of us can begin to consider, said he was deeply affected by the young woman's murder.

"The animal —" Byrth caught himself. "Excuse me. The *suspect* who we believe committed this atrocity is up to something else in your city. We have evidence that this particular drug trafficker has also begun bringing to Philly what he started in Dallas. That is to say, the sale of a drug that combines a cold medicine with heroin. Its street name is 'cheese' — and this guy markets his variety with a snappy blue logo under the catchy brand name 'Queso Azul,' or Blue Cheese. It's particularly heinous because he targets kids as young as middle-school age. Two dollars a hit — and then they're hooked on heroin."

This news triggered more murmurs in the crowd.

An attractive young woman in a striped pantsuit was seated just to Byrth's right. She raised her left hand. Byrth could not help but notice the giant gleaming diamond wedding ring. She held a pen and small piece of paper in her right hand.

"Sergeant, how do you spell that?"

Byrth spelled Queso Azul, and the young woman thanked him as she wrote it down.

"Yes, ma'am."

Byrth then saw a hand go up at one of the back tables.

*I guess we're already into the Q & A.*

*But Matt did say this was a loosely structured meeting.*

The hand belonged to the friend of the inbred one, the bearded one.

"Yes, ma'am?" Byrth said. "I mean, sir?"

The bearded one stood. He had a look that was antagonistic.

*Small wonder.*

*We hardly became buddies earlier.*

"Yes, I'm Dr. Stanton Hargrove —"

"You're a medical doctor, sir? Pardon the interruption. Everyone here is new to me."

"I have a double Ph.D.," he said with obvious pride. "I chair Marsupialia Studies in the Biology Department at Bryn Mawr."

"'Ph.D.'?" Byrth repeated. "Of course. And the order Marsupialia? Aren't those the pouched mammals. Right? Kangaroos, bandicoots —"

"Yes, they are," Hargrove interrupted, clearly pleased someone recognized his chosen field of work.

"— opossums?" Byrth finished. "We have opossums in Texas."

"Yes," he replied, a bit bewildered. "And opossums."

There were muffled chuckles in the crowd.

*This pompous ass wants to be called "doctor."*

*He doesn't have a clue what it's like to be a real doctor, one like Mitchell.*

*I'm damn sure not going to give him the satisfaction.*

"Thank you, sir, for clarifying that for me," Byrth said. "And your question?"

"It is this: As horrible as these acts today were, how do they possibly affect someone, hypothetically speaking, of course, enjoying, oh, shall we call it some recreational marijuana?"

As he sat back down, Byrth immediately said, "Well, for beginners, it's an unlawful act —"

"I'll take that one," Denny Coughlin interrupted, his hand extended for the microphone.

Byrth passed him the microphone, and Coughlin went on: "As Sergeant Byrth was I think about to say, possession or consumption of an illicit drug is illegal in the Commonwealth of Pennsylvania and will find your hypothetical example duly arrested and quite possibly incarcerated."

He paused for a sip of water.

"But there is a bigger point to your query that I want to make. While I am not able to give further details, I can tell you that the two injured in the explosion at that motel this morning come from two very fine families. Were it not for illegal drugs, those two young people from the Main Line would not have been at the back of some seedy motel at two o'clock in the morning. And they would not have jeopardized what otherwise would have been wonderful, productive futures."

He started to hand back the microphone to Byrth, then stopped.

"I might add one other thing," Coughlin said, "and Sergeant Byrth here can put it in better perspective than I. There are those who devoutly believe, and I count myself among them, that those who take so-called recreational drugs are funding not only these criminal gangs and their street wars, but also funding terrorism around the world."

He then handed the microphone to Byrth.

Byrth saw that Professor Hargrove — the bearded one now had a name — called from his seat, "You can't be serious!"

Coughlin's Irish face looked to be reddening. But he simply nodded his answer, taking the high road by choosing not to get into a verbal battle.

"Count me in with Commissioner Coughlin's crowd, too," Byrth said into the microphone. "It's unequivocally a fact that terrorists are funded by drug money. And it's easy to understand why: The amount of money is beyond belief."

He started pacing in front of the lectern.

"Anyone have an idea how much money from illegal drugs leaves the United States each year for Mexico and Colombia?"

"Tens of millions!" a young man in a tan blazer called.

Byrth smiled and shook his head. "Perhaps that much in a week," he said. "Our friends in the federal government estimate that just those two DTOs — the Mexican and Colombian drug-trafficking organizations — take out of the U.S., either physically or by laundering it, somewhere between nine billion and twenty-five billion dollars. That's *billion*-with-a-'b.' Every year. And that's a lot of available cash floating around."

The room fell silent.

Byrth added, "And that's just from the wholesale distribution of marijuana, methamphetamine, and heroin from Mexico, and cocaine and heroin from Colombia. Doesn't begin to count the other Central and South American countries, nor, say, heroin from Afghanistan, which basically supplies the bulk to the world markets."

"That's staggering," a male voice said.

"Anyone want to take a guess at how much was budgeted in a recent year for the Merida Initiative, the U.S.'s antidrug program?"

No one took a guess.

"About three hundred million to Mexico," Byrth said, "and another hundred million to Central America. *Million*-with-an-'m.' Meanwhile, not long ago, in a single raid in Mexico City, agents seized more than two hundred million in U.S. currency. Just from a single supplier of chemicals for making meth. That's only one-fifth of one billion bucks. Imagine the logistics of keeping safe the multiple billions in cash of a wholesaler of final product."

"Absolutely mind-boggling," another man's voice declared from the middle of the room.

"Small wonder there's so much corruption

south of the border," the young man in the tan blazer added.

Byrth was silent a moment, clearly considering his words. "Not just south of the Rio Grande. . . ."

Someone grunted.

Byrth paced again, then went on: "So, for just two countries, something between nine and twenty-five *billion* dollars in illicit money. And it's a cash business. None of those annoying things we honest folk have to deal with, like taxes." He paused. "But they do, however, have to deal with death. And sometimes that comes to them a little sooner than they expected."

Byrth smiled. "Here's a bit of trivia. There are a hundred one-hundred-dollar notes in a banded packet. That's a stack worth ten grand, and it's not quite a half-inch high. A hundred of those banded ten-grand packets equals one million bucks. And call it — what's fifty inches? — call it four feet high. Or two stacks of two feet high."

A very distinguished-looking silver-haired lady in a navy blue linen outfit raised her hand. She looked perhaps fifty-five or sixty years old.

"You could carry around a million dollars in a briefcase. No one would be the wiser," she said in a very soft feminine voice.

"Yes, ma'am. Or in a UPS or FedEx box. A million bucks delivered overnight."

Some of the faces looked incredulous. Most appeared shocked.

Byrth then said, "But a billion is . . . ?"

"A thousand million," a young man's voice offered. "Using your ballpark figure, that'd be a pair of stacks two hundred feet high."

"Right," Byrth said. "And multiply that by more than twenty-five billion a year. Every year. And it's not all in hundred-dollar notes. Twenties are common."

The faces continued to look incredulous and shocked.

"The logistics of moving the money push the bad guys to the point of desperation," Byrth said. "With so much cash, they smuggle it by truck, car, Greyhound bus. They will even ship it like a Christmas fruitcake via UPS, FedEx, or even the U.S. Postal Service. The drug traffickers drive out to suburbia and find a house with its yard littered with newspapers, indicating the homeowner's out of town. Then they phone down to their stash house along the border and give them the address. Next day, a box gets delivered, no signature required. The courier just rings the doorbell and drives off. Soon as it's dark, the traffickers drive back out and collect their package. If they lose a few in the process, it's just the cost of doing business. Cash gets shipped back the same way."

"So how is this cash laundered?" the distinguished woman asked.

"With U.S. law requiring that any cash transaction in excess of ten thousand dollars be reported to the U.S. Treasury, it's a real challenge to move nine billion, let alone twenty-five billion. Year after year."

"Then how —" she repeated.

Byrth put his right hand to the side of his head, the pinky at the corner of his mouth and the thumb to his ear. "Hello, Western Union?"

He put down his hand. "Not only that, of course. Lots of money moves through electronic transfers and other types of wire remittances. Prepaid Visa gift cards are popular. There's also the Black Market Peso Exchange; you can guess how that works — the dirty dollars buying clean pesos at a steep premium."

Matt Payne was writing down "Black Market Peso Exchange" and "FedEx" on a piece of paper. He saw Tony Harris move suddenly.

Harris had felt his cell phone vibrate.

He pulled it from its belt clip and tried to discreetly check its screen.

Both Payne and one of the waitstaff, a male, noticed him. Payne then saw the male walk over and slip what looked like a business card on the table before Harris.

Byrth looked over at it and read:

---

**LEAGUE POLICY:**

No Cellular Telephone
Conversations Permitted
Kindly *Turn Off* All Such Devices.
Thank You.

---

Payne rolled his eyes.

He whispered, "I've collected enough of those to start a fair-size bonfire."

Harris showed Payne the screen.

"Shit!" he whispered after he'd read: 1 OF 2 CARS BURNED IN W KENSINGTON WAS CHEVY CARJACKED BY MATT'S SHOOTER.

"Forget getting any fingerprints or blood from that burned hulk," Payne whispered.

Harris nodded as he put the phone back on his belt clip.

Payne looked back at Byrth.

He was pacing again as he spoke: "And, of course, often they don't even bother to launder it. They just smuggle bricks of cash across the border. They do it exactly as they brought in the drugs, but, of course, in the opposite direction. Once it's out of the country, it's easier to clean. Want to guess how many of those multimillion-dollar high-rise condos on the water from South Beach Miami to West Palm got bought with squeaky-clean pesos?"

*And all those Porsches,* Payne thought, recalling his car search on the Internet.

Byrth made a face. "I know you've heard of the annual list of the world's richest people published by *Forbes* magazine."

The crowd responded quickly with "Of course" and "Yes" and "Uh-huh."

Byrth went on: "In 1989, that list ranked Pablo Escobar, the cocaine drug lord based in Medellín, Colombia, as the seventh-richest man in the world. Net worth of twenty-five billion. And that was in 1989-valued dollars. Here was a man responsible for murdering countless of his enemies, including hundreds of police, thirty judges, and an unknown number of politicians."

"Mind-boggling," the young man in the tan blazer said. "But, hey, he's dead."

Byrth nodded. "Yep. Score one for The Good Guys — our U.S. Army Special Forces by name. But there's been plenty of

536

boys ready and willing to take his place. The head of the Sinaloa cartel, for example, one Joaquin 'El Chapo' Guzman — who happens to be a fugitive, having 'escaped' from a Mexican prison — recently earned a place on that Billionaire Boys' Club list."

The room was quiet.

Then the distinguished-looking silver-haired lady in the navy blue linen outfit raised her hand again. She looked clearly concerned.

"I'm sorry, everyone," she said softly. "I seem to be taking over this meeting. But I have to ask: What would you say is the solution, Sergeant? Is there one?"

"Ma'am, I don't begin to suggest I'm smart enough to have the answers. But there are highly intelligent people who have spent a lot of time studying exactly that. And, as part of that, they have stated the obvious: We could follow the model of Thailand."

"I am not familiar with that," the distinguished lady said.

"In 2003, Thailand began embracing Mao Zedong's example. The Royal Thai Police reported that in a three-month crackdown, some twenty-two hundred drug runners were summarily shot and by year's end another seventy thousand arrested. Those seventy thousand were lucky. Chairman Mao's communists, calling illegal drug users and suppliers social parasites, just outright killed them all."

Professor Hargrove's inbred buddy called out somewhat indignantly, "That's never going to happen here."

Byrth nodded. "I agree. Nor is the other option, what the economist Milton Friedman, among others, calls for — legalize drugs and end the war. Get rid of today's Prohibition, which is what some of those on that side call it."

"That won't happen either," the inbred buddy called out, this time somewhat disappointedly.

"And I agree again."

"So, what do we do?" the silver-haired lady said softly.

Byrth was quiet a moment, before he answered with: "Dante said, 'The hottest places in hell are reserved for those who in times of great moral crisis maintained their neutrality.'

"And I agree with that," Byrth said after another moment. "As well as with those who've said that the illegal drug problem is (a) not going away and (b) is going to get worse if we do nothing — that is, 'maintain neutrality.' And these brighter minds have said that the solution is very simple. The laws are already in place. Start with real border security. Start applying RICO — that's the federal Racketeer Influenced and Corrupt Organizations Act, which has been successful at so many levels. Use all the other laws on the books. And use those twenty-five billion dollars a year as funds to enforce the laws. Nothing more, nothing less." He paused, and sighed audibly. "I believe I've overstayed my welcome up here. I'll say one final thing: Continue your fine support of those in law enforcement. Thank you very much for your kind hospitality."

He turned to Commissioner Coughlin. "And for your hospitality, Commissioner."

He handed back the microphone to him.

The room, with the notable exception of Professor Hargove and his pal, erupted in applause. D. H. Rendolok was pounding his table and calling out, "Hear, hear!"

Coughlin said into the microphone, "If there are no other questions . . ." He waited a long moment, and when no one raised a hand or called out, he added, "Then we're adjourned till next time. I hope to see everyone again then."

As Payne was standing and taking a sip from his fresh drink, Professor Hargrove said in another stage whisper, "Better start next time without me. What unmitigated bullshit propaganda. . . ."

Payne walked around to that part of his table, then suddenly found that his left shoe had become snagged on the thick woolen carpeting. Luckily, he caught himself and his very full cocktail glass from falling.

But it had been an absolute shame that his trip caused him to dump a perfectly good Famous Grouse onto the head of Professor Stanton Hargrove, the distinguished chair of Marsupialia Studies in the Biology Department of Bryn Mawr College. Some even managed to strike his inbred buddy.


# X

## [ONE]
## 4606 Hatcher Street, Dallas
## Wednesday, September 9, 9:06 P.M.
## Texas Standard Time

There were only the women and children and teenagers now with Jorge Ernesto Aguilar and his TEC-9 in the kitchen of the old wooden house.

Almost all were either whimpering or

outright sobbing. Each toddler, innately understanding that something was terribly wrong with Momma, cried uncontrollably. The mothers made what limited efforts they could to try to soothe them. They could see that El Cheque was becoming more and more agitated by all the commotion.

Minutes earlier, Miguel Guilar, after grabbing the older male by the back of the shirt collar, had taken him and a length of medium-size chain and a lock back to the smallest of the house's five bedrooms. Juan Paulo Delgado had done the same with the teenage boy, but had gone to the master bedroom, which he considered to be his room when in town. Both handcuffed men had protested loudly and made some effort to resist being moved. And both men had been quieted when struck on the side of the head with the black Beretta semiautomatic pistol.

And so began the women's whimpering and sobbing and uncontrollable crying.

While it was the least of their immediate problems, the women could see that the house was squalid. It clearly had been a long time, easily years, since there had been any kind of upkeep — never mind preventative maintenance — performed on the sixty-year-old house. The same could be said for any housecleaning. The dirty appliances in the kitchen had last been replaced when the fashionable color had been a dark avocado green. The single kitchen sink, chipped and rusty, was filled with filthy dishes and glasses. The countertop suffered the same misfortune as the floor — both had linoleum that had separated at the glued seams and both had places where the linoleum had been ripped away long ago, revealing the raw plywood beneath.

Dirt had actually piled up in the corner of the kitchen by the back door, where there was an industrial-size thirty-gallon plastic garbage can. The trash was overflowing.

The women had found that the bathrooms were no better. Worse, there was no running water. The toilet tank, which had no top, had to be filled manually from a heavy plastic ten-gallon water bottle.

And soon they would learn the same was true, if horribly worse in other ways, in the bedrooms.

In the master bedroom, Juan Paulo Delgado led the teenage boy to a back corner. The room was furnished with a somewhat new queen-size bed — it was Delgado's bed, after all — a bedside table, and an older set of dresser drawers. A crudely cut sheet of plywood was nailed over the window.

Delgado kicked the boy's feet out from under him. The teenager, unable to break his fall because his wrists were still zip-tied behind his back, yelled as he fell and struck the floor forcefully, smacking his head on the matted green shag carpeting. It stunned him to the point where he just lay there groaning softly.

Nearby, there was a black iron natural gas heater bolted to both the floor and the wall. Delgado began threading the chain around one of the heater's iron feet, then took the two ends and made a single wrap around each of the teenager's wrists. Then he took the small steel padlock and, removing all the slack in the chain so that the links squeezed the boy's flesh, ran its hasp though the two loops of chain and snapped it shut.

He turned and walked over to the dresser, which had three rows of two drawers. He opened the bottom right one and was relieved that no one had touched his stuff. He removed a handheld digital voice recorder and a roll of duct tape.

He tossed the roll of tape over by the boy's head.

He then walked over and put the recording device on the bedside table.

*I'll make two,* Juan Paulo Delgado thought. *One with him making noise and one with his mouth taped shut.*

Then Delgado went back out into the kitchen.

All eyes turned to him. He saw that the pretty girl in the tight jeans and pink shirt had fire in her eyes. Others' eyes showed a mix of anger and fear. Clearly, everyone had heard the teenage boy's yell and the sound of his fall, and then the quietness.

El Gato smiled at them.

They watched as he walked over to a kitchen cabinet beside the dirt-smudged faded-white Kenmore refrigerator, opened the cabinet, and took out a bottle of Jose Cuervo tequila. He uncapped it and took a long swallow, then held out the bottle, waving it as an offering to the women. There were no takers. He shrugged and took another pull.

Miguel Guilar walked into the kitchen and wordlessly looked around the group for the next person to be chained in the bedroom. He shook his head out of annoyance and grabbed the nearest girl by her upper right arm. It was the pudgy eighteen-year-old with the streaks of bleached hair. She pulled back from him, but when Guilar used more force, and El Cheque motioned menacingly with the TEC-9, she reluctantly went with him.

Delgado walked over to the very attractive girl in the tight jeans and pink lace blouse. She narrowed her eyes at him.

He smiled, reached out with his index finger, and stroked the soft skin of her throat on up to her chin.

The fire in her eyes grew, and she made an angry face and slapped away his hand. Then the look on her face and the fire in her eyes changed to fear as she recoiled at the thought of his response.

El Gato laughed aloud.

"Come," he said, holding out his hand for her to take. "Let us go show your boyfriend a thing or two."

She stood frozen. He grabbed her by the upper left arm and jerked, herding her toward the hallway that led to the master bedroom. She shook free of his grip and walked ahead of him.

When they entered the master bedroom, the pretty girl in pink saw her boyfriend lying on the carpet at the far end of the room and ran to him. He was still somewhat groggy from hitting his head on the floor.

Delgado went to them, grabbed the boy by the shirtsleeves at his shoulders, pulled him into a seated position, and leaned him against the gas heater. Then he slapped him.

The girl whimpered.

The boy opened his eyes, dazed. But it was clear that he recognized the girl and, when he made a face, Delgado, too.

*"Bueno,"* Delgado said.

Then El Gato stood.

The eyes of the boy and girl followed him as he walked over to the small table between them and the bed, then picked up a small electronic device and pushed a button on it. A pinhead-size red light came on. He put the device back on the table and walked back over.

Then he bent over, grabbed the girl by the waist with both of his hands, lifted her completely off the floor, and threw her onto the bed.

The pretty girl in pink started screaming hysterically. The teenage boy began yelling. The girl kicked at El Gato and flailed with her arms, fighting off his advances with a great effort.

But El Gato only laughed as he tore off her clothing.

The great effort of a ninety-five-pound girl proved no match for the strength of a muscular man twice her size.

When the women in the kitchen heard the screaming from the boy and girl, their crying intensified.

After a moment, El Cheque sighed disgustedly.

"Just shut the fuck up!" he shouted.

They were quiet a moment. Then their sad noises began again.

El Cheque shook his head.

Miguel Guilar came back into the kitchen.

El Cheque walked over to him and without a word handed him the TEC-9. Then he walked back across the kitchen and grabbed two of the teenage girls he'd eyed as they got out of the van, pushing them toward the hallway.

He said to Guilar, "Your turn to keep watch, *mi amigo*."

Five minutes later, the women in the kitchen heard a girl cry out from one of the smaller bedrooms. From the master bedroom, they could no longer hear the teenage boy's terrified shouts of "Stop! No!" over and over.

Now only the muffled cries of the pretty girl could be heard.

*"Someone! Anyone! Help me! No . . ."*

After another twenty minutes, El Gato reappeared in the kitchen, wearing only his desert camouflage cutoff shorts. In his left hand he carried the recording device. His right hand had the roll of duct tape.

He looked absently at the two mothers and their toddlers who had not yet been locked up in one of the bedrooms. The women glared back at him.

Miguel Guilar was drinking from the bottle of tequila. He grinned at El Gato and held out the bottle. El Gato grinned back and took it.

Then El Cheque came into the kitchen and removed the last of the group.

Delgado looked at Guilar and held up the recording device. "Want to hear? It came out better than I thought. The boy shouting is the better of the two, I think."

"I already did hear. . . ."

Delgado shrugged and said, *"Bueno."*

He looked around the kitchen.

"Where is the bag of stuff?"

Guilar pointed to the doorway that led to what originally had served as the dining room.

El Gato took another swig of tequila, then went through the doorway. Guilar followed.

The onetime dining room now contained a long folding table with a battered top and rusty steel legs. It had three of the white plastic stackable chairs around it.

Against one wall were gray plastic storage bins stacked five high. These contained the various paraphernalia — the mixing bowls, the digital scales, the empty packets, et cetera — for the manufacturing of Queso Azul. One bin also held at least a dozen brand-new prepaid cellular phones, all unused and still in their original clear plastic containers.

"There on the table," Guilar said.

On the folding table was a black thirty-three-gallon plastic bag commonly used for the collection and disposal of lawn clippings.

Delgado went to the table and sat in one of the plastic chairs. As he reached for the top of the bag, he noticed that it had been put on top of an official-looking envelope. The return address of the envelope read: CITY OF DALLAS, WATER UTILITIES DEPARTMENT, CITY HALL, 1500 MARILLA STREET, DALLAS, TX 75201. Across the envelope in big red lettering was printed: FINAL NOTICE!

*No wonder the damned water's turned off. The idiots didn't pay the bill.*

The house was still listed under Delgado's grandmother's name. The utilities were under a phony name and were supposed to be paid in cash every month. In lieu of proving their creditworthiness, they'd had to put up a five-hundred-dollar deposit in order for the city to agree to begin service. But that had been a helluva lot better than giving a social security number or driver's license number — genuine or stolen — that would then be part of the City of Dallas database and could somehow come back to bite them in the ass.

Delgado noted that the envelope also had a familiar stain across the words FINAL NOTICE! And there was some white powder residue.

He licked a finger, wiped at the residue, and touched it to his tongue.

*Coke.*

*No wonder they forgot to pay the bill.*

*Too damned coked out. . . .*

Miguel saw what he was looking at and raised his eyebrows.

"Ramos was supposed to pay that," he said.

Delgado shook his head, disgusted at the idiocy of the seventeen-year-old Ramos Manuel Chacón.

*And it's probably the same stupidity that's the reason we haven't heard from him.*

*Los Zetas didn't grab him.*

*He's down there throwing coke at those gringo college girls to get in their pants.*

"It needs to be paid, Miguel. We don't want the city thinking this is now an abandoned property, and come around for a look. You take care of it tomorrow."

*"Sí."*

Delgado grabbed the top of the big black bag and untied the overhand knot that held it closed. Inside he saw almost fifteen individual zipper-top clear plastic bags. In each of the bags was a cell phone or a small address book or a spiral notepad or a wallet — or a combination thereof. Each bag had a number written on it in black permanent marker ink along with a brief description. One, for example, had "#6 Fat girl, 18, w/ striped hair."

Delgado knew that if he went to the bedroom where the pudgy girl had been taken, somewhere on her body, probably on top of her hand, he would find "#6" written in black ink.

He dug around in the large bag until he found one labeled "#10 hot teen girl w/pink top."

He removed it from the black bag and put it on the table. In the bag was a cellular telephone with a pink face. The back side had rhinestones hot-glued to it in the shape of a heart.

The phone was on, and he pressed keys until he was scrolling through its address book.

"Ahhh," he then said, reading on the small screen: MADRE. *"Bueno."*

He readied the digital recorder in his left hand, putting his index finger on the PLAY button. Then he pushed the green key on the cellular phone's keypad.

Three rings later, he heard the cheerful voice of an older woman.

"*Hola,* Maria!" she said in Spanish. "How are you?"

Delgado barked back in Spanish: "We have your daughter!"

Then he held the digital recorder to the cell phone and played the audio recording. It was the one with both the boy and girl screaming.

He gave that to a count of five, pushed STOP on the digital recorder, and put the pink-faced phone back to his ear.

"Do as I say, and you get the girl back alive!"

He listened for a response. But he heard only silence, and then, in the background, a concerned young voice saying, *"Madre? Madre?"*

Delgado looked at Guilar and said, "Shit! I think she fainted!"

He pushed the red END button on the cellular phone.

Then he reached across the table and picked up the black ink marker. He wrote on the bag: "1. Called 'Madre' 9/9 9:50pm.

Woman fainted?"

Then he stuck the phone back in the bag. And fished out another. And repeated the calling process.

This time, he speed-dialed the number on the menu linked to the listing that read HOME, and when the man answered, he began their exchange by playing the audio clip of just the girl screaming.

Delgado knew that it did not matter that the recording was of another girl. When parents heard a female's voice screaming and were told that it was their child, they tended to believe exactly that. And not believing carried serious consequences. If the receiving telephone had caller ID, so much the better when Delgado called using the girl's personal cell phone.

Then he barked in Spanish: "We have your loved one! Do as I say, and you will see her alive again!"

Delgado carefully explained that he wanted the two thousand dollars that was to be paid to the coyote. He said that it was to be sent to Edgar Cisneros at the Western Union, Mall of Mexico, Philadelphia.

Delgado had a fake Texas driver's license with that name and his picture. He'd bought it for three hundred dollars. It had been made by the same counterfeiter who lived in a loft apartment near that expensive private school, Southern Methodist University. He sold to the sorority girls and other students there what the kids simply called "fakes."

"If you do not do as I say, and especially if you contact the police," Delgado said in an angry tone of voice, "your loved one will be dead this time tomorrow. When we get your money, she will be taken to Dallas and released."

He put the recorder and the cell phone face-to-face and hit PLAY.

*"Someone! Anyone! Help me! No . . ."*

After a few seconds, he broke off the call.

Delgado looked at Miguel Guilar. Guilar smirked. He knew damn well that Delgado had no intention whatever of releasing the girls. They were all, or at least the more attractive ones, going to be moved to Philadelphia.

Miguel Guilar's phone then buzzed once. He pulled it from the clip on his belt, then read the text message.

"Uh-oh!" Guilar said. "Look at this! And a Mexico City number."

He held out the phone for Delgado to read it.

"What do you think that means?" Guilar said.

011-52-744-1000

ramos here . . . i borrow amigos fone . . .
am in houston jail . . . u bail me out? . . .
police want me 2 say i live on hatcher . . .
y is that?

Juan Paulo Delgado's eyes went to the envelope.

His stomach suddenly had a huge knot. He had to consciously squeeze his sphincter muscle — he thought he might have shit his pants.

*Why? Because you didn't pay the water bill, you fucking idiot!*

*And they obviously found it in your car, then bluffed you!*

Right about then, El Cheque walked in, holding up his cell phone. He had a confused look.

"Ramos just sent me a text . . ."

*Dammit!*

Delgado bolted out of the chair and grabbed the black plastic bag.

"Throw everything important into the trucks!" he said.

"What? Why? And about them?" El Cheque said, gesturing in the general direction of the bedrooms.

Delgado nodded at the black plastic bag.

"This is all we need. We leave them. Let's go."

Holding the top of the black plastic bag, Delgado spun it to make a gooseneck, then secured it closed with another overhand knot. When he picked it up, he saw the envelope with FINAL NOTICE!

"Fucking moron!"

From inside the black plastic bag, the pink phone with the heart of rhinestones began ringing.

# [TWO]
## Society Hill, Philadelphia
## Thursday, September 10,
## 8:36 A.M.

Chadwick Thomas Nesbitt IV drove up South Third Street in his cobalt-blue BMW coupe. He'd just left his home at Number 9 Stockton Place in Society Hill and was headed for his office at the corporate headquarters of Nesfoods International. He wore expensively tailored slacks and blazer, a custom-made French-cuff dress shirt, and a fine silk necktie.

Nesbitt was talking on the telephone with his secretary, Catherine Taylor, going over his calendar of appointments and meetings for the day. She had just said, "You have a nine o'clock with Feaster Scott, the art director on the new international line of organic soups." Then, as he approached Lombard Street, he heard the phone beep in his ear and he checked the screen.

It read: CALL WAITING — PACO ESTEBAN.

He said, "Let me call you right back, Cate. Or I'll see you in a minute."

Then he hit the button and took the incoming call.

"Hello?"

"Meester Nesbitt, this is Paco Esteban."

*I know that. But it would take more time explaining I have caller ID than it would to ignore the obvious.*

"How are you, Paco? Better? Is everything okay?"

"Is *bueno,*" Paco Esteban said. Then, in a tone that revealed both his pride and his determination, he added, "I have found the evil man."

"What!" Nesbitt said, the news causing him almost to drive off the street. "Hold on."

He braked heavily, came almost to a stop, then, because there was no on-street parking, gently rolled up over the low curb and onto the sidewalk to get out of traffic.

He had stopped shy of Pine Street, right across from the Thaddeus Kosciuszko National Memorial. The Polish-born soldier had bitterly battled the Russians — in the Kosciuszko Uprising — before coming to fight in the American Revolutionary War. As a colonel in the Continental Army, he became a hero — later rising to a one-star general — and then had become an American citizen.

*Wonder what ole Thaddeus would think of this craziness that's come to the country he fought so nobly for?*

*These new immigrants only seem to fight and kill among themselves. . . .*

"Okay, Paco," Nesbitt said somewhat calmly. "Tell me all that again."

"I know where El Gato is," El Nariz said.

"This is the evil one?"

"*Sí.* The evil one. El Gato. Means 'The Cat.' "

"And you have seen him?"

"I have seen his evil house. Where he keeps the girls prisoner."

Nesbitt glanced at the clock on the instrument cluster. It showed eight forty.

*I'm going to be late. I've got that nine o'clock. . . .*

"And I have pictures," Esteban added.

*"Pictures? Of what?"*

"Of the girls who El Gato forces to have sex for money."

Nesbitt could not believe his ears.

*This is getting worse by the moment.*

*How much of this is going to stick to me?*

"Where are you, Paco?"

"I am at my house. On Sears Street."

"Over by the Mexican Market?"

*"Sí."*

*That's really not far from here,* Nesbitt thought.

Nesbitt glanced at the clock again: eight forty-five.

He sighed, then reached for the pen and gasoline station receipt that were on the console near the hand brake.

"Give me your address," he said, turning to the back of the receipt. "I'll be right there."

Ten minutes later, Nesbitt turned off South Eighth Street and pulled the shiny M3 to the curb across the street from 823 Sears Street. On the way, he'd just had time to call back Catherine and ask her to reschedule his nine o'clock with Feaster Scott and put anything else on hold.

He looked around.

*Jesus, that wasn't even a mile — but here it's a world away from Society Hill.*

He was well aware that the sports car and his clothing contrasted sharply with the neighborhood. He was more than a little worried about leaving the car unattended — at best it might get keyed, at worst it might disappear altogether.

He hit the master locking button on his car key, locking the doors with an audible click and arming the alarm with an electronic *chirp.*

He glanced up and down the street, and thought:

*Thanks a lot, Skipper, ol' pal.*

*What was it that Matt said? Right . . .*

*"No good deed goes unpunished."*

Nesbitt knocked on the painted metal front door of the row house. He heard footsteps on the other side of the door and, after a moment, the sounds of multiple locks being opened.

The door swung inward, and Paco Esteban greeted him with a warm smile.

Looking at the short, heavyset man with coarse coffee-colored skin, Chadwick Nesbitt would never have guessed they were the same age.

"Come in, please, Meester Nesbitt."

Inside, Chad Nesbitt saw that there was a small gathering at the back of the house, four Hispanic women in what appeared to be a parlor. It was sparsely furnished, and the majority of the chairs looked as if they belonged outdoors. The women stopped talking to look toward him, then looked away and went back to their conversation.

"Come into the kitchen, please," Esteban then said.

The kitchen was still a mess from the making of breakfast. Nesbitt could hear the coffeemaker burping steam as it finished brewing a fresh pot.

Esteban had two cheap coffee mugs in his hand. He did not ask if Nesbitt wanted any; he simply poured coffee in both, then handed one to him.

Nesbitt didn't feel he could refuse.

"Milk? Sugar?" Esteban said.

"Black is fine. Thank you." Then he said, "You said you had pictures?"

"Sí. I thought that a smart man like you could get them to someone who could help." He hesitated as their eyes met. "I am not comfortable speaking with authorities."

Nesbitt nodded.

Esteban brought out his cell phone. He

punched a few keys, then handed it to Nesbitt.

"Push this one here to go from one to another," El Nariz said, indicating a particular key.

As Nesbitt keyed through the images, El Nariz gave him a running commentary as to how he'd gotten the pictures and who was in them. He got to one that had been taken inside the convenience store, the bottom of the frame cut off, showing, barely, the two young Hispanic girls sitting at the folding table and flipping through old magazines.

"Rosario said those two are from Mexico."

"They don't even look fourteen years old!" Chadwick Thomas Nesbitt IV said indignantly, almost spilling his coffee.

He felt shocked to his very core.

"*Sí.*" El Nariz said softly. "Fourteen, Rosario says."

Nesbitt clicked again. The next image was shot at a forty-five-degree angle, but the subject miraculously was completely within the frame.

"That is their guard, who watches over them. And, sometimes, forces them to have sex with him."

Chadwick Nesbitt shook his head in disbelief.

He clicked some more, but the images either repeated what he'd already seen or captured display shelving of automotive motor oil cans and toilet paper. Then the first image came back on screen. He handed back the telephone to Esteban.

"And you say you have the address of this evil man's house?"

"*Sí.* Where El Gato keeps the girls. Hancock Street — 2505 Hancock Street. I will never forget that address as long as I am alive."

Nesbitt wrote "El Gato" and "2505 Hancock" on the back of the gasoline station receipt.

"And I have the number of the van they drive the girls around in," Esteban said with more than a little pride.

Nesbitt looked him in the eyes, clearly impressed.

"Give it to me," he said.

Esteban recited, " 'GSY696.' It is a Ford van. No windows. The color is tan. And very dirty."

Nesbitt nodded as he wrote it down, trying to squeeze all the information on the small slip of paper.

Nesbitt looked at Esteban. "And is the . . . the girl's . . ."

Esteban nodded. He crossed himself, then

said, "May God take pity on me, Ana's head is still in the freezer in the basement."

*Unbelievable!*

*A severed head in the freezer!*

*And fourteen-year-old girls forced into pros-titution!*

*What the hell next?*

*I do not want to know.*

*But I know I can't let this guy get near —* *what did he call him? — El Gato.*

He pulled out his cell phone and hit a speed-dial key.

*Okay, Matt. Now it's a lot later.*

*Answer your goddamn telephone!*


# [THREE]
# Philadelphia Police Headquarters
# Eighth and Race Streets, Philadelphia
# Thursday, September 10, 8:16 A.M.


Sergeant Matt Payne and Sergeant Jim Byrth came into the Homicide Unit and saw Detective Tony Harris across the room at his desk, holding two telephones to his head. His left hand held a cell phone, his right shoulder held the receiver of his desk phone to the other ear, and he was taking notes with his right hand.

When Harris saw them approaching, he mouthed, *Give me three minutes.*

Payne nodded, then touched Byrth on the shoulder.

"Coffee?" Payne said.

"Sure," Byrth said.

Payne led him to the observation room between two holding rooms that also served as the Homicide Unit's commissary. Its windows were two-way mirrors for observing those being interviewed in either holding room. It had a Mr. Coffee brewer, as well as an open cardboard bakery box of somewhat fresh doughnuts and, surprising Payne, banana nut muffins. Next to them was an old glass beer mug that someone had obtained from Liberties in what could be termed "a midnight acquisition," or simply "pilfered." It had a sign taped to its side that read: REMEMBER TO FEED THE KITTY. Inside were coins and dollar bills.

As Payne poured coffee into two foam cups, Byrth stuck two bucks in the glass mug.

"Welcome to hurry up and wait," Payne

said as he glanced at Harris. "But he sounded really excited when he called."

Payne sipped his coffee. Then he said, "There. He's hanging up."

They walked over to Harris's desk and drew up two chairs.

"Good morning, Tony," Byrth said.

"Good morning," Harris said a lot more pleasantly than he looked. "That said, it may well turn out to be a great morning."

He pushed a short stack of computer printouts toward Payne.

"Look at those," Harris said.

Payne flipped through them quickly. They looked familiar — printouts of *The Philadelphia Bulletin* website pages — but nothing unusual.

"What am I looking for?" he said, then passed the pages to Byrth.

"I had an early breakfast with Stanley Dowbrowski."

Payne shook his head. "Name doesn't ring a bell. Should it?"

"Maybe not. He's sixty-five; been retired from the department some fifteen years now. He lives around the corner from me, over on Brocklehurst Street, and we stay in touch. When I got home last night just shy of midnight, I found that he'd left me a message on my machine. It was too late to call him — he's always been a morning guy — so I set the alarm for five. Then I called him at oh-dark-thirty. Turns out he's not as early a riser as he used to be. I woke him —"

Payne chuckled.

Byrth grinned as he put the papers back on Harris's desk.

"— but he wouldn't admit it. He said he had something really interesting" — he nodded at the papers — "and said to drop by for coffee and he'd show it to me."

Harris reached for the heavy china mug on his desk that had a representation of the Philadelphia Police Department logotype and gold lettering that read: DETECTIVE ANTHONY HARRIS — HOMICIDE DIVISION. He took a sip of his coffee.

"I really need to quit. I've been sucking this stuff down since five-thirty. Anyway, I swung by the store and grabbed a couple boxes of doughnuts and assorted muffins. Stanley's in really bad health — on oxygen, thanks to a life of chain-smoking cigarettes — and doesn't get out. So I figured he could use something fresh from the store."

Payne gestured toward the commissary. "There're some —"

"Yeah, that's some of them. Stanley refused to keep all I brought to him. Said that the guys at the Roundhouse deserved them more."

"So what did he show you?" Byrth said.

"It's curious," Harris said. "It may not mean anything. But —"

" 'Turn over the stone under the stone' sayeth the Great Black Buddha," Payne said, almost perfectly mimicking Jason Washington's sonorous voice.

Harris knew Payne was not mocking Washington. But still his eyes darted across the room to Washington's glass-walled office. It was empty.

Harris picked up the pages. "Stanley likes to add comments at the end of the newspaper articles."

He flipped to the page that had the article on the shooting at the Temple University Hospital. He pointed to it.

Payne and Byrth looked and read:

---

**ARMED MAN MURDERS BURN VICTIM BEFORE FLEEING HOSPITAL, FIRING AT POLICE**

**While police remain mum on details of the murder, witnesses claim gunman fired shots at man who shouted "Police!" while chasing gunman from hospital.**

---

"Stanley likes to use as his screen name 'Hung.Up.Badge.But.Not.Gun.' Here's what he posted in the comments section."

Payne and Byrth then read it:

---

From **Hung.Up.Badge.But.Not.Gun (2:56 p.m.):**

*I talked to an inside source, too, and was told that this was a hit job. Maybe not a professional one, but the burn victim (there's more to that story that I cannot share) was targeted. So sad to see this happening in Philly. I'll say it again: Shoot 'em all and let the Good Lord sort 'em out.*

---

"Interesting perspective on shooting 'em all," Byrth said. "Probably good thing he is retired."

"So," Payne said, "who's his inside source?"

"Not for dissemination. No reason to get her in trouble just for talking shop with her uncle."

It was clear by his expression that Payne was trying to figure out who Harris was talking about.

"'Her'?" Payne repeated. "You mean that chunky female who was posted outside of Skipper's ICU? Stephanie Polish-Something?"

Harris nodded. "Police Officer Stephanie *Kowenski,* age twenty-five."

"That's the one," Payne said.

"She's Stanley's sister's girl, and his pride and joy. She joined the department because he loved it so much." Harris paused. "Remind you of anyone, Sergeant Payne?"

Payne made an expression that said he took Harris's point.

"I guess sometimes there is something in our DNA that makes us hardwired to do this crazy job," Payne said.

Then he looked at the printouts. "So, what're we looking for here?"

He saw that someone had circled the time stamps at two different places on the page.

One was on the reader comment that followed Stanley Dowbrowski's comment:

---

From **Death.Before.Dishonor (3:20 p.m.):**

*What about "Thou Shalt Not Steal"??
The only sad thing about what*

---

"'Skipper'?" Payne read aloud. "How the hell did he know it was Skipper? That's not exactly a common name."

"Clearly, there's some significance to 'steal,'" Byrth added.

Tony Harris shrugged. Then he pointed to the other time stamp that was circled.

They read that one:

**Update (5:44 p.m.):** **According to the anonymous source inside the hospital, the patient who was shot to death was J. Warren Olde, Jr.**

"Is the source there the girl, too?" Payne said.

"I don't think so," Harris said, "because she knows Stanley would never leak to reporters, and she follows his example." He paused. "The interesting thing here is that the newspaper did not even mention the victim's name until more than two hours after this guy, this Death.Before.Dishonor *person,* wrote what he or she wrote."

Byrth offered, " 'Death before dishonor' is something the gangbangers stole from the old mafia types. It's a badge of honor that they've bastardized, like everything else they've stolen. They get the phrase tattooed on them, usually in prison."

Harris nodded, then went on: "When Stanley noticed that the poster had (a) mentioned Skipper and (b) mentioned him by name two hours before the paper reported the formal name and (c) then took into account the tone of the posting itself, he remembered something. He remembered that both the name Death.Before.Dishonor and the anger were familiar."

Harris flipped the pages of the printout.

"And so he went back through the newspaper web pages, trying to find this article."

He pointed to the printout of an article with the headline 2 DEAD AFTER METH LAB EXPLODES, BURNS PHILLY INN MOTEL.

"Here at the bottom" — he pointed — "Stanley posted this comment."

Payne and Byrth read it:

"Really is a good thing he's not wandering around with a gun and a badge anymore," Byrth repeated.

Harris chuckled. "That's just his sense of humor. Stanley's not the type to go postal."

Byrth snorted. "I remember when we had that rash of post office workers shooting their coworkers. Somebody said that it just wasn't right for them to be shooting each other — dramatic pause — because it was only fair that their frustrated customers should get to do it."

Harris and Payne chuckled.

"Anyway," Harris then went on, "apparently that shoot-'em-all comment provoked the Death.Before.Dishonor person, because she or he posted a pretty raw comment."

"About?"

"Stanley said it said pushers sold drugs because people wanted them. And it was no different than what got sold legally — booze, cigarettes."

He paused and looked between Payne and Byrth.

Harris then said, "And this is where it gets interesting: Stanley said he seemed to recall that comment ended by suggesting that drug dealers clean up after their own."

Payne was shaking his head.

Harris went on: "And ended with something along the lines of 'We clean up the rats like those in the Philly Inn.' "

"Jesus!" Payne said. "It actually used the name?"

Harris shrugged. "I don't know. And Stanley's not sure. But there was no question that he meant that motel."

He pointed to the printouts.

"The reason he doesn't know is because that comment is gone. When Stanley clicked back, he found his comment, but the one from Death.Before.Dishonor, which had been immediately after his, was gone. And this one was next in line."

Payne and Byrth read:

"Stanley said that he guessed there were enough reports of the comment's abusive language that the online editor at the paper pulled it off. That's what I was trying to figure out when you guys came in; I was on the phone with different folks at the newspaper."

Payne said, "It shouldn't be a problem finding it. It's at least got to be in the backup files on the *Bulletin*'s computer system mainframe. What I'm wondering is if we'd have any luck tracing the postings back to their source."

Harris nodded, then looked at Byrth. Payne followed his eyes.

Payne noticed that Byrth was deep in thought.

And that he had the dry white bean going across the fingers of his left hand. That had been what caught Harris's attention.

Byrth said, "It is common for, say, an arsonist to stand in a nearby crowd to watch the firemen put out his handiwork."

Payne considered that, then picked up on his train of thought.

"Yeah," he said, "and these comments could very well be just another manifestation of that behavior."

Payne then felt his phone vibrate in his pocket.

He pulled it out and saw that he'd received a text message from his sister.

It read:

---

Amy Payne

Against my advice as a professional and a friend, I tried to steer her away . . . You better take care of this one, Wyatt Earp!!

---

Payne shook his head.

*What in hell is she talking about?*

He made a face as he slipped the phone back into his pocket.

Harris and Byrth noticed that.

"Everything okay?" Harris said.

"Hell if I know," Payne said, shaking his

head. "Women."

That triggered appreciative chuckles.

Then Payne felt another vibration in his pocket.

*Sonofabitch! Now what does Amy want?*

Harris and Byrth saw that, too.

He made another face and said, "Sorry. I should just turn the damn thing off."

He glanced down at the color LCD screen:

---

unknown number

OK . . . I gave it some thought.

Even consulted with my favorite shrink.

I'm game, Matt.

See, I promised myself . . . well, I'll explain later. -A

---

Payne thought his heart was going to burst though his chest.

*Amanda!*

*Unknown number? Shit!*

*Wait! Amy has to have it!*

His thumbs flew as he replied to his sister's text.

He put down the phone and looked between Harris and Byrth.

"What?" Payne said innocently.

"Should we wait?" Harris said, sounding a little exasperated.

"No, go ahead," Payne said.

Just then, the phone vibrated with her reply.

"Sorry," Payne said, and glanced at the screen:

---

Amy Payne

I was going to ignore you but knew you'd get her number somehow & then hold it against me that I withheld it . . . 609-555-6221.

---

*Great!*

Then he stuck the phone back in his pocket.

"What I was going to say," Harris then said, his tone still suggesting mild annoyance, "was that I agree with Matt. That we could get our people to see if they can trace these to an IP address."

Payne and Byrth nodded.

Every device connected to the Internet had to have a unique Internet Protocol numerical address, and, at least in theory, every IP address of every router had to have a legitimate physical address associated with it as well. So they could track backward and find the IP address . . . and find their doer.

"Failing that," Harris went on, "we can get the *Bulletin* to seed an article that might incite the Death.Before.Dishonor person to reveal more about him- or herself. One of those phones to my ear when you came in was with Lee Bryan" — he looked to Byrth to clarify — "Bryan is the editor at the *Bulletin*. He agreed. With conditions, of course."

"Of course," Payne said dryly. "Damn sure worth a try."

Payne gestured toward Harris's desk telephone. Harris pushed it across the desk toward him. Payne picked up the receiver, thought for a second, then punched in a short string of numbers.

"Corporal Rapier," Payne said into the phone. "Is the ECC free? Anyone in there?" He listened a moment and then grinned. " 'Just Sweet Dee on the big screen.' I see. Then that means you'll be available in the next ten or so minutes. And we'll need someone from Information Systems Division."

Payne hung up the phone.

He looked at Byrth. "ISD falls under the department's Science and Technology division."

Byrth was nodding when he felt his cell phone vibrate.

"Sorry," he said, slipping the white bean into his pocket and reaching for the phone. "Apparently, I'm not any better than Marshal In Lust here."

He read the screen. His eyebrows went up.

"Excuse me," he said.

He pushed a speed-dial key and put the phone to his ear.

Harris and Payne exchanged a glance.

"Yeah, it's me," Byrth said into the phone. "What do you have?"

And he remained stone-faced and silent for the next few minutes, breaking his silence with only a few grunts and "*uh-huh*"s.

Then he said, "Okay. Thanks. Keep me posted."

Byrth looked at Payne and said, "Remember that kid running drugs I told you we nabbed in College Station?"

"Shoney?"

"Close," Byrth said. "Ramos Manuel Chacón. Good memory, though."

He turned to Harris and brought him up

to speed on Ramos Manuel Chacón.

"What about him?" Payne then said.

"When they booked him, they didn't really get anything beyond the phone numbers on his cell phone. But then they went through his car with the proverbial fine-tooth comb. In addition to the drug residue — he'd already delivered the drugs to his vendors — there was all kinds of trash. And, apparently, there were a few bills that had not been mailed, including a City of Dallas water bill."

Payne and Harris were nodding.

"Water bills have service street addresses," Payne said.

"Right," Byrth said. "So they called Company B in Garland; that's the Texas Rangers office in DFW. And Sergeant Kenny Kasper — really good guy — gets the address and drives by in his personal vehicle. Doesn't see anything of interest. So he gets an idea. He drives over to Dallas City Hall. Craziest damn place; the building looks like a triangle turned on its head. That I. M. Pei designer did it. Anyway, he pulls some strings. Now he's wearing a water meter reader's outfit and he's got a city vehicle with all the appropriate stickers on the doors."

Payne snorted. "Pretty good trick."

Byrth nodded and said mock-seriously, "That's why we're Texas Rangers."

He went on: "So then Kenny drove over to the house and banged on the front door, prepared to say he's there to turn on the water. No one answered, but he thought he could hear muffled moans. He went around to the backyard. But all the windows and the back door were covered. He banged on that door and — you know what? — the damnedest thing happened. It swung wide open."

Payne chuckled. "That's called a Size 10 Steel-Toe Universal Key."

After a moment's thought, Byrth went on: "What he found wasn't pretty. But it could've been worse if he hadn't taken the door."

"What?" Harris and Payne said at almost the exact same time.

"It's a stash house in a struggling neighborhood near downtown. And inside he found eighteen undocumented immigrants, mostly women, all but the two toddlers chained and locked up. Everyone had duct tape on their mouths, toddlers included. Kasper said he's pretty sure some of the young girls had been raped."

"My God!" Harris exclaimed.

Byrth nodded. "And there was drug-manufacturing paraphernalia. Empty packets of Queso Azul scattered all over the dining room. They don't know how long the bad guys had been gone, but it appeared that they just missed them. And judging by the way things were thrown around, they're not going back to the house."

"They just left those people to die?" Payne said, shaking his head.

"Happens all the time in the desert," Byrth said. "Doesn't make it right, of course."

They were all quiet, lost in thought.

"Then this El Gato is back in Dallas?" Payne said.

Byrth shrugged. "No one knows. None of the immigrants are talking. At least, not saying anything of help. Forensics is going through the scene, but that'll take forever to process. There're eighteen sets of prints from the immigrants alone. Lord knows how many from the bad guys. And even then who knows if we get a match to any."

After a long moment, Payne suddenly said: "The Hispanic girl who got beheaded!"

"What about her?" Tony Harris said.

"That's the story we seed in the *Bulletin*. It may not get this Death.Before.Honor guy, but it might help us locate El Gato or someone who knows him."

"You sure, Matt?" Byrth said. "Seems like a long shot. One based on a lot of ifs. Beginning with (a) if this guy even reads a newspaper, and (b) if he has a computer, and (c) if he reads an online newspaper, and (d) if it's the *Bulletin*. And putting that story out, well, it's a whole lot easier letting the cat out of the bag than it is putting it back."

Payne shrugged. "True. But it costs nothing to try. And the deputy commissioner's let the cat out already. Even though last night at the Union League was supposed to be off the record, no one keeps secrets. This will get us looking under the rock that's under the rock. We find nothing there, we move on to another rock."

He started to stand up.

"Shall we go to the ECC?"

On the way upstairs, Payne tried to discreetly type a text message.

Byrth and Harris exchanged glances and shook their heads.

Payne shrugged sheepishly, but grinned as he continued thumbing the message:

---

got your number from amy.

that's great news!

why the change of heart? not that i'm complaining.

---

> can i buy you lunch?? dinner??
>
> a vine-covered cottage on the side of the road??

Then he hit the SEND button.

# [FOUR]
# Philadelphia Police Headquarters
# Eighth and Race Streets, Philadelphia
# Thursday, September 10, 8:45 A.M.

Corporal Kerry Rapier was waiting in the Executive Command Center when Matt Payne, Tony Harris, and Jim Byrth entered. He was with a young man who had skin as dark as the Black Buddha's. The young man was sitting in a motorized power chair.

*The kid in that fancy wheelchair doesn't look like he's old enough to be in college,* Payne thought.

He felt his phone vibrate. He read the screen:

---

609-555-6221

Lunch? Dinner? Vine-covered cottage?

Methinks you might be getting a little ahead of the game, Romeo . . .

But . . . do I have to pick just one? (wink)
–A

---

He grinned, and sent:

---

all three . . . might even throw in a white picket fence . . .

---

Payne hit SEND, then grinned again as he reread her message.

He realized he could feel his heart rate beating faster.

He slipped the phone back into his pocket as Corporal Rapier called to them, "Gentlemen, this is Andy Radcliffe."

Radcliffe had a round kind face with

gentle coal-black eyes. His full head of dark hair was evenly shorn almost to his scalp. He wore blue jeans that had an ironed crease and a white cotton button-down dress shirt that looked a size or so too large. The shirt also had been carefully ironed. His navy blazer was a little big for his narrow frame, and he had on athletic shoes.

Rapier went on: "Andy's in his second year at La Salle, and he's been interning here at the department. He and I have worked on projects this summer. He's really good —"

*Did Radcliffe just blush at the praise?* Payne thought.

"— and, even more important," Rapier said smiling, "he's all that's available right now from ISD."

"Then I guess we'll just have to make do," Payne said solemnly.

Radcliffe turned quickly to look at Payne, who calmed his fears by smiling.

Payne introduced the others, then said, "That's one helluva wheelchair, Andy. It looks like a high-dollar office chair on a space-age rocket pod."

"Thank you, sir. It's pretty much as you describe. Watch."

Using the joystick on the right armrest, he maneuvered the chair around the command center. It made a soft humming sound as he showed off, the joystick controlling speed and direction. With six wheels — four small ones in each corner and two larger ones directly below each armrest — the power chair could spin in its own space. And Andy had it do exactly that.

"Impressive," Harris said.

Payne said, "Mind if I ask the rude question . . . ?"

Andy shrugged. "Doesn't bother me. I got robbed three years ago. Was walking home — we live in North Philly — from work. I was bringing my mom and little brother dinner. I couldn't outrun them. They got my wallet. I got a knife in the back. It nicked my spinal cord. So now I'm a sophomore at La Salle, doing a double major in computer science and criminal justice."

*Nice kid,* Payne thought, genuinely impressed. *He projects nothing but a positive outlook.*

*Not sure I could do that if I were in his shoes.*

"Good for you, Andy."

He shrugged again.

"What are my alternatives?" he said logically. "Sit in a corner and wither while I complain bitterly about the cards I've been dealt?"

Payne didn't trust his voice to speak.

He squeezed Andy's shoulder and nodded softly.

After a moment, Payne turned to Byrth and said, "La Salle University is just west of Broad Street, a few miles north of Temple University Hospital where the shooting took place."

Andy Radcliffe's face lit up at the mention of that.

"We were watching that video loop," he said, nodding at the flat-screen TVs. "That was one pretty cool foot chase, Sergeant Payne."

Now Payne felt a little embarrassed by the praise. He nodded his thanks.

Radcliffe pushed the joystick so that the power chair spun, then moved with that soft humming sound to the command center's control panel. Radcliffe popped the black-and-white surveillance video up on the main bank of sixteen sixty-four-inch flat-screen TVs.

"We've already seen Marshal Earp's chase," Jim Byrth said.

Andy Radcliffe grinned at the nickname.

He said, "I can't watch it enough. You know, before I got robbed and all, I never thought twice about cops. Except to avoid them on the street. But the patrolman — Will Parkman? They call him 'Pretty Boy'

589

— the cop who got my case?"

Payne shook his head. "Don't know him."

"I do," Rapier said. "Because of Andy, of course. Really good guy. Ex-Marine. Did some amazing things in Southeast Asia. Not just 'Nam."

Payne nodded appreciatively.

"Anyway," Andy said, "Pretty Boy — he's not really pretty at all, you know, more like kinda dumpy, which is why they call him that — he kept coming around the hospital to check on me. Then he came by the house, made sure my mama and baby brother were . . ."

He looked away for a moment. He cleared his throat. When he looked back at Payne, Matt could see the boy's eyes were glistening.

*Tears. He's holding them back.*

"So, this Parkman, you're saying, didn't have to do what he did," Payne said. "That he was a pretty good guy?"

"Yeah," Radcliffe said. "*Is.* He's helping out with my tuition at La Salle till I get on with the department here. He's what some call an M&M."

"How's that?" Payne said.

"Like the candy. Hard shell on the outside. All sweet and soft inside."

Payne grinned and nodded.

*Obviously a damn good guy.*

*I should look into starting a scholarship fund for guys like Andy.*

*I'm embarrassed that this Pretty Boy Parkman's already thought of it before me.*

"Okay, Matt, what's going on?" Rapier said. "What do we need to do?"

Payne explained.

Then Harris handed them the printouts from Stanley Dowbrowski.

"The *Bulletin?*" Andy Radcliffe then said.

"Yeah."

At the main keyboard, he began typing. After a moment, the main bank of sixteen TVs showed an unusual Internet browser window. Then that window filled with the front page of the online edition of *The Philadelphia Bulletin.*

"A school buddy of mine works in the paper's ISD. He's also interning over at the FBI," he said, and pointed his thumb back over his shoulder.

The FBI's William J. Green Jr. Building was a couple blocks away, over at Sixth and Arch.

Andy Radcliffe then pulled out his cell phone and hit a speed-dial key. When his buddy came on the line, he explained what they were trying to do.

"Can I access it remotely?" Andy Radcliffe said.

Then he tilted his head to hold the phone to his ear. With both hands on the keyboard, his fingers flew. The Internet browser window with the image of the newspaper then shrank to fit on only the left eight TVs. A new browser window opened on the right eight flat-screens.

The new window was mostly blank. There was a single box in the middle. He moved the cursor to it.

"Okay, I got it," Radcliffe said, and began typing as he said "uh-huh, uh-huh."

In the box a string of asterisks appeared, clearly obscuring the password's string of letters and numbers.

Radcliffe hit RETURN and the box went away. Another flashed ENTRY SUCCESSFUL, then it went away and a new page appeared in the window. It was a tree of coded hyperlinks, the blue-colored links a series of alphanumeric file names.

"I'm in," Radcliffe then said into the cellular phone. "I'll call you back."

He broke off the call. Then he typed some more, and the second browser window shrank to fit only the top right four sixty-four-inch flat-screens. Another new window opened on the four panels beneath it.

"What sort of browser is that?" Payne said. "I've never seen one quite like it."

Radcliffe looked at Kerry Rapier, then at Payne. "If I told you, I'd have to kill you."

Byrth and Harris chuckled.

Payne looked at Andy and saw he was grinning ear to ear.

"It's a custom-built browser," Radcliffe then said. "Comes from a skunk works at MIT. The code was written basically to strip out all the commerce parts you find on junk like Explorer and instead concentrates on making the program super-secure."

"It looks pretty bare-bones."

"Looks are deceiving."

"You might want to write that down, Sergeant Payne," Byrth said with a big grin.

"It's one robust browser," Radcliffe said, concentrating on his work.

They watched the cursor move to the window with the newspaper articles. And then they saw that when he floated the cursor over a headline, one of the tree's hyperlinks in the browser window on the upper right became a brighter blue.

"The upper right browser shows the meat of the newspaper, all the files and such, stripped of the coding that makes the GUI so pretty."

" 'Gooey'?" Byrth said.

"GUI, for graphical user interface. It basically means what makes a computer page look nice."

"So how's it going to be possible to do the trace?" Payne said.

"Yeah," Ratcliffe said. "ICANN."

"You can what?" Payne said.

"No, ICANN. The Internet Corporation for Assigned Names and Numbers. ICANN."

"You're making this up," Payne said.

Byrth put in, "I think you may be right, Marshal."

"I'm not making it up. Hey, can I call you 'Marshal,' too?"

Payne didn't respond.

Radcliffe explained, "ICANN is a private nonprofit corporation out in Marina Del Rey, California. It was started in 1998, and tasked to assign and track every website, et cetera."

Radcliffe moved the cursor into the new browser window. He typed in a website address and hit ENTER.

A pleasant blue page filled the browser. It had the ICANN logotype — it looked like a stylized pound symbol inside a circle meant to resemble a globe — and line after line of hyperlinks. Radcliff clicked on SITE MAP at the top of the page. And a new page appeared with an eye-crossing number of additional hyperlinks. He went immediately to the one he wanted and clicked.

"Okay. A unique numerical identification, what's called its logical address, is assigned to every device — every computer — so it can join the network and communicate with another computer. If IP addresses were not unique, there'd be all sorts of conflicts. It'd be chaos. Once we have the IP address, we go to ICANN and find out where the address is registered."

He moved the cursor to the left browser window.

"Okay, now we go back to the newspaper and find those comments you're hunting."

He flipped to the printout with the first comment. Then he clicked around in the left browser, working his way through the newspaper until he found the article. The others noticed that the blue hyperlinks in the upper right browser brightened and dimmed as he went through the various pages.

"The two pages are connected," Payne said aloud. "Interesting."

One blue hyperlink then stayed brightened.

He moved the cursor over to it and clicked.

Up popped a window. In it was:

"Well, I'll be dammed!" Payne said. "There it is! The missing jewel."

At the top of the pop-up window was: IP ADDRESS X.173.57.92.234.

"Now we take that" — he put the cursor over the address, copied it, then put the cursor in the bottom right browser window — "and feed it to ICANN."

He clicked.

Another pop-up window appeared. It not only had a street address with city, state, and zip code, but there also was a small street map with an arrow pointing to the exact address.

"Amazing!" Jim Byrth said.

"Anchorage, Alaska?" Payne said. "The guy's way the hell up there?"

Andy Radcliffe shrugged.

"Let's check the other one," he said.

When it came up, Payne said, "Jesus Christ! That one says he's in the Florida Keys."

Andy Radcliffe looked in deep thought. He clicked around and double-checked a couple links.

"That's just not possible," he then said. "Both of those comments were typed in the same day — yesterday. No way someone could've traveled from Alaska to Florida. And there's no way for two people to have the same screen name; the software that sets up the screen names only allows for unique ones. For obvious reasons."

Radcliffe thought a bit. "There is one possible explanation. If this guy had some way to mirror another computer, he could create confusing IP addresses. And mirroring computers is easy. It's just that generating an artificial IP address, in essence an alias, can cause havoc. But it is the electronic equivalent of a shell game. And that'd work."

Payne sighed.

"Looks like we're at what's known as a dead fucking end," Payne said.

Then he saw Radcliffe staring at him with a look of dejection.

*Andy looks like he's truly sorry this went nowhere.*

*Like it's his fault.*

"Hey, it happens, Andy," he said.

Harris offered, "Maybe he will write again, and we can draw him out."

Payne turned to Byrth. He saw that the Texas lawman not only appeared to be in deep thought but that he had that dry white bean tumbling again across his left fingers.

"What're you thinking?" Payne said seriously. "You look damned introspective."

"Thinking about Plan B," Byrth said. "We let your cat out of the bag."

Payne nodded.

Harris said, "I can call Lee Bryan at the paper and give him the story he can write and post."

Payne felt his phone vibrate, and he found himself in what he realized was a Pavlovian moment. He was grinning, and it was because he'd already conditioned himself to associate the phone vibration with a text message from Amanda Law.

But then it vibrated again. And when he

picked up the phone, the smile quickly went away.

The cellular telephone instead had been ringing. The color LCD screen flashed: SOUP KING — 1 CALL TODAY @ 0902.

*Well, I've put him off long enough.*

*Now certainly qualifies as "later."*

"Hey, Chad," Payne said into the phone after hitting the keypad. "What's new?"

# XI

## [ONE]
## Philadelphia International Airport
## Thursday, September 10, 9:01 A.M.
## Eastern Standard Time

Juan Paulo Delgado pulled out of the parking lot at the Avis Rent A Car facility, the tires of his Chevy Tahoe squealing, speeding off so fast that he almost snapped off the white barrier arm at the security booth.

Delgado was pissed off. The causes were many, and growing, the most recent being the attitude of the Avis assistant night manager.

They had had a long-running arrangement in which Delgado could park in the employee parking lot for as long as he wanted, in exchange for which Delgado saw that the guy got an occasional FedEx envelope of heroin, sometimes cut and mixed and packaged as Queso Azul, sometimes pure, uncut smack. The guy sold it to supplement — very damn nicely — the income he got from the Avis gig, which he said he kept only because he needed the health benefits for his daughter's sickle-cell anemia.

*But now, like the others, that's not good enough anymore.*

*No. The bastard wants more.*

*Just like that fucking Skipper Olde was always squeezing me.*

*And that* pendejo *who worked with him and cooked Skipper's meth.*

*They both got their payback. . . .*

Delgado was also still pissed, of course, at Ramos Manuel Chacón and his incredibly stupid mistake.

*Make that mistakes.*

*First, not paying the bill.*

*Then sending that text from jail.*

*Who knows what he had to promise the other inmate so he could use that phone?*

Delgado knew that all kinds of contraband existed in Texas jails. Almost anything could be had for a price paid to the right guard. And that included cell phones.

It was well known that in the state slam in Huntsville, Texas, the Mexican Mafia handled their outside business dealings using cell phones. The gangbangers called in hits on rival gang members, for example. Once, they'd even phoned a judge at his home, threatened him, then named his daughter and said they knew where she went to high school.

That, of course, had triggered a clean sweep of the cells. Contraband was always confiscated at these things, but then the bribes to the guards would begin again. And then there'd come another sweep. And on and on.

*It's only a matter of time before that phone he used gets picked up.*

*And then who knows how long till they track down the phones that were called from it.*

*If Miguel and Jorge are smart, they'll get new phones.*

*Me, too. I've had this one a week now.*

*And Ramos can rot in jail.*

*I'd be careful not to drop the soap, if I were you,* mi amigo. *And keep your back to the wall. . . .*

Then there'd been that newspaper photograph and story this morning.

That one really pissed him off.
*Stupid doctor bitch.*

After they had fled the Dallas house, Delgado got the hell out of Dodge as fast as he could. He'd had Miguel Guilar and Jorge Ernesto Aguilar drive him the twenty-five miles out to Dallas–Fort Worth International Airport so that he could catch the first direct flight to Philadelphia. Dallas Love Field didn't have anything departing for Philly till hours later, and those flights made stops en route. His American Airlines Boeing 727 had left DFW at four thirty Texas Standard Time.

When the American Airlines plane had landed in Philly at eight thirty Eastern Standard Time, he'd turned on his phone.

The phone had pinged three times, announcing three new text messages. One was from Guilar. He'd written that he and Jorge Ernesto Aguilar had driven the Suburban back past the stash house — and reported that the place was crawling with cops. And ambulances.

Delgado had replied that the sooner he and El Cheque got on the road headed for Philly with the guns and money and drugs, the better. Especially if they were going to finish with the ransom calls; that window of financial opportunity was quickly closing now that the people had been found in the house. It would slam shut very soon.

They could establish another stash house in Dallas, or maybe even Fort Worth, or both, sometime soon.

Delgado, still on the plane, had next sent a text message to Omar Quintanilla:

> meet me @ mall de mejico in 30 mins
>
> it's payday

Then, as he was walking from the concourse to get his bag, he passed a newsstand with three neat tall stacks of the Thursday edition of *The Philadelphia Bulletin*.

*Actual paper newspapers,* he thought.

*No computer required.*

As best as he could recall, Juan Paulo Delgado had never bought an actual newspaper. And he'd had no intention of doing so.

But then he noticed the big color photograph, on the newspaper's front page, of an attractive blond woman in a white medical lab coat. She stood behind a bank of microphones at what looked like a hospital.

The headline above the photograph read: DOCTOR CONFIRMS BURN VICTIM SHOT

TO DEATH IN ICU BED.

He picked up a copy and unfolded it. Then he read the caption:

Dr. Amanda Law, MD, FACS, FCCM, spoke late Wednesday at a news conference and confirmed that a patient had been shot to death in the Temple University Hospital's Burn Unit ICU around 11 A.M. She confirmed the identity of the murder victim, first reported in Wednesday's editions of *The Bulletin*, as that of twenty-seven-year-old J. Warren Olde, Jr., of Philadelphia. His murder was one of four in Philadelphia on Wednesday. "The cowards who carried out these killings are despicable," Dr. Law said at the end of what became an emotionally charged statement. "Shooting a helpless patient as he lay unconscious in his hospital bed is a vile act. And then there were those helpless bystanders shot in the Reading Terminal Market. I would personally like to stare these evil people in the eye and see that they suffer real justice." Police said the investigations continue in both shootings. See full story on page A3 and online at www.

"So you would, Dr. Law?" Delgado said aloud, bitterly. "Well, I'd like to meet a lovely girl like you, too."

He looked at the stand that held the stack of newspapers. The sign on it said the paper cost seventy-five cents.

*No wonder I don't buy papers!*

He dug in his pocket, and found three quarters among his change. He left them on the stack of papers, then went to Baggage Claim for his duffle. And then he caught the Avis shuttle bus to the lot.

When Delgado turned off South Sixth Street into the parking lot of the Mall of Mexico, he saw Omar Quintanilla sitting on the sidewalk.

Slender and wiry, the twenty-two-year-old Quintanilla stood five-eight and weighed 110 pounds. He had dull, vacuous eyes and kept his dark hair cut close to the scalp. Baggy jeans hung loosely on his thin frame, as did a white droopy sleeveless T-shirt.

Quintanilla saw Delgado's SUV pull into the lot and stood slowly, then more or less sauntered across the parking lot. He did so slightly bent over, making it look as if it annoyed him to expend the effort.

Delgado watched, and shook his head.

*That's not the same guy I played football with in high school.*

*Around the drugs, he's a really different guy. . . .*

Delgado found a parking spot in the shade of a small tree. The spot not only provided him relief from the morning sun, it gave him a view of the front door and the sidewalk along Sixth Street.

Quintanilla walked up to the driver's door. Delgado already had the window down.

*"Hola,"* Quintanilla said absently, reaching in with his right hand to bump fists with Delgado.

"Everything's gone to shit in Dallas," Delgado said.

*"Sí,"* Quintanilla said, nodding. "I heard from Miguel. That's some bad shit."

Delgado nodded. He scanned the parking lot. There was nothing unusual. Just a steady stream of cars and trucks coming and going. A white Ford pickup was stopped at the sidewalk along Sixth. Three Hispanic male day laborers were at its driver's window and negotiating some business.

*Hell,* Delgado suddenly thought, *we could*

*just pull up in the van, negotiate some bullshit price for some bullshit construction job, and those idiots would just jump in the van.*

*Then we could ransom them back to their illegal families. If they have any money.*

*Need to give that some more thought. . . .*

Delgado looked at Quintanilla and said, "Everything good here?"

Quintanilla nodded.

"How's Jesús?"

"Sleeping again. Those pills Angel gave him make him very sleepy."

*Or Jiménez is just being his usual lazy nineteen-year-old self,* Delgado thought.

"Where's Eduardo?"

Quintanilla looked at his wristwatch and said, "Should be back at the house by now, getting the cutting crews going."

Delgado considered that. It was important to keep the lawn-mowing schedules, if only for the cover the business provided for their other activities. Should anyone ever question them, they'd simply mumble that they were humble yard boys.

Then he reached into his wallet. He removed a driver's license and handed it to Quintanilla.

Quintanilla looked at it. He recognized it as Delgado's counterfeit license from Texas, the one with Delgado's picture but the name

Edgar Cisneros.

"What am I supposed to do with this?" he said.

Delgado nodded toward the mall.

"Go in there to the Western Union counter. There should be a two-thousand-dollar wire transfer waiting for Edgar Cisneros."

"But this has your picture on it. Why don't you do it?"

"Because I want *you* to do it!" El Gato snapped. "That's why."

He did not want to tell Quintanilla that he thought there was a slight chance someone could be looking for him in there, waiting for him to show up at the Western Union counter.

And the reason he did not want to tell him was that he didn't really know why the thought had come to him.

Delgado had had time to think on the plane, and he didn't want to admit it, but he'd realized that coming so close to getting caught in Dallas had both shaken him up and made him at least a little paranoid.

Which really pissed him off.

*All because that idiot Ramos made a stupid mistake.*

*And now I'm upset to the point I might make a mistake.*

*So that is why I want you to go in, Omar.*

608

*But I'm just not going to tell you that. . . .*

"But," Quintanilla protested, "do you think they'll let me get the money with this ID's photo?"

Delgado was about to snap again, then looked at Quintanilla's dull gaze — *Nobody home . . . why bother?* — and decided against it.

He said slowly, "How would you know to come and get the money if you weren't who you said you were? *That* is what you tell the teller. *Bueno?* "

Quintanilla shrugged, showing absolutely no confidence.

Delgado then added, "And if that does not work" — he pulled a wad of folded bills from his pocket and peeled off one note — "then slip this to the teller under the license."

Delgado gave him a hundred-dollar bill.

"Nobody says no to Ben Franklin, especially in Philadelphia," Delgado said with a smile.

Quintanilla took it, then turned, and sauntered toward the front door of the Mall of Mexico.

In the twenty minutes that Quintanilla was in the mall, Delgado sat in the SUV, watching the patrons come and go. Occasionally, he would glance at the picture on the front

609

page of the newspaper, which was on the front passenger seat.

The more he looked at it, the more he thought about the bitch's comment. And the more he thought about that, the more he really wanted to fulfill her wish.

*Teach her a lesson to say things she knows nothing about.*

*And why not?*

*A doctor makes a lot of money . . . somebody would pay to get her back.*

*And pay good.*

*Or we could just have some fun with her.*

He looked at the picture of Dr. Amanda Law.

*Yeah, why not . . . ?*

Delgado then saw Quintanilla come out of the Mall of Mexico carrying a letter-size envelope. As he sauntered across the parking lot, a ten-year-old battered Chevrolet Venture minivan pulled into the parking space two spots away. An elderly Hispanic woman, so squat that she barely could see over the dash, eased the dirty black vehicle to a stop. She was alone.

As Delgado looked at the van, he remembered that they had had to tigertail their minivan. It had been the one he'd used to take the dead headless girl to the river.

*All we have now is the big Ford van. I don't*

*want to use it.*

*So we need another minivan.*

*And Abuela's looks like it'd work just fine. Price is right.*

Delgado got out of his Tahoe and walked toward Quintanilla.

He told him, "The keys are in my truck. You get in it and wait till I text you when and where to go. Got it?"

Delgado saw Quintanilla's vacuous eyes staring back.

"Got it?" he repeated.

Quintanilla nodded, then handed over the envelope. "It worked. License is in with the cash."

Delgado took the envelope and looked around. No one was paying them any attention. And the elderly woman, who wore a rumpled tan sack of a dress, was just getting her door open and unbuckling her seat belt.

He folded the envelope and stuffed it in his back pocket.

"Follow me to the truck, then get in it."

"Okay."

Delgado walked quickly toward the Tahoe, then turned toward the Chevy minivan. The woman didn't hear him approaching.

*"Abuela!"* he called out affectionately, as one would one's grandmother. *"Hola!"*

She turned in her seat in time to feel Delgado stepping into the minivan and quickly shoving her across the bench seat.

She screamed.

The keys were still in the ignition, and he fired up the engine, then threw the gearshift into drive.

She screamed again.

Two blocks later, Delgado pulled to the curb. He motioned for her to get out. She quietly complied.

As he drove off, Abuela screamed again.

Delgado drove another two blocks, then pulled to the curb and sent a text message to Quintanilla.

# [TWO]
# 823 Sears Street, Philadelphia
# Thursday, September 10,
# 9:21 P.M.

Detective Anthony Harris pulled Sergeant Matt Payne's white rental Ford sedan to a stop in a parking spot behind a bright blue BMW M3.

"That's Chad's coupe," Payne said.

"And 823's right there, across the street," Sergeant Jim Byrth of the Texas Rangers said from the backseat. He had The Hat on his lap.

As he got out of the car, he put on The Hat.

With Payne's announcement that they might have found the girl's head, Byrth was anxious to add another piece to the puzzle that would help hunt down El Gato.

Harris and Byrth were halfway across the street when Byrth looked back at Payne. He was standing at the curb, checking his phone.

"You coming, Marshal?"

When they had approached the rental car at the Roundhouse, Harris saw that Payne had his cell phone out. He appeared to be anticipating either a call — or, more probably, a text message — at any moment.

"Give me the car keys, Matt," Harris had said with mild disgust. "You're damned dangerous with that phone. Can't believe what it'd be like with you on that and trying to drive, too."

"I'll take my usual spot in the back," Byrth said, looking at Payne. "You, Marshal, can ride shotgun."

Harris drove from the Roundhouse over to Sixth Street and took it toward South Philly.

With one eye on his phone, Payne went

over with Jim Byrth the little bit of information Chad Nesbitt had told him in the diner by the Philly Inn. And he gave Byrth more background on his relationship with Nesbitt and Skipper Olde, both long-term and specific to the previous day.

He glanced again at his phone.

*Nothing! Dammit!*

He checked to make sure it was still on, that the damned battery hadn't crapped out or something. It was still on, but the battery was low.

It had been almost a half hour since Matt had sent that text message to Amanda. And she hadn't replied. And that worried him.

*Did I say something wrong?*

*Did I open a wound, one of those things that caused that pain in her eyes?*

*Jesus, her silence is killing me.*

*And that's the part of text and e-mail conversations I absolutely hate — the silence of no reply.*

*In person, if they're silent you can read the eyes and face. On the phone, you can pick up on their tone of voice.*

*But e-silence is e-fucking deafening.*

*And if I send another, it might annoy her more.*

*That is, if she's annoyed.*

*How's that saying go?*

*"When you find yourself in a hole, Payne, stop with the damn digging."*

Matt thought that the message had been pretty simple and straightforward.

*But women are always trying to read between the lines.*

*What could she possibly read into mine?*

*Or maybe it was too simple . . . it's damn hard communicating emotion in a text or e-mail. Even a missing comma can have a huge impact.*

*"Let's eat, Grandma" changes a helluva lot without the comma.*

*Then it's "Let's eat Grandma" — who probably won't willingly come to the table.*

He scrolled back in the string of messages and reread what he'd sent, which simply had repeated part of the earlier text:

---

you never answered . . . why the change of heart?

---

*Maybe* that's *it. I'm pushing. . . .*

Then suddenly his phone vibrated.

And his heart automatically began beating faster.

When Matt looked at the text message, he was at first shocked at its length.

*Jesus! It's a tome.*

*What in the world did I trigger?*

That's *what took her so long.*

*It'd take me days to thumb-type one that long on my phone.*

Then he remembered seeing her cell phone at Liberties.

It was one of those really new ones, actually more of a small computer that happened also to be a phone. The computer-phone was one and a half times the size of a playing card, and damn near as thin, and if you tapped the icon labeled TEXT, a window with a facsimile of a typewriter keyboard popped up. It was a qwerty one, like a real full-size keyboard only smaller, and allowed for much faster writing than most cell phones.

Phones such as Payne's.

He read Amanda's text:

---

609-555-6221

Hi . . .

I have to be honest. (If only because without that, why have a relationship?)

Didn't get much sleep last night, what with all this running through my head.

---

See, I was — maybe still am — afraid of getting close to a cop.

I remember, not exactly happily, all the sacrifices my father made to be a cop. How hard it was on our family, especially my mother, seeing him every day walk out the front door for work and not knowing if that would be the last we'd see him alive.

And then dad got shot.

Matt, I didn't want that again.

But then I saw what that bastard did at the hospital.

And what you did! Wow! How you were all over that guy without a second thought.

We can't have people like that loose on the streets.

And to do that, we need people like my dad and you.

And I think I need someone like you . . . (smile) -A

Payne just stared at his phone.

There was a lump in his throat that felt like the size of a Lincoln SUV.

He thought he might cry.

*How do I reply to that?*

*My God!*

*No wonder she took so long to reply.*

"You okay?" Harris said, looking askance at Payne.

Payne tried to clear his throat. The Lincoln SUV budged a little. He was about to reply, but didn't trust his voice. He simply nodded.

Then his phone vibrated again.

It was another text from Amanda:

---

609-555-6221

Something else I need to get off my chest.

Recently I've lost a couple of people who were very close to me.

That made me rethink a lot of things.

Plus, my specialty can be kind of rough on the psyche.

---

Especially seeing the kids across the street at shriners. Anyone who thinks they have a tough life hasn't taken a walk through a pediatric burn ward and visited with those poor kids.

Anyway, all that made me pretty introspective.

And so I promised myself that i'd do what my friend — Carl Crantz was his name — said before he passed: to live every day like it's the last.

Sorry. You asked . . . (smile) -A

Now Payne was crying. He turned his head so Tony Harris wouldn't see.
*And how the hell do I respond to* that?
*What a wonderful woman. . . .*
After a moment, he thought, *Well, when in doubt, tell the truth.*
He texted:

i'm speechless.

that, like you, was beautiful.

thanks for sharing. -matt

A second later, his phone vibrated:

609-555-6221

Matt?!? Oh no! Wrong Payne!

I thought I was texting my therapist!

Just kidding (smile) I meant it for you. -A

He grinned. Then he had a thought and really grinned broadly as he typed:

cute.

just so you know, my favorite part was where you mentioned your chest . . . (big grin)

609-555-6221

You're so bad!

I share my soul and that's the thanks I get.

Some sexist caveman comment on my anatomy.

Next thing you know, we'll have our first argument. (smile)

---

no chance of that. for one, i could never argue with you.

for another, i've been told that there are two theories to arguing with a woman.

and neither work. (smile) so why try?

A minute passed, and there was no reply.

Harris said, "What happened with your phone? You finally break it? You're pounding that thing with your thumbs like it needs life support."

Payne looked at him and shrugged.

He looked back at the phone and thumbed:

oh . . . and nice story in today's paper!

you looked terrific.

how is your day going?

---

609-555-6221

Thanks. That was a difficult press conference. But, it explains why I was out of sorts at the bar later.

And my day is great, thank you.

We still on for that lunch?

---

*Lunch? We never planned lunch.
Oh! "Lunch, dinner, cottage."*
Payne thumbed and sent:

---

yes! that'll knock lunch off the list.

one down, two to go. (grin)

let me get back to you in just a bit.

He sent the text just as Harris pulled the rental Ford in behind Chad Nesbitt's BMW.

Harris, Payne, and Byrth stood at the painted metal door of the row house at 823 Sears Street. Payne knocked loudly with his knuckles three times.

They could hear on the other side of the door the sounds of feet approaching. Then, a moment later, there came the banshee wail of a woman. Followed by the sounds of heavy footfalls pounding away from the door.

On the stoop, the three exchanged glances as they heard a woman's Latina-accented voice. It cried out, *"La Migra! La Migra!"*

And then they thought they heard a back door slam shut.

Payne and Harris looked at each other, then at Byrth.

" 'La Migra,' " Byrth explained, "is a Spanish pejorative for immigration enforcement officers."

They nodded their understanding.

"Can probably thank The Hat for that," Payne said, and chuckled.

A moment later, they could hear two male voices on the other side of the door, having an animated discussion. Finally, there came the sounds of the three locks on the door being turned.

The door swung open.

Paco Esteban stood there. Chad Nesbitt was behind him.

El Nariz's eyes fixated on The Hat.

"Thanks for coming, Matt," Nesbitt said, then looked between Harris and Byrth and added, "Gentlemen."

Nesbitt saw Payne looking at Paco Esteban.

"Paco," Nesbitt said, motioning in Payne's direction, "this is my friend the policeman I told you about."

Then Byrth spoke up. "I'm not La Migra, Paco." He held out his hand. "I'm Sergeant Jim Byrth of the Texas Rangers. And I've come after the man known as El Gato."

El Nariz looked at the Texas lawman warily. He shook his hand and said, *Mucho gusto* without much gusto at all.

But there seemed to be some relief in his eyes at the mention of El Gato. It told him that maybe this authority wasn't after anyone in his home.

Payne introduced Harris and himself.

"Come in," Esteban said.


Chadwick Thomas Nesbitt IV felt the bile rise in his throat one more time. He was on his knees, his expensively tailored slacks

624

now soiled by the dirty floor of the bathroom in Paco Esteban's basement. His fine silk necktie was loosened and the collar of his custom-made French-cuff dress shirt unbuttoned. There were wet spots of vomitus on both garments.

Just outside the door, on the closed white door of the horizontal Deepfreeze, Paco Esteban had opened the black plastic bags containing the severed head of Ana Maria Del Carmen Lopez.

He had peeled back the bloody white towel with which he'd wrapped her head.

And there Harris, Byrth, Nesbitt, and Payne had had their first look at the face of what once had been a pretty seventeen-year-old Honduran.

Now, however, her light-brown skin was blotched and bruised, her long straight black hair matted, her dark eyes glassy.

Nesbitt had lost it when he noticed her soft facial features had what had been cute little freckles across her upper cheeks and pixie nose.

"What's that?" Payne said, pointing toward her left ear.

Esteban turned the head slightly.

They saw there on the neck, at the hairline, a small black tattoo. It was a gothic block letter D with three short lines.

"El Gato and his whiskers," Byrth said.

Payne shook his head in shock. "What's the D about?"

Byrth shrugged. "Maybe, probably Dallas."

Then Nesbitt shared the information about El Gato's girls and the house on Hancock.

*What a helluva break!* Payne thought.

And then he thought, *Amanda and lunch!*

He began thumbing:

---

how's your day going?

just had an interesting development in the case . . .

---

He pushed SEND, but then his screen flashed with ERROR — NO SERVICE.

*Dammit!*

*Must be because we're in the basement.*

He looked at the signal strength. None of the five bars were present. He also noticed that the battery was almost drained.

*That's not good.*

*Worse, I'm not sure I have a charger in the rental car.*

Payne walked across the room. The smallest of the five bars flickered on, indicating the weakest of signals.

He hit SEND again. And a second later the screen flashed MESSAGE SENT.

Then his phone chirped twice. And its screen went black.

*Fuck!*

*What if Amanda tries to reach me?*


# [THREE]
# 3519-A North Broad Street, Philadelphia
# Thursday, September 10, 9:56 A.M.


Dr. Amanda Law had just paid for her usual morning double cappuccino with nonfat milk at the Cup O'Joe's Internet Café location across Broad Street from the Shriners Hospital for Children.

She stepped outside and looked up at the morning sun and smiled. Her cellular telephone chimed once. She looked at the screen and her smile became larger.

The box showed the first two lines of the message. It read:

> matt
>
> how's your day going?

And she thought, *I haven't felt this good in a long time.*
*I'd forgotten what it was like to have someone thinking about me.*
*And being genuinely affectionate.*
Amanda slid her left thumb across the bottom edge of the big glass of the computerphone and the touch screen lit brightly. Now she could clearly read the box that had popped up in the middle:

> matt
>
> how's your day going?
>
> just had an interesting development in the case . . . need to postpone lunch (frown)
>
> sorry . . . i'll make it up to you . . . promise!

She thought somewhat sadly:

*And so that begins, or continues . . .*
*But I can deal with it.*
She tapped out:

---

I'm still fine.

Same as the last time you asked — what?
— a half hour ago? (wink)

And that's fine about lunch. I have a busy
day, too.

Besides, I told you I know how your days
can go.

So, be safe! -A

---

Then she hit SEND. She had no way of
knowing that it would be some time until it
would be received and read.

Dr. Amanda Law took a sip of her coffee
and prepared to cross the street and enter
Temple University Hospital.

She looked left, checking for southbound
traffic. There was a package delivery truck,
a big boxy brown one, accelerating down
Broad. She glanced right, trying to judge the
northbound traffic, wondering if she could

go after the delivery truck flew past her at the hammers of hell.

A block south, the traffic light had all the vehicles on Broad stopped in both directions. A taxicab was parked in front of the hospital, and behind that a beat-up old black minivan was rolling to a stop. She saw a skinny dark-skinned man in baggy jeans, a zipper hoodie sweatshirt, and a wife-beater T-shirt get out of the sliding door on the far side, walk to near the front door of the hospital, and stop to look back at the minivan.

Suddenly, there was the enormous sound and wind of the delivery van blowing past. It went so fast it left a huge wake. Amanda caught herself clutching at her phone and coffee, afraid she'd drop one or the other, or both.

Then all was calm again. She glanced left and saw that no other vehicle was coming, and stepped off the curb. Just shy of halfway across, she glanced to the right. The taxicab was now rolling forward. It made the right turn onto Tioga just as Amanda stepped around its rear bumper.

As she stepped up on the sidewalk, she noticed movement to her right.

The black minivan, too, was rolling.

And the man in the T-shirt was moving away from the front door of the hospital.

Then all of a sudden the minivan accelerated and was right behind her.

And the man in the T-shirt was running right at her. He charged into her, his right shoulder hitting her just above the stomach, at the same time wrapping his arms around her, like a football tackle. It knocked the wind out of her.

The impact also caused her to squeeze and crumple her cup, the hot coffee spilling on her and her attacker, and she dropped her phone on the sidewalk.

As she slowly went backward, Amanda Law began anticipating hitting the hard concrete sidewalk.

But the next thing she knew, she was down, and it hadn't been hard concrete. It had been a softer landing. Then she realized that she was now on a blanket inside the black minivan, its sliding side door still locked in the open position.

There was no middle or backseat in the van, only open carpeted floor.

She tried to scream or yell, but the wind knocked out of her left her gasping for air.

She heard the driver, a male, yelling: "Phone! Get the fucking phone!"

The driver had been yelling at the man who'd tackled her, because with a grunt he pushed off her. He ran back to the sidewalk and retrieved the phone.

She tried to sit up and make a try for the open door. But then she painfully felt a hand grab her hair at the back of her head. It pulled her back down.

She heard some woman's voice on the sidewalk yell, "Stop them! Someone call the police! Stop!"

Then the man who'd tackled her jumped back into the minivan and onto her. The hand let go of her hair. And the minivan roared away from the hospital, wind rushing in through the open sliding door.

Some three or four blocks later, the mini-van stopped. The man in back slammed shut the sliding door. There was the sound of tape being ripped from a roll. Despite her desperate attempts, Amanda Law very shortly found her wrists bound with duct tape, then her ankles. Then a strip of the tape was placed over her mouth, and finally a pillowcase pulled over her head and held there with a wrap of tape around her neck.

Amanda Law, her head still covered by the pillowcase, knew that she was in some sort of house not too far from the hospital. She had tried to track the direction and distance the van had driven her since she'd been abducted, but had become pretty disoriented after the first four or five turns. On two of the turns, the driver had taken them so fast that she'd rolled around on the open back floor, and that had really thrown off her sense of direction.

The distance had been easier to track only because it had not taken long at all to reach the house. It had been maybe eight, ten minutes at most before the driver had stood heavily on the brakes, then bumped up over a curb.

Someone — it must have been the skinny dark-skinned one in the T-shirt — had gotten out the front passenger door, and there had been the sound of a chain being pulled from around a metal pole, then of a metal gate dragging across what sounded like rock. The van had eased forward, its tires crunching on the gravel. And the gate was closed and locked.

One of the men had then picked her out of the back of the van, thrown her over his right shoulder, and carried her into the house. There, in what smelled like the kitchen, she had been put into what felt like an old wooden armchair. There came a tugging at her duct-taped wrists, and she realized after a moment, when the pressure of the wrap began easing, that her hands were being released.

But only for a moment. As she flexed her fingers and wrists to get the feeling back in them, someone grabbed her left wrist, and there came the sound of more duct tape being torn from a roll. Her left wrist was then taped to the left armrest of the wooden chair, and it was repeated on the right. Then her ankles were taped to the bottom of the chair's front legs.

She could hear the sound of someone walking across the room, the door of a refrigerator opening, the clanking of what sounded like beer bottles being removed. Then the door closed and bottles were opened with a *pffft* sound.

And then the clanking of glass bottles again.

*They just toasted the success of my kidnapping!* Amanda Law thought.

*What the hell is going on?*

*What do they want with me?*

*Is this . . . is this* it?

"So, Dr. Amanda Law," a male Hispanic voice said.

*He knows me?*

*How the hell does he know who I am?*

*That's the same voice as the driver, who shouted about getting the phone. . . .*

There was the sound of a newspaper being opened.

The voice then said, " 'The cowards who carried out these killings are despicable' —"

Despite the tape covering her mouth, she suddenly gasped.

*He's reading that from the front page of the paper!*

The voice went on: " 'Shooting a helpless patient as he lay unconscious in his hospital bed is a vile act . . . I would personally like to stare these evil people in the eye and see that they suffer real justice.' "

There was a long silence. It ended with the sound of a glass bottle being put heavily on a table.

"That bastard Skipper wasn't helpless, Dr. Law. Same with that Jamaican bastard in the market. No, no. And I would think someone as smart as you would know things are never as simple as they appear." He took a sip of his beer. "So maybe now you do. Too bad it's too late."

*These are the killers . . . ?*

*Dear God . . .*

Then she heard another male Hispanic voice: "It's busted a little, but still works."

"Give it to me," the first male said.

Amanda could hear the *click-click-click* sounds the computer-phone made when the touch-screen buttons were tapped.

"Well, look what we have here. Dr. Amanda Law has a new boyfriend sending her texts. Looks like his name is Matt."

*Oh, no! What happens now?*

*Especially if they find out Matt's a cop . . .*

"Wonder if the boyfriend will pay to get Dr. Amanda Law back. And how much more to get her back safely?"

The other man grunted.

"Well, only one way to find out," the first said.

Amanda heard a different clicking sound, like the pushing of a button.

*That's not my phone.*

Then she heard the terrifying sound of the screams of a young girl and the shouts of a young boy.

*That's a recording!*

*Of somebody being — what? — tortured!*

Then there was another click. The recording stopped.

"Here we go," the first man's voice said.

She heard the familiar clicking sound of her phone.

Then quiet.

Then one more click.

"I'll be damned! It went into voice mail," He added bitterly, "What's the matter, *Dr. Law?* Doesn't your boyfriend take your calls? Maybe this bastard Matt *won't* pay to get you back! How is that for your *justice?*"

Amanda felt a sob welling up. She fought it back.

"Well, what the hell. We'll just leave the boyfriend a message."

There came the clicks, then she could hear the male breathing heavily.

*He's getting some sick satisfaction out of this!*

*It sounds almost sexual!*

*Oh, God help me!*

Then she heard, after enough time had passed for Matt's phone to answer and roll the call into voice mail, the man shout: "We have your girlfriend, Matt!"

Then came the audio recording of the teenage boy's terrified shouts of "Stop! No!" and the girl begging, "No! Don't!"

That went on for maybe five seconds.

Then the man shouted: "Do as I say, and you get your Dr. Law back alive! No cops!"

Then there was the sound of more clicks.

And then the kitchen was terribly quiet.

Except for the soft sobbing of Amanda Law.

# [FOUR]
# York and Hancock Streets, Philadelphia
# Thursday, September 10, 11:01 P.M.

Matt Payne, Tony Harris, and Jim Byrth were seated in the passenger seats of Paco Esteban's white Plymouth Voyager minivan. It was parked on the corner, a block shy of the dilapidated row house at 2505 Hancock Street.

Esteban was in the driver's seat. And that almost had not happened.

At Esteban's house, a fairly charged discussion ensued as to what to do with the information — not to mention the head — that Esteban had provided.

Chad Nesbitt, seeing where the debate may have been leading, excused himself. He'd said he'd done more than enough putting Paco Esteban together with Matt Payne. And he left, presumably to go home for a bath, clean clothes, and a good mouthwash.

638

In the basement, Harris had automatically said that he'd call in the information to the Roundhouse. That would get the official wheels turning. And someone farther up the food chain, certainly one in a white shirt, if not a white shirt with one or more stars pinned to its collar points, would decide how many assets to throw at 2505 Hancock Avenue.

"Slow down, Tony," Payne had said. "Until ten minutes ago, we pretty much did not have a damned thing on where this guy was."

"Yeah. And?"

"And I think it could blow up on us if suddenly there were a dozen Aviation Unit helos buzzing the rooftop of the place just so they can send video back to the Executive Command Center."

"You don't know they'll do that, Matt."

Payne nodded.

"True, Tony. But I also don't know that they *won't* do it. Which is what I'd prefer — that they don't fucking do it." He paused for a moment. "This guy is bad, and it's an important bust. I don't want someone doing it for the glory. I just want the sonofabitch off the streets. Period." He gestured at the Deepfreeze. "No more little girls losing their heads, for starters."

Paco Esteban grunted and nodded.

Tony Harris nodded. "Matt, you know I agree. But there are other ways to do this."

"Yeah, but they involve a whole helluva lot more people, which we don't need. And more time, which we don't have." He paused. "Look, you're welcome to call it in, if that's what you feel you have to do. But God knows what this animal is capable of doing next."

"Tony," Byrth said, "I'm afraid that I have to agree with Matt."

Payne looked at Byrth. He wasn't at all surprised that a Texas Ranger would have no trouble going it alone.

He'd read all about "One Ranger, One Riot."

Tony Harris looked between them, then held up his hands in a gesture of surrender.

"Let the record show that I have dutifully played devil's advocate and hereby subscribe to whatever operation Marshal Wyatt Earp has in mind."

Payne smiled. He knew Harris wasn't mocking him.

"Tell you what, Tony. Call the Roundhouse, give whomever you feel can be trusted the address of this row house *and* the strict order (a) to say and do nothing with it and" — he glanced at Byrth — "(b) to have the cavalry ready to ride in should you call for it. Give it a code name if you want. *Prairie Fire* was one that the guys in Special Forces in 'Nam used for when the shit hit the fan. I'm partial to *Get Me the Fuck Outta Here!* Leaves no room for confusion or misinterpretation."

Harris grinned. Then he nodded agreeably.

"I can live with that," he said. "Okay, so what do you propose?"

Sergeant Matthew M. Payne, Philadelphia Police Department, Badge Number 271, turned to Paco Esteban.

"Señor Paco Esteban, I hereby officially offer to you a position as confidential informant for the Philadelphia Police Department. In this capacity, you agree to assist in any way that (a) you can and (b) you feel is within your capabilities. In return, the department will make monetary payments and certain other tokens of compensation as mutually agreed."

It was common practice for Philadelphia Police Department ongoing investigations to use confidential informants. And it was entirely within the rules and regulations of the department. For example, the police not only paid confidential informants for tips that led to arrests for illegal guns and drugs, they also provided the funds to make those purchases. It wasn't unusual for the money to run into the tens of thousands of dollars.

Of course, there were rules governing the use of confidential sources. Among them was that there had to be a professional relationship. Strict procedures and policies were in place to ensure an arm's length of professionalism between a police officer and an informant.

Paco Esteban shook his head.

"You don't or you won't?" Payne said somewhat incredulously.

"I don't."

"You *don't?*" Payne repeated.

Paco Esteban shook his head again.

"I don't want one dollar. I want that bastard caught. What do I do?"

"Everybody ready?" Matt Payne said, sliding open the side door of Paco Esteban's Plymouth van, using his left hand. Payne and Harris were seated in back on the bench seat; Byrth was in the front passenger seat. On the console between the seats was a white paper bag. Printed on it in somewhat Asian-looking lettering was: TAKE OUT TASTY CHINESE. The van reeked of greasy fast-food wontons.

Byrth said, "Yup."

Harris said, "Uh-huh."

Esteban said, *"Sí."*

Everyone but Esteban was armed with a semiautomatic pistol. Payne had his Colt .45 ACP Officer's Model in his right hand. It was cocked but unlocked, ready to fire. Harris held his Glock Model 17 nine-millimeter between his legs, the muzzle pointed at the floorboard. Byrth's black Colt Combat Commander .45 ACP, with its inlaid star of the Texas Rangers, was on top of his right thigh, pointed at the dash.

Payne watched as Byrth put his left boot on the dash and pulled up on his cuffed pants leg, then reached to the right of his calf and pulled out a pistol from the boot top.

*I'll be goddamned,* Payne thought.

*That's that Officer's Model he told me he carried as his backup.*

Byrth racked the slide back, then reached to the floorboard, where he had an open plastic box of .45-caliber cartridges. He pulled a single round from the box and slipped it into the chamber. Then he let the slide slam forward. With the hammer now back, he set its lock, then fed it a full magazine. Finally, he slipped the pistol back inside his boot top and pulled down his pants cuff.

Byrth caught Payne's stare and, over his shoulder, said, "I'd rather have my twelve-gauge pump with buckshot for this, but it wouldn't fit in the boot."

Payne chuckled.

"Okay, Paco," Payne said. "Let's roll."

The minivan began driving slowly toward 2505 Hancock.

As Esteban approached the row house, he steered to the left side of the street, then up and over the curb. Payne had told him to stop the van there so it could provide them at least a little cover and concealment.

Esteban then got out and reached back in for the bag of fast food.

Esteban was dressed in somewhat ragged khakis and a T-shirt, and on his head wore a big orange ballcap with the logotype TAKE OUT TASTY CHINESE. Payne had actually taken the cap off the head of one of the employees when they'd bought the food. He'd tossed the kid a twenty and smiled. The kid had thought him a fool, but kept the cash nevertheless.

Jim Byrth covered the right side of the front door, Payne the left. Tony Harris had gone around back to cover that possible exit.

Paco Esteban rapped on the wooden door.

No one answered.

He knocked again, harder.

After a few minutes, they heard the sound

of shuffling footsteps. Then the door cracked opened.

A short, sleepy Hispanic male with a bad mustache stood there. He wore only boxer shorts and had a bandage around his left thigh.

"Your order," Esteban said, holding out the bag of Chinese takeout. "It is prepaid."

"We didn't —" Jesús Jiménez started to say. Then through his sleepy haze he heard the "prepaid" part. The groggy teenager decided he was hungry.

Esteban had been told not to stand too close to the door.

Jiménez had to reach out of the house in order to grab the bag.

And when he did, Jim Byrth grabbed his arm and spun him. He threw him to the floor and had the surprised kid handcuffed in no time. He stuck the muzzle of his .45 into the kid's mouth. The kid's suddenly widened eyes suggested that he'd instantly understood the message.

As Payne moved closer to enter the door, he looked down at the Hispanic male.

*That's the shooter from the hospital!*

*The sonofabitch who killed Skipper!*

*And who I shot!*

*I should just —*

Bryrth then quickly jerked Jiménez down

645

to the van, practically carrying the small teenager. He unlocked one of the handcuffs and clipped it to the sliding door handle.

As Byrth returned, Payne wordlessly signaled Paco Esteban to go to the van. Esteban shook his head, then very reluctantly did as ordered. When Jesús Jiménez started to shout a warning, Esteban surprised both Payne and Byrth by punching the teenager in the face, knocking him out cold.

*Well, that just earned him monetary payments and certain other tokens. . . .*

Payne and Byrth looked each other in the eye. Byrth nodded for Payne to take the lead.

Even with the front door open, it was dark inside because of the front windows being covered.

They walked in a crouch, staying close to the walls. There was almost no furniture.

Payne heard voices coming from the back of the house.

They entered a room that appeared to be the dining room, and which held only a couple of wooden armchairs. On the far wall was a swinging door, with light from the far room leaking around its edges.

Payne moved fluidly toward it, Byrth on his heels. As they approached the swinging door, the voices became louder and more clear.

Payne could distinguish at least two — both males, both with Hispanic accents.

They listened for another minute. There was no additional voice.

Then one of them yelled, "Jesús! You okay? Who was at the door?"

Matt looked at Jim. They were both half-lit by the dim light bleeding around the door. Jim signaled for them each to take a side of the door.

Matt moved to the left, Jim to the right.

Matt could see the rusty gold-colored hinge by his head. He tried to peer into the kitchen, but the gap between the door and its frame wasn't large enough and there was a piece of painted wooden trim on the far side.

Then they heard the first voice again. He barked: "Go look!"

And a second later, the door swung into the dining room, as Omar Quintanilla sauntered through, absently holding a pistol along his right leg.

When the door had opened, light momentarily flashed into the dark dining room, almost blinding Matt and Jim.

Then the door swung shut. Jim, his eyes not quite adjusted from the sudden light, instinctively jumped in Omar's direction. He hit him square, getting his left arm around Omar's throat.

They then went to the floor, making a helluva noise.

"Omar!" the male inside the kitchen yelled. "What the hell'd you just do?"

As Jim punched Omar in the face, Omar's pistol went off. The round went into the ceiling.

Matt had his pistol aimed at the pair, but could not see well enough in the dark to get a good aim.

Then he heard Jim mutter, "You sonofabitch."

The pistol went off again. This time, the round found Omar, who suddenly stopped fighing. He moaned and clutched at his chest.

Then Payne suddenly heard and saw the swinging door get kicked open — and he saw and felt it hit him, pushing him back against the wall.

He instinctively kicked the door back.

And there he saw the other Hispanic male. He was bringing up the muzzle of a bullpup-style weapon, about to get an aim on Jim Byrth.

Matt Payne followed Jim Byrth's lead — and jumped at the man, wrapping his left arm over the man's left shoulder and grabbing the forearm of the weapon. As he pulled it upward, the gun went off, the muzzle spraying a stream of lead up a wall and across the ceiling.

Payne began pummeling the man's head with his pistol, and threw him to the ground. And then he felt another pair of hands on the man's body — Jim Byrth was stripping him of the bullpup weapon.

Payne hit him in the head again. And the man went limp.

Payne cuffed him and left him on the floor.

Matt and Jim stood. Jim had the P90 submachine gun slung on his right shoulder.

"Nice work, Marshal."

"You okay?"

"Yup. No more holes in me than I came with."

"Let's clear the kitchen and the rest. Then you can get this asshole trussed up."

They found the kitchen clear but for one person who looked to be a woman. There was a pillowcase over her head, and she was taped to a chair. They immediately deemed her not a threat.

Payne went to the back door and looked out the window. He just barely saw Tony

Harris to the side of the door, waiting for someone to flee.

"It's me, Tony!" he called. "Matt Payne!"

Matt thought he heard the woman whimper.

He unlocked the door and opened it.

"C'mon in, and clear the rest of the house with Jim!"

Tony Harris entered and said, "Jesus, Matt! What's with all the gunfire?"

"Just another day at the OK Corral, Tony."

Through the open swinging door, Harris saw a stream of blood on the floor. He moved for a better look, then saw the dead body of the Hispanic male on the floor of the next room.

He raised his eyebrows. Then he raised his pistol and followed Byrth out of the kitchen.

Matt Payne glanced at the kitchen table and saw a plastic storage box containing a score or more of used cell phones. On the table itself was a battered fancy phone with a big glass touch-screen.

He slipped his .45 in the small of his back and turned to the woman bound to the chair.

"It's going to be okay," Payne said softly.

"I'm a Philadelphia policeman."

As he pulled out his folding pocketknife, he thought he heard her start sobbing heavily.

"I'm going to cut open the top of this pillowcase, okay?"

Her head bobbed enthusiastically, the pillowcase moving in a rapid manner.

"Okay, now don't move your head."

Taking great care, he grasped the pillowcase's seam at the top of her head, pulling it up and away from her head so that if she suddenly did move again, his knife blade would be a safe distance away.

Very carefully, he slipped the tip of the serrated blade into the fabric. He sawed slightly, and the blade slit the fabric all along the seam.

*Well, she's a blond,* was the first thing that he thought.

Then he tugged the case down so it fell to her shoulders.

"Jesus Christ!"

Payne had to force himself to go slowly while unbinding Amanda Law, first removing the strip of gray duct tape from her beautiful face — the strip literally went from ear to ear — then removing the tape from her wrists and ankles.

What made it harder was that he was shaking.

*Are my emotions taking over?*

*Not good.*

*It'd be better if it's just the adrenaline kicking into overdrive. . . .*

He started by kissing her on the forehead and saying, "This might hurt . . ."

Then, as gently as possible, he began pulling the tape from her left cheek and, a moment later, her right cheek.

"Oh, Matt!" Amanda cried out.

Excitedly, she tried to sit up higher so that she could kiss him, but, still bound to the chair, she collapsed back into it.

"Slow down, baby!" Matt said, smiling, then leaned down and kissed her softly on the lips.

He looked her in the eyes. They were all puffy and wet from the crying.

"Are you okay?" he said in a soft tone. But there was anger in it, too. "Did they . . . do anything to you?"

Her eyes were big and expressive. She shook her head vigorously.

"Thank God," he said, then kissed her again. "Now, let me get the rest of this tape off."

She nodded gently.

He put the knife blade on the tape securing her left wrist.

"You heard the girl screaming on your voice mail?" Amanda asked.

Matt paused and looked at her.

"No," he said, shaking his head, slightly confused.

"They left a terrifying message on your voice mail. They were holding me for ransom. But it wasn't me. On the message, I mean."

Matt nodded as he tried to digest that.

*A voice-mail message?*

*I wouldn't have gotten it because my battery is dead.*

He glanced at the box on the table, then went back to cutting the duct tape. He was really worried he might accidentally cut her in his haste. He had to saw slowly through the tape. They had made at least four wraps of each wrist and ankle, and it took more slow sawing than he could believe.

Paco Esteban came into the kitchen.

"Sergeant Byrth — he said tell you 'house clear,' " Esteban said.

"Thank you."

Payne reached into his pocket and pulled out his phone.

"Paco, would you look in that box of phones and see if you can find a battery that works with this phone? Or maybe a charger,

653

if there's one in there."

"*Sí.*"

Jim Byrth walked into the kitchen.

"Okay, I've got El Gato secured in there," he said, and grinned. "Taped to the chair just like he likes."

He handed Payne's handcuffs back to him.

Then he said, "The guys in Dallas described that stash house they raided. This place is set up just like it. It's a damn prison. Actually, our Texas prisons are nicer."

Byrth then tossed a nice tan leather wallet on the kitchen table. And two State of Texas driver's licenses.

"El Gato is one Juan Paulo Delgado, aka Edgar Cisneros. I called it in to the office. He's got a few priors, but nothing serious like this. Born at Parkland in Dallas at taxpayer expense — both parents undocumented Mexican nationals, later given amnesty in that law President Reagan signed — and educated in Dallas at taxpayer expense. Too bad he learned all the wrong lessons."

Payne raised his eyebrows at that.

*So he is a U.S. citizen, and preying on illegals, ones like his parents. Unbelieveable.*

*But an animal's an animal, no matter the circumstances.*

"Here, Sergeant Payne," Paco Esteban said, holding out Payne's cell phone.

Payne took it and saw that Esteban had already pressed the 0/1 button. The phone was coming to life.

It vibrated three, then four times. Its small screen announced that he had five missed calls, including two voice-mail messages and two text messages from Amanda Law.

Payne hit the speakerphone key. He played the first voice mail; it had been blank.

The second voice mail was El Gato's threat, with the screaming boy and girl recording and the threat to kill Amanda.

Payne saw Amanda start to shake visibly.

He knelt and held her as he turned off the telephone.

When she'd stopped, he stood. He looked at the beers on the table.

He walked over to the refrigerator, opened it, and found it packed with bottles of beers. He grabbed three and brought them back to the table. When he opened one, it made the sound of gas escaping. He thought he saw Amanda recoil at it. But when he handed her the open bottle, she quickly grabbed it and took a big swallow.

He opened another and offered it to Byrth.

"Maybe in a minute. Thanks."

He offered the bottle to Esteban, who took it.

Then he opened the third. He put it to his lips and turned it upside down, drinking at least the first third.

He then kissed Amanda again on her forehead.

"I'll be right back, baby."

Juan Paulo Delgado looked up when he heard Matt Payne enter the dining room. Byrth had taped his wrists palm-up, and Matt saw the "D" tattoo. Payne felt a level of anger he did not know was possible.

"So now what?" Juan Paulo Delgado, his head bruised and bloody, said with an odd smile.

His tone did not reveal any fear. In fact, it sounded taunting.

With the beer bottle in his left hand, Payne pulled his Colt from the small of his back with his right hand.

He took another healthy drink of the beer, then looked the animal in the eyes.

*What did Amy say about psychopaths?*

*You can't rehabilitate them. They'll kill again and again.*

*And in prison they'll be thrown in solitary.*

*So why not just fucking kill him now?*

*He probably was going to do that to Amanda*

*. . . after doing God knows what.*

The image of the girl's head in Paco Esteban's freezer flashed in his mind.

*Sonofabitch!*

*No one will miss you, Delgado.*

*No one will give a rat's ass you're dead and gone and burning to a crisp in hell.*

Payne raised his pistol, pointing the muzzle at Delgado's forehead. He thumbed back the hammer.

He saw him flinch, if only slightly.

*And shits like you get killed every day in drug deals gone bad.*

Payne held the gun there for what seemed like five minutes.

*But I can't do it.*

*Even as badly as he deserves it.*

*It would make me little better than him.*

*I am not judge and jury.*

*Stanley Whatshisname is wrong.*

*We can't just shoot 'em all and let the Lord sort 'em out.*

Payne brought down his pistol. He locked it.

"This is your lucky day, you sonofabitch."

El Gato grinned defiantly at him.

Payne added, "You really must be a goddamn cat. But you just burned one of your nine lives. Eventually, you'll run out."

Payne looked down a moment. At Delgado's feet he noticed there was a bean, similar to the one Jim Byrth tumbled across his fingers. But this one was black. He shook his head.

Payne turned.

Byrth and Esteban were standing there, backlit in the open doorway to the kitchen. Both now wore the tan-colored surgical gloves the crime-scene technicians used.

*Nice and professional of Jim.*

*And what the hell . . . time to move this case to the next phase.*

Payne looked between them, then wordlessly walked back into the kitchen.

Payne saw that Tony Harris was handing his handkerchief to Amanda Law. She was standing, leaning against the counter by the sink.

She ran toward Matt. He went to her, his arms open, and wrapped them around her. She sobbed uncontrollably.

Payne then heard Jim Byrth enter the room.

Payne whispered to her, "It's okay, baby. It's all over."

And then there was the sound of a gun going off in the dining room.

# [FIVE]
## Terminal D
## Philadelphia International Airport
## Thursday, September 10, 5:21 P.M.

"Well, Matt," Jim Byrth said. He wore clean slacks and shirt, his white Stetson atop his head. "I'd say Juan Paulo Delgado got his wish."

Payne looked at him a long moment. "I don't follow you."

" 'Death before dishonor'?"

"Oh." He shrugged. "I dunno, Jim. He looked pretty dishonored in that chair."

Byrth grinned. "My granddaddy had an expression. He told me, 'Jimmy, in life you'll find three kinds of men. There're the ones who can learn by reading. And there're the ones who can learn by observation.' "

He paused to let that sink in.

"And?" Payne said.

" 'And then there's the rest of them who have to pee on the electric fence to find out for themselves.' "

Payne laughed aloud. "Sounds like one of Ron White's lines."

Bryth and Payne looked at each other. " 'You can't fix stupid,' " they said, simultaneously quoting the Texas comedian.

"And thankfully, most bad guys are stupid," Byrth said.

"That .45 Officer's Model had the serial number ground off," Payne said, but it was more of a question.

"What .45?" Byrth said with a straight face. After a long moment, he added: "Oh, the one a certain informant carried?"

Payne nodded.

"No idea what you're talking about, Marshal."

After a moment, Payne said, "So, what's with the beans?"

"Beans?"

"The ones you tumbled on your hand."

Byrth nodded. The Hat accentuated the act.

"John Coffee Hayes?"

Payne shook his head.

Byrth explained: "He became a captain in the Rangers round about 1840. Helluva reputation for dealing with lawless Mexicans and marauding Indians. A couple years later, one of his men, who guessed he was as good as his boss, got involved with a bunch of other Texans who were planning an invasion of Mexico. The Mier Expedition?"

Payne shook his head again.

"Well, they failed miserably. The Mexicans captured them, including Samuel H. Walker — that was Hayes's man — and a fellow named Big Foot Wallace. The order came down to execute every tenth man."

Payne was nodding. "Then they let the rest loose to take the message back to Texas. 'Don't mess with Mexico.'"

"Exactly. You know, Texas actually uses that in an antilitter campaign. But that's another story."

"But what about the beans?"

"To decide who died, they had a drawing. The prisoner who drew a white bean lived. A black bean meant death for the poor bastard. Both Walker and Wallace drew white ones, and that's how the story got back to Texas."

Payne had a mental image of the black bean at Delgado's feet.

Byrth looked in his eyes and sensed it.

"Look, Matt, the way I see it, our informant friend just saved the Commonwealth of Pennsylvania and the Lone Star State countless dollars in the housing, feeding, and prosecution of the deceased gangbanger. Plus, my favorite part — no more paperwork."

Payne did not look convinced.

"Prosecuting a capital murder charge," Byrth went on earnestly, "costs from two hundred thousand to three hundred thousand bucks. If you get a conviction and a long jail sentence, then it's about thirty grand a year per inmate. That's another three hundred grand every ten years." He looked at him. "The way I figure it, El Gato getting shot when he attacked the Philly PD's confidential informant saved the lawful taxpayers a million bucks. At least. You ought to factor that in when you compensate Paco. It was self-defense."

Payne shook his head.

"Matt, you really don't think that I came here planning on taking that piece of shit back to Texas?"

Payne said nothing.

Byrth grinned, and quoted, " 'All warfare is based on deception.' "

Payne nodded. "Sun Tzu."

"Yup. So you *do* know this has been going on for millennia."

Byrth held out his hand. As Matt shook it, Byrth said, "Come visit us in Texas, Marshal. We could use someone like you. We've got plenty more bad guys like Delgado. And it's only going to get worse."

Texas Rangers Sergeant James O. Byrth then affectionately patted Philadelphia Homicide Sergeant Matthew M. Payne on the shoulder. He turned and joined a crowd walking down the concourse.

And then The Hat was gone.

As he was driving out of the airport, Matt Payne thought about what Jim Byrth had said. He couldn't quite reconcile all of it. At least not yet. But he already was seeing there was some truth to it.

*Cops have held the line between civilized society and the barbarians forever.*

*And that's not going to change as long as there're bad guys.*

*Even Amanda said she understood that.*

He felt his cell phone vibrate. And the Pavlovian response was triggered.

As he looked to the screen, his pulse quickened.

He read:

663

— no number -

Dinner gets delivered at 7 o'clock.

Just found this cute cottage on the Internet.

To hell with lunch. . . . -A

# ABOUT THE AUTHOR

**W. E. B. Griffin** is the author of six bestselling series: The Corps, Brotherhood of War, Badge of Honor, Men at War, Honor Bound, and Presidential Agent. He has been invested into the orders of St. George of the U.S. Armor Association and St. Andrew of the U.S. Army Aviation Association, and is a life member of the U.S. Special Operations Association; Gaston-Lee Post 5660, Veterans of Foreign Wars; China Post #1 in Exile of the American Legion; the Police Chiefs Association of Southeast Pennsylvania, South New Jersey, and Delaware; and the Flat Earth Society (Pensacola, Florida, and Buenos Aires, Argentina, chapters). He is an honorary life member of the U.S. Army Otter–Caribou Association, the U.S. Army Special Forces Association, the U.S. Marine Corps Raider Association, and the USMC Combat Correspondents Association. Griffin lives in Alabama and Argentina.

**William E. Butterworth IV** has been an editor and writer for more than twenty-five years, and has worked closely with his father for seven years on the editing of the Griffin books. He is the coauthor of the bestselling OSS Men at War novels *The Saboteurs* and *The Double Agents* and *Death and Honor* in the Honor Bound series. He lives in Texas.